She should run.

Escape before she reached a place from which she couldn't retreat. Before the life she lived lost its worth.

And yet, she stayed.

She didn't know how it happened, but suddenly she was wrapped in his arms, both of them trembling, both seeking, mouth and tongue and teeth, desperate to get closer, as if they could climb inside each other.

And oh, was this what it was like to want? To feel a hunger deep inside you, to the core of your womb, where life had eluded her? His hands moved erratically, as if he could hardly imagine he was sweeping along her hip, her thigh, the edge of her ribs. His mouth burned her throat, her shoulder, the swell of her breast, and she suddenly wanted that mouth everywhere. She wanted him to brand her with his touch so that no one else could ever claim her.

PRAISE FOR THE
DRAKE'S RAKES SERIES

Always a Temptress

"4½ stars! Readers would never suspect that Dreyer earned her reputation writing contemporary romance. Her novels have every hallmark of a memorable historical romance: passion, unforgettable characters, an engrossing plot. May she continue to deliver her fantastic historicals!"
—*RT Book Reviews*

"Fueled by a surfeit of sizzling sensuality, chilling suspense, and delectably dry wit, *Always a Temptress* brings Dreyer's first historical trilogy to a smashingly successful conclusion. Strong secondary characters add depth and humor to the book's emotionally compelling, impeccably researched plot as Dreyer again deftly combines deadly intrigue and sexy romance in a swoon-worthy read."
—*Booklist* (starred review)

"A Perfect 10! The characterizations make *Always a Temptress* an awesome read…a tantalizing tapestry of romance."
—RomRevToday.com

"One of the jewels within the story is the wonderful band of supporting characters we encounter…I enjoyed this book for the suspense, the romance, and the humor that was beautifully mixed together in a wonderful story."
—FreshFiction.com

"A super Regency undercover romance starring a tough combat veteran and a courageous heroine. Their pairing make for a fun thriller, but it is the support cast at Rose Workhouse and an orphanage that brings a strong emotional element to an exciting, complicated historical."

—GenreGoroundReviews.blogspot.com

Never a Gentleman

"Exquisite characterization; flashes of dry, lively wit; marvelous villains; and a dark, compelling plot that unfolds in tantalizing ways."

—*Library Journal*

"A pure joy to read! Dreyer displays her phenomenal sense of atmosphere in an emotionally powerful and beautifully rendered love story...the consummate storyteller makes the conventional unconventional. Combining beautifully crafted, engaging characters with an intriguing mystery adds depth."

—*RT Book Reviews*

"As always, Ms. Dreyer has written an engrossing story which will entice the reader into the world of the Regency...If you loved *Barely a Lady,* you won't want to miss the second book of the series."

—FreshFiction.com

"Superb...an intoxicating read. If not having the first book stops you from reading this one, get the first one.

The next book promises to be just as exciting and sexy as this one, so just go and buy all of them. You won't want to miss out!"

—TheRomanceReadersConnection.com

Barely a Lady

One of *Publishers Weekly*'s Best Books of 2010

A Top Ten *Booklist* Romance of the Year

One of *Library Journal*'s Best Five
Romances of the Year

"Dreyer flawlessly blends danger, deception, and desire into an impeccably crafted historical that neatly balances adventurous intrigue with an exquisitely romantic love story."

—*Chicago Tribune*

"Vivid descriptions, inventive plotting, beautifully delineated characters, and stunning emotional depth."

—*Library Journal* (starred review)

"Romantic suspense author Dreyer makes a highly successful venture into the past with this sizzling, dramatic Regency romance. Readers will love the well-rounded characters and suspenseful plot."

—*Publishers Weekly* (starred review)

Also by Eileen Dreyer

Once a Rake

Eileen Dreyer

FOREVER

NEW YORK   BOSTON

Copyright © 2013 by Eileen Dreyer
Excerpt from *Twice Tempted* © 2014 by Eileen Dreyer
All rights reserved. In accordance with the U.S. Copyright Act of 1976, the scanning, uploading, and electronic sharing of any part of this book without the permission of the publisher is unlawful piracy and theft of the author's intellectual property. If you would like to use material from the book (other than for review purposes), prior written permission must be obtained by contacting the publisher at permissions@hbgusa.com. Thank you for your support of the author's rights.

Forever
Hachette Book Group
237 Park Avenue
New York, NY 10017
www.HachetteBookGroup.com

Printed in the United States of America

First Edition: October 2013

10 9 8 7 6 5 4 3 2 1

OPM

Forever is an imprint of Grand Central Publishing.
The Forever name and logo are trademarks of Hachette Book Group, Inc.

The Hachette Speakers Bureau provides a wide range of authors for speaking events. To find out more, go to www.hachettespeakersbureau.com or call (866) 376-6591.

The publisher is not responsible for websites (or their content) that are not owned by the publisher.

To Karyn
Who always sees the things I don't.
Thanks. Chinese is on me.

Acknowledgments

Once again I would like to extend my thanks to everyone who helped me create my worlds. Of course to Andrea Cirillo and Christina Hogrebe of the Jane Rotrosen Agency, my family at Grand Central; my brilliant ADD sister Amy Pierpont, for directing my wandering path, to Lauren Plude for her priceless assistance, Claire Brown and the peerless Grand Central art department for my exquisite covers, and Leda Scheintaub for copyediting. Special mention to my assistant, Maggie Mae Gallagher, for keeping me sane. To my writing families: always the Divas, MoRWA, the Published Author's Group, the As Yet Unnamed Plotting Group in a Penthouse. To all my fans and supporters out there who make it worthwhile to write stories.

Specific thanks to everyone who helped me research and write a trilogy that suddenly involved early nineteenth-century science (I have a bibliography on www.eileendreyer.com). To the generous people of Lyme

Regis who shared their stories with me. To my hosts in Ireland who let me run away to write. To my friends at Wired Coffee, and, of course, to my Rick, who kicks me out to write when it's needed and never asks if the damn thing's done yet. The damn thing's done.

Once a Rake

Prologue

October 1815

Later, no one would be able to agree as to exactly what happened on the HMS *Reliance* that night. The witnesses were too many and the action too sudden to gain a coherent story.

What everyone did agree on was that about two hours after dusk, the Duke of Wellington came up on the deck of the ship, a fast brig that was carrying him home from France. Surrounded by several of his staff, the very recent hero of Waterloo and military governor of France was in an excellent mood, the distinctive bray of his laugh carrying out over the choppy water as he cupped his hands to light a cigarillo. The waxing moon slung a thin necklace of diamonds across the water, and the wind was freshening. Off to port, the coast of Dorset appeared a black void against the diamond-rich sky, which put them two days out of the port of London.

The second fact no one could dispute was that when

the group came up on deck, one man could easily be
distinguished among them. Standing well over six feet,
Colonel Ian Ferguson of the Black Watch towered over
his commander. It wasn't only his height that made him
memorable. Even in the uncertain light of the night-
running lanterns, his hair shone like fire, and his shoulders were as wide as a Yule log.

In the few days he'd been with the duke, Ferguson had
proved himself to be loud, funny, fierce, and uncompro-
mising. And even though he proclaimed himself a loyal
Scot, he swore he was Wellington's man. Which was why
it was so puzzling that he would pull out a gun and point
it right at the duke.

"A gun!" someone yelled. "To the duke!"

Chaos erupted on the deck. Men scattered, shouting
warnings and commands. Others threw themselves in
front of the great man. Swords were drawn. Several men
must have had guns, because suddenly there was a staccato pop-pop-popping. Acrid puffs of smoke cut visibil-
ity, and the ship heeled a bit as the steersman ran to help.
Some men prayed, one wept, and the Duke of Wellington,
much as he had on innumerable battlefields, stood his
ground, a cigarillo in hand and a bemused expression on
his face.

"What the devil?" he demanded, looking down to
where a man lay on the deck at his feet.

The deck stilled suddenly, the smoke writhing about
the men and sharpening the air as the sails flapped uselessly above them. Bare feet thundered below as the crew
roused to the alarm.

"He tried to shoot you!" one of his aides accused, already on the run to the railings.

"What?" Wellington barked, his focus still down. "Simmons here? Don't be ridiculous. Get more lamps lit. Let's see what's going on here."

There was no question that Simmons was dead. A sluggish pool of black blood spread out from behind his head, and his eyes stared open and fixed on the heavens. One of the crew retrieved the man's pistol from his outstretched hand and stood.

"No, sir," one of the officers said as he bent over Simmons. "Ferguson."

"Who?" Wellington demanded, finally turning to look.

"That Scotsman. The one who tried to shoot you!"

"Ferguson?" Wellington stopped on the spot. "Bollocks."

One of his newer aides, the Honorable Horace Stricker, stepped out of the shadows, holding on to a bleeding arm. "Saw him myself, your grace. Pointed that popper right at you."

Wellington pointed at the body on the deck. "And Simmons here?"

Everyone looked around, as if seeking answers.

"He must have gotten in the way of Ferguson's bullet," Stricker said. "I shot the Scot. Where is he?"

Two people pointed over the side of the ship. One of Wellington's staff pocketed Simmons's pistol. The bo'sun ran up with several lighted lanterns, which cast an eerie, wavering light over the scene.

"Well, find him," Wellington demanded. "I'll be in my cabin."

All came to attention as he passed, but Wellington didn't seem to notice. He seemed preoccupied, shaking his head slightly, as if wiping something away. More than one sailor commented that he looked sadder at the news of who his attacker was than the fact that he'd been attacked at all.

"Hard aport!" the captain bellowed, and men scrambled into the rigging. The ship heeled again, more sharply. "Man the halyards! Prepare to shorten sail and come about!"

Beneath the quick little ship, the water of the channel passed in choppy, frothed waves. The wind was stiff this night, ten knots from the northeast. Any man out in that water would be sorry.

* * *

Ian Ferguson was damn sorry. Bobbing up like a punctured cork, he shook the water from his eyes and looked up at the slowing ship, a hand pressed to the sharp ache in his chest. He couldn't figure out what had just happened. He'd come up on deck to share a cigar with Wellington. The next thing he knew, that little *riataiche* Stricker was pointing a gun at the general.

Ian had reacted instinctively, pulling his own gun and firing at Stricker. Immediately there were guns everywhere, a succession of shots, and suddenly he'd been knocked hard in the chest and catapulted right over the railings. He'd hit the cold channel water with barely a splash.

Did he save Wellington? Had he hit Stricker? God and the Bruce, he hoped so.

Come to think of it, what about that hit to *his* chest? Kicking hard to stay above the swells, he took a second to look down. He wasn't sure what he expected to see in the dark water. Blood, maybe. There was a hole in his jacket; he put his finger through it. No injury, though, except for a tender spot over his ribs. He was breathing well and didn't feel that awful disintegration that came with real injury.

"There he is!" somebody shouted above him.

Ian looked up to see the lighter being hoisted out. A bouquet of heads appeared at the rail, haloed by the thin light of the lanterns. Ian lifted a hand to wave. He heard a sharp snapping sound, and the water near him leapt. Ian froze. Hell and damnation, they were firing at him!

He opened his mouth to shout. Another gun fired.

"Shouldn't we get him on board?" Ian heard from the first officer.

"And waste time with a court martial?" came the furious answer.

Ian cursed. He hadn't killed Stricker after all. Now he had to find a way to prove that it was Stricker who had fired the first shot. That Stricker's cabin was where he'd found the flask. The flask that should have been back at Horse Guards. The flask that he'd . . .

Ian laid his hand back against his chest. He smiled. No wonder he hadn't been hurt. The silver flask wouldn't hold a dram anymore, but sure, he bet it held a flattened bullet.

So, Stricker wanted him dead. He'd just see about that.

"Reloaded, sir," came the faint call.

"Get him before the moon disappears."

Ian saw the muzzle lowered over the side. A Brown Bess. He sucked in a lungful of air and dove. The pain and the crack came at the same moment. Blast. The bastard had hit him. The air whooshed out of his lung and Ian sank.

This time he didn't come up.

Chapter 1

Ten days later

Sarah Clarke was not going to let a pig get the best of her. Especially not this pig.

"Willoughby!" she called as she scrambled over the broken fence.

Blast that pig. She had even tied him up this time. But the pen was empty, the wood on one side shattered, and precise little hoof prints marched away through the mud.

Sarah took a brief look at the stone outbuildings that clustered around the old stable. She could hear rustling and creaking, which meant the animals had heard Willoughby escape. But there were no telltale porcine snortings or squeals. If she knew her pig, he was headed due south, straight for disaster.

Sarah rubbed at her eyes. "The cliffs. It had to be the cliffs."

She hated the cliffs. She hated the height and the uncertain edge and the long, sudden drop she had almost made on more than one occasion all the way to the shingle beach below. Just the thought of facing them made her nauseous.

"I have better things to do," she protested to no one.

It was closing in on evening, and she should be feeding her animals. She needed to help Mr. Hicks rescue the sheep who had taken advantage of another fallen fence to wander in among Sir Magnus's prized Devon Longwools. Then she needed to inspect the debris that seemed to be diverting the stream into her wheat field. Instead she would be dancing on the edge of death to collect her pig.

She sighed. She had no choice. Willoughby was Fairbourne's best source of income. And he was in imminent danger of tumbling off the edge of Britain.

Ducking into the barn to retrieve her secret weapon, she picked up her skirts and ran for the path that snaked through the beech spinney. It was the same route Willoughby had taken the day before and the week before that.

Oh, why couldn't he become enamored of an animal in his own farmyard?

"If it weren't for the fact that you are such a good provider," she muttered, pushing her hair out of her eyes with one hand as she ran, "I'd leave you to your fate. Stupid, blind, pig-headed...well, I guess you would be, wouldn't you?"

Both pig-headed *and* blind. One of her husband, Boswell's, few good ideas, Willoughby was a new breed called the Large Black, which produced lovely gammon and even lovelier babies. He also had ears that were so large they flopped over his eyes, making it difficult for him to see. The problem was, Willoughby didn't seem to notice until he was trapped in mire or running right over a crumbling escarpment.

Why couldn't Fairbourne have been situated farther away from the sea? Sarah mourned as she wove her way through the wood. Somewhere like, oh, she didn't know, Oxford. Quiet, dry, and relatively clean. Away from oceans or high cliffs, with libraries that held more than Debrett's and gothic novels. Yes, especially libraries.

Not that she had ever actually seen Oxford. But she had always thought how wonderful it must be to stroll the stone walks and smooth greens that stretched beneath golden spires, soaking in the history, the culture, the learned discourse of men in flapping black robes. Books and lectures and good dinner conversation. No mud, no mucking out, no pigs of any stripe. But especially no Great Blacks with a predilection for falling in love with inappropriate species.

His latest *amour* resided in Squire Bovey's pastures, which were reached by way of the coastline. The coastline, which at this point was a cliff several hundred feet above the Channel and apt to crumble for no reason.

Sarah was still running when she burst through the trees into a hard blast of cold Channel wind. She stumbled to a halt, her heart stuttering. Beyond her the land rolled away, barren of all but bracken as far as the jagged, uncertain cliffs. She could see the better part of a mile both ways. She did not see her pig.

Oh, lord, please don't let him have gone over. He's the difference between getting by and going hungry.

She was still standing fifty feet from the cliff working up the nerve to get close enough for a look down when she caught the sound of a plaintive squeal. Whipping around, she gaped. She couldn't believe it. There, tucked into the spinney not ten feet away, stood Willoughby, securely tied to a tree. He didn't look happy, but Willoughby never looked pleased when his plans were thwarted.

Sarah looked around, expecting to see the squire's boys, or Tom Scar, who did odd jobs in the neighborhood and could always be seen walking this way at end of day.

But there was no one there. Just the grass and bracken and never-ending wind, which tugged impatiently at her skirts and tossed her hair back in her eyes.

Could it be her mysterious benefactor again? For the last few days she had suspected that she had a guest on the estate. She had been missing eggs and once found evidence of a rabbit dinner. Probably a soldier, discharged after ten bloody years of war and left with no job or home. He wasn't the first. He certainly wouldn't be the last.

At least he had attempted to repay the estate's meager bounty. Sarah had come out each morning to find some small task done for her. The breach in a dry stone wall mended. Chicken feed spread, old tack repaired, a lost scythe not only found but sharpened. And now, Willoughby.

Another aggrieved snort recalled her attention. Willoughby was looking at her with mournful eyes. Well, Sarah thought he was. It was difficult to see past those ears. She walked over to let him loose and was butted for her troubles.

Whoever had tied him had known what they were about. It took ten minutes of being goosed by an anxious pig to get the knot loose. Wrapping the rope around one fist, Sarah reached into her apron pocket for the piece of coarse blanket she had plucked from the barn. Fluttering it in front of the pig's nose, she tugged at the rope. Willoughby gave a happy little squeal and nudged her so hard she almost toppled over. She chuckled. It never failed. She pulled him into motion, and he followed, docile as a pet pug.

It had been Sarah's greatest stroke of genius. Willoughby might not be able to see all that well, but a pig's sense of smell was acute. So Sarah collected items belonging to Willoughby's current *amour* to nudge him along. Her only objection was the fact that her pig couldn't tell the difference between her and the squire's mare.

"Come along, young man," she coaxed, striding back through the spinney with him in tow. "You truly must cease this wandering. Your wife and babies are waiting for you. Besides, I have four very pretty sows coming next week to make your acquaintance, and you needs must be here. It is iniquitous, I know, but I need that money to tide us over the winter."

If Willoughby finally did manage to tumble off that cliff, she would have no money at all to make it through. She would have no pig to sire new babies, and no stud fees. So the first thing she must do when she returned was fix the pen. Then she still had lost sheep and a diverted stream to attend to before finishing her evening chores.

As she did every autumn, when the farmyard was perennially muddy and her skin chapped, Sarah wished she were somewhere else. It wasn't as bad in spring or summer, because then she had growing things, new babies to raise, the comfort of wildflowers and warm skies. Every spring she imagined things could be better. Every autumn she admitted the truth. She was caught here at Fairbourne, and here she would stay. She had nowhere else to go.

She wouldn't think of that, though. It served no purpose, except to eat away at her heart. Tucking the bit of blanket on the fence where Willoughby could smell it, she tied him up with a scratch of the ears and an admonition to behave. Then, rewrapping her muffler against the chill, she went about her work, ending with a visit to the henhouse.

It was when she slipped her hand beneath Edna the hen that she knew for certain who had tied up Willoughby. Edna was her best layer, and yet the box was nearly empty. Sarah checked Martha and Mary and came up with similar results. Someone had taken their eggs. And it hadn't been a fox, or at least one of her birds would have been a pile of bloody feathers.

Well, Sarah thought, collecting what was left. Her visitor had earned his meal. She wished she had seen him, though. She could have at least rewarded him with a few scones for rescuing Willoughby from sure disaster.

On second thought, she considered with her first real smile of the day, maybe not scones. They would be Peg's scones, and Peg's scones could be used for artillery practice. No one should be rewarded that way.

Sarah might have thought no more of the matter if the men hadn't ridden up. She was just shoving the chicken coop door closed when she heard horses approaching over the rise from the Pinhay Road. She sighed. Now what?

Giving up the idea that she would eat anytime soon, she gave the coop a final kick and strode off toward the approaching riders. She was just passing the old dairy when she caught movement out the corner of her eye. A shadow, nothing more, by the back wall. But a big shadow. One that seemed to be sitting on the ground, with long legs and shoulders the size of a Yule log.

It didn't even occur to her that it could be anyone but her benefactor. She was about to call to him when the riders crested the hill and she recognized their leader.

"Oh, no," she muttered, her heart sinking straight to her half-boots. This was not the time to betray the existence of the man who had saved her pig. She closed her mouth and walked straight past.

There were six riders in all, four of them dressed in the motley remnants of their old regiments. Foot soldiers, by the way they rode. Not very good ones, if the company they kept was any indication. Ragged, scruffy, and slouching, they rode with rifles slung over their shoulders and knives in their boots.

Sarah might have dismissed them as unimportant if they had been led by anyone but her husband's cousin, Martin Clarke. She knew better than to think Martin wished her well. Martin wished her to the devil, just as she wished him.

A thin, middling man with sparse sandy hair and bulging eyes, Martin had the harried, petulant air of an ineffectual law clerk. Sarah knew better. Martin was as ineffectual as the tides.

Just as Sarah knew he would, he trotted past the great front door and toward the outbuildings where he knew he could find her at this time of day. She stood where she was, egg pail in hand, striving for calm. Martin was appearing far too frequently lately.

Damn you, Boswell, she thought, long since worn past propriety. *How could you have left me to face this alone?*

"Martin," she greeted Boswell's cousin as he pulled his horse to a skidding halt within feet of her. She felt sorry for the horse, a short-boned bay that bore the scars of Martin's spurs.

"Sarah," Martin snapped in a curiously deep voice.

He did not bow or tip his hat. Martin knew exactly what she was due and wasn't about to let her forget it. Sarah wished she had at least had the chance to tidy her hair before facing off with him. She hated feeling at a disadvantage.

"Lady Clarke," the sixth man said in his booming, jovial voice.

Sarah's smile was genuine for the squire, who sat at Martin's left on an ungainly-looking sorrel mare. "Squire," she greeted him, walking up to rub the horse's nose. "You've brought our Maizie to call, have you? How are you, my pretty?"

Pretty was not really a word one should use for Maizie. As sturdy as a stone house, she was all of seventeen hands, with a Roman head and a shambling gait. She was also the best hunter in the district, and of a size to carry Squire's massive girth.

Maizie's arrival was met by a thud and a long, mournful squeal from the pigpen.

The squire laughed with his whole body. "Still in love, is he?"

Sarah grinned back. "Caught him not an hour ago trying to sneak over for a tryst."

The squire chuckled. "It's good someone loves my girl," he said with an affectionate smack to the horse's neck. Maizie nuzzled Sarah's apron and was rewarded with an old fall apple. Willoughby sounded as if he were dying from anguish.

"Thank you for the ale you sent over, Squire," Sarah said. "It was much enjoyed. Even the dowager had a small tot after coming in from one of her painting afternoons."

"Excellent," he said with a big smile. "Excellent. Everyone is well here, I hope? Saw Lady Clarke and Mizz Fitchwater out along the Undercliff with their paints and hammers. They looked to be in rude health."

Sarah smiled. "They are. I will tell them you asked after them."

"This isn't a social call," Martin interrupted, shifting in his saddle.

Sarah kept her smile, even though just the sight of Martin sent her heart skidding around in dread. "To what do I owe the honor then, gentlemen?"

"Have you seen any strangers around?" the squire asked, leaning forward. "There's been some theft and vandalism in the area. Stolen chickens and the like."

"Oh, that," Sarah said with a wave of her hand. "Of course. He's taken my eggs."

Martin almost came off his horse. "Who?"

Shading her eyes with her hand, Sarah smiled up at him. "Who? Don't you mean what? Unless you name your foxes."

That obviously wasn't the answer he'd been looking for. "Fox? Bah! I'm talking about a man. Probably one of those damned thievin' soldiers wandering the roads preying on good people."

Did he truly not notice how his own men scowled at him? Men who undoubtedly had wandered the roads themselves? Well, Sarah thought, if she had had any intention of acknowledging her surprise visitor, Martin's words disabused her of the notion. She wouldn't trust Napoleon himself to her cousin's care.

"Not unless your soldier has four feet and had a long bushy tail," she said, genially. "But I doubt he would fit the uniform."

The squire, still patting his Maizie, let out a great guffaw. "We'll get your fox for you, Lady Clarke," he promised. "Not great hunt country here. But we do. We do."

"Kind of you, Squire. I am certain the girls will be grateful. You know how fatched Mary and Martha can get when their routine is disturbed."

"Martha . . ." Martin was getting redder by the minute. "Why haven't I heard about this? You boarding people here? What would Boswell say?"

Sarah tilted her head. "I imagine he'd say that he was glad for the eggs every morning for breakfast, Martin."

For a second she thought Martin might have a seizure, right there on his gelding. "You're not going to get away with abusing your privilege much longer, missy," he snapped. "This land is . . ."

"Boswell's," she said flatly. "Not yours until we know he won't come back."

"Bah!" Martin huffed. "It's been almost four months, girl. If he was coming back, he'd be here."

Sarah stood very still, grief and guilt swamping even the fear. Instinctively her gaze wandered over to what she called Boswell's arbor, a little sitting area by the cliff with a lovely view of the ocean. Boswell had loved sitting there, his gaze fixed on the horizon. He had planted all the roses and fitted the latticework overhead.

His roses, though, were dying. His entire estate was dying, and Sarah was no longer certain she could save it.

"He will be back, Martin," she said, throwing as much conviction as she could into her voice. "You'll see. Men are returning from Belgium all the time. The battle was so terrible it will be months yet before we learn the final toll from Waterloo."

It was the squire who brought their attention back with a sharp *harrumph.*

Sarah blushed. "My apologies, Squire," she said. "You did not come here to be annoyed by our petty grievances. As for your question, I have seen no one here."

"We've also been told to keep an eye out for a big man," the squire said. "Red hair. Scottish. Don't know that it's the same man that's raiding the henhouses, but you should keep an eye out anyway."

Sarah was already shaking her head. After all, she hadn't seen anything but a shadow. "Wasn't it a Scot who tried to shoot Wellington? I saw the posters in Lyme Regis. I thought he was dead."

The squire shrugged. "We've been asked to make sure."

"I'm sure you won't mind if we search the property," Martin challenged.

He was already dismounting. Sarah's heart skidded, and her palms went damp. "Of course not," she said with a faint wave. "Start with the house. I believe the dowager will be just as delighted to see you as the last time you surprised her."

Martin was already on the ground and heading toward the house. With Sarah's words, he stopped cold. Sarah refused to smile, even though the memory of Lady Clarke's last harangue still amused her.

"Just the outbuildings," he amended, motioning to the men to follow him.

Sarah was a heartbeat shy of protesting when she heard it. Willoughby. The thudding turned into a great crash and the heartfelt squeals turned into a near-scream of triumph. She turned just in time to jump free as the pig came galloping across the yard, six hundred pounds of unrestrained passion headed straight for Squire's horse.

Unfortunately, Martin was standing between Willoughby and his true love. And Sarah sincerely doubted that the pig could see the man in his headlong dash to bliss. Sarah called out a warning. Martin stood frozen on the spot, as if staring down the specter of death. Howling with laughter, the squire swung Maizie about.

It was all over in a moment. Squire leapt from Maizie and gave her a good crack on the rump. With a flirtatious toss of the head and a whinny, the mare took off down the lane, Willoughby in hot pursuit. But not before the boar had run right over Martin, leaving him flat in the mud with hoofprints marching straight up his best robin's egg superfine and white linen. Sarah tried so hard to keep a straight face. The other men weren't so restrained, slapping legs and laughing at the man who'd brought them as they swung their horses around and charged down the lane after the pig.

Sarah knew that she was a Christian, because she bent to help Boswell's unpleasant relation off the ground. "Are you all right, cousin?"

Bent over and clutching his ribs, Martin yanked his arm out of her grasp. "You did that on purpose, you bitch."

The squire frowned. "Language, sir. Ladies."

Martin waved him off as well. "This is no lady, and you know it, Bovey. Why my cousin demeaned himself enough to marry a by-blow . . ."

Sarah laughed. "Why, for her dowry, Martin. You know that. Heavens, all of Dorset knows that."

The only thing people didn't know was the identity of her real father, who'd set up the trust for her. But then, knowing had been no benefit to her.

"What Dorset knows," Squire said, his face red, "is that you've done Boswell proud. Even kind to his mother, and I have to tell you, ma'am, that be no easy feat."

Sarah spared him another smile. "Why, thank you, Squire. That is kind of you."

The squire grew redder. Martin harrumphed.

"Climb on your horse, Clarke," Squire said. "It's time we left Lady Clarke to her work. We certainly haven't made her day any easier."

Martin huffed, but he took up his horse's reins. He was still brushing off his once-pristine attire when the soldiers, bantering like children on a picnic, returned brandishing Willoughby's lead, the pig following disconsolately behind.

With a smile for the ragged soldier who'd caught him, Sarah held her hand out for the rope. "Thank you, Mr. . . ."

The man, lean and lined from sun and hardship, ducked his head. "Greggins, ma'am. Pleasure. Put up a good fight, 'e did."

She chuckled. "I know all too well, Mr. Greggins." Turning, she smiled up at her neighbor. "Thank you, Squire. I am so sorry you had to send Maizie off."

The squire grinned at her, showing his gap teeth and

twinkling blue eyes. "Aw, she'll be at the bottom of the lane, right enough. She knows to get out of yon pig's way."

Tipping his low-crowned hat to Sarah, he turned to help Martin onto his horse. Sarah waved farewell and tugged a despondent Willoughby back to his pen. She was just pulling the knot tight when she caught sight of that shadow again, this time on her side of the coop. Casting a quick glance to where the squire had just mounted behind the pig-catching soldier Greggins, she bent over Willoughby.

"I wouldn't show myself yet if I were you," she murmured, hoping the shadow heard her. "And if it was you who let Willoughby go a moment ago, I thank you."

"A search would have been...problematic," she heard, and a fresh chill chased down her spine. There was a burr to his voice. A Scot, here on the South Dorset coast. Now, how frequently could she say she'd seen that?

"You didn't by any chance recently shoot at someone, did you?" she asked.

As if he would tell the truth, if he were indeed the assassin.

"No' who you think."

She should turn around this minute and call for help. Every instinct of decency said so. But Martin was the local magistrate, and Sarah knew how he treated prisoners. Even innocent ones. Squeezing her eyes shut, Sarah listened to the jangle of the troop turning to leave.

"Give you good day, Lady Clarke," the squire said, and waved the parade off down the drive.

Martin didn't follow right away. "This isn't over, missy," he warned. "No thieving by-blow is going to keep me from what is mine. This land belongs to me now, and you know it. By the time you let go, it will be useless."

Not unless the shingle strand sinks into the ocean, she thought dourly. The only thing Martin wanted from Fairbourne was a hidden cove where boats could land brandy.

Sarah sighed, her mind made up. She simply could not accommodate Martin in this or anything. Straightening, she squarely faced the dyspeptic man where he stiffly sat his horse. "Fairbourne is Boswell's," she said baldly. "Until he returns, I am here to make sure it is handed back into his hands in good heart. Good day, Martin."

Martin opened his mouth to argue, and then saw the squire and other men waiting for him. He settled for a final "Bah!" and dug his heels into his horse. They were off in a splatter of mud.

Sarah stood where she was until she could no longer hear them. Then, with a growing feeling of inevitability, she once more climbed past the broken pigpen and approached the shadow at the back of the coop.

And there he was, a very large red-headed man slumped against the stone wall. He was even more ragged than the men who had ridden with Martin, his clothing tattered and filthy, his hair a rat's nest, his beard bristling and even darker red than his hair. His eyes were bright, though, and his cheeks flushed. He held his hand to his side, and he was listing badly.

Sarah crouched down next to him to get a better look, and saw that his shirt was stained brown with old blood. His hands, clutched over his left side, were stained with new blood, which meant that those bright eyes were from more than intelligence. Even so, Sarah couldn't remember ever seeing a more compelling, powerful man in her life.

"Hello," she greeted him, her own hands clenched on her thighs. "I assume I am speaking to the Scotsman for whom everyone is looking."

His grin was crooked, and under any other circumstance would have been endearing. "Och, lassie, nothin' gets past ye."

"I thought you were dead."

He frowned. "Wait a few minutes," he managed. "I'll see what I can do."

And then, as gracefully as a sailing vessel slipping under the waves, he sank all the way to his side and lost consciousness.

Chapter 2

Sweet lord, Sarah thought, staring at the unconscious man at her feet. What do I do now? He was huge. At least four inches over six feet and fifteen stone, all of it seemingly muscle, which meant he would be impossible to move. She had a feeling that she would get halfway across the yard, the Scot's feet in her hands, and Martin would come thundering back. And wouldn't that set the seal on the disaster that was her life?

"Sir?" she asked, nudging the unconscious man's shoulder. "Sir, you must wake."

The posters had said the assassin was a soldier. Her shadow was clad in what was left of civilian clothing: well-made tweed hacking jacket, buckskins, turned boots that had seen a lot of scuffing. Good lawn shirt and brown brocade waistcoat, his blood-stained cravat wrapped around his waist rather than his throat.

She knew she should assess how bad the injury was. Instead, she stood up. There was a good chance this man was guilty of attempted murder, if not treason. If she helped him, she would be just as guilty as he. She should call Martin back to take him.

Martin. Sarah's stomach lurched. She took another look at her guest, his features ashen and blood beginning to seep over his fingers. She couldn't do it. If she announced this man's presence, it would give Martin the perfect excuse to search her property, to harass her little family. She could not allow either, for more reasons than Martin knew.

Besides, she thought, she didn't know for certain that this was the man they sought. Looking at the size of him, though, she was more certain that he was the one who had kept Willoughby from tumbling into the sea. She owed him something for that.

"Sir, please," she urged, crouching back down to push at the man's shoulder. "You cannot stay here."

She couldn't help it. She had to know how bad the situation was. She laid her hand against his broad forehead and all but groaned aloud. He was burning up. She didn't think there was any way he was going to leave under his own power.

Sarah took a quick look around, just to make sure they were alone. The outbuildings were quiet and the house silent. Only Willoughby showed any curiosity, sticking his snout between the fence slats to sniff at the intruder.

"Do not dare fall in love with him," Sarah warned the pig. "He's leaving."

"Do you think I'm no' worthy o' love, then, lass?" came a faint, gravelly voice. Gasping, she looked down at the stranger. His eyes still weren't open; he hadn't moved. But that had been his voice, hadn't it? She wasn't just imagining it?

"I have no idea what you are worthy of, sir," she answered. "But I am certain you would not want it from a six hundred pound pig."

That earned her another smile that all but set her back on her heels. *Oh, don't do that,* she thought desperately. That smile did something dangerous to her. Something surprising, disorienting. Something she did not have the luxury of feeling. Ever.

"Not a very discriminating porker, is he?" the man asked, struggling to sit up.

Sarah helped until he was vertical. "Heavens, no. Quite capricious, in fact."

He managed to get one eye open. Blue. Sky-over-the-sea blue, when the sun shone and clouds rode high. Promise blue, infinity blue. Sarah couldn't quite catch her breath.

"You've named him Willoughby?" he said, his voice gravelly and deep.

She allowed a small smile. "After another unfaithful pig in a book I read."

"*Sense and Sensibility.*" He gave a tiny nod. "Grand book."

"You read it?"

He got the other eye open. "Och, lass, a man has to do more with his time than assassinate beloved national figures."

Sarah found herself on her feet, hands clenched. "Then you did try to kill . . ."

"Wellington? Nae. But someone is tryin' hard to blame me, now, aren't they?"

She couldn't decide what to do. How could she possibly know whether he was telling the truth? "Why would they blame you if you are innocent?"

He gave a minimal nod. "Och, weel, hasn't that been somethin I've been ponderin' the last few days? Could be because I saw who did do it, o' course."

"You did?"

"Oh, aye. And for my troubles I was shot and sent swimming in the Channel."

Sarah couldn't take her eyes from him. "Why should I believe you?"

He smiled again. Damn him. "I canna think of a reason you should."

It was getting harder to breathe. "If you are innocent, you should go to the authorities."

"If I go to the authorities, I'll be dead in a day. The people involved in that assassination attempt are highly placed. No, lass, I need to get to London."

"You've been trying to get to London all this time and only made it this far? The alert has been out on you for almost two weeks."

He grimaced. "Wheesht, lassie, I'm not in my best form. And it seems every tree in Britain holds my likeness. It's hard to hide a Scotsman as big as me in the brambles."

"But you've lingered here for at least three days."

He shrugged. "It's this blasted gunshot. What with everything, it's begun to fester. It seems to have taken the meat out of my legs entirely."

She was wringing her hands now, as if that would help. "You need a doctor."

He closed his eyes, as if the effort to keep them open was just too much. "Nae, lass. I just need a night or two under a roof. A bit of soap and water, a chop or two. I'll be gone before you know it. Unless you want to help me to London."

She backed away. "No. I cannot."

"Wellington is in grave danger."

She looked around her, suddenly sure Martin would hear them and gallop back up the drive. Certain one of the women in the house would wander out and spy her conversing with an injured Scot. It would take only one mistimed witness to bring disaster down on them all.

She should see him on his way. If she did, though, she didn't think he would last the week. He was so pale, so thin, as if he'd burned away too many pounds in the last few days. His eyes were smudged and sunken, his lips cracked. And that blood. Could she so easily condemn him?

Could she condemn her own family if he was lying? Her home?

Her home.

Oh, Christ, she thought with weary frustration. *I am so tired of always being an inch away from disaster.*

"You put my family in terrible danger," she finally said, taking another step back.

"Family?" he asked. "You have children?"

Her laugh was sharp and dry. "Not in the strictest sense of the word. But there are three women who would suffer if I were brought up on charges of abetting a traitor."

Some of the starch seemed to go out of him. Sarah stopped herself from reaching out to him. Guilt was an old companion. Why should it bother her so much now?

"You don't understand...," she protested, her hands caught in her apron.

He afforded her another wry smile. "Och, lass, but I do. Ye'd be a fool to believe such a disreputable stranger, just because he saved your pig from going over a cliff...at personal risk to himself."

She took another step back. "Do not *dare* . . ."

But his eyes were open and they were amused. Self-deprecating. Inexplicably, shadowed with grief. Sarah knew it was absurd, but she felt as if she were falling into them, her hard-won balance sacrificed to his pain.

She closed her own eyes. "You don't understand . . . ," she repeated pointlessly.

"Then help me up, lass," he said, sounding unbearably weary, "and I'll move on."

She didn't budge. She didn't open her eyes, as if that could indefinitely delay her need to act. She might have stayed that way if she hadn't heard a voice from the house.

"Lady Sarah! Are you comin' in f'r dinner soon?"

Sarah jumped. The last thing she needed was for anyone to come looking for her.

"I will be there in a minute, Mary!" she called, staring down at the Scot with dread. "I'm securing Willoughby!"

"Mizz Hardy says to hurry please, ma'am!"

The thin, hesitant tones of Mary Sunday's voice were punctuated by the slamming of a door.

"Come along, then, lass," her surprise guest said, lifting a hand. "Gi' me a hand up, and I'll be off."

She stared at that hand as if it were a puzzle. She tried so hard to be practical. To be realistic. She couldn't. "No," she said with a shake of her head. "You won't."

She simply couldn't do it. She could not condemn him.

She should, God knew. She should get him as far away as possible before Martin returned. If the man was a traitor, there would be no mercy for her, none for anyone on the farm. But her instincts, developed over a lifetime spent balanced on the edge of security, had served her well. And her instinct said that no matter how it looked, this man was telling the truth.

He rolled and pushed himself to his feet. "Don't be daft, lass. Help me leave."

He swayed so alarmingly that Sarah put a hand around his ribs to stabilize him. It was like trying to balance a standing stone. "You wouldn't get off my property before you went down again," she said, "which would surely attract the wrong kind of attention. It happens that I have several empty outbuildings you could use for a night or two. We just need to get you there."

His hand on her shoulder, he shook his head, as if to clear it. "What if yon lassie stumbles over me?"

Sarah actually laughed. "No one goes into these outbuildings but Mr. Hicks, our man of work, and me. And Mr. Hicks never sees anything I do not want him to."

The Scot squinted at her, his eyes creased with humor. "Don't tell me. You do a wee bit of smuggling on the side."

She stiffened. "Now you're being ridiculous. I run my husband's estate. And make certain that his cousin who does smuggle remains at a safe distance."

The Scot tilted his head. "I think you have no man to protect you."

"My man went off to war."

"He fought at Waterloo?"

She looked away so he could not see her fresh guilt. "Yes. The 35th Foot."

He nodded. "Good lads all."

Odd how this stranger's praise could make her feel a bit better about Boswell. "Thank you. I heard the Black Watch fought heroically as well. You were an officer?"

"A colonel. Still am, unless this brangle has cost me that as well."

For a few moments, Sarah concentrated on getting the man into motion. Tucked right under his shoulder, she was struck by the solid weight of him. A *frisson* of energy seemed to shudder between them. Unbidden heat in a cold dusk. The sensation was so unfamiliar that she stumbled with the surprise of it. He didn't seem to notice, thank heaven. She would simply have to ignore it.

Drawing in a breath, she pushed on, stumbling over the cobbles of her stable yard. That was when it truly struck her what she was doing. Without her permission, her heart sped up. Her chest suddenly seemed too tight, as if a bubble of air were caught in it. She hadn't been beset by such feelings often, but she knew what they were. Exhilaration. The impermissible excitement of trodding along the edge of rebellion.

The last time she had felt it, she had been helping her friend Fiona run away from school. She could easily remember the heady thrill she'd felt as their coach had jolted and swayed across Berkshire. She swore she could still smell dust and leather seats.

"That cousin of his is nae wrong, lass," the Scot suddenly said. "Four months is a long time."

As quickly as that, the exhilaration died. "Not long enough to give up. Now, come along. I refuse to miss my dinner."

Bearing more of his weight, she guided him into the potting shed, not much in use at this time of year. He stumbled over his own feet, and shivered alarmingly as they entered through the listing wooden door. The floor was dirt, but it was dry and the temperature tolerable. He could at least rest a night or two before moving on.

It took some minutes, but they got him settled on the chair Mr. Hicks kept for his bad back. Sarah ignored the chair's groan of protest as all fifteen stone sank onto it. Shoving aside empty pots so the man could lay his head on the bench, Sarah gathered together what empty sacks lay about.

"This is the best I have for cover," she apologized, laying them in his lap. "I'll return later with blankets. Will you be all right?"

He never opened his eyes. "This'll be grand."

Still she hesitated. "It isn't much."

He chuckled. "Lass, this little stone hut is a palace compared to some of the places I've called home. Dinna fesh y'rself."

"Oh." She nodded. "Of course. I heard conditions on the Peninsula were terrible."

Strangely enough, that was what got his head up and his eyes open. "Aye," was all he said, wearing the oddest expression. "The Peninsula."

She gave a jerky nod. "Well, good-bye for now," she said, wiping her hands on her apron. "I hope you like rabbit stew. That is what is for dinner."

"May I ask one favor, lass?"

She shrugged. "You can certainly ask."

"Your name. I don't know what to call my angel of mercy."

She fought a furious blush. Suddenly she felt uncomfortable, as if her act of charity had just become very personal.

"Sarah, Lady Clarke," she finally said. "And you?"

He stared at her as if she had two heads. "You don't know my name?"

She shrugged. "Evidently whoever drew up the posters felt a description was sufficient. 'Tall, large Scot with red hair, blue eyes, multiple scars and tattoo of thistle and dagger on left upper arm. Weight sixteen stone.'" She tilted her head a bit. "It seems you have added a scar to the collection. And lost a stone or two."

He shrugged. "Swimming is nae my best sport. And it's nae a dagger. It's called a *sgian dubh*."

Sarah blinked and surrendered a faint smile. "Oh. Of course."

He looked surprised. "You know what a *sgian dubh* is, do you, lass?"

"As a matter of fact, I do. I had friends in school from Scotland. They had *sgian dubhs*." She couldn't help but smile, thinking of how her friend Fiona had sewn a special pocket in her sleeve to hold the little knife at the ready. "We wove some pretty elaborate plots involving those little knives and certain academy mistresses."

It was his turn to grin, and it softened his face, easing those hard lines that bracketed his mouth and punctuated his forehead. "Ferocious wee thing, aren't you?"

Her humor died. "When necessary. Now then, sir. I would appreciate a name."

Before she could think to intervene, he climbed unsteadily back to his feet and bowed. "According to you English," he said, his deep voice sliding over her skin like honey, "my name is John Edward George Ferguson Hawes, Viscount Hawes."

She blinked up at him, an odd sense of familiarity nagging her. "You're a peer?"

Again, he shrugged, as if it were unimportant. "So it seems."

"It seems? Are you not certain?"

His smile twisted. "Oh, aye. I'm afraid I am. The thing's just a bad fit. I prefer to hear the name I carried until the day the toffs found me."

He began to sway again. She reached out to grab his arm. "Then what name will you allow?" she demanded in exasperation. "So I can get you off your feet before you fall all on your own."

She had no intention of being in the way when he did.

Thankfully, he didn't attempt another bow. "If it's all the same to ye, lass," he said, "I would rather you call me Ian. But if you've a need to be formal, then it would be Ferguson. Colonel Ian Ferguson."

In that moment, everything changed. Sarah felt as if she had been felled by a tree, by a house. By an iceberg.

"You stare, lass," he said, listing a little more.

"You cannot be," was all she could manage. She wanted to step back, to get a better look at him. But she knew if she let go, he would drop like a rock.

"Can I no'?" he asked.

Suddenly that sense of familiarity made sense. It was the color of the hair, that dark, rich auburn. The blue, blue eyes and the height. The story she should have remembered about how Ian Ferguson became Viscount Hawes.

Anger began to bubble deep in her. Resentment.

"The girls I was speaking of who attended school with me at Miss Chase's Academy outside Slough," she said. "The ones with the *sgian dubhs*. Their names were Fiona and Mairead Ferguson."

Immediately his features lit up. "You know Fiona and Mairead?"

This time she did step away. His legs immediately gave out, landing him with a thud on the chair.

"*You* are their brother," she accused.

He frowned at the venom in her voice. "Aye, lass. I am."

She nodded sharply. "When was the last time you saw them?"

He looked bemused. "Two...nae, three years."

"Indeed," she said, knowing her voice was cold with condemnation. "In that case, it might be better for both of us if I bid you farewell right now. You will undoubtedly be able to find your way in the morning."

Before he had a chance to react, she turned about and slammed out the door.

Chapter 3

Sarah's indignation propelled her on a march around the outbuildings.

Fiona Ferguson's brother. How could he be? Fiona had been born and raised in Edinburgh. She was now living somewhere in West Riding. How could her brother wash up on the south coast and end up on Sarah's farm? How was Sarah supposed to deal equably with him, when all she wanted to do was wallop him in the head with a fence post for neglecting her friends?

There had been few enough of those in Sarah's life. Her birth assured that. But for those precious few years at school, she had been able to claim four. Her roommates: Pippin Knight, Lizzie Ripton, and the Ferguson sisters. Fiona had shared four years of boarding school with Sarah. But Fiona's twin, Mairead, had lasted only weeks, overwhelmed and miserable by the upheaval in her life. And none but her sister and friends had cared.

Fiona had always been quick to excuse her brother for abandoning her and her sister so thoroughly. "He found us a school," she would say. "And when that didn't work for Mairead, he sent one of his friends to make sure she got home safely."

He had found them what the students had dubbed Last Chance Academy, the worst school in Britain, in which dozens of girls had been left to languish behind the cold walls of arbitrary discipline, mediocre academics, and parental indifference. The only time Sarah thought of her marriage with anything but regret was when she remembered that it had saved her from another day in that prison.

And Ian Ferguson had not once visited his sisters or interceded on their behalf. He hadn't so much as asked exactly why it was that Mairead went home. Only Fiona had fought for her sister. Fiona and her school chums.

Sarah finally came to rest against Willoughby's enclosure, still too angry to go inside.

It wasn't that easy, of course. It never was. Her feelings for Ian Ferguson were far more complicated than mere anger, and had been for years. But she wasn't about to kick at that nest now: It would be pointless.

Inevitably, Sarah's gaze swept over to the arbor. *Oh, Boswell. How did it come to this?* Even before Boswell's flight, she had worked herself raw to hold on to Fairbourne. She had cobbled this place together with her callused fingers, her wits and her determination to finally belong somewhere. She would do anything to protect it. She *had* done anything, and the secrets weighed on her like grief.

How then, could she think of risking it all for one man? All Martin Clarke had to do was discover Ian Ferguson crouching in her potting shed, and Fairbourne would be emptied like a plague house. The family Boswell had asked Sarah to protect would be destroyed, and the only real home she'd ever had lost.

Her instincts said to leave Ian Ferguson to rot. To hand him over forthwith to the militia, where he would no longer be a threat to her or to Fairbourne.

Rubbing at her eyes, she sighed. She couldn't. Fiona would never understand. Even after her brother's neglect, Fiona still loved the beast. She still insisted that it would have been impossible for Ian to do more for her, since he was busy fighting on the Continent. She would never understand if Sarah turned him in. Sarah would never forgive herself if her actions hurt her friend again.

As if expressing his scorn, Willoughby snorted, butting up against her leg. Sarah instinctively bent to scratch his ears.

"I should do it, should I?" she asked the pig, often the recipient of her thoughts. "I should just turn him over to the militia. That way he would be safe from Martin, and I would be safe from him."

And yet, even as she said it, she knew that she would do nothing of the sort. She would patch him up as best she could, and show him the way up the coast. And when he was gone, she would return to the gray monotony of her life. And she would never tell a soul he'd been there.

* * *

"About time you showed," Sarah heard the minute she opened the kitchen door. "Dinner's been ready this while."

Reaching behind her to untie her work apron, Sarah smiled at Peg Hardy, who was setting a steaming cobbler on the work table. Behind her, little Mary Sunday was stirring soup in the cauldron, and covered dishes sat out on the serving table. The air was redolent with a bouquet of scents from dinner: yeasty bread, roasting mutton, the last of the blackberries tucked into a cinnamon-scented crust.

Every time Sarah walked in the kitchen door, she marveled that Peg could produce such delectable smells and such bad food. It was even worse that Sarah seemed to be the only one who noticed.

"I apologize for being late, Peg," she said as she pulled her apron off over her head. "I was forced to waste time dealing with Cousin Martin."

And hiding a possible traitor in the potting shed. Just the thought sent Sarah's pulse skyrocketing. She couldn't imagine that Peg didn't notice how upended she was.

Peg was too busy making the evil eye sign with flour-dusted fingers at the sound of Martin's name. "Well, you'd better get in there all the same. Them termagants is about to start poundin' their silver on the table."

Sarah stopped short. "They came down for dinner?"

Oh, hell. She'd been counting on sitting at Peg's table for dinner so she could run back out. Now she would have to do the pretty for at least two hours.

Peg rolled her expressive brown eyes. "Aren't you the lucky one? Poor ole Parker's been pourin' sherry like lemonade, and Miss Fitchwater's wavin' smelling salts like incense in a Papist church."

Poor old Parker being their butler, the last of the old servants, who had claimed deafness when retirement was suggested.

Sarah felt a headache coming on. "What happened this time to set them off?"

Hand on hip, Peg snorted, sounding a bit like Willoughby. "Her grand ladyship slipped out on the cliffs and lost some of her paint pots to the ocean. Miss Artemesia got a letter from one of her school chums."

Sarah sighed. "Poor Artie. She was so happy there."

"Well, she ain't now. So you'd better be wearin' armor when you walk in there. Parker'll only be able to hold 'em off so long." Reaching over, Peg gave her a little shove. "Go on up the back stairs, now. Mary brought up a can of hot water and laid out your lavender dress."

Sarah planted a kiss on Peg's cheek. "I don't know what I'd do without you, Peg."

Peg's lean, hard face went all red, and she waved Sarah off. "Don't be daft. Haven't left you yet, have I?"

Sarah's mother had never forgiven her when Peg followed Sarah to Fairbourne upon her marriage. Sarah didn't want to think what might happen to her loyal friend if Martin succeeded in taking over. There would be no other place for any of them to go.

* * *

It took Sarah no more than twenty minutes to freshen up and change. Even so, by the time the cadaverous, smiling Parker ushered her into the rose parlor with creaking dignity and a full glass of sherry, the three women waiting for her looked as if they had been holding off starvation with roots and rainwater.

"Can you never arrive on time for a meal?" Lady Clarke asked as she fidgeted with her Norwich shawl where she sat on one end of the faded straw silk settee. "Hunger is not good for my heart."

Calm, Sarah thought, standing so still that Parker turned to stare at her. *It isn't Lady Clarke's fault that I feel as if I can't breathe. She isn't breaking the law for a handsome man.*

Her hand shaking only a little, she accepted the glass from Parker, took a too-big gulp, and strode into the fray. "I apologize, Mother Clarke," she said, deftly avoiding the feathers the woman always wore in her hair at dinner so she could give her a quick buss on the cheek on the way by. "I was delayed by Cousin Martin and the squire."

As for Lady Clarke, Sarah suspected her heart was the soundest mechanism on the estate. Not that Lady Clarke had ever allowed that to affect her pretense of fragility. A deceptively frail-looking woman of middle height with faded blond hair and papery skin, she had perfected the art of ruling via vapors. But then, Sarah thought, if she had been forced to spend thirty years with Lord Clarke, she would have been a bit vaporish herself.

"Good evening, Miss Fitchwater," Sarah said with a real smile for the tall, storklike lady perched beside the dowager, a full glass of ratafia in her hand. "Did you have a good day out on the Undercliff?"

"A disaster," Lady Clarke moaned, hand to forehead. "I am all over bruised."

"I heard," Sarah said, taking a seat beside young Artemesia on the matching settee that bracketed the sputtering fire. "I am so sorry. It is a testament to your fortitude that you are here, Mother Clarke. Do you not think, Miss Fitchwater?"

"Oh, indeed," the woman agreed, patting at the dowager's hand. "Indeed."

One of the few blessings of living at Fairbourne was

that it was situated right along one of the most beautiful coastlines in England, famous for not only its very paintable flora, but its retrievable fossils, which kept both women busy. A mixed blessing, in Sarah's opinion.

Sipping at her sherry, Sarah looked over to ask Artemesia about her day, but the petite blonde was glaring at the far wall, her eyes suspiciously damp, her hands picking at the coliquet ribbon that fell from the waist of her much-turned cherry kerseymere. It seemed that once again Peg's assessment was accurate. The girl and her mother were in a sour enough mood to strip the remaining paper from the walls. Thank heaven for Miss Fitchwater, who had a happy knack of pouring oil on turbulent seas. Sarah simply didn't have the patience to negotiate peace tonight.

"It was a lovely day, though," Miss Fitchwater said. "Was it not, dear? Brisk."

The dowager resumed fluttering, which, with the layers of pastel fabrics she wore—mint, peach, lavender, and cream—caused her to look like a trapped butterfly. "I fail to see how. I found nothing new to paint. I vow, I thought I would have years' worth of material for my comprehensive catalog of Devon and Dorset flora and fauna."

"There was that wonderful late Dorset Heath," Miss Fitchwater offered, patting again. "I thought it an exceptional specimen."

"So it was," Lady Clarke mused. "Do you think I should sketch it?"

"It might take your mind off the half-mourning butterfly you never found, dear. Why not go early tomorrow? I thought I saw a lovely gryphaea I'd like to chip out."

"And you, Miss Fitchwater?" Sarah asked, wondering

why Parker hadn't announced dinner yet. She was beginning to wonder if she would have the patience to last out the evening. "Did you have any luck today?"

The horse-faced woman smiled back with a nod. "Oh, yes. It was a most productive day for me, thank you. An ammonite and lovely devil's toenail."

Sarah chuckled at the acquisitive light in the fossil-hunter's eyes. "Definitely more productive than my day. I spent much of it rescuing Willoughby from his latest obsession. He has developed quite a passion for the squire's mare."

A vaguely distempered light appeared in Lady Clarke's soft brown eyes. "Sarah, please," she begged in die-away tones. "That is not at all an appropriate topic of conversation for the parlor."

To Sarah's left, Artemesia giggled behind her hand. "No wonder no one invites you to local functions, Sarah. You sound like a farmhand."

No one invited Sarah to local functions because she was a by-blow, especially since Boswell had gone. Even the squire, who was more than happy to help her in the fields, succumbed to his wife's delicate sensibilities when invitations went out. Sarah might have minded more if it didn't afford her the chance for blessed solitude. And truthfully, social exclusion had long since lost its sting.

"A farmhand, Artie?" she echoed with a smile for the fidgety fifteen-year-old. "And so I am. Isn't it wonderful that I enjoy it so much?"

"Sarah, must you use that awful nickname?" Lady Clarke asked, her hands fluttering in protest. "You make Artemesia sound such a guy."

"But Artie specifically asked me to," Sarah said. "I

think a girl should be able to choose how she calls herself. I always wanted to call myself Cecily but Mrs. Tregallan thought it suspiciously sibilant."

Artie giggled again.

"And that is another thing," Lady Clarke protested. "I insist you cease calling your dear mother Mrs. Tregallan in that odious way. Especially after all she did for you."

"It is what she wished," Sarah reminded the older women. "As you know, she advocated honesty in all things. And she was not my mother. My mother was dead."

"Well, I see no reason I should not be called Artie," Artemesia spoke up with some hauteur. "It is what the girls called me at school. I think it . . . speaking."

"It is *vulgar,*" her mother protested weakly, reaching a trembling hand to Miss Fitchwater, who passed her vinaigrette. "If that is all you learned in that school, then it is just as well you left."

"I did not *leave,*" Artemesia retorted. "Sarah ran out of money. If not for her, I would still be singing duets with the Duke of Thurston's daughter."

Ah, Sarah thought, *here it comes.* Artie was definitely in the mood for a quarrel. Maybe she will be so irritable we can shorten dinner and I can get back outside.

"The Tate girl?" Miss Fitchwater asked Artie, her long face creased in delicate distress. "A brass-faced hoyden if ever there was one."

Artemesia let loose a practiced titter. "Oh, Rosie, you don't know anything. Gillian Tate is top of the trees. Everyone wants to be her."

Lady Clarke stood up, startling them all. "Do not *dare* show such disrespect to Miss Fitchwater," she snapped, aristocratic brow as clenched as her hands. "She is my dear friend and has sacrificed much to bear me company in my trials. And if I hear you use those childish nicknames once more, you will spend the week in your room. Her name is Rosamunde, not *Rosie,* and you will address her as Miss Fitchwater. Did you learn nothing from your time at school?"

In a flurry of skirts, Artemesia followed to her feet. "Of course I did, Mama. I learned how backwards we all are here. Oh, how can I bear it? No one cares for my feelings. I think Sarah made me return home out of spite. She knows how popular I am and she can't stand it because nobody wants her. Even her family would never have kept her if they weren't paid. And he was a vicar. Why, even Boswell ran away from her!"

She is fifteen, Sarah reminded herself when she wanted to slap the girl. *She is lost, and frustrated and seeing her friends live the life she should have.* A dilemma Sarah was far too familiar with. And yet tonight, she couldn't pretend sympathy.

Fortunately, Lady Clarke reacted before Sarah could betray her frustration. With a wail worthy of Siddons, the elder woman fell back onto the settee in a classic pose of distress. "Oh, horrid girl!" she cried. "How could you mention our missing boy, our dearest Boswell, and distress your mama so..."

Taking her cue, Miss Fitchwater retrieved the vinaigrette and the dowager's hand. She waved one and patted the other. "You distress us all, Artemesia," she gently chastised, which sent Artie crashing back onto her own seat in a flurry of skirts.

"I didn't mean...You know...." Huge tears spilled down her cheeks.

Opening her mouth to defuse the situation, Sarah reconsidered. After all, Artie didn't lie. Boswell had run away from her. Once he'd realized that it would be Sarah and not he who was saving the estate, he had escaped to find his glory in the most time-honored fashion. He had taken the rest of Sarah's dowry money and gone off to be a soldier.

And Sarah, left behind, felt guilty for it, for feeling nothing but relief on seeing him walk away, because she would be left behind, she the one with the least right to call Fairbourne home.

Oddly, it made her think of her surprised guest. Ian, the soldier who had been a hero, the man blessed with devout siblings. Even when he didn't deserve their devotion. Sarah wondered if he would ever understand how much she resented him for it.

And not, she admitted to herself, merely because he had hurt his sisters. Because his sisters, no matter how he ignored them, how often he disappointed him, loved him without question. Without reservation.

As she sat in this threadbare parlor with its meager fire and the displeasure of her companions, Sarah stared into the nut-brown sheen of her drink and admitted the truth. She wasn't just angry at Ian Ferguson. She was jealous. She had spent her entire life seeking inclusion, envying her four friends the fact that they were wanted for no other reason than their existence. A feeling Sarah couldn't comprehend.

Ian Ferguson would never understand. No matter what he did or didn't do, Fiona and Mairead would stand by him, believe him, and love him. They would never think to hurt him in return.

It wasn't fair. It wasn't right. For the first time in years, it hurt.

"Sarah? Are you all right?"

Sarah blinked and looked up to Miss Fitchwater. "Oh. Yes. Yes, I'm fine, thank you."

Fortunately, her lapse had been masked by the inevitable end to the scene between Artie and her mother, with Artie on her knees by her mother apologizing for being such a beast and her mother whimpering, as if Artie had been the one to send Boswell to war. Boswell, who was never mentioned unless his mother was feeling unattended.

Miss Fitchwater, an old player on this stage, kept her attention on Sarah. "I believe Artemesia owes you an apology," she said.

Sarah looked up, startled. "Pardon?"

"An apology?" Artemesia cried, back on her feet. "Why? If it weren't for Sarah, I would be back with my friends right now planning the autumn cotillion."

Sarah looked up to see tears blossom in the girl's eyes, and her own frustration eased. At least she had had her chance. "Is that what your letter was about?" she asked.

Artemesia seemed to collapse into herself. "I should have the chorale solo. Everyone says. And yet, I'm *here*."

"That does not excuse bad manners," her mother chastised, her voice calm for the amount of frenetic movement that was going on. "Dear Rosamunde is right. You owe Sarah an apology."

Sarah almost gaped. Lady Clarke never defended her. Maybe the older woman had hit her head when she'd fallen that afternoon.

"I apologize," Artie muttered, her face down to hide the stain on her cheeks.

Lady Clarke sighed and fidgeted with her shawl. "Much better. My heart could not have tolerated being ashamed of my daughter, after all the care and affection I have devoted to her. After all, a lady is judged not by how she treats the daughters of dukes, but how she treats the daughters of...the lesser among us."

Sarah almost laughed out loud. Ah, so that was what she was now. The daughter of the lesser among us. Sarah assumed the dowager was referring to her mother's unmarried status, since that lady's birth had been in every way equal to the dowager's. She'd just had the great misfortune to believe the wrong promises.

"Thank you, Artie," Sarah said, briefly laying a hand on the girl's.

Fairbourne was all she needed, Sarah reminded herself when Artie pulled her hand away. That was what her marriage had bought her. Not the love of her husband; she hadn't expected it. She didn't love him either. Mostly she pitied him, a weak man given too big a task. Not the respect or love of his family. They resented the need for her.

Her marriage had bought her this wonderful old pile of Elizabethan bricks. She loved to wander the wainscoted rooms, listening to the echoes of its three hundred years. She loved to walk land she had saved. She loved to care for the animals who needed her and the fields that were once again greening with wheat and barley under her care. Most days, she could even love the people who needed her more.

It had been enough for a long while now. She refused to let Ian Ferguson take that away from her.

"My lady," Parker finally announced in stentorian tones from the doorway. "Dinner."

Finally, Sarah thought, setting her sherry on the side table and getting to her feet. One more minute and she would be weeping and tearing her clothes. And there was quite enough drama in this house without her.

* * *

Dinner seemed interminable. After the fireworks in the drawing room, conversation lagged, punctuated by little flare-ups between mother and daughter over one imagined slight or another. For once, Sarah failed to get involved. She was too preoccupied with her own problems.

By the time the runny blancmange had been set out with the nuts, signifying the end to another nightmarish meal, Sarah had her plans for her surprise guest well in hand. She just had to get away so she could implement them. Before anyone could start another argument, she excused herself and got to her feet, her attention already on the supplies she would have to purloin.

Usually she was able to escape without interference. Not so tonight. Sarah had just reached the bottom step of the old oak staircase when Artemesia stepped in front of her.

Oh, no, Sarah thought. *Not tonight.* She hadn't been paying enough attention at dinner. Artie was twisting that poor coliquet ribbon into shreds. There were once again tears in her eyes and a definite wobble about her mouth.

"Why do you put up with me?" the girl demanded, her voice rising dangerously. "I'm a beast. I'm so sorry, Sarah."

Oh, lord, Sarah thought uncharitably. *This could be a long session if I don't head her off.* Even as she thought that, she realized that she couldn't simply abandon the girl. All Artie wanted was to be like her friends. Sarah understood that all too well.

"I know, sweetheart," she said, and gathered the teen into her arms.

Shaking with gusty sobs, Artie collapsed against Sarah's shoulder. Sarah murmured and stroked her hair and waited for the storm to pass. It was the least she could do. Lady Clarke certainly wasn't any help. Miss Fitchwater tended to look on Artie like a wild creature who might bite. And Sarah was usually too busy about the estate to listen to her.

"You really need to guard your tongue a bit better, my dear," Sarah said, brushing the straggling strands of honey-blond hair off the girl's forehead. "The hallmark of a good society lady is the ability to lie with a smile, no matter how you feel."

Artie looked up, her pretty brown eyes swimming in tears. "I was doing beautifully tonight before you got there. I didn't even tell Mama she looks quite dreadful in that new dress. I knew it would hurt her." The tears swelled. "And then I hurt you instead. I *am* sorry, Sarah. Truly."

"I know, my dear. We have all been under a strain since Boswell went off to be a soldier. And I'm afraid the strain won't ease until he comes home."

"I just…wanted…to stay," Artie sobbed. "They'll all go on without me. They will have their season and marry and live real lives, and I'll be stuck…*here*…waiting for Boswell to come home."

Sarah stroked her hair. "Oh, love. I wish there had been another way."

"I...I know..."

Her own chest growing tight with the girl's misery, Sarah briefly closed her eyes. "If you promise not to share with your mother, shall I tell you a secret? It seems we have two extra appointments for Willoughby's, er, services. If he is successful, I might be able to put money away for next term's tuition. Can you wait that long, do you think?"

Artie pulled back to meet Sarah's gaze, her features frozen. "You...you mean it?"

In her head Sarah ruthlessly shuffled aside the new milch cow she had hoped to buy. They would survive with two for a while longer. "I do. Now, go wash your face. You look a fright."

Artie gave her a smacking kiss on the cheek. "You're the best thing that has ever happened to us, Sarah..." Suddenly, her eyes lit and she giggled. "I mean, Cecily."

And without another word, she scampered up the steps. Sarah knew she shouldn't have crumbled beneath the girl's tears, but she couldn't really feel bad about it. She would manage. She always had.

"She's right, you know."

Startled by the new voice, Sarah whipped around to see Miss Fitchwater standing in the shadows by the parlor. "Oh. You startled me."

The lady smiled, her long face softening. "You *are* the best thing that has happened to us. I hope you know that."

For once in her life, Sarah blushed. "Don't be silly. Is there something you need?"

Miss Fitchwater paused a moment, as if deciding. Finally, though, she stepped forward. "I hate to add to your burdens, but are you going into Lyme soon?"

"I do have a few commissions to execute," she said, anxious to be away from Miss Fitchwater's sharp gray eyes.

The woman gave a hesitant nod. "Lady Clarke has need of just a few new paints."

It was all Sarah could do to keep from sighing. She shouldn't have been surprised, really. If Lady Clarke were sleeping on the floor of a workhouse, she would consider herself entitled to "just a few new paints." Ever since Sarah had found herself in charge of the devout artist, she had been struggling to find a way to restrict her spending.

"Here," Miss Fitchwater said abruptly.

Sarah opened her eyes to see the woman holding out her hand. Cupped in her palm was the diamond and ruby brooch she always wore with her best gray dress.

"This should do for a bit," Miss Fitchwater said.

Sarah made no move to take it. "No."

Miss Fitchwater harrumphed. "Take the thing. I don't want it if it means my dear Winnifred is unhappy. And think about how fretful she would be if forbidden her art."

Sarah felt so torn. She honored Miss Fitchwater's sacrifice. It was a lovely thing to do for her friend, to sacrifice her most cherished possession. But all it did was keep Lady Clarke nestled in cotton padding, her world composed of watercolors and hiking gear.

"I shall record every flower, butterfly, insect, and bird of the south coast," the older woman had once boasted. And she had been doing it too. The egg money went into her hobby. Artemesia's school fees. Funds for the roof.

Lady Clarke only noticed the world around her if her paints ran out or the weather kept her from the Undercliff.

"You don't understand," Miss Fitchwater said, as if hearing Sarah's thoughts.

"I imagine I don't," Sarah answered. "But then, I cannot imagine spending my day grinding something called Egyptian Mummy into a paint color."

Or refusing to sell the resultant artwork for coal. Or her daughter's school fees, so Artie might have a chance at a decent marriage.

Miss Fitchwater almost smiled. "Oh, Egyptian Mummy is a lovely brown."

Sarah laughed. "But it is from a *mummy.* Surely all finer feelings are revolted."

For the first time in weeks, Sarah won an almost impish grin from the older woman. "Not when it can put just the perfect shading on a Lulworth Skipper butterfly."

Sarah wanted to say no. No more wasteful spending. She knew she wouldn't, though. There was little enough here at Fairbourne to soothe a soul. She herself loved the wind, the untidy folds of land, the little mutterings of excitement with which her animals greeted her. Lady Clarke loved to paint. And Miss Fitchwater loved Lady Clarke. How could Sarah disdain such devotion?

Surrendering, she plucked the brooch from Miss Fitchwater's palm. "If you refuse to be dissuaded," she said, "I can do nothing but what you ask. I will take it into Lyme when I go, and we will pawn it. That way it will be waiting for you to recover."

Sarah was disconcerted to see tears sparkle in the older woman's eyes. "Thank you," Miss Fitchwater said, clasping Sarah's hand in her own. "I meant what I said before."

Her face grew grim, her posture unconsciously rigid. "Winnie might not be able to say it, but you truly are the best thing that has happened to this family."

Sarah felt the unfamiliar burn of tears block her throat. She knew what it took for Miss Fitchwater to say that. She couldn't remember ever receiving such a sweet gift.

Even knowing how uncomfortable she would make the ungainly woman, she gathered her into a quick, fierce hug. "And you are the best that has happened to me."

Which was why, in the end, she had to see Ian Ferguson on his way.

* * *

Sarah wasted not another moment. While Lady Clarke and Miss Fitchwater perused the latest watercolors in the art studio–cum–second parlor and Artie plunked her way through a Scarlatti piece in the music room, Sarah raided the linen closet for extra blankets and the still room for bandages and a few herbs for poultices. Peg saw her, but Peg was another who never thought to challenge Sarah's actions. So Sarah felt free to snatch a bowl of stew, a hunk of bread, and a mug of ale to go with her supplies.

"You have to stop feeding that pig like he was human," Peg said, appearing beside her to pull open the back door.

Sarah resettled her loot and smiled. "Oh, no, Peg. This is for me. I've decided that I wish to actually enjoy dinner tonight. So I shall have it in the stables."

Peg's response was a soft *hmmph,* but she didn't object.

Sarah stepped out into the dying evening. The fading light cast a golden glow over fast-moving clouds, and the wind fretted about Sarah's ankles. She smelled rain and knew they were in for more. She should be thinking about how she could get the man in the shed off her land. Instead, she found herself once again fighting that perfectly ridiculous surge of exhilaration.

She knew better than to feel anything of the sort. She didn't have the time or the right. She refused to admit that she'd run up to tidy her hair before running out the door.

It wouldn't matter. It *didn't* matter. Even so, she clutched her supplies to her chest like new schoolbooks as she strode past the shorn garden and through the various stableyards. As she passed Willoughby's enclosure, he grunted in greeting.

"Good thing you're here," she told him. "Tonight I am not so sure I'd chase you."

She wouldn't have believed a pig could look resentful. This one did. It made her chuckle as she grabbed the shed door and gave it a pull. She felt giddy and silly and anxious; she felt as if something alien had taken up residence in her chest. She tried very hard not to smile as the hinges screeched in protest.

"Mr. Ferguson—"

Her smile died unborn. She looked around the shed, sure her eyes were deceiving her.

They weren't. The shed was empty.

Chapter 4

Yorkshire

The last time Alex Knight saw Fiona Ferguson, he delivered the best news of her life. This time he brought the worst.

"If you will wait here, my lord," the rotund little butler intoned with a bow. "I will notify the marquess."

Alex didn't even bother to respond. He just walked across the vast salon to look out the window. It was better than looking around what was one of the coldest, grimmest rooms he had ever entered. Not that it was dingy or dark. The windows were at least ten feet tall and facing south, so the sun should have warmed him. But there was something off-putting about the unrelieved white of the marble floor, the spare blue and gold décor, and surgically precise positioning of the various priceless porcelains.

The Leyburn marquessate was older than Noah, a venerable title built up over centuries with royal loans, favorable marriages, and the judicious switching of allegiances. Alex might have expected this house to reflect such history, much as his own home, a gray stone behemoth of venerable splendor that rambled over the ground like a hodgepodge of the ages of Britain.

He couldn't have been more wrong. He suspected the house truly was as old as the title. But recently the exterior had been tightly wrapped in severe, geometric Palladian sterility, the footprints of history well camouflaged by acres of stark white marble.

He should have anticipated it, really. After all, the only other time he had met with the marquess had been at his townhouse in St. James Square, and that home had been just as bleak, a gleaming white sepulcher decorated in marble statues and condescension.

Alex hated it. He wondered where in this mausoleum Fiona would find comfort from the news he was about to impart.

I am so sorry, Miss Ferguson. I have some bad news. Will you sit?

Fiona, sit down. This is going to be hard.

At least you're safe here with your grandfather. Ian accomplished that at least.

Alex had been testing his script since he'd received the order to break the news to the Hawes family. Surely there was a better way of telling the girl.

Doesn't it help that you're living in luxury instead of the slums of Edinburgh, where you grew up? Don't I get a reprieve for helping to find your grandfather?

Miss Fiona . . .

"Mr. Knight!"

Alex spun around to see Fiona Ferguson stepping

through the open door. The sight of her literally took his breath.

Four years ago he had predicted that Fiona Ferguson would mature into a rare beauty, a redhead majestic enough to shame Boadicea. And she had. Standing at least five foot seven, she was blessed with statuesque proportions and magnificent auburn hair caught up in a thick knot that ruthlessly contained the lush curls he remembered. Her square face was high-cheeked, her mouth broad, her eyes a startling blue.

She took a step forward, and he realized he'd been staring. "Lady Fiona," he greeted her with a bow.

She dimpled. "Mr. Knight," she responded, dropping a matching curtsy. "No, that's not right. I heard that your uncle passed away. I am so sorry. That makes you Lord Whitmore now, doesn't it?"

"Guilty as charged, ma'am."

She motioned to one of the ice blue velvet chairs that had been positioned before a white satin settee, and took the other herself, lowering into it with all the poise of a duchess, her jonquil dress a splash of life in the sterile room.

That was when Alex noticed that something was...off. Not her looks; she had more than fulfilled the promise he had recognized four years earlier when he'd first caught sight of her hanging from a carriage window. Her elegance did not disappoint, nor her kindness. But something...some spark was missing. Some animation.

His impression sharpened as he watched Miss Ferguson order tea. She was paler than he remembered, the saucy scattering of freckles missing from her nose.

Her movements were tidier, smaller, as if meant to fit into a less expansive space. The Fiona Ferguson he remembered had stood toe-to-toe with him, eyes flashing lightning, nostrils flared like a horse scenting battle, hands on generous hips. Now she seemed...dimmed. Oddly colorless, even with her magnificent looks.

Was this the natural outcome of her years spent learning to fit into her new role as granddaughter to a marquess? Or was it something more? Did the opulence of this place weigh her down too?

"It is so very good to see you," Fiona said, her smile quiet and her hands crossed demurely in her lap. "What brings you so far north?"

Alex blinked. Oh God, he thought. He had been so caught up in her metamorphosis, he had all but forgotten his intent here. He had come to break her heart.

"I need to speak with your grandfather and sister as well," he said, trying hard not to betray his own distress. "Did the butler tell you?"

"Mims is getting grandfather now. I believe he is in his office. As for Mairead—" Her smile was rueful. "She is still asleep. She was up most of the night, after all."

He lifted an eyebrow. "She is not ill, I hope."

Fiona chuckled. "No. She is just Mairead. I will share your message with her when she rises, if that will serve. Can you not tell me what the news is? It might help to anticipate grandfather's reaction."

He didn't answer right away, still badly off-balance. He had brought bad news before. But *this* . . .

He must have given something away, because suddenly Fiona's smile died. Her hands tightened in her lap, as if she were holding onto something. Her gaze sharpened, and her breath caught. "Oh, God," she whispered. "Ian."

Alex was reaching for her hand, as if he could somehow cushion the impact of his words, when the door swung open. Alex found himself back on his feet as an older man strode through. Fiona's grandfather. Alex recognized the sharp blue eyes and square face that was replicated so exactly in the old man's grandchildren.

The marquess was much smaller than they, in height and bone, but handsomely turned out. Leonine white hair, the posture of a cavalry officer, and a hooked proboscis that would have put Old Nosey himself to shame. But he had cold eyes. Impatient eyes, as if the world was meant to serve him, and forever fell short.

"Lord Whitmore?" the man asked, his bushy white eyebrow raised. "Ah, yes. I remember now. Old Whitmore's great-nephew. We do go to great lengths to secure heirs, don't we?"

The marquess's voice was soft and deep. Nonetheless, Alex heard the unbending steel beneath. Alex gave a formal bow. "Indeed, sir."

"Grandfather," Fiona said, her voice sounding strained. "Allow me to introduce Alex Knight, Earl of Whitmore. Alex, my grandfather, the Marquess of Leyburn. I think Alex has news of Ian, grandfather."

"We have met, granddaughter," the marquess said, again in that curiously quiet voice. "You need not belabor the relationship."

Again she sat. The two men followed suit. Alex snuck a look at Fiona to see a betraying flush in her pale cheeks.

"Is it?" the marquess asked, his tone changing not at all. "About John?"

Alex saw now that the older man's fingers were digging into his knees, and he felt a fresh grief for the news he brought.

Clearing his throat, he faced the marquess. "Ten days ago," he said, wishing he could instead watch Fiona, who had lost that brief color, "an attempt was made on the life of the Duke of Wellington."

Fiona gasped. Her grandfather sat unmoving. Alex did not want to share the rest. He wanted to walk out right now and leave them with something. Anything.

He couldn't. "Reports have come that Ian was the one who fired the shot."

"No," Fiona said very clearly, very definitely. "Absolutely not."

The marquess waved off her objection. "The duke?" he asked, his voice brisk.

"Is unharmed. Other men protected him."

The marquess let out his breath, as if the news relieved him.

Fiona leaned forward. "That is absurd. You know Ian. He has too great a respect for the duke. He would never harm him."

Alex almost smiled. It was true. Often enough when in his cups, Ian had declared to all and sundry that the Duke of Wellington was the only Sassenach worth the powder to blow him to hell, and that even a Scot would be a fool not to follow him.

"Miss Ferguson, I promise," Alex said, finally taking her hand. "We are doing everything we can to learn the truth. But I'm afraid there were witnesses."

She had no answer. Her hand was cold, though, and trembling.

"Where is he?" the marquess asked.

Alex snapped back to attention. "Wellington?"

"John."

Alex noticed that the older man had not once called Ian by his Gaelic name or identified him as his grandson. It made Alex remember the day four years earlier when he had tracked the marquess down to bring him long-awaited news. The marquess's grandson, missing since childhood and long since given up for dead, had been found. He called himself Ian Ferguson, and was a colonel in a Highland Brigade. Until the truth had been revealed to him, Ferguson had believed himself and his sisters bastards.

Anyone would have thought the old man would have been over the moon. The search for an heir had been protracted, the marquess's only son having died four years earlier without other legitimate sons. If Ian had not been found, the title would have most likely reverted to the crown upon the marquess's death.

But upon reading the official notification, the marquess had crumpled the letter up and tossed it in the fire, his only words, "Damn Scottish witch."

Alex had not been there when the marquess had finally met his grandson, but it seemed that he had not gained any affection for him.

"He's dead," Alex said anyway. "Ian is dead."

Alex braced for tears, for denials and recriminations. Instead, he was met by silence. The marquess looked pensive. Fiona turned to her grandfather, perfectly composed, except for her eyes, which had grown large and glittered with unshed tears. She was trying to gauge the old man's reaction, Alex realized.

"Are they certain?" the marquess demanded, his voice unchanged.

Alex nodded. "I'm sorry, but it is almost certain. He was shot and went off the side of a ship in the Channel. An extensive search was mounted without success."

The marquess nodded, as if Alex had imparted news no more disturbing than a cancellation in his schedule. "In that case," the man said, abruptly getting to his feet, "I will need to go to London to see the Prince Regent. He will not refuse to help me protect the title. I will not forfeit everything this family has built up because of one traitor."

Alex stared. He had been so stunned by Ian's death, he hadn't even considered the ramifications. If it was proved that Ian as Viscount Hawes had committed treason, all titles, lands, and possessions belonging to the marquessate could well be forfeited.

"He is *not*—" Fiona objected, rising as well.

One cold look from her grandfather silenced her. "After I see to that business," he said with a sharp nod, "I must contact my new heir."

Fiona, her eyes bright with unshed tears, abruptly looked up. "Ian was your only heir."

The marquess glared down at her. "Not only. Only, unavoidably, the nearest. It would have been far better if he had never been found."

Without another word, the marquess stalked from the room. And Alex was left alone to bear witness as Fiona, in perfect silence, broke her heart against the rocks of loss.

* * *

Near Richmond

"He's dead, then," the gentleman said, never slowing his pace as he strode across the harvested field, a Manton shotgun broken over his elbow.

Alongside him a thinner, younger man attempted to keep up in boots not meant to be scuffed on the jagged remnants of broken wheat. "We assume so, sir."

The older man stopped so suddenly that his guest almost caromed off him. "You *assume*? Why does that not comfort me, Stricker?"

Stricker wished he could wipe his brow. Even with the autumn chill, he was suddenly hot and uncomfortable. "We've searched now for almost two weeks, sir. No one could have survived that sea. No one."

"What about the flask he is supposed to have had?"

"He had it. He took it from my belongings. It is also lost."

The older man looked off, as if able to pull up the scene. "Then it is either at the bottom of the Channel, or Ferguson has it."

"And he is at the bottom of the Channel." It was all Stricker could do to keep from fidgeting. "Believe me, sir, I had reason to make sure. If Ferguson could have proved the thing had been in my possession, I would have been hung. So I have as much reason as you to make sure."

His companion turned on him. "No, Stricker," he said, his voice too quiet for Stricker's peace of mind. "You do not. You don't have the welfare of this empire on your conscience. If Ferguson manages to throw a spoke into this plan, we could lose everything, and what would happen to us then? You think the French Revolution cannot happen here? *Do* you? Just leave that fool prince in charge another year, and you'll see."

For a long moment, the old man was silent, the furrow between his graying eyebrows deep. Stricker held absolutely still. He knew what happened if a person displeased these men. He had met their pet assassin once. He didn't want to again.

"Consider this, though, sir," he finally said. "Even if Ferguson survives, we have so discredited him, no one will believe him, no matter what he says."

The older man nodded absently. "How is your arm healing up?"

"Fine, sir. Almost back to form." As if he'd tell the old goat if it weren't. Damn Ferguson for his quick reactions. The blackguard had damn near shattered his elbow.

"Excellent. Go back and make absolutely certain that neither Ferguson nor that flask ever show up again. Get whatever help you need. *I* will determine when you have looked long enough."

Waving to the loader who followed a good twenty paces behind, the old man accepted two shotgun shells, slipped them into the barrel, and snapped the gun closed. Stricker was about to step back when the man abruptly swung the shotgun right at his chest. Stricker's instinct was to shriek and fall. Instead, knowing exactly what that would cost him, he stood stock still.

Lightning fast, the older man pulled the gun a few scant inches to the left and fired twice, bringing down a quail Stricker hadn't even heard. Stricker felt deafened, and his bladder threatened to loose. It didn't help his peace of mind that the old man then cast a speaking glance at him.

"Just to make sure you have all the help you need," he said. "I believe I will contact Madame Ferrar. She can be most... persuasive, if needed."

She could be most lethal. Stricker wanted so badly to say no. To tell the old man that he was finished. That he could no longer associate with people who hired monsters like Madame Ferrar. Instead, before the man had a chance to reload, Stricker bowed in acknowledgment and walked away.

* * *

Ian felt a bloody idiot. He had meant to be so thoughtful, sneaking out of Sarah Clarke's shed before anyone could find him and accuse her of harboring a fugitive. He had imagined he could make it at least as far as the next farm along the coast.

He hadn't made it a hundred feet. Now he sat once more, his back against the cold, wet stone of the stable, sucking an egg from one hand and holding onto an old scythe with the other, just in case he needed to defend himself.

It was too lowering for a Scot who had survived ten years on the Peninsula to have been brought down by a fever. But here he sat with no more strength than an infant, and a brain that wandered aimlessly about. He was more cold and wet than the stones at his back, and afflicted with a peculiar tightness in his chest. Even the damn scythe felt too heavy to lift.

Without warning, the stable door creaked open and early sunlight washed in.

Ian blinked. "Blast," he muttered, disgusted with himself. He'd left it too long.

He knew he should scramble to his feet, prepare to fight. He could manage no more than to just sit there, squinting into the light, an empty eggshell in his hand, the scythe on the dirt floor. He heard the footsteps first; a quick, precise staccato. A shadow separated itself from the door. He closed his eyes rather than face what was to come.

He waited for a cry of discovery. For condemnation, for recognition, for death; he almost didn't care which anymore. What he got was a wet snout in the neck.

"*A bhidse!*" His eyes jerking open to find himself being delicately sniffed by a porker almost the size of the redoubtable Willoughby. Just as pitch black, this one was more delicate about the face, with liquid black eyes.

Ian blinked. "I gather I am addressing the lovely Marianne?"

His voice came out scratchy and thin, which irritated him anew.

"Elinor, actually," came Sarah Clarke's voice from the doorway. "She is much too pragmatic to be Marianne. The last time Willoughby returned to her from one of his fancies, she kicked him in the face."

Determined not to betray the relief he felt at a familiar voice, he dropped the scythe to scratch the porcine lady's ears. "A stalwart female."

His reward was a grunt and a burrowing at his shoulder. It was his turn to grunt as the movement sent a sharp pain slicing through his side.

"What are you doing here?" Sarah Clarke asked, still not moving from the doorway. "I searched for you last night."

He carefully shrugged. "One of my best talents is the ability to seem invisible."

"Of course." Her voice was dry as dust.

Ian made the mistake of looking up then, to see Sarah Clarke approach. Her form was suddenly limned by in the dawn light. Her hair, which had seemed so mousy, gleamed in a nimbus of old gold around her soft face, and her movements seemed imbued with grace. She was not a beautiful woman. Her looks could only be labeled as modest. And yet, like a thunderclap, they leveled him.

Her face, so unremarkable, looked suddenly soft and feminine, her mouth the perfect size and shape to be kissed, her chin rounded, with just a hint of a dimple. And her breasts, which he hadn't even noticed before, pulled at the practical cotton of her brown dress, inexorably drawing Ian's attention. Breasts to cushion, to comfort, to support a weary man when the world grew too heavy.

That would have been bad enough, but as she stepped closer, a bucket in her hand and the other up to brush back a tress of hair, he saw that her hands were trembling.

So, the cool voice was only a front. He looked more closely to see that faint lines had blossomed at the corner of her eyes, and her rather pink lips had flattened out. She was distressed.

He wanted to pull her into his arms. He wanted to ease the taut line of her shoulders and bring a smile to that face. He wanted to stroke her cheek, unwind her tightly bound hair, and reassure her that all would be well.

With no warning, desire surged like an overfed river; his cold body flushed as if he were slouched beneath a Spanish sun. It had to be the fever, he thought desperately. There could be no other reason for his reaction. He liked women. He'd had his share; he'd regretted a few. But he had never been laid low like a lad seeing his first milk-maid.

She was approaching, her expression tentative. His heart sped, and his fingers itched to move. He clenched his hands into fists as the pig, hearing her mistress's voice, turned and grunted.

"You really came back?" he heard himself ask like a calfling.

She scowled. "I did not think I would be able to move you on without food."

"I appreciate that."

Stopping before him, she set down the pail. "Don't be," she said as if she found injured soldiers in her stable every day. "You are just another chore."

He attempted a smile. "Does it help at all that I am a very grateful chore? You could so easily have set the militia on me."

Flushing, she ducked her head. "I regret what I said last night," she said. "I did not mean for you to leave while you were still sick."

"Ah, wheesht, lass. Ye are a true friend to my sisters. I canna ask for more."

She stood rather stiffly, as if absent an answer. Silence stretched, punctuated by the rustlings and fretful mutter-ings of the inhabitants of various stalls.

"Tregallan," he said, squinting up at her.

She froze. "Pardon?"

He gave her the best smile he had in him. "I was fes-hing here all morning, trying to remember you. Fiona wrote regularly, you know, all about school and her friends. Lizzie Ripton, Pippin Knight, and Sarah. Sarah

Tregallan. It's why I did nae remember you earlier. I remember her telling me that her friend Sarah Tregallan had contracted a marriage...contracted. Sounds as if you'd come down with the ague, doesn't it?"

Poor Sarah, Fiona had described her to him. *The example of how we would be treated if the world knew we had no father either. If it were not for Lizzie and Pip and me, she would have no friends at all, and that is simply wrong.*

It was, he thought, seeing the strain in her soft hazel eyes. He and Fiona had been lucky. They had found a father after all, and he had been a viscount. A rank bastard in behavior, but definitely not in lineage. A viscount who had passed on his name. Evidently Sarah Tregallan hadn't been so lucky.

"This was the marriage?" he asked. "To the missing Boswell?"

"It was. It is."

"And was it a good thing?" he asked, knowing he had no right.

She tilted her head, the sun seeping through her tousled hair. "Why, yes. I have a home, and work to do, and animals to enjoy."

"Like Elinor here?"

She gave an abrupt nod. "She accompanies me on rounds each day," she said, giving the pig a scratch. "She likes to make sure everyone is behaving. Off with you now," she said, tapping the pig on the rump. "Your babies are hungry."

Elinor obligingly turned and trotted back out of the stables. Ian battled a useless wish for her owner's touch. A tap on his own rump wouldn't have come amiss at all.

His body was already anticipating it, shivers chasing up and down his spine.

His attention returned with a snap when Sarah crouched down before him and plucked the emptied egg from his fingers. "Yes," she said, considering it. "I thought you might still be close when I came away from the henhouse with a lighter basket."

"Apologies, ma'am," he said with a lopsided bow of the head. "Your hens were most obliging."

She shook her head. "Yes, they are quite silly enough to be susceptible to a handsome man. It is your hair. Reminds them of a cock's comb."

"Well, it's fitting," Ian admitted. "I'm feeling a bit of a coxcomb."

"And so you should. Exactly what was the point, sir, in moving from my potting shed to my stable?"

"The company, of course. A gelding, a donkey, and two goats, from my counting."

"Were they so intimidating that you felt the need of some support?" She reached out to the scythe.

"Don't touch that," he snapped, closing his fist around the handle.

She yanked her hand back.

He gave her a rueful smile. "It's nae much," he said. "But it gives me the illusion that if needed, I can fight my way past my foes."

It also kept his hand safely away from her hair. He was positively twitching with the need to run his fingers through it. His filthy, sweat-slicked fingers, which he was sure she would not appreciate.

Without asking permission, she reached out to lay her hand against the side of his face. "As I suspected. You are hot as an oven. And still wet. What am I to do with you?"

"You are to push me out the door and on my way," he answered, his voice humiliatingly uncertain. "Then, when the searchers inevitably return, you may show them your empty buildings with impunity."

"Don't be daft," she said, not moving. "It would not matter if I had nothing in these buildings but cobwebs. It is still a principle of mine never to allow Cousin Martin to set foot over my threshold."

"But you don't argue that I should be on my way."

She had been rising, but his words stopped her. "No, Colonel," she said, bending back down. "I do not."

She was crouched before him, her skirt puddling in the dirt, her sun-streaked hair untidily scraped back. Her eyes were hazel, he thought. Plain eyes, plain brows. And yet they mesmerized him. There should be nothing special about her eyes. About her small, practical hands. And yet he couldn't keep himself from reaching out to take hold of one.

The connection was instantaneous. Something in her, something deep and bright and strong, infused him with heat. Something in the slightly rough texture of her skin shook him to the core. He swore that a current snaked between them, like fire arcing across treetops.

Her expression didn't change by an iota. She went so still Ian wasn't sure she breathed. And yet he knew that she felt it too.

She was the one who first broke contact. Lurching to her feet, she grabbed for her pail and strode over to the stall that held a pedestrian-looking bay hack, who knickered at her approach.

"Yes, Harvey," she soothed him with a rub on his nose.

"Your food is coming. First, though, I must care for the foolish human."

"I can hear you," he reminded her.

"I know." Setting down the pail, she bent out of sight. "I don't believe you will be wandering about for a while, but if you do, it would be best to stay away from Harvey here. He bites."

"I know," Ian said ruefully, holding out his arm to display his mangled jacket. "He attempted to breakfast on me earlier."

Chuckling, she returned to the horse. Reaching into her apron, she pulled out a misshapen lump of biscuit. "If you wish to gain his favor," she said, smiling up at the horse as he daintily lipped the mass from her outstretched hand, "he does love my cook's biscuits. I believe it is because he is the only one with teeth strong enough to chew the things."

Giving the nodding horse a final rub, she picked up two blankets and carried them back to Ian. "Here," she said, briskly arranging them over him. "These will have to do until I can get back out here. Old George might have some clothing that would fit you."

"He must be a good size, Old George," Ian retorted, snuggling under the scratchy, horse-scented wool.

She straightened. "Something to keep in mind. Now, I will go about my day so my actions here don't raise suspicions. After breakfast, I will tend to that side of yours and bring you food. Unless you prefer hay, that is."

"Thank you. I'd not say nae t' a steak."

She scowled. "You'll not say nae to porridge. That is what we have. We usually have eggs, but someone ate them."

He tried his best smile. "Offer oats to a Scot? Lassie, I ken I'm in love."

Pursing her lips, she looked down at him. "It occurs to me that your brogue is as capricious as my pig."

He actually felt exhilaration bubble up behind his sternum. "It serves its purpose."

"If you wish to be underestimated," she said, "I imagine so."

She flashed him a quick grin, and his stomach swooped. Her teeth were white, even in the gloom of a dark stable.

"Stay away from my hens," she said briskly, walking over to retrieve a pitchfork. "I can only explain missing eggs so long. And you will please remain in one place so I can find you. When I have cleaned out the extra stall, you can hide there."

"Let me help," he said abruptly, hating the sight of that pitchfork in her hand. "I can clean stalls better than most."

"Thank you, no. I wish you to do nothing that will delay your departure or imperil my animals."

She turned back to her work, her drab brown dress swirling gently behind her. Ian couldn't take his gaze from her. It was because he was sick, he thought again. He wasn't able to mount his usual defenses. But he suddenly couldn't bear the idea that after this, he would never see this kind woman again.

When she stepped into an empty stall, Ian noticed that the door was listing. In fact, much of this little estate was listing. Listing and crumbling and faded.

"From what I see," he said, "you have need of that reward."

She didn't hesitate in her work. "Are you asking me to turn you in to be hung?"

"I suppose I'm asking why you don't."

For long moments she continued to bend and straighten, her focus entirely on pitching hay. Ian waited, not even sure what answer he wanted. He caught sight of her hands and suddenly felt angry. They were elegant, long-fingered, and lean. They should have been manicured and soft, callused by no more than the keys of a pianoforte. Instead her nails were short and ragged, and he could see scars on her knuckles, as if she were the warrior instead of he.

"I don't turn you in," she finally said, turning to gravely consider him, "because no matter what you have done, amazingly enough, your sisters love you."

Her answer made him feel even worse. She was right, of course. "You are very loyal to them."

"They are the best of friends."

"Even Mairead?" he asked, wanting her smile back.

Well, that got her hackles up. "Do not dare disparage Mairead," she snapped, pointing at him. "Just because she is not exactly like every other primped and pretty miss is no reason to make light of her. Mairead is . . . special. And she is lucky to have a twin who has sacrificed so much to watch over her. Her brother certainly doesn't."

Ian raised both hands in defense. "Guilty. And he knows it."

It would do no good, after all, to explain exactly why he had been unavailable to be there to help the girls all these years. No woman wanted to hear about scraping for pennies, of surviving great battlefields and small, sordid skirmishes and even more sordid spying just to be able to send more money home for food, of volunteering for every extra duty he could in the chance he could profit. Of always falling short, no matter how he tried. Of being so far away when his mother died that by the time he'd found his way home his sisters had been living in unspeakable conditions.

He had made up for it, though. He had found Drake's Rakes, gentlemen who helped the government in clandestine ways, and they had led him to Miss Chase's Academy for the girls, where his sisters should have been safe and happy and carefree, their every want seen to.

But that hadn't worked out very well either, had it?

"You're right, of course, lass," he admitted. "I've been a dismal failure as a brother. Please believe me, though. It isna' for want of trying."

He would not fail them again. He would not fail anyone. If he hadn't already made that vow to his grandfather, he would make it here.

Sarah Clarke considered him in silence for a moment, her fingers wrapped around the pitchfork, her color rising. "I fear, Colonel," she finally said, her voice tight, "that I don't believe you." She shook her head. "Three years. If you were my brother I would never let you back in the door."

A tough critic indeed. "Well, there was a war on," he reminded her.

"A war that had a year-long lull, if memory serves. A lull during which you spent quite a bit of time with your grandfather securing your inheritance."

"In Vienna. We were both there for the Congress. I never—"

He was going to say he'd never made it back to England, but of course that would be a lie.

"Never in England?" she retorted. "Nonsense. You were here several times. Fiona mentioned seeing you in the society columns. Let me see... 'that rascally Scot with a temper managed to delight the very weddable Lady A L at Almack's last evening.'"

"You memorized a newspaper clipping?"

"I remember when someone has so hurt my friend. Fiona wanted desperately to see you that summer, but your grandfather would not allow her to leave Yorkshire, and you refused to travel that far. London seemed much more to your taste."

He wanted to snap at her, to tell her she was being unrealistic. To make her understand how hard he had worked in the last two summers coming to peace with his new future as heir to a British marquess. Working with both his grandfather and Drake's Rakes to cement his position so he would never again be helpless to protect those who depended on him. But to his shame, he had been so determined to indelibly secure his family's comfort that he had mistaken their happiness.

"I promise," he said. "First thing after this, I will see my sisters and beg their pardon. And explain who Lady Ardeth Langstrom is." Another flash of guilt, an unfamiliar need to justify himself. "My grandfather introduced me to Lady Ardeth in Vienna. She and I are to marry next summer."

A sensible lady with a sensible eye to marriage. Far more beautiful than Sarah Clarke. The perfect wife for a future marquess with big plans, even though he had never once reacted to her as he had just now to Sarah Clarke.

"My sisters dinna know yet," he said. "Lady Ardeth has been in mourning, so the official notice has nae been sent out."

He wasn't certain in the half-light of the barn, but he thought Sarah Clarke went suddenly pale. She opened her mouth. Shook her head. Instead of answering, though, she spun back to her work, forking hay with the determination of a zealot, her body unyielding, her slim arms strong with muscles she'd built while protecting this little estate on the edge of nowhere.

Somehow, with only that silence and industry, she made him feel even worse.

Chapter 5

By the time Sarah finally approached the stables again, her carefully collected supplies hidden in her bucket, the sun was fairly high in the sky. She had attempted to return twice before, but her courage had failed her. It threatened to again, right where she came to an uncertain halt mere feet from the stable's stone side.

Everything had been so clear last night. Because of her friendship with Fiona and Mairead Ferguson, she had committed herself to help their brother on his way to London. Nothing more.

She had even remained calm this morning when she had walked into the stables to be surprised by the morning sun washing over Ian Ferguson as he sat against the stone wall, his long legs stretched out and that ridiculous eggshell cradled in his hand. The sight of him had been a surprise, certainly, but it hadn't leveled her. She had been more concerned with the pulled, pale cast of his features, not the way his auburn hair turned to dark fire where it curled at his neck. She had, of course, noticed his body, bold as a stone castle defending a hill, his square face carved from the same granite. But that was only to evaluate his weight, so she would know better how to help him. She swore it.

But then he had smiled, and everything changed. Sweet heavens, that smile should have been painted into every Bible in the kingdom as a warning against sin. It was the kind of devilish, boyish smile that took the strength right out of a girl's knees and demanded a smile in return. It was a smile that forced one to admit that her feelings for him were far more complicated than anger and jealousy.

Oh, she was angry. She was jealous. But that smile had done something far worse. It had resurrected feelings she swore she'd packed away where they could never be found; the unformed yearnings of a young girl.

The first time Sarah had heard of Fiona's notorious brother, she had been twelve, freshly exiled to the cold stone halls of Last Chance and aching for comfort. Mail call had been announced, which did nothing but make Sarah feel more alone. She seemed to be the only one without a letter or package. Rather than admit it, she'd tried to sneak out.

Pippin had intercepted her with her hand on the door. "Come on, then," she'd urged, pushing Sarah toward her bed. "Lizzie has biscuits."

She did indeed. After the roommates had congregated on Pippin's bed, she passed them around. Pippin showed off the lavender soap her sister had sent. That scent could still make Sarah smile. She remembered so clearly the comfort of it, the scratch of wool beneath her knees as she curled up next to Pip, the sharp tang of ginger biscuits on her tongue. She remembered the crisp crinkle of paper as Fiona unfolded the letter her brother had sent.

And she remembered that letter, word for word.

Dear Brat,
    Well, we've made it to Bombay. What can I say about India? It is a cacophony of sound, of color, of smells. A teeming, steaming, whirling madhouse of life. I think I'm going to like it here . . .

And from that moment, Sarah had dreamed of a different life. She dreamed of adventure, travel, challenge. She dreamed of fording rivers, facing implacable enemies, discovering new worlds. And she would do all of those things by the side of Ian Ferguson. He would teach her to laugh, and she would make a home for him.

It had been a lonely girl's dream, nothing more, put away with her school jumpers and French primer, good for nothing but measuring the confines of her prison. That deadly smile had resurrected it. Worse, it had imbued it with color.

Did he have to be so bloody handsome? So vital that even ill and injured, he fairly pulsed with life? Did he have to be even more magnificent than her younger self had imagined, tucked away up in that cold dormer?

Again her gaze drifted over to Boswell's arbor, whether for apology or permission she wasn't certain. She was being disloyal. Worse, she was being unfair. Poor Boswell. How could he ever compare to Ian Ferguson? Boswell had tried so hard, but he was a small, soft man with no real sense of himself. Sarah had the feeling that even feverish and wobbly, Ian Ferguson knew exactly who he was.

It might have been different if her marriage had been different. If she hadn't been foisted on Boswell as much as he'd been foisted on her, the only option offered for a bleak future. For both of them, really. She had brought Boswell money and he brought her respectability. Only Boswell had spent the money with nothing to show for it, and she was still a bastard. And no matter how they'd tried, they had neither known how to keep resentment at bay.

She took one last look at the arbor, where she had re-planted Boswell's rosebushes. She could so clearly see him standing there the day he'd gone to war, a thin, pale man clad in the perfectly tailored, unblemished uniform he had spent the seed money on, his gold braid gleaming as brightly as the untested sword that rode his thin hip. He had looked as out of place in the crimson and gold of the 35th as he always had in work boots and broadcloth. Not a man with a purpose. A boy playing dress-up and hoping this latest costume fit. She wished, for his sake—for both their sakes—that the last one had.

That quickly her outrage died, and she was left with nothing but the same gnawing regret and grief she carried to bed with her every night. He had tried. They had both tried so hard. But only one of them had meant it.

There were no more answers here. Lifting her bucket, she continued on to the stables. She had just reached for the door when she heard boots crunch on the path.

"Milady!"

She whipped around to see Old George striding toward her, a bundle under his arm. Forcing a smile, she went to meet him. "Good morning, George."

Standing even taller and broader than Ian Ferguson, Old George pulled off his crumpled slouch-brim hat to reveal the strong, handsome features and thick, curly black hair that made all the local girls sigh. Only a few years older than Sarah, he carried himself with an oddly formal dignity. He was in his town clothes, black broadcloth and heavy shoes.

"You were askin' f'r these," he said, holding out the parcel. "You said old ones."

She held out her free hand for the bundle. "Thank you. I believe I owe you."

Handing it off, George grinned, showing big white teeth. "No you don't. Seems to me as how I been owin' you for a while now, haven't I?"

In all truth, he had. Old George was the land agent for the smugglers hereabout. It was George who crept across the back acres of Fairbourne with pack ponies on moonless nights, sometimes using her outbuildings when authorities came too close.

Old George knew that Sarah couldn't actively participate in smuggling. Boswell hadn't stood for it, what with the war on and all. But neither could Sarah turn against her neighbors who had for so long depended on the gentlemen to survive. So when she saw the thin white ribbon tied onto the old oak by the barn, she kept away from the path through the far woods.

It was one of the reasons she trusted George to keep quiet about the loan of his clothing. That and the fact that George had always watched out for the tenants of Fairbourne, especially since Boswell had left.

"Any word from Belgium?" he asked, just as he did every time he passed.

Sarah shook her head, wishing she could reassure him. "Nothing."

He absently nodded. "Got some…acquaintances go over. I asked 'em to look. They heard nothin' either. It's like Boswell just disappeared."

"Things are still so unsettled over there," Sarah said, looking away. "We *will* find him."

George gave her a tilt of his head. "We better. I'm thinkin' Martin Clarke won't be held off much longer."

For that Sarah had no answer.

"He c'n be taken care of, you want," George said, leaning closer. "Prob'ly should anyway. Ole George isn't happy with Martin Clarke these days."

Sarah let out a bark of laughter. "Oh, George. Don't tempt me. But thank you. I'll think of some way to hold him off."

This time George looked her square in the eye. "You don't, then you call George. Hear?"

She wouldn't. Too many people depended on George to put him at risk. It cost her nothing to nod anyway.

He gave another quick tilt of the head, George's version of a nod. "There's somethin' else. Somethin' queer-ish."

A *frisson* of portent slithered down her back. George was slapping his hat against his leg, a sure sign he'd waited to bring her trouble. "And what is that, George?"

"Martin Clarke," he said, looking down at her. "Who else? He been by here?"

"He has. Yesterday."

Another nod. "He bring anybody with him? Soldiers an' the like?"

"And the squire," she said, wishing George would get

to the point. "They were looking for a vagrant who has evidently been in the area. Why?"

He nodded. "Says he be huntin' that soldier went in the water over to Exeter. The one tried to kill the Duke of Wellington. But it's not the water nor beach he be searchin'. Only the farmland beyond the cliffs."

She shrugged. "They mentioned that. But I wouldn't worry."

"He also been talkin' to all the men what work with me at night. Makin' sure they knew he had his eye on 'em."

Sarah frowned. "What could you all have to do with such a thing?"

"We could be scapegoats, comes to that. It's no secret Martin Clarke has done his share o' dabblin' in brandy and lace. Word is he's decided to help himself to our territory." He kept turning his hat in his hands.

Yet another stone of worry to add to her load. "I wish I could disagree," she mused. "But I have a feeling that might be the reason he is so anxious to acquire Boswell's land. His own estate is much finer. But it has no coastal access."

George nodded. "Might be time to worry. Especially since he brings help."

Sarah huffed impatiently. "Oh, lord, George, that motley crew couldn't find chickens in a henhouse."

"Not that lot what's been followin' him around," he corrected. "Regulars. A whole troop of 'em, taking their orders from Clarke and some prissy little toff named Stricker. Showed up this mornin'."

George was right. That was definitely queerish.

"You're quite certain they have been searching for the dead man?"

"Hear they be goin' house to house from Exmouth to Charmouth offerin' a reward for that Scotsman dead or alive. I b'lieve they be comin' back this way. And I don't think they be in a mood to be told no."

Sarah thought George must have heard the sudden thundering of her heart. "I don't suppose they are all moving together."

"So that maybe you could get around 'em somehow? No. They be spread out like a flock of sheep in a high wind. Mighty convenient, you ask me."

"They're really spending all that effort to look for a dead man?"

"I be thinkin' they ain't so sure he be dead. And I'll vow Clarke means to find him with one of my lot holdin' his hand. Arrestin' us'n would make it real easy to get us out of the way, give him the whole coast."

Sarah's stomach clenched into a knot. "That would be terrible."

"More'n you know, ma'am. Martin Clarke has taken to runnin' with an evil crowd. Bad reports comin' from over to Torquay. Coercin' men to work for 'em, threats, fires, witnesses disappearin'. Evil."

She briefly closed her eyes. "I can't believe it."

"A shifty one is your cousin."

She couldn't help a smile. "Not my cousin, George."

He should have looked more amused. He merely gazed at her, his soft brown eyes troubled. "We might should make sure he's got no reason to worry, m'lady. Ya think? Be right sad he was able to bring down one of our own."

George's words almost stripped Sarah of control. There wasn't another argument George could have made that could have caused more havoc.

Our own. He was including her, which was the greatest honor any Dorsetman could give her. Especially since she wasn't a native.

Tell him about Ian Ferguson. Let him share the burden. Better yet, let him take it off your hands.

She only needed to look at George to know she couldn't. If George were caught with Ian Ferguson, far too many people would suffer. Not just a few poor gentlewomen, who might be excused a mistake. Entire families. Villages. Martin would use that excuse to wipe out every man who participated in the trade and usurp what they left behind.

"Might be good to make sure they got nothin' ta find," George said gently, his eyes on the clothing. "Ole George don't hold with traitors."

It was all Sarah could do to keep from flinching. If she couldn't convince George to leave well enough alone, they could all be in the suds. She prayed George didn't see that she trembled.

"I don't hold with traitors either, George," she said, meeting his gaze. "You have never had reason to question my judgment before. I hope that has not changed."

Again, George held his answer a bit too long, the silence punctuated by the lowing of a cow and the chatter of birds in the spinney. But just when Sarah had given up hope, he smiled. Not a big smile, like he gave to the barmaids down at the Three Tuns. A small, knowing smile that spoke volumes.

Plopping his hat on his head, he nodded. "Well, then, I be off to find me a new mare. I'll be back on Tuesday next to finish puttin' up that hay."

"Thank you, George. For everything."

He threw her an offhand wave and ambled off down the drive. Sarah remained where she was, clutching the roughspun clothes to her chest as if it could help bolster her courage.

*   *   *

Ian didn't mean to frighten her. It was just that it had been three hours since he'd last seen her, and he was growing anxious. When he finally ran out of patience, he dragged himself to the stable door and held on for dear life as he took a peek outside.

He reached the door just in time to see a behemoth striding toward her with a bundle in his arms. A behemoth who seemed to behave with far too much familiarity, to Ian's way of thinking, especially considering the fact that the man had the rough looks of a first-class rake. Black hair, dark eyes, and a smile Ian recognized for the deadly weapon it was. Christ, the bastard even had a dimple in his chin.

"*That* is Old George?" he demanded the minute Sarah stepped through the door.

She shrieked and jumped back, the pail she carried clattering to the ground and spilling out sticking plasters and jars and scissors. "What in blazes are you doing?"

"Protecting you, it seems. You can't mean to tell me you trust that lummox."

She was standing there, a hand to her chest as if holding in her heart, her eyes wide in the gloom, and suddenly he had the most irrational urge to kiss her. It would have been easy. She was no more than a few feet away, her face tilted back to berate him, her lips parted. He swore he could taste them, plump and sweet as strawberries. He could feel the soft comfort of her in his arms.

"I beg your pardon?" she demanded, shattering the fantasy.

Ian almost grinned. She deliberately turned away and bent to pick up her supplies.

Ian knew he wasn't acting the gentleman, but he couldn't help watching the pull of her dress across her bottom. Predictably, his own body tightened and warmed. "You didn't answer. That was Old George?"

"It was."

"Just how old is *young* George?"

She actually grinned over her shoulder. "Four."

Ian scowled. "You deliberately led me to believe the man was...was..."

"Old enough to have a young child?" she asked, and stood. "Why, so he is. It is Young George who insists on the names. Now, come along," she said, standing to wrap her arm around his waist. "You need to sit down before you break something and I find myself stuck with you forever."

She was right. His head was spinning like one of Whinyate's rockets. Her breast was pressing against his chest, and he could smell fresh lavender soap on her hair, which made the dizziness worse. Suddenly he couldn't breathe; his body was no longer merely warm. Every inch him that touched her seemed to be on fire. He wrapped his own arm around her and swore he felt her tremble.

She couldn't be unaware of that odd, enervating heat that flared between them. He wouldn't allow it. Surely her nostrils flared, just a bit. He swore she stumbled, just a little. Just enough that they both had to hold on to each other more tightly.

In the end, he wasn't quite certain who dragged whom as far as the little milking stool against the wall.

"Let go," she told him the minute he plopped down. Her voice sounded a bit breathless as she bent over him, caught in his hold. Her body was stiff as starch. He was certain that she sounded breathless, as if her heart were beating as quickly as his.

"Then you do feel it," he muttered as he nuzzled her neck. "I thought so."

"*Colonel . . .*"

"Ian," he corrected, right there into the tender skin of her throat. "Call me Ian."

She knelt, her hands behind her neck to try to peel his fingers away. "I'll call you toothless, if you don't stop."

He couldn't bear to release her. He felt as if she were the only true thing he could find. As if the smell of soap was a reward for bravery.

"Let. *Go,*" she demanded, her brisk voice perilously close to his ear.

He did. Eventually. But for that long, heart-stopping moment, he held onto that soft, sweet-smelling, stalwart woman and wondered if this was how a man rested.

"Colonel!"

He let go, only to start swaying again, his balance quite lost. He didn't really mean to do it. But somehow as she tried to catch him, their mouths met. Ian's reaction was instinctive. He wrapped his arms around her and held on.

Sweet Jesus, he was dying. He couldn't remember a kiss tasting so sweet. So soft and tender and delicious.

She tasted like coffee and cinnamon. She felt like silk against his tongue. He wanted to devour her.

For an inexcusable length of time, he thought she was as stricken as he was. She leaned into him, opened her lips, moved with him as he tasted her. He could feel her heart thrumming and swallowed her gasp of surprise. He wanted to let a hand go to explore her contours, but he had enough sense left to hold still. He didn't want this moment to end, this astonishing, hot, hungry meeting that should never have happened.

She was the one who jerked back. Her eyes were stark, appalled. Her mouth was open, as if she couldn't find the words to express her anger.

But she wasn't angry; he could tell. She was hurt, and he'd never meant that.

"I'm sorry, lass," he apologized, even more ashamed because he wasn't. "I didn't mean . . ."

"I think you might do better on the ground," she said, her voice as suddenly brisk as her actions, once again immersing him in her scent as she pulled him off the stool and plopped him on the hard ground.

Ian still couldn't catch his breath. There was something tight and urgent in his chest, as if he were balanced on the edge of a sharp precipice and looking down.

"Don't let go," he heard, and couldn't believe it was his own voice.

The ache in his chest sharpened. What was he doing? He knew better. He had learned a long time ago never to hold on to any person, even his sisters. People left. They died or they disappeared, and the heart could only stand so much.

But he wanted to hold on to Sarah Clarke. He wanted

it so badly it robbed him of breath and crowded his throat.

This time there was no answer from her, only a quickening of her breath. Did she hold him more tightly? Was she as upended as he was?

"Colonel, I . . ."

He shook his head hard, as if he could reorder his thoughts. It did nothing to ease the fire in his chest. "My apologies, lass. I seem to be all about in the head."

Kneeling, she carefully separated herself from him, her chest still rising quickly, her soft mouth swollen. He swore he could still taste her.

"In my defense," he said, not having even enough courage to meet her gaze, "you do smell wonderful."

She smelled like open fields and soft summer evenings.

"I smell like soap," she said, and lurched to her feet, her hand brushing against her lips, as if she couldn't quite comprehend what happened. "Something with which you appear to be quite unacquainted."

He couldn't help a quick grin. "Only recently . . . well, to be fair, it *was* quite precious on the battlefield, but I swear I made amends the moment I could."

"Well," she said, reclaiming her bucket and taking over the milking stool. "If you keep trying to discommode me like that, I believe you'll be able to call this a battlefield."

It wasn't what he wanted. It was, he knew, what was needed. So he grinned. Thankfully, her lips curved up in response.

"Coat off," she said, briskly setting to it, "then shirt out and pulled up."

He knew it only took moments to pull him out of his jacket. It felt like years, and left him even more shaken and sweaty.

"Now, the hard part."

He braced himself. Lifting his shirt, she began to unwind the cravat he had used as a dressing. As she reached the last bit, the linen caught on dried blood. She was as careful as she could be, damping the linen as she peeled it away. He grunted with the flare of pain. Dropping the soiled linen, she bent to peer at his side.

"Oh, my," she murmured, laying soft fingers against his skin. "You weren't exaggerating about your wound. It looks terrible."

He looked down and was distracted by her frown. He wanted to lick that frown. "Not so bad," he disagreed, seeing the same angry, weeping gash she did. The only thing to be glad of was that the ball had gone straight through his side, and that he wasn't pissing blood. The poxy thing hurt like the devil. Penance for his sins, he thought wryly. "If you can just...oh, clean it up and get me on my way, I'd be grateful."

She shook her head. "I am not so certain it will be that simple. You really should have had this looked at quite a while ago." She pressed against the skin above the wound. Ian grunted again. She looked up. "That was what I was afraid of. This is badly infected. What have you been rolling in, Willoughby's pen?"

He shrugged. "A marsh or two. Several barns. A chicken coop."

It was her turn to grunt. "Well," she said, straightening. "I am very good at treating fever in a pig. I am not so certain about oversized soldiers."

He couldn't help grinning. "What would you do for the pig?"

"A good cleaning. Garlic poultice and feverfew. I don't think that will be enough here." Clucking softly to herself like a mother chastising a child for falling out of a tree and scraping his knee, she turned to her bucket and rifled through her contents.

"We will use the garlic," she told him. "I have rarely seen it fail. And for the fever . . ." Pulling out cloths and soap, she set them aside. "Some fever is good. It kills the poison. But I think you have overdone yours. I have some willow bark tea."

Jumping up, she carried the pail out of the barn. She returned with water, grabbing a crate on the way in so she could lay out what looked like instruments of torture. Ian watched in appalled silence.

"You've done this to Willoughby?" he asked, casting a wary eye.

She smiled to herself. "Oh, yes. Large Blacks are notorious for tripping over their own hooves and cutting something. And though they are exceptionally clean animals, they do live in barnyards and roll in the mud to cool themselves."

She bent to wash the wound. Ian grimaced. "No wonder he keeps running away."

She didn't look up, but he could see a smile. "They also don't talk back when one is doing them a favor."

"That's only because they don't know the words."

She chuckled. "Clunch. Now, please pull up your shirt so I can work."

Still a bit off-balance, Ian immediately complied. "Sarah . . ."

She immediately stiffened. "I did not give you leave to use my name."

Lord, she made him want to smile. "You don't think formal manners are a bit pointless right now?"

She glared at him. "I think it would behoove us both to keep our relationship as formal as possible. Familiarity lowers barriers, and I truly don't wish to go to all this trouble only to have to brain you with a shovel. We must concentrate on getting you safely away before the soldiers find you."

Ian opened his mouth to gently chastise her, but just as quickly realized she was perfectly right. He had crossed the line.

"Soldiers?" he asked, knowing he wouldn't like the answer.

She nodded. "It seems that not everyone believes the reports of your death."

"But the soldiers were already by."

"Not hired ex-soldiers. It seems a troop of regulars is scouring the hills for you. If it is all the same to you, I would prefer they not find you here."

He found himself looking toward the door, as if he could see a troop clattering up the drive. He couldn't possibly stay here any longer. Every minute he stayed put Sarah Clarke in worse danger. "You need to get me to London."

She looked at him with implacable eyes. "I need to get you off my land. If I have to put you in a dinghy out to sea, I will do it."

Ian had never really thought about what he *wanted* in a wife. He only knew what he needed in a marchioness, and he'd found it. But at that moment, seeing Sarah Clarke's soft hazel eyes glinting and her posture iron rigid in defense of her little home, remembering the fire in her kiss, Ian wished he'd had the choice.

Maybe it was better she was already married.

"Are you sure your husband's coming home?" he asked anyway.

She looked only a bit more stunned by the question than he felt. He almost stumbled into an apology, until he saw the fleeting panic, the grief and anger skim those earth-soft eyes before she turned deliberately back to her work.

"Yes," she said, and he didn't believe her. "He's coming."

He was about to question her when she picked up his jacket from where he had laid it on his lap. "We need to move this."

She was standing up to hang the jacket from a nail when Ian caught the sound of a thud. Sarah must have heard it too. She bent over to retrieve something from the floor.

"What is this?"

Ian looked up to see silver glint in her palm. "Ah," he answered, hand out to accept it. "This is what both landed me in this mess and saved me from it. Behold the evidence that providence blesses me."

"A pocket flask?"

"With a rather large dent in it." He handed it to her. "This was the shot that should have cut my stick for me. Instead it left me with a bit of dented silver and an achy rib."

For a moment she did no more than run her finger over the uneven dimple. "I don't often consider drink to be a good habit," she finally said. "In this instance, I may have to make an exception."

"Oh, I dinna drink," he said. "At least not from this flask. This flask I lifted from the poncy little Sassenach who did try to shoot Wellington. It seems to be a signal of some kind. What kind I'm not sure. But behold."

With a flick of his thumb, he snapped open one side to reveal a hidden panel of ivory bearing the beautifully painted miniature of a smiling blond woman in indecently transparent attire.

"Oh," she said, finger running over the coyly smiling face. "She is lovely."

"Very. I don't think you'd like her, though."

"Why?"

"This, my lass, is Madame Minette Ferrar. She was an agent for the French during the war, and one of the most ruthless assassins in Europe."

Sarah Clarke stared at the smiling picture. "My. Is she the one who shot at Wellington?"

He smiled. "No. A chinless weasel named Stricker did that. Compared to our Madame Ferrar, a rank amateur. Madame Ferrar is a virtuoso of her craft."

With knives. Obscenely. But Sarah Clarke didn't need to know that.

Suddenly he realized that she was staring at him. "What?"

"Stricker?" she asked. "But that is the man who is leading the soldiers. He and my husband's cousin."

For a moment, all Ian could do was stare at her. "Wheesht," he finally said with a sore laugh. "It seems he is nae the idiot I took him for."

If nothing else, Stricker could make sure Ian was shot

before telling his side of the story. There was absolutely no question now. Ian had to leave.

Lurching like a drunk sailor, he tried to gain his feet.

"Stop that!" Sarah snapped, giving him a shove. "What do you think you're doing?"

It was far too easy for her to get the upper hand. Ian landed back on the ground, his side again on fire, his head spinning. "*Mac an donais,*" he grated, shutting his eyes.

"I'm going," he said. "Before Stricker can find me here and bring you up on charges."

"Well, you'll go nowhere like this," she retorted, pressing something against his side and setting loose a fresh shower of pain.

"You don't understand . . ."

"Oh, but I do. You need to leave. I don't dispute that." Pulling something else from her bucket, she wiped at his side with, he thought, a pad of sandpaper. "What I do dispute," she said, sounding exactly as his mother once had when he'd misbehaved, "is that you will be able to leave with this fever. So you might as well let me finish."

He could smell her hair again, a fresh, flowery scent that battled with the coppery tang of blood and sweat.

"Fortunately," she continued, "you were obliging enough to soak this for a time in salt water. That might help get you through the next two days."

Alerted by the sharp tone of her voice, he looked up. "Why the next two days?"

She sat back on her stool and tossed the bloody rag into her pail. "Because I believe you are about to be very ill. I suspect the only reason you have yet to succumb is because you doused the wound with lashings of salt water. You might have been free and clear, except you then insisted on wallowing with farm animals."

"You make it sound as if I was bored and looking for a diversion."

He got a huff for his troubles. "Don't be absurd. You were doing what all men do. Acting before you thought." She didn't look away from the slash on his side. "I imagine the salt water hurt."

"Stung like a horse whip."

"Rather like pouring brandy on it, do you think?"

"Very much."

"Well then, this shouldn't hurt much worse."

And without warning, she took the flask, unscrewed it, and upended what must have been a pint of pure alcohol along the gash, sending Ian straight to his feet.

"Christ, woman! What are you trying to do, torture me?"

"Yes," she said, on her feet as well, the flask in one hand and his arm in the other. "Isn't it obvious? I get so little entertainment here. Now sit down."

He did just that. She followed, setting the flask in his lap. And then, as if she couldn't help herself, she touched him again. Laid her palm against his skin just above the wound, as if bestowing a blessing. Her attention was on her actions, so he knew she didn't see his face. He was glad.

He was beset by the most unaccountable sense of yearning. Loss. He couldn't remember the last time anyone had laid such a gentle hand on him. Buffets and cuffings and bracing handshakes he knew. The strong, callused clasp of a fellow soldier or the precise acknowledgment of his grandfather. Quick sisterly hugs, the purposeful strokings from bed partners, and the perfunctory raising of a cheek for a kiss by his fiancée. But none that offered comfort. None that bestowed grace like the callused palm of this farm woman.

He was being unforgivably maudlin, he thought, briefly closing his eyes. He needed to get away from this place before he succumbed to more than a fever.

He was so distracted by the thought that he almost missed the creaking of the door. Sunlight splashed his closed lids. He was halfway off the stool before he got his eyes open to find a large shadow in the doorway.

"I wouldn't move if I were you," a cold voice warned. "I have a gun on you. And at this range, I can't miss."

Chapter 6

Sarah almost welcomed the intrusion. Anything to break the tension that had been building. Dear God, she had only touched him, and her arm tingled as if she'd caught hold of Dr. Mesmer's galvanizing machine. Her entire body seemed energized and enervated at the same time.

And that kiss . . .

"George." She stood and faced the intruder, hands on hips. "Put that thing away."

The great lummox ignored her, walking right up to Ian and pointing the big coaching pistol at his head. "I will not," he scowled. "''E's the one they be huntin' for."

"Yes . . ."

Before she could get another word out, the point became moot. If she hadn't seen it herself, she would never have believed it. Ian, who could barely get his knees to hold him up, suddenly exploded into action, knocking the gun away and flipping George right over his head. With a crash that made the ground shake, George landed flat on his back and was rolled into a headlock by an ashen, sweat-sheened Ian, who again knocked over the bucket. Sarah saw the water slosh over the dirt floor and knew she should rescue the gun in its path.

"Ye never pull a gun on a lady," Ian snarled in George's ear. "Didn't y'r ma nae teach you aught?"

Sarah gaped at them. For the last five years, George had earned extra money for his family by bare-knuckle boxing at county fairs. To her knowledge, he had never been bested. And yet Ian held him facedown, as helpless as a day-old calf.

"Get the gun, m'lady!" George rasped in spite of Ian's arm held tightly around his throat. "Stop him."

Ian looked up. "Milady?"

Sarah couldn't manage a response. She saw, for the first time, the threat in Ian Ferguson. The power. He was paler than death, the sweat sliding down his temples, and yet he held George absolutely motionless.

And his eyes. Oh, his eyes. He was weak and ill and injured, and yet the light in his eye was indomitable, fierce, the kind of light she thought would be seen in the Highlanders of old as they came streaming down a glen in full battle cry. He must have been a magnificent soldier.

"This is *Lady* Clarke," George grated, still caught tight in Ian's grip. "And you'll treat her with respect or I'll . . ."

"You'll what, laddie?" Ian said to him with a sudden grin.

Sarah wanted so badly to laugh. But she had spent enough time with men to know that it was the last thing George needed. Bending, she finally picked up the gun.

"You can let him go now, Ian," she said. "He would never hurt me." Dropping the pistol into her deep pocket, she once again rescued her poor bucket from where it had fallen. "And thank you for protecting me, George. But I spoke the truth before. I am in no danger from the colonel."

Ian complied, and George stumbled to his feet. Ian's head dropped. He was on one knee, panting and waxy and trembling. George was trying to stretch out the shoulder Ian had strained.

Sarah bent to check Ian. He was bleeding again. "Come, George. Give me a hand."

George scowled, but he settled Ian back against the wall and crouched before him. "Colonel?" he asked, scowling.

Ian grinned. "Highlanders. Ye?"

George gave that quick quirk of his head. "HMS *Indefatigable*."

Ian grunted. "A tar. I might have known."

George glared. "Bo'sun."

For a long moment, they just stared at each other, locked in a silent battle of wills.

Sarah sighed. "If you both will let me know when you have come to some accommodation, I will occupy myself making the garlic poultice."

"I'm sorry, m'lady," George said, not looking away from Ian. "But I think you should give me back my gun. I know you saw the posters in town."

"I did, George," Sarah said, once again rescuing her supplies. "But the colonel says that he did not shoot Wellington. I believe him."

George stared at her as if she had just told him she was a French spy. "You *believe* him? Just like that?"

Rescuing a cloth, she put it into Ian's hand, then laid both against the wound. "No. I went to school with his sisters. If he is the man I grew to know through his letters, he would never harm the duke." She lifted the now empty bucket. "Now, if you would get me some more water, I will tend his wound so that eventually he can move on."

"He'll be moving on right now," George protested, arms crossed. "I have a horse outside."

"Water, please, George," she challenged, the bucket held up. "And be careful of Harvey as you go by. He is in a snappy mood today."

Finally conceding with a grunt, George grabbed the pail and stomped out, taking a wide berth around Harvey's stall. Harvey lunged for him anyway, great horse teeth clacking together as George scooted past. Turning back to her task, Sarah pulled out the garlic mash she had prepared and opened it. The sharp scent stung her nose, reminding her of just what she would have to do the next few days to see Ian Ferguson off her land. If his fever was any indication, she was going to have to sneak out time and again to apply poultices, dose fevers, and change bandages.

She should let George take Ian off her hands, just as he wanted. George would get Ian away, and she would be left with no more to burden her than her daily struggle to survive. There would be no more divided loyalties, no speeding heartbeats or damp palms, no sudden, unfamiliar yearnings. No danger of any kind. Well, no *new* danger.

But Ian would be gone. And no matter how she should wish for that, she didn't.

She realized suddenly that George had returned, pail at his feet. "Well?"

Her options collected in her chest like rocks. But then

she saw the resignation in Ian's eyes. He would agree with George, just to protect her. But he was too ill to travel. And George was too vulnerable to help him. At least that was what she told herself.

"No." She turned back to spreading the garlic over a piece of linen. "Thank you, though, George."

"But I can get him away," George protested. "The ship's in."

She nodded. "And don't you think Martin is waiting for you by the pier?"

Ian Ferguson abruptly looked up. "Bloody hell," he said. "You're right."

She looked over to see the frustration written on those deathly pale features.

"Is that what you were planning?" Sarah asked him. "To steal a boat?"

He shrugged. "I've had so little luck traveling over land, and I'm running out of time. Wellington needs to know of the danger to him, especially from Stricker."

George stared. "Stricker? The little ferret who's taken up with Martin Clarke?"

Ian faced him. "The traitorous little reptile who did shoot at Wellington. I ken he's leading the soldiers so he can silence me before I can accuse him."

"Why?" George asked. "Why shoot the duke now, when the fightin's done?"

Ian rubbed at his forehead. "Because a group of Englishmen are trying to topple the throne, and they know the general would be the first to stand in their way. Until Wellington is dispatched, they canna move. Which is why he is in such grave danger." George stared hard at him. Sarah held her breath.

"Tell me again he be no traitor," George said, never looking away from Ian.

"He is no traitor," Sarah said as calmly as possible.

"How do you know?" George demanded. "He mighta cozened you, Scot 'n all."

She felt her heart give a little hiccup. Had he cozened her? Had she allowed her own loneliness and drudgery to so consume her that she would believe any man who looked at her with desire in his eyes and kissed like a starving man? Could she truly be ready to put everything she had left in this world at stake for a man she barely knew? A man who had been such a constant disappointment to his sisters?

She was suddenly so afraid that she would do just that. She would put all her trust in this man, merely because he was the first man who looked at her as if she were not an unpardonable mistake, as if, God help her, she were the answer to his needs. She was afraid she would protect him because he had *seen* her.

Oh, sweet lord, she thought, barely able to keep from touching her suddenly sensitive lips. It was humiliating to realize how frail she really was.

Then she realized that Ian was silently watching for her answer. And blast him if his expression wasn't one of understanding.

Ian...no, she thought, with a shake of her head. Not Ian. The *colonel*. That was how she would think of him, not as the man whose exploits had been dramatic reading through four years of school, every girl's dream. Not the handsome man with the devilish smile. A distant acquaintance. A formal relationship centered on his sisters. Not on his kiss. That *damn* kiss. That exquisite kiss.

"He is not a traitor," she repeated, and turned back to her work.

"All right then," George conceded. "What about Weymouth? We could get him on a ship there. It's beyond where Clarke be searchin'."

Sarah shook her head. "Princess Charlotte is in residence. The entire Royal Navy is attending her." Leaning over, she exchanged the bloody cloth for her poultice, rousing the smell of garlic. "Here. Hold this."

Ian wrinkled his nose at the pungent aroma. "I smell like a Spanish cook," he complained, before looking up at her. "Could you get in to see her?"

She stared at him, sure she'd misheard. "The princess? Are you mad? What would make you think I knew the heir to the throne?"

"Your friend Pippin Knight does. And the other one. Lizzie something. Fiona is always writing me about it."

"Pippin also lives in Wiltshire and is the daughter of an earl." She hoped he wouldn't notice that she didn't speak of Lizzie. The last thing she wanted to do was involve Lizzie.

"You're the daughter of some toff too," George offered diffidently.

Sarah shrugged. "Some toff who never acknowledged me. Princess Charlotte would never receive an unknown by-blow, no matter how close I am to her friend."

She didn't want to see Ian Ferguson's reaction to her admission, so she bent to retrieve a length of muslin. Pulling him away from the wall, she began to wrap the poultice against his bare torso. His skin was so hot, she kept thinking. He was expending far too much energy when he was so sick. He was hard, though, his body sculpted from heavy work. If nothing else, she thought, running her hands around his back, he was in excellent shape. *Excellent* shape.

Which, by heaven, she shouldn't even notice.

"What do you think the princess could do?" George asked, still frowning.

Ian sighed. "Nothing, probably. It was just a thought."

For a good few minutes as Sarah finished her work, nobody spoke. Over in his stall, Harvey gave the wall a good kick, and one of the goats bleated nervously. Sarah had just begun to hope that she would escape soon without any more distractions when Ian stirred. The *colonel,* she amended angrily. As if that would make a difference.

"You could mail a letter for me," he blurted out.

She and George turned to him. "To the princess?"

His grin was fleeting. "To my friends. I'm nae the only one trying to protect Wellington. If I can get word to the right people, they can warn him."

Again Sarah froze, a scissors in her hand. *No,* she thought. *No.* Agreeing to his request would take her from life-saver to co-conspirator. She could just see the soldiers coming upon her with that damning letter in her pocket. *Dear sir, I have Colonel Ian Ferguson in my stable. If you have the time, could you come collect him?* There could be no explanation adequate enough to keep her out of gaol.

"I cannot," she said, and knew he could hear the distress in her voice. "It is too much."

He was rubbing at his forehead, his eyes briefly closed. If possible, he was looking even worse. "Dinna you have a friend you can trust? Somebody you could write, who might forward a letter tucked inside a missive? So we could masquerade where the note actually came from?"

"Of course I do," she retorted. "Your sisters. Who are half an island away. But I would never put them in that kind of danger."

He shook his head. "It would take too long to get a message to them anyway."

She split the end of the bandage in two, aware that the colonel would not give up.

"What about Pippa, Alex Knight's sister?" he asked. "You know her."

"Visiting relatives in Ireland."

"You shouldn't do this, m'lady," George protested. "Woman like you shouldn't be mixed up in such dirty doin's."

"None of us should," she said. "But that does not get Colonel Ferguson out of my stable or the Duke of Wellington protected."

Oh, dear God. What had she just said? She couldn't be considering it.

"Another classmate from Miss Chase's, maybe," Ian said. "Any one of them would do. After all, they weren't sent to that school because of the color of their hair."

Sarah blinked in confusion. "Pardon?"

Now it was Ian's turn to look confused. "You know why you were sent there."

"Of course. Because I was incorrigible."

Because they had all been incorrigible.

Ian was staring. "*You?*" he and George retorted in unison.

"Bollocks," Ian said.

"Daft," George agreed.

Sarah had to smile. "Not misbehaving incorrigible.

Shameful love child incorrigible. My adoptive parents believed that they would never get me off their hands without at least a semblance of training in the womanly arts." She swept out her free hand, encompassing her world. "And of course they were quite correct. I don't know what I would have done without the pianoforte lessons, proper use of cutlery, and, of course, globes. Although French actually has come in handy. I can converse with the odd smuggler who washes ashore."

"You been a great help, m'lady."

"Thank you, George. I can't think how French or the proper use of a bouillon spoon could help you, though, Colonel."

"Surely you know the real purpose of the school," Ian protested.

Suddenly his mouth shut and he looked over at George. George looked at Sarah. Sarah sighed. "You might as well tell me. George will not leave 'til this is settled, and he is close as a clam. You rather have to be in his line of work."

George scowled. "An' then he can tell me how you got involved in all this." Sarah thought Ian was about to, when Harvey whinnied. Sarah looked up to see him turned to the door.

Hoofbeats out on the drive. A lot of them.

"Bloody hell," Ian snapped. "Not again."

Sarah was almost too afraid to look outside. Tying the last knot in Ian's bandage, she climbed to her feet and shook out her skirt. Passing Harvey another biscuit on the way by, she strode over to crack the great door open and look out.

A phalanx of mounted men in bright red were trotting

up the drive. Sarah fought a surge of panic. At least they didn't have Martin with them. They did have a chinless civilian wearing a bright yellow jacket with impossibly large brass buttons and a tall beaver hat riding alongside the officer.

They were stopping at the front portico, which gave Sarah a few extra minutes. There were times it was a benefit to have an octogenarian butler.

"Who is it?" George asked, never moving from where Ian sat.

"Soldiers," Sarah said, returning to them. "Real ones."

"What are they doin' here so soon?" George demanded, standing.

It was a silly question. "If this man Stricker is noticeably absent of a chin and taste," Sarah announced, closing the door. "He has accompanied them."

Ian tried to push himself up. "That's it, then," he said. "I have to get away."

"You won't get fifty feet," Sarah said. "George. See if you can get him to the chicken coop. I think that will be safer. They certainly won't look for you there."

"Not the coop," Ian protested. "Those hens hate me."

George ignored him. "You can't face those men, m'lady."

"I cannot ignore them, George. Now go, both of you. I will wait for a moment and head for the house."

"I have a better idea," George suggested, suddenly sounding diffident again. "Let's put him in the west wing cellars. They'll never find him there."

Sarah shot him a scowl. "*I* will never find him there, George. The cellars are impossible to reach. The floors and stairs are rotted all the way down."

By all that was holy, George was giving her a sly smile.

"What?" she demanded.

"Well," he said, head down like a lad caught red-handed with a fistful of cookies. "Happens when Boswell and me was lads, he showed me a secret way in. Happens . . ."

Sarah felt the blood draining yet again from her head. She truly couldn't stand too many more surprises. "You have used them?" she demanded, he voice rising. "You have stored contraband in those cellars? In the *manor house*?"

George ducked his head. "Once or twice. Nubody thinks to look there."

"And where," she asked, striving mightily to hold on to her temper, "is this way in no one knows about?"

"Over by Boswell's arbor."

Sweet Jesus. Sarah almost fainted on the spot. "His *arbor*? Where his good roses are planted?"

"On the other side. Down the hill a bit. There's a little door tucked into that little hollow facing the sea, the one with all the bracken. Goes right to the cellar."

She knew she was wasting precious seconds, but she simply couldn't assimilate all this at once. Certainly not with a troop of soldiers knocking on her front door.

"You and I will speak later," she warned the big man. "For now, wait 'til the soldiers enter the house and then get yourselves to safety. I will find you later."

"You *will* remember I'm down there," Ian said much too lightly. "Won't you?"

His face was sweat-sheened and flushed, his balance gone. Sarah knew he was really ill, and liable to become even more ill soon. At this point, though, she had to focus on the soldiers. "Take the blankets down with you. It will be chilly."

She met his gaze then, just for a moment, soaking in that bright, bold blue as if those eyes were the first promise of dawn. Of hope and renewal.

"You're *sure* now . . ." George protested.

Sarah sighed. "Go, George."

George helped Ian to his feet and turned for the back door. Sarah couldn't help watching Ian as they passed. His arm slung around George's shoulder, he stood the shorter by an inch or two, but was just as broad. Stronger, she was sure, when he wasn't wracked with fever. Dangerous to her peace of mind in any state.

"George, wait!" she called, furious that in all the mayhem she had forgotten the most vital thing. Quickly she gathered up the supplies she had brought and crammed them back in the bucket. She caught up with George by the back door and handed it all to him. "I have willow bark tea in here. Give him a cup now. The sooner we break his fever, the sooner he will be gone."

Ian shot her another grin. "And here I thought we were getting along so well."

"Not with soldiers on the property. Now, go."

Giving them both a final shove, she took herself off for the house.

* * *

Peg was standing at the back door when Sarah arrived. Together they got Sarah's apron off and exchanged her half-boots for slippers. Quickly tidying her hair, Sarah managed a quick wash-up and spent a moment brushing the bits of straw from the bottom of her skirt. Then, drawing a calming breath, she strode through the green baize door into the main house.

"What seems to be the ruckus, Parker?" she asked as she reached the foyer.

Fourteen soldiers of varying height and disposition were crowded together on her black and white marble floor along with the civilian who was staring through a rather silly jeweled lorgnette at the line of rather risqué statues Boswell's grandfather had looted on his Grand Tour the previous century. Parker, short, bald, and asthmatic, seemed to be holding them all back with his bare— well, gloved—hands. At any other time, Sarah would have considered this high farce and smiled.

"Oh, my lady," he gasped the minute he saw her. "These ... these men seek to ... to *search* my lady's house. I have tried to tell them they have no business disturbing three such fine ladies, but they ... *insist*."

Coming to a halt before the tall, effete lieutenant, Sarah clasped her hands before her and raised an imperious eyebrow, all the while thanking Lizzie for teaching her the trick. It had been a good thing to have a duke's daughter for a friend. "Good heavens, gentlemen. What are you about?"

His shako tucked under his arm, the lieutenant dropped a perfectly good bow, as if he weren't seeing Sarah in an outdated dress of questionable origin.

"Madame," he began.

"My *lady*," Palmer huffed. "You are addressing Lady Clarke, and don't be forgetting that, you pup."

Sarah couldn't help smiling. It certainly was a day for

gentlemen defenders. "Thank you, Parker. Now, Lieuten-ant . . ."

How calm her voice was, she thought. Her heart was thundering as if she'd run in.

"Swyzer, my lady," he said. "Lieutenant Lord Elvin Swyzer of the 54th Foot."

"A pleasure, Lieutenant," she responded with her own nod and allowed him to bend over her hand. "To what do we owe the honor? As you may imagine from Parker's distress, we rarely entertain officers from the king's army here."

The lieutenant briefly bowed again over her hand and then stepped back. "Your husband is . . ."

"Not home from service. He is also in the army. 35th Foot. Until such time that he does return, I fear you are left with me." She made it a point, then, to look over at the civilian. "And you, sir?"

He immediately bowed. "Horace Stricker, ma'am. I am here at the behest of the Duke of Wellington himself."

She raised one eyebrow, just as Lizzie had taught her. "Indeed. In relation to what, may I ask?"

The young lieutenant gave Stricker a sharp look. "If I am not mistaken, Lady Clarke, you have had cause to be visited by others recently, searching for a vagrant?"

"Not king's soldiers or militia," she disagreed. "Unless the standards of the army have taken a precipitous drop. I believe these were mercenaries hired by Mr. Martin Clarke to harass innocent women."

The lieutenant flushed, proving to Sarah that Martin was behind the surprise visit. "Mr. Clarke might have been a tad precipitous," Lieutenant Swyzer said in his most official voice, "but his caution was valid. We have reason to believe a traitor to the crown is hiding in the area."

Sarah put her hand to her throat. "Not that man they were searching for last week. I thought he had...well...I thought he had perished."

Stricker stepped forward. "We can't take any chances," he said a bit too eagerly. "Ferguson is a dangerous man."

Lieutenant Swyzer cast another jaundiced eye Stricker's way. "We must be certain, in any case. We are searching all along the coastline."

"Oh, is that what it is?" Sarah asked. "I had heard that soldiers were searching houses around Sidmouth. Was that you? You certainly seem to be moving quickly."

Swyzer flushed a bit and dipped his eyes. "Yes, well, certain intelligence has led us to believe that the traitor might be in this area."

Sarah smiled. "Ah. Would the intelligence have come from Martin Clarke himself? Yes, I see it did. Did Mr. Clarke tell you that he objects to my running my husband's estate in his absence, or that Mr. Clarke has been seeking a way to take my place? He is my husband's cousin, you know." From the reaction, most probably not. "I thought that might have been the motivation behind his last visit. But if there is a traitor loose, please feel free to check the grounds. We are only three women and a few staff here, and I would not wish my dear mother-by-marriage to be distressed or threatened."

"She is not here now, ma'am?"

Sarah looked over to the long-case clock with the plump little angels painted around the face. "She should be here soon, Lieutenant. She has been out painting."

If only the lieutenant had waited an hour, the dowager

would have been the one to greet him, and neatly kept him from searching. Sarah, however, had not the histrionic talent to frighten the soldiers off. And, if what George said was true, the safest way to convince the soldiers to move on was to let them search. If only her heart would quiet. She felt as if she were suffocating.

"Thank you, ma'am. I assure you, my men will be most respectful in their search."

"Of course you will, Lieutenant. I would sincerely regret having to notify my friend the Duke of Dorchester of any...depredations suffered at your hands."

From the way his posture abruptly straightened, the lieutenant was well acquainted with the language of power. What he did not need to know was that the Duke of Dorchester would rip out his eyes rather than acknowledge Sarah Clarke.

Offering another perfect bow, the officer turned and briskly issued the orders that sent the men in different directions.

"Oh, dear," Sarah murmured as they prepared to disperse. "I should go down and warn cook. The last time a man set foot in her kitchen he was met with a meat cleaver."

The small band skidded to a halt.

"Oh, and Lieutenant, I should warn you. We have closed off the entire west wing because of rot. The floors and stairs are unstable. Please be careful."

Sarah spent the next hour on tenterhooks, expecting any moment to hear a shout of discovery as the men tromped up and down stairs. She would have preferred to spend the time in the kitchen with Peg and Parker soothing herself with tea and biscuits. Instead she sat alone in the Rose Salon quietly working on some mending as if her entire life weren't in upheaval. *Oh, Boswell,* she thought, stabbing the needle into the worn linen with far too much force, *if you were here, this wouldn't be happening.*

Sighing, she set down her work. No, if Boswell had been here Ian Ferguson would have been handed directly into Martin's care, and Sarah never would have known what a close call she'd had. She would never have found herself racked with guilt over feelings she seemed to have no control over. Feelings that filled her chest to bursting and set her hands shaking. Feelings she had never thought to hope for or want.

She almost laughed. She had a possible traitor in her cellar and soldiers searching for him. And that wasn't what upset her the most. Which made her feel guiltiest of all.

By the time Sarah heard the front door open, she wondered just where else the lieutenant could find to search. At least he had kept out of the west wing. He had tested her assertion about the floor and ended up with an injured soldier and shattered floor. But now the search was over, even if the lieutenant didn't yet know it. Setting her mending aside, Sarah prepared for the fireworks. She shouldn't, but unforgivably, she was smiling with anticipation. After all, she loved theater as well as anyone.

"What is this?" she heard in strident tones that echoed through the entryway. The dowager had returned. "Parker, who are these people intruding on a gentleman's home?"

Lady Clarke might have been more timely, Sarah

thought. But at least she would impress on the lieutenant how little he would want to return.

Parker must have answered, because the lady cried, "What? Oh, my heart! Rosamunde, my salts. I am so faint. Soldiers, *here*, as if we were common brigands!"

Sarah heard running boots and the lieutenant's voice, reassuring the ladies. She almost felt sorry for the poor man. He wasn't a bad sort, really. He just hadn't expected anything like Lady Clarke.

Sarah was already on her feet when the parlor door slammed open and a squad of soldiers escorted Rosie and the dowager to the sofa, leaving a trail of blue Lias clay and fallen scarves across the good carpets.

"Dear me," Sarah gently exclaimed. "Mother Clarke, are you all right?"

"My nerves!" the dowager cried, her hands in flight, her redingote half off. "My heart! It is fluttering so, I can hardly breathe! I hold you accountable, sir, mark me. To barge in on peaceful ladies like this. It is not to be borne!"

Lady Clarke fluttered her various shawls so wildly she could have put a fire out. Rosie proffered the vinaigrette, but Mother Clarke was too busy wailing like a tired child to take advantage of it. As for Sarah, she was struggling to keep a straight face.

"I don't understand at all. Sarah, what is this about? You know my heart cannot tolerate surprise. These men say they searched my rooms. My *rooms*, Sarah. How could you allow this?"

"I had no choice, Mother Clarke," Sarah responded gently as she picked up the fallen scarves. "It seems a dangerous traitor might be lurking in the linen closets."

That stopped the dowager midwail.

"Traitor?" Miss Fitchwater echoed.

"Indeed. I assured them that we would never consort with such a low person, but the lieutenant had to make sure."

The lieutenant, standing ineffectually by the door, nodded. Lady Clarke went off in a full fit of vapors and the search was immediately suspended. Sarah took her first full breath in hours.

She would have felt worse about her treatment of the older woman, if after showing the soldiers out, Sarah hadn't stopped by the salon door to hear Lady Clarke's brisk voice.

"Honestly, Rosie. The idea that these jackanapes can simply *invade* a person's home. I hope he loses sleep over his disregard of my nerves."

Sarah waited, and sure enough, she heard Miss Fitchwater chuckle. "I fear the poor lieutenant may never recover, dear."

Walking away, Sarah smiled to herself. It never did to underestimate the women.

Now, if she could only find a way back to the cellars without alerting them.

*   *   *

Ian did not wait well. Ever since he'd spent four months imprisoned in a French cell in Portugal, he especially didn't wait well in the dark. And this bloody cellar was dark. Dark, cold, and damp. Even with two blankets and dry clothing, he was shivering.

Before the candle George had left winked out, Ian had caught sight of geometrically shaped mountains in the gloom. Boxes and barrels, if he weren't mistaken, tidily piled up in the dim corners, just begging for exploration.

Not today, he thought, resettling himself on the hard floor. Today his attention was taken up by the lengthening silence. The mounting worry that Sarah Clarke would run afoul of Stricker, and Ian would never find out. How long had he been down here, he wondered, wishing for the thousandth time that his pocket watch hadn't ended up at the bottom of the English Channel. If he were still outside, he could gage the time by the light, the position of the sun, the animals. Here in the darkness he was lost.

He shifted again, thinking that the weight he'd lost must have all been in his posterior. The stone floor seemed especially hard and sharp. The least they could do, he thought, disgruntled, was provide a fellow a bed.

That thought almost made him laugh. He could count on his fingers the number of times he had slept in a real bed in the last ten years. There were better things to focus on, surely. If only he didn't feel so fuzzy. If only he could pace. If only he knew what was going on over his head.

For now, all he could do was wait and plan. How to get out. How to get help. How to get that bastard Stricker. Ian had survived too much over the years to let one nonentity of a low-level secretary bring him down.

The question, though, was how the little snirp had gotten hold of the flask. The last time Ian had seen it, Marcus Drake had held it in his hand. The Rakes had gathered to consider the mystery of the thing, a seemingly innocuous trinket that had been more ferociously sought than Wellington's battle plans. Drake had said that he was handing the flask over to Horse Guards, so the government could decipher its import.

How had it ended up in Stricker's possession? Who in the government had intercepted the thing? Or, he thought, considering the only British aristocrats he chose to call friends, could one of the Rakes themselves have turned coat?

No. He would not accept it. He knew them too well. He trusted them, and trust was a hard thing to earn from Ian Ferguson.

Reaching into his pocket, he pulled out the flask he'd carried from the *Reliance.* This, then, was the crux of the matter. An enigma wrapped in a mystery. An easily overlooked item that, passed from one hand to another, seemed to signal action.

Absently he flicked open the back of the flask and held it so the faint light washed over the small portrait inside. Sarah was right. The woman in this painting was beautiful.

Blond, voluptuous, with the kind of blue eyes and coy smile that toppled men like trees. A perfidious enemy who had almost singlehandedly toppled the Rakes.

Ian had spent the last eleven days focusing on her face so that when he saw it again, he could stop it. He could put a bullet right between those laughing blue eyes and end the evil that crouched behind. Right after he wrung every secret from her he could.

The problem was, here in the dark and cold, it wasn't the beautiful blond face of Madame Ferrar he kept seeing. He was plagued by the memory of a truer face, a less beautiful face. Quiet beauty drawn in simple strokes and painted in softer colors.

A casual acquaintance would not see Sarah Clarke's beauty, because it required study. It *deserved* study. A chance-met person would see plain brown hair, a heart-shaped face and pleasingly rounded body. That person wouldn't notice the warmth of the mossy green eyes, the sharp intelligence and compassion in their depths. He wouldn't be permitted contact with that soft body to realize what a pillow of comfort it was.

He was mad. He knew it. The last thing he could afford right now was to be so drawn to any woman. He needed to heal. He needed to get away from this refuge before he was discovered. He needed to warn Wellington, clear his name, and keep his promises to his grandfather, including the one to marry Lady Ardeth Langstrom. Sarah Clarke needed to hold on to her estate until her husband returned.

It was then Ian knew that he was unredeemable. Because all he could think was that he hoped that husband never came home.

Chapter 7

It took Sarah all of two hours to finally escape the house again without being seen. The door to the cellars was right where George said it would be, tucked behind the bushes that masked a hollow in the steep hillside. Sarah couldn't believe it all hadn't simply slid down the under-cliff any time this past decade.

Feeling unbearably stretched by the day she had already passed, Sarah found herself prey to nastily swinging emotions as she passed Boswell's arbor, from unwarranted anticipation to perfectly excusable dread to all-too-familiar guilt. She kept wanting to look over her shoulder as she negotiated the door with an arm full of lanterns, nostrums, and food, as if expecting Boswell to catch her out in her anticipation of seeing Ian. Then, two feet into the tunnel, she walked right through invisible spiderweb. It was almost the last straw.

She was still making jerky swipes at her hair when she reached the main part of the cellars. "Four years I have lived in this house," she muttered, stumbling on the uneven stone. "Four years, and I had no idea this was here.

None. Boswell didn't tell me. His mother didn't tell me. Old *George* didn't tell me." She shuddered. "I hate spiders."

Ian's voice came out of the darkness. "My intrepid Sarah afraid of an arachnid?"

"Absolu...good heavens," she exclaimed, finally realizing that the Stygian gloom wasn't merely a contrast to the outside sun. "Did George not leave you a lamp?"

"Nothing but a ha'penny candle," Ian said, sounding so forlorn Sarah almost smiled. "And that lasted no more than an hour."

He was on his feet, Sarah realized, leaning against the stone wall. Odd, she thought, standing perfectly still, she didn't need light to locate him. She didn't even need his voice, which echoed around the cavern like a ricocheting bullet. She could *feel* him, a physical force. Heat, life, power. Sunlight against the eyes of a blind woman.

The sensation so distracted her that she almost missed the sound of a weapon being uncocked. "Is that a gun?" she demanded, peering into the impenetrable gloom.

She heard him shuffle. "George left me his pistol. We weren't sure who'd be comin' to visit, were we?"

"Well, I have brought no one with me but the odd spiderweb, so you may sit."

She heard him ease himself onto the floor and made for that direction. Except for the pitifully small light thrown off from her lantern, it was black as pitch down here.

"Since you're back I assume everything went well with the army?" he asked.

She felt guilty again. His question was offhand. His tone of voice was anything but. "Oh, yes. By now they are undoubtedly enjoying a wet down at the Three Tuns."

Catching sight of a jumble of blankets on the floor, she set down her supplies. "I cannot believe George left you in the dark."

"He said there were no lanterns down here."

"He lied. If those bundles and barrels are what I think they are, he would make certain there is quite enough light down here. He just doesn't like you."

"I figured that. Right about the time he threatened to prevent future generations of Fergusons if I brought you to harm." It sounded as if he smiled.

Pulling out her tinderbox and setting to work, Sarah smiled back. "George feels the need to protect me while Boswell is gone."

"I see." There was no mistaking that tone of voice either.

"No, you don't. George is Boswell's brother." She tilted her head, amused. "We seem to be awash in by-blows in Dorset. Fortunately for George, no one minds."

"Especially if he supplies them with brandy."

She grinned. "You're beginning to think like a Dorset-man, Colonel."

"Ian."

Light flared, and she set about lighting her lanterns. Leaving one on the floor, she lifted the other high enough to illuminate this section of the undercroft. Low-vaulted brick chambers bled damp from the walls. Well-packed dirt floors spread out in all directions. Sarah walked the corners to orient herself and counted at least a dozen lanterns hung from hooks driven into the brick.

She had walked far into the dark when she stumbled over something. Lowering her lamp, she highlighted the uneven floor. Her breath caught in her chest. Spilling out from behind a little outcropping were the remnants of supplies: more blankets, a pewter mug, and a plate. An untidy pile of cast-off stockings, as if someone had hidden down here in the darkness. Sarah felt the shock back up in her throat.

Oh, she thought, her heart clogging with old, thick pain. *So this is where he was.*

"Sarah?"

Briefly squeezing her eyes shut, she turned her back on the telling little cache and returned the way she'd come. Hanging her lantern from a hook, she stopped a moment to consider what else cluttered up the cellar. Packing crates shared space with a mountain of barrels, all tucked neatly beneath the arching supports.

"I should toss everything in a pile and burn it," she muttered, hands on hips.

Ian grinned. "You might want to remember that these barrels are full of brandy."

"Good thing for George," she huffed, and began lighting more lanterns. "I would hate to risk the house."

"Good thing for me too," Ian admitted. "I'm not movin' vera fast right now."

"Oh, I don't know. You were moving pretty quickly a while ago. I believe you cost George a year of his life."

His chuckle was a bit mad. "Never underestimate the element of surprise, lass."

She was grinning again, an odd effervescence building in her chest. "Well, you certainly surprised me. I cannot remember anyone taking George down."

He huffed. "No sailor could stand up against a Highlander."

Closing the last lantern, she blew out her spill and

turned back. "If you shared that sentiment with George, it shouldn't surprise you that you are currently making a bed of the floor."

"Oh, it's nae bother. I've slept on the ground before."

"I imagine you have." Retrieving her pail, she turned to Ian's care. "I made up another poultice for your side," she said, pulling out a covered bowl. "This infection worries me. How are you feeling?"

"Like I've been strapped to the end of a twelve-pounder."

"But do you feel any better?" She took her first good look at him. "Good heavens, you're wet. Did you bathe?"

He should have looked pitiful, sitting there in the corner on the little nest he'd made from his blankets. Sarah's heart did clutch uselessly at the sight of his pale, drawn face. But his hair curled in damp disarray at his neck, which gave him a piratical look, especially with that scruff on his face. How could so ill a man look so virile?

His mouth was canted in a wry grin that took her breath. "George said he refused to allow me in his good clothes until I didn't reek like last week's fish. There seems to be a spring in that hollow before you reach the cellar."

"Yes, so I found." Her boots were soaked. "Well, here," she said, rummaging for a towel. "Dry your hair."

She wished the soft cotton shirt he wore had a neck cloth. As it was, once again she could see a glimpse of Ian's chest, and that intriguing little notch at the base of his throat, which seemed to deepen as he raised his hand to rub at his head. For some reason, just the sight of it sent her pulse racing again. There was something so erotic about that little hollow, so intimate, as if it was made just to dip one's tongue into.

She froze, mortified. Good heavens, where had that thought come from? Perhaps the low light was a godsend after all. She thought she was blushing to her toes.

Bending to work, she cleared her throat. "I will ask again. Are you feeling better?"

His smile was blinding, even on half power. "Now that I can see you."

She huffed impatiently so he couldn't see how his words affected her. "Well, at least your tongue is still well-hinged."

Suddenly she was nervous. Shy, as if she had never cared for a man before, never seen a naked chest or touched bare skin. There was something about this man, though. That life force drew her to him, a primal power that both attracted and disturbed. That deadly half-smile that took the stuffing from a girl's knees. She wanted so badly not to be so attracted to him. To feel nothing but a stranger's concern.

If only he still smelled rank. But he didn't. He smelled like lye soap and tobacco. If he could have been thin and unprepossessing like Stricker. Like, God help her, Boswell. But he wasn't. Ian Ferguson was broad and hard and muscled. He was the size of a man who could cushion falls, who could ward off pain and provide protection.

He was everything she had never had the courage to wish for.

"Sarah?"

Ian's voice startled her. His touch electrified her. He had reached out a hand to brush a strand of hair from her forehead. She felt as if she had caught lightning. Looking up, she realized that he was just as startled. His hand hovered an inch from her face.

She leaned back. "Uh, sorry. Woolgathering. I need to change that poultice, please. Can you lift...?"

Wordlessly, she gestured to his shirt. She almost shook her head, so furious was she to clear it. She needed to get this man out of here and reclaim the even tenor of her life. The stultifying boredom, loneliness, and drudgery of her life.

"All right?" Ian asked. He had gathered the linen in his hands and lifted it.

Giving a jerky nod, she bent to cut off the wrappings. "I wish the redness had receded a bit."

Lifting the bandage away, she bent close and sniffed. Beneath the garlic, she caught the thick miasma of infection. The wound was weeping and, she thought, more swollen, which might mean that the garlic was drawing. It was difficult to tell in the uncertain light. There was no question that his skin was hotter. The fever pulsed off him. Picking up a knife, she once again slathered mashed garlic onto linen.

"Garlic again?" he demanded, still holding his shirt high. "Are you treating a gunshot or serving me up with tomatoes and sausage?"

She chuckled. "Garlic is wonderful for drawing infections. We'll try it for two days. If the infection is no better, we might change. Bread and milk, clay. Honey."

"I take it back. I'm to be on the menu for tea."

"It will be hot this time," she said, and felt him brace.

She pressed the pack against the wound. He hissed. She began wrapping, desperately trying to ignore the intimate proximity of his body. He didn't notice. His eyes were closed against obvious pain.

"Tell me about the soldiers," he asked, his voice a hiss. "They searched?"

"Oh, yes. Very thoroughly, until Lady Clarke returned home to vanquish them with an episode of vapors that scattered sheep four farms over."

He chuckled. "So that was what that terrible noise was. I thought it was the banshee coming to announce my death."

"You are Scottish, Colonel," she reminded him, the silly banter effervescing in her veins. "Hold this." He did. "The banshee only warns the Irish."

His eyes opened, clear, water-blue, and they were laughing. "My great-gram was an O'Hanlon," he said. "It's well known the banshee follows the O'Hanlon clan."

"Good," Sarah said. "It will save me from wasting my time keeping watch down here. I can just listen for her to give me the news."

He chuckled. "Ye are a cold woman, Sarah Clarke."

She stopped, glared. "I told you . . ."

"And I'm ignoring you, lass. Wheesht, how can a man bare his chest to a lady and remain on formal terms?"

She should say no; she knew it. Instead she focused on getting him wrapped so she could retreat to a safe distance.

"Your Mr. Stricker was everything you promised," she said, hating that she sounded breathless. "I cannot think how he should be believed over you."

"Stricker is a viscount's whelp."

"As are you."

He shook his head. "I'm also a Scot who's made no bones about his allegiance. Scots are valued for throwing against cannons. Not for much else. I canna think ye'd understand."

She huffed. "Try not to be absurd. Of course I understand. Society believes bastards should be drowned at birth, like unwanted kittens. No person is wanted less."

He frowned up at her. "Your husband wanted you."

She smiled. "He wanted my dowry. My father was a man with deep pockets and an even deeper reservoir of guilt. Both have seen me this far."

Stupid girl, she thought, frowning. *You sound like a whiny child.*

She was going to turn away then, ashamed at her lapse, when Ian took her hand. Her head snapped around and she stared. She shouldn't have. His eyes were so gentle, suddenly. So warm, inviting her in. His hand was strong and protective.

"Fiona and Mairead get nothing from their friendship with you," he said, "but I think they'd have my liver and lights if I hurt you. And there might not be as much to recommend me, but lass, I'd be your friend as well."

She couldn't breathe. She couldn't move. She was going to weep, and that was inexcusable. And yet she couldn't seem to draw back the hand that suddenly seemed so warm in his. She couldn't break the odd current that connected them. "You would say anything right now," she said, trying desperately for humor. "You have yet to be fed."

His grin was conspiratory. "Och, from what ye said, that's ta be no treat at all."

She smiled back, her eyes burning. She had no place to put this awful feeling, this nameless, faceless yearning.

She was lying to herself. It had a face, which made it hurt all the worse.

"I would like to be your friend, Ian Ferguson," Sarah said, and thought how like a vow it sounded. "If you, worthless Scot that you are, will be mine."

And then he did the most daft thing she had ever seen. He lifted her hand, and without looking away from her, kissed it. Sarah flushed to her toes. How did she survive such a thing? She felt as if she were being crushed.

"Wheesht, lass, ye've gone and done it now," he said, and Sarah thought he sounded a bit unsettled himself. "Ye've put yourself in the power of the mad Fergusons."

She had to turn away. "Not so powerful," she said, bending back to her work. "You're the one sitting on the floor, after all."

He chuckled, and then winced, focusing Sarah's attention right back on his wound. On his torso. On her hand, which she finally retrieved to smooth the linen beneath it, which did nothing to ease her distress. If anything, it made it worse.

Sarah tried so hard to ignore the ridges of muscle and bone that crossed Ian's massive chest, or how tight his belly stretched beneath her fingers. He was so very masculine. Taut and well muscled and intriguing with soft red hair that spread across his chest and trailed down his torso. She so wanted to play with it, to measure the expanse of his chest and cradle those shoulders. To stroke each nick and scar with her fingers as if she could ease pain long gone.

"You've collected quite a road map of the war here," she said, her voice unforgivably wobbly.

He didn't look away. "Ten years worth. It's hard to miss a target my size."

"What is this from?" she asked, touching a stellate scar almost under his arm.

He shivered and she yanked her hand away. "That was from shrapnel going over the wall at Badajoz."

"And this?" A long, puckered slice just above his belly. An inch lower or higher and he would surely have been dead.

"Dragoon's blade. Busaco, I think...no, Vimeiro. Quite a scrap, that."

She shivered herself, thinking of how often he had been close to death.

"You are a good soldier," she told him, not knowing how else to acknowledge his tenacity and strength and courage.

He shrugged. "It was the only way to support the girls."

Sarah looked up to see the ghosts in his eyes. She felt them all the way to the pit of her stomach. "Surely there was an easier way."

"Not for a bastard from the streets of Edinburgh."

She shook her head, thinking of the damage done to the Ferguson children. "If only the marquess had found you sooner. He could have saved you from this."

If only their father had not been such a monster that their mother had spent her life hiding them from him.

"I would have fought no matter," Ian said. "The only thing he could have changed was my rank. But it's pointless to speculate. The old bastard didn't bother to come looking for us until the girls were almost full-grown and my mother long dead. Fat lot of good he did us then."

"He did," she insisted. "*You* did. Fiona and Mairead are safe. They have status and wealth and a family, where before they only had you . . ."

"And I wasn't much to brag of."

"Don't say that!" It should have amused her that she defended him. For so long she had disdained Ian's place in his sisters' lives. But one look at these scars told Sarah just what he had sacrificed to keep them safe, and she hurt for him. She wanted, suddenly, to protect him. Not only from physical scars, but those that had scored his soul.

"I was wrong before," she said, clenching her hands. "I should never have said those things to you. You did everything you could to support your sisters until they had a chance for more."

He shook his head. "Do you know the condition I found them in when I finally got leave to look for them after my ma died? Do you know where I found them?"

"Of course I do. Fiona told me. They were living under the South Bridge."

"Do you know what it's like under that bridge, Sarah? It's darker than this cellar. No light, no air, no hope. No bloody help from anyone. Just crowded together like vermin. That is what I left them to."

His face was raw with grief. Sarah couldn't bear it. "You did not," she insisted, reclaiming his hand. "You left them in a mid-level apartment on North Gray's Close. Fiona should have told you your mother's illness ate up the money you sent. She confessed as much to me when she told me what an amazing brother she had."

Sarah couldn't look away from the bottomless pain in Ian's eyes. It was all she could do to keep from wrapping him in her arms like a child.

She did the best she could. She lifted her other hand and cupped that rugged cheek. "You risked your life for ten years so they never have to risk theirs. You got them into Miss Chase's. Do you know what I would have given for one person who loved me so?"

He shook his head. "I'd like to take credit," he said.

"But I was nae the one got the girls into the school. I was the reason they went."

She retreated, hands in her lap. "What do you mean?"

He stared at her for long moments. "Do you know why *you* were there?"

She frowned. "I told you before. Because I was incorrigible."

He was already shaking his head. "No, it wasn't. There was only one reason you would have been sent there. Do you know who your father was, lass?"

"My father?" She suddenly felt as if she were fighting a surprise current. "What would he have to do with it?"

"Do you?"

She looked away. "As a matter of fact, yes. When I was very young, my adoptive parents snuck me in his side door on my birthday to pay obeisance. His wife was far kinder than she should have been. She was certainly kinder than he was."

Sarah remembered a smiling, sunlit woman with a soft voice and still hands. She also remembered wasting far too much time wishing for that mother. But those wounds were too old to inflict sharp pain. For a long time now, they had done no more than ache like worn muscles.

"Will you tell me who he is?" Ian asked.

"No." She met his gaze head-on. "I will not. My father is dead. I haven't been welcome in his home in a long time. Besides, I cannot imagine what he would have to do with any of this."

Ian ran his hand through his tumbled hair. Suddenly Sarah realized he was shivering.

"Oh, heavens," she gasped, her scissors clanging into the pail. "You're freezing. Let me get you covered up and fed. Then we shall have time to satisfy my curiosity."

His answering smile was telling. Rueful, a bit relieved. Warmer than the moment warranted. Just the sight of it incited a like warmth, a longing for what wasn't hers. Sarah tamped it down, like every other wish she had ever had, and got to work setting out his meal. And then she felt even worse, when Ian fell to eating as if he'd been starving. He didn't even seem to notice that Peg's stew was gelatinous or that her fairy cakes would have sent the wee creatures crashing to earth. He just sighed in appreciation and downed the rest of the tea.

"Next time," Sarah said, "I shall just slaughter Willoughby and drag him down here for you to enjoy at your leisure."

His grin was brighter by far. "No, you won't. You could nae kill that beast if you were all starving and the reaper was at your door."

Sarah sniffed. "I should never have named him."

"You dinna live merely from him and his get, do you?"

"No. We have sheep and a few milch cows and goats for cheese. And we have acreage planted in wheat. And you met our hens."

"It sounds prosperous."

"Not for a long time," she said, and settled herself next to him on the blanket. "Now. You are warm, treated, fed, and safe. I have an entire ten minutes before I am expected back. I believe I am owed a story."

She shouldn't have pressed. She could see he was wearing thin. But with evening coming on and his fever inevitably climbing, she had a nasty suspicion this was the last time she would get sense from him for a while.

Finally Ian shrugged. "Fair enough, lass. But I can't tell it all. Too many lives would be at stake. Especially yours."

She felt unaccountably betrayed. "You think I would share the information some evening as parlor chat?"

"I think it is better that if you are pressed you have nothing to say."

She tilted her head. "And that includes your sisters and the academy?"

Again he paused. Again she battled a flush of resentment.

"I don't have the right to expose the people involved," he defended himself, as if he could hear her. "No more than I have the right to put you in harm's way. The people we are seeking wouldn't hesitate a second to harm you for information."

Finally there was nothing left to do but nod. "Will you tell me what you can?"

His smile was rueful. "It's actually quite simple. All the students at the academy are relatives of gentlemen in government service. Men who might hold sensitive positions. One of the ministers realized that a man's family—especially his vulnerable sisters and daughters—could make him vulnerable to attack or blackmail. It was decided they could be best protected in a boarding school."

Sarah was gaping now. "Miss Chase's was supposed to be a...safe haven?"

Ian smiled. "Exactly."

The idea was so ludicrous she almost burst out laughing. "Who exactly chose it?"

"I know this will go no further."

Not unless she ever met the man. She had a lot to say to

the nodcock who thought Miss Chase competent to protect innocent girls.

"His name is Baron Thirsk," Ian said. "He is Miss
Chase's cousin. I was assured that there was no more secure place for the girls than Miss Chase's. There hasn't
been a girl kidnapped or threatened since Thirsk began
sending them there."

Instead of the men, it had been the girls who had paid
the price. But she couldn't tell Ian that. He didn't need to
know what a hellhole the academy had been until Alex
Knight swept through and replaced Miss Chase with a no-
nonsense director named Miss Barbara Schroeder.

Alex. She blinked. "You don't mean to tell me that
Alex Knight is in a sensitive position. Why, he's in no
position at all." She smiled. "Unless you count being a
member of Drake's Rakes. But I don't think profligacy is
the kind of sensitive position you were speaking of."

"You know of Drake's Rakes?"

Her smile grew. "Oh, yes. We followed their exploits
in the society pages. I admit to some jealousy. They all
seem to enjoy themselves so much."

Something about his sudden stillness alerted her.
"What could Alex possibly do?"

"You'd be amazed what information can be gleaned in
ballrooms and salons, lass."

She was staring now. "He's a *spy*? Alex Knight?"

"Let's say he gathers information. But that is nae
something to share. Even with his sister. Although, from
what I know of that wee lass, she knows more than Alex
would like to think."

"She never told me." Sarah kept blinking, as if it would
help all this make sense. "What about you?" she asked.

"Do Scottish soldiers occupy sensitive positions as well?"

He seemed discomfited by the question. "They do if they find themselves doing a bit of extra work for the government."

"Like trying to protect Wellington?"

"Like that. And other small tasks."

She didn't believe him, at least about the "small" part. She had a feeling that Ian Ferguson had waded through the worst of the war, no matter how he discounted his part.

"And you thought Fiona and Mairead might be threatened?"

His smile was rueful. "Not really. But school was better than life under a bridge."

She looked off into the darkness. What could her father have done to warrant her inclusion into the school? He'd been barking mad. At least that was what she'd heard.

"All right, then," she said briskly rather than revisit those old memories. "What exactly is this present business about? The people wanting the throne and Wellington."

"There are men who believe that they would be better at running the country than what we have now. I think the reformists distress them almost as much as the mad king. What they would like is to put Princess Charlotte on the throne instead under their aegis."

"And they're afraid the Duke of Wellington would stop them?"

"Can you imagine the duke allowing these men to clear the way for Princess Charlotte to become queen?"

"The . . ." Sarah's stomach dropped. "Oh, dear God. She can't be on the throne unless the king and the prince regent are . . ."

"Dead. You see why I canna wait. If they get to Wellington, they silence the crown's most ferocious defendant. And if they can make it look as if a radical reform group was behind the assassination, people would fall in behind them like ducklings." He paused, his eyes shadowed. "You can understand why I need your help."

Sarah suddenly found it hard to breathe. "But I don't want to be involved in plots against the throne. I want to get my hay in and protect my pig."

Ian shrugged. "None of us do. Imagine my surprise that I'm trying to save the life of a British king. A generation ago, I would have been booted from my clan."

She shook her head. "Clan, nonsense. You're a British viscount, one day to be a marquess. It is your duty to protect the throne."

Leave it to Ian to grimace. "Ah, and isn't that the unkindest cut of all?"

She couldn't help it. She chuckled. "Yes, I remember how delighted Fiona was to find out that rather than being a Scottish rebel she was actually mostly an English miss. Her letters could have caught fire from the outrage."

"She does seem happy there, doesn't she?" he asked.

Sarah stopped, thrown off balance by the sudden change in direction. Something about Ian's expression told her that she would learn no more of plots and traitors. He was deliberately turning the conversation.

"With her grandfather," he clarified.

"With *your* grandfather," she clarified instinctively. Why the question disconcerted her, she didn't know. But he seemed so anxious, suddenly, so uncertain.

"Yes. I think so. I know that Mairead is happy."

She noticed that he was still frowning. "What about

you?" she asked. "Are you reconciled to your paternity? The war is over, after all. You have lost your excuse to avoid your duties."

His expression didn't ease. "The duties, yes. I think so. The paternity?" He frowned. "Who would want a monster for a father? Fiona told you . . . ?"

"How you all came to land in the slums of Edinburgh?" Reaching out once again, she laid her hand over his. Her life story was squalid. His was tragic. "She said your mother feared your father so much she spirited you three away without his knowing."

Ian's expression grew distant, as if seeing old ghosts. "He was a coward who hit women and abused the help. My grandfather used his power to protect that monster. To protect the name of Ripton, above all else. I have better things to do with power like that."

She sat back and smiled. "Then you have made your mind up to it."

He looked up, and she was surprised to see a deep purpose in those bright blue eyes, a flame kindled she hadn't noticed before. "You have a lot of time to think on your future when you're in a camp waiting for the dawn," he said. "And I had a lot to think on. I'll be a marquess, and isn't that a right knockabout? I'll be everything I've distrusted my whole life. Have you met my grandfather?"

"No. Fiona says he is . . . consumed with his position."

He nodded. "I'm not sure the old tartar ever takes off the ermine." His eyes grew sly. "I think he must have had a spasm when he realized I was alive. My mother was everything he hated; Scottish, a rebel laird's granddaughter, and strong. But he had to find me or the title died. And isn't that a lovely thing? It means he canno' change his mind. I am the heir whether he likes it or not, and his every dime is entailed. Even when I take my place with the reformers." His grin grew a bit mad. "Can't you see it? A strapping Scottish lad like me in Lords railing against clearances and proposing bills for universal vote and Irish rule? Maybe I should do it wearin' my kilt."

Sarah smiled. "Good thing he'll be dead by then. You'd give him a seizure for sure."

He chuckled. "He insists on teaching me the world of power. Well, I'm learnin'. I'll gather every tool he gives me and use it to help change the face of this country."

"And your fiancée? Does she agree with you?"

He grinned. "That's the best part, isn't it? The marquess arranged the marriage so I would toe the line. But what he doesn't know is that Ardeth is as passionate about reform as I am. Can you imagine the difference we can make?"

Sarah deflated suddenly. She had begun to fantasize, she thought. It was so easy to do in the cave, pretend that the future could change out of all recognition just because you wanted it to. But the real world waited, and it included the perfect wife for a future marquess and nascent reformer. Doors would open and people would listen. And none of that would ever happen if he appeared with an unknown bastard on his arm. And unknown bastard who had no business even toying with such an idea in the first place.

Foolish girl.

"There's only one wee problem, lass," he said, his expression again serious.

She looked away. "You cannot stand for Lords if you're hung for treason."

"I was actually thinking that I wouldn't want to be in a parliament if the traitors managed to grab the country." He shrugged. "But I canna think a treason charge would help much either. Will you help?"

She made the mistake of meeting his gaze. Sweet heavens, his eyes could draw her to her death. Now that she understood their depths, they were even more impossible to withstand. She really didn't want to be involved. She wanted nothing to do with spies and royalty and villainous women. It was all she could do to get by day by day.

But how could she walk away? How could she put him at greater risk? How could she ignore the very imminent threat to her country?

She could not deny it anymore. She believed him. Not just because he was Fiona's brother. Not because she wanted him to be the person he seemed. Because he *was* that person.

Abruptly standing, she strode toward the door. She wanted to walk, to take to the hills, as if she could outdistance the decision she had to make. As if walking out of this cellar could separate her from what had to happen here. She stood in the doorway for what seemed an eon listening to the faint call of birds, a bark of a dog.

"A letter," she finally said, turning on her heel and crossing to him. "One letter."

"You do have a friend, then, who can forward a message for me?"

The answer sat heavy in her chest. She hated to involve Lizzie in this mess, for so many reasons. But if anyone could get a message to Ian's friends, it would be she.

"I do."

Sarah might have thought Ian would brighten with her answer. He only seemed to look immeasurably wearier. Struggling to his feet, he faced her. "I'm sorry I have to ask it of you, lass. I promise I'll be gone as soon as I can."

Sarah rubbed at her own eyes. It was better than betraying the fact that his promise suddenly hurt. It shouldn't have. It should have relieved her mind. But for just a moment, she had had a taste of what it meant to know this remarkable man, and like the first taste of sweet on the tongue, it compelled her to want more.

"Sit down," she commanded, waving him away. "Or I will find myself forced to house you in this cellar for weeks. I had already planned to go into Lyme Regis tomorrow. When all are abed tonight, I will bring you writing material."

"Thank you, Sarah," he said, and took her hand.

She felt it again, that searing heat that seemed to leap from his fingertips when they touched. She looked down, sure she should see fire. But they were just ordinary hands, his big enough to surround hers, like a shield, hers callused and scarred, as if to remind her of her place.

He could protect her, she thought. Under any other circumstances, Ian Ferguson could have helped her fight her battles and cushioned her hurts.

And yet he wouldn't. And she had no right to ask for anything more. It hurt, but she pulled away. "Thank me by getting better."

Chapter 8

Dearest Lizzie,

Do you remember that favor you owed me for finding those books on anatomy for you? Well, my dear. I am calling it in…

It was the next morning, and Sarah was trying to finish her missive before hitching Harvey to the small gig for the trip into Lyme. Sarah wished she could be writing this letter to anyone else but Lizzie. Proper, regal, self-contained Lizzie who had so rarely flouted the rules, yet who still wrote Sarah the occasional letter. The more Sarah thought about it, the more she hated the idea that she was putting Lizzie in a dangerous position. But she didn't know whom else to contact.

She had Ian's note in her pocket. She had obtained it the night before after dinner when she had arrived to find him ashen and trembling, the letter sitting on one of the packing crates and the ink carefully recapped.

She wished she could have been more surprised by

his condition. But she wasn't. She thought of the fierce energy he had expended to keep George pinned to the ground, and how he had collapsed afterward. The same had happened in the cellar. The minute Ian secured her cooperation, he seemed to fold in on himself. His temperature soared, and the stuffings went out of him.

Even with the poultices and lashings of willow bark tea and yarrow, he had spent a bad night. What disturbed Sarah was that she feared it was only the beginning. She was getting nowhere with her poultices. And she knew the fever would soar again when night returned. She was so afraid that she would return from Lyme to find him in desperate need. How could she care for him without giving him away?

I need your help, Lizzie. You see, Boswell still has not been heard from. I need to learn what has happened to him without my mother-by-marriage knowing. She is distraught enough that we fear for her health. But she checks every letter that leaves this house, certain I am somehow being unfaithful.

Sarah hoped Lady Clarke never saw this bouquet of lies. The relationship they had built out of mutual tolerance would rip into tatters.

The man I need to reach is Lord Marcus Drake. I have been assured he can help me. Will you forward the enclosed letter, Lizzie? I will be forever grateful.

She wanted to say more. She wanted to tell Lizzie everything that had happened since she had first discovered

Ian Ferguson behind the chicken coop. She wanted to share the astonishing sensations, the maelstrom of emotions, the confusion that had been her constant companion the last two days.

Dear lord, she thought. Has it only been that long since Ian Ferguson had blown into her life like a strong gale and tumbled the tidy bits of her quiet existence into chaos? Could she truly be so undone by only a few hours' acquaintance?

She wanted to ask her friend—any of her friends—for advice on how to go on.

She wanted to tell Lizzie how her fingers still hummed from where they had touched Ian's. How she had to fight the most absurd impulse to smile at nothing every time she remembered their kiss. How she yearned to be cradled in those magnificent arms and be nourished by his laugh, his honor, his courage.

And his eyes. Oh, his eyes, so blue it was like looking straight up into the sky, like bathing in the clear water that tumbled over a small fall. Like life itself. Sarah fought the warming of her body at the thought of that clear, night-rimmed blue.

But not just that; his size, his smell, his smile. His sharp wit and bright mind, which seemed just as intoxicating as his broad chest. She had been married four years; she had always thought she and Boswell had done well enough together. But not once in that time had she felt the sizzling energy that had flooded her body when Ian kissed her. She had never felt her breasts go taut or her belly kindle. She was having trouble sitting still; her body wanted to move, to curl in on itself, to stretch like a cat in a warm windowsill. For the first time in her life, she wished she were prettier, younger, softer. She wished she didn't have calluses on her palms and wind-chapped cheeks.

She knew better. And yet she wanted nothing more than to slip down that secret tunnel like a girl sneaking out of school. She wanted to warm her hands on him like a hot fire, to soothe herself on his smile. To hear more of his story, his plans, his dreams, to savor the sense of a strong man.

For the first time in her life, Sarah knew what it meant to really want a man, deep in her belly where they said hunger lived. In her heart, which hadn't found a steady rhythm since first meeting him. In the warm core of her soul, which none had touched before. Not her friends, not her parents, not her husband. She had never allowed them to, knowing too well the cost.

She was terrified, though, that this rough-hewn Scot had awakened something in her, a need for union, for belonging, for a life she had never allowed herself. She was terrified he would make her vulnerable.

She was terrified he already had.

Dear Lizzie, she wanted to write. *I think I may have done something very foolish. I think I have tasted temptation. And oh, Lizzie. I think I like it very much.*

"I thought you were going into town," Artemesia spoke up suddenly behind her.

Sarah startled so badly she splattered ink on her letter. She wasn't taking surprises well right now. "Yes, so I am. As soon as I finish a note to my friend."

Artie plopped down on the other desk chair. "Take me with you. I need to purchase a new ribbon for my bonnet and mail a letter to Cecily Tate." Suddenly dropping her head, as if to watch the tangle she was making of the lemon ribbon that tied her sprig muslin, she shrugged. "Please, Sarah." She looked as uncomfortable as if she had reported for punishment.

Sarah touched the girl's hand. "I would be delighted, Artie."

Well, she thought. Delighted might be an exaggeration. Artie's mood was still swinging in unpredictable directions, which made her a less than comfortable companion. At Sarah's answer, Artie gave a jerky nod, her focus still on her writhing hands.

"Artie?"

The girl all but flinched. "Did you mean it?" she asked in a near whisper, as if the question were too frightening to be asked.

"Did I mean what, dear?"

That beautiful young face lifted and Sarah saw the raw pain of hope strain those soft brown eyes that looked so much like Boswell's. "About school. Can I go back?"

Reaching over, Sarah took the girl's hand. "I mean to try, Artie. It is all I can promise. Boswell and I made a vow to contain our spending for a few more years, until we could get out from under the worst of the mortgages. But I am hopeful."

She and Boswell had done no such thing. She had told him during one of the rare times he had been willing to listen. It had been soon after that, he had taken the last of her dowry and bought his commission. But that was something Artie didn't need to know.

Artie began nodding again, her head back down. "It's just...I got a letter today," the girl said, abruptly on her feet and pacing. "My friends are...they're planning their debuts, and all I can think is that by the time I am free of this place, it will be too late, and I'll be too old for a season! I'll be too old for *anything*!" Big tears welled in her eyes and spilled over.

Sarah ached for the girl. Done with hesitation, she intercepted her and wrapped her arms around her.

To Sarah's surprise, Artie nestled right in, sniffling against Sarah's shoulder. "Do you realize," the girl asked, "that Cecily is attending a house party near here for Princess Charlotte?" She pulled a scented, watermarked paper from her pocket and held it up. "All of my particular friends will be there. Cecily, and Letitia Weems, and Amelia Tulley. Cecily says that the guest list will include all the cream of society. It is to be given by the Duke of Dorchester. He isn't married, Sarah, did you know that? He is undoubtedly looking for a wife, and he'll probably choose someone vile like Penelope Susson simply because I won't be there."

"The Duke of Dorchester?" Sarah scoffed, brushing Artie's golden yellow hair off her forehead. "You don't want him. He's far too old. Why, I believe he wears stays and puts his teeth in a glass."

It was better than admitting to Artie that even if she had stayed at her boarding school, she never would have been invited to such an exclusive gathering, especially as any relation to Sarah.

Artie gurgled with laughter. "He's a duke," she said. "What does it matter what he does with his teeth?"

Sarah grinned. "Tell me that the first time he appears at dinner without them."

He wasn't too old, of course. Not by society standards. No more than thirty. Sarah still wouldn't want Artie to waste herself on him, dukedom or not. The duke was a petty man, a poor brother, and worse landlord.

But if he was indeed having a house party at Ripton Hall, Sarah would have to make sure her letter to Lizzie got out quickly, otherwise it might be lost in preparations for a royal visit. It was the lot of a duke's sister, after all, to help supervise and entertain.

Leaving Artie to her ribbon, she sat down to finish her missive.

Please do not let your brother frank the letter, Lizzie. I would rather he doesn't know about this. She would rather no one knew that Lizzie was involved at all. *When I see you again, I will explain why.*

She was just slipping the letter into her apron when the door slammed open.

"I'm...s-s-sorry," little Mary Sunday said with a lop-sided curtsy, her hands wrapped in her stained apron. "Parker is chasing the pig round the yard."

For a moment Sarah couldn't even think how to react. Her ancient butler was chasing livestock? "Pardon?"

The painfully thin tweeny nodded her frizzy blond head. "He be pullin' down the washing and layin' on it, ma'am."

"Parker?"

"The pig. Mizz Peg thinks them wool things you been lettin' him sniff has give him a taste. She says, you don't get him from her laundry, he'll end up in her skillet."

"Oh, good," Artie giggled, jumping up. "It's been ages since we've had gammon."

Sarah ignored her and ran for the kitchen. She could hear Peg even before she pushed open the door into the yard, and Parker's gasping protests as he tottered across the kitchen garden after Willoughby, who seemed to be trailing a clean blanket.

"Parker!" Sarah called after her panting butler. "Stop! Willoughby! Sit!"

Parker stopped. The pig sat. Right on the newly cleaned laundry Peg had just put up on the line. Before anyone could reach him, he proceeded to lie down and roll.

Sarah couldn't help it. She started laughing. Peg was screeching, Parker was gasping for breath, a gloved hand to his mud-spattered chest, and Willoughby was grunting in ecstasy because he had captured a blanket.

"Get that pestilential pig out of my sight!" Peg screamed, setting the hens clucking and Heloise and Abelard, their goats, bleating in distress.

Sarah kept laughing, tears running down her cheeks. Oh, she thought, wouldn't Ian love this. She couldn't wait to share it with him.

She froze, her laughter abruptly dying. She felt as if she'd been doused with cold water. No, she thought. Not Ian.

"What do I do with these blankets, Miss Sarah?" Peg demanded. "They're ruined. And we don't have many more. I swear, this pig's been eatin' 'em behind my back!"

Parker was still gasping. "I couldn't...stop him, my lady...I'm so...sorry..."

"Are we going into town or not?" Artie demanded by the kitchen door.

Sarah saw all the faces looking to her for direction: Artie and Peg and Parker and Mary Sunday, all looking for answers. For instruction. There was no one here to share her burdens. No one to share her joys. Except for that brief few years with her friends, there had never been. Not with her parents, not with Boswell, not with his family or neighbors. Damn Ian Ferguson for briefly making her forget that.

"It's all right," she said as if it didn't matter. "Parker, go inside and lie down. Peg, we have other blankets. I shall take Willoughby. And Artie. If you want to go into town, hitch up Harvey."

"What?" was Artie's instinctive protest. "No. He bites. Besides, a lady doesn't . . ."

"This one does," Sarah answered without turning away from the pig. "Take a couple of Peg's scones with you. You can either help, or you can stay. Decide."

And then, before anyone could argue with her, she walked off toward the pens, yanking the pig behind her. When Peg, hands on hips, muttered, "Well, finally," Sarah didn't bother to find out what it was that was finally happening. Since she heard Artie stamp back into the house, she thought she knew, though.

It didn't make her feel any better. She was suddenly remembering that twelve-year-old Sarah who dreamed of adventure and companionship. Of sharing it all with a heroic man. Instead she had gotten a man who had been forced into marriage and resented every minute of it. A homebody she had inadvertently harried from home.

Her life had been set from birth, and she should never forget it.

Especially with Ian Ferguson sleeping in her cellar.

* * *

Sarah usually enjoyed her trips to Lyme. That day she did not. She drove there with a treasonous letter in her pocket that would pull her dear Lizzie into the mess, and she spent the day both anxious to get back to Ian and dreading it, beset by the suspicion that he needed her.

She reached the cellars that night to find her worst fears realized. She found Ian confused and incoherent, the wound angry and weeping, with red streaks snaking up his side. He was restless, beset by chills and shakes. So she maneuvered him back to the nest he had made for himself from the blankets and covered him. She cooled him with spring water, reapplied the poultice, and urged barley water and willow bark tea on him.

As the hours passed, he grew inexorably worse. She stayed. His fever raged, and she bathed him. He grew delirious, and she held him. As if she were paying her penance for wanting to share something with him, she shared the private demons that escaped to torment him. All night she sat in that cold cellar with him as he fought one battle after another, sought lost comrades, crept through enemy territory toward safety. She lived in terror that he would be heard. His voice rose and fell, a haunting refrain of pain and loss.

"Andrews! Back! Get back, damn you! You're too far!"

"Let me go! I have tae get ta them. They're dead men else!"

This was a good man. He shouldn't have to suffer so. And yet, relentlessly, as if locked too long and too ruthlessly behind that mad, manic grin, every phantom he had fought came to find him. And Sarah, her heart bleeding, was left to murmur, to bathe his face and hold his hand when the memory grew too sharp and the cost of his battles grew sharp-etched on his broad, bold face. He had seen too much. He had suffered more. And here in deepest night, within the earth where phantoms lived, he paid the price.

"Brace up, men! They're comin' again!"

For three days the fever waned in daylight and roared at night. Sarah sat by him hour after hour when she could and worried over him when she couldn't. Outside the world went on. The weather grew sharper; the first crunch of ice crusted the mud. Willoughby claimed the ruined blanket, and Peg sulked. Sarah and Mr. Hicks reinforced the pen for the tenth or twelfth time, Lady Clarke nagged at her for news of the Egyptian Mummy watercolor, and Artemesia bewailed missing the house party of the century. Another fox disrupted Sarah's henhouse, making off with two of her favorite layers, and Old George put up the hay, all the while trailed by his chattering four-year-old son and Sarah's six hundred pound pig.

When he could, Old George also relieved her in the cellar. She was too tired to berate him for carrying on his smuggling so close to home.

"If you can smuggle brandy in here," was all she said, "you can get a cot."

The next time she returned to the cellars, Ian was tucked up on a camp bed with a feather pillow. It wasn't George's fault Ian was so tall his feet hung over the end.

Sarah entered the cave to find George standing next to the cot, a rag to his bleeding nose.

"Good heavens," Sarah said, dropping her things. "What happened?"

"*Buaidh no Bàs!*" Ian thundered and came straight off the bed.

Sarah jumped back. "What does that mean?"

George ducked a wild swing. "I suspect it means 'kill the Englishman.'"

"Here," she said, stepping past George to Ian.

George tried to stop her. "No, m'lady. He'll hurt ya."

"No, George," she said, kneeling by the cot. "He won't."

He didn't. Not once. By the fourth day George sported more than one bruise and a new twist to his nose. Ian was a fighter. A berserker, his sister had once called him. If George tried to hold him down, he fought like a madman, and he packed a wallop. But the minute Sarah spoke, Ian stopped. Listened. Quieted down. It confounded George. It tortured Sarah to know that this man who fought with such tenacity and strength, who had been trained to war and fought it in his mind, would, even in the throes of delirium, know to treat a woman so gently.

She knew now what her wish for human contact would cost her. She knew that no matter what, every cry and shudder, every name called to in the night would follow her into her own sleep. If she ever slept again.

* * *

On the fourth day, Sarah was delayed in getting to the cellars. Another length of fence had gone down that day, letting sheep into the squire's pastures and leaving one dead in the road. It was the fifth time in a month it had happened.

Picking up one of the boards where it lay in the trampled dirt, Mr. Hicks scratched his grizzled head and spit on the ground.

"Sawed," he growled. "Almost clean through."

Straightening from where she was laying out tools, Sarah stared at him.

He waved the board in her face like a sword. "Sawed!"

Sarah looked at the obvious saw marks, then at the condemning light in the old man's eyes. She sat suddenly on the stile. "Who would...?"

Mr. Hicks spit again and threw the board away. Sarah looked up at him, wanting him to say he'd made a mistake. That he had jumped to conclusions.

"Pardon my sayin' so, m'lady. But you know damnall who would." He pointed at the board. "This were malicious business. I got a good suspicion who did it, and I think as maybe he's done it before."

Sarah looked around, as if an explanation would be forthcoming.

No. Not that. Not now.

But it was. She knew it as surely as she knew the culprit's name. She was suddenly disgusted that she hadn't suspected it long since. Mr. Hicks was right. It had been a harder summer than usual. Surprise deaths, inexplicable damage that had cost money she didn't have. And who else but Martin Clarke would profit? According to the entail, he was the only heir.

Had she wrongly blamed Willoughby for all the times he had gotten loose? Could human hands have clogged the stream that had ruined part of her wheat crop? And her chickens. A fox was the logical assumption. What if the predator had possessed only two legs? Could Martin Clarke truly be that malicious?

She felt sick. Why hadn't she seen it? What could she do about it? She couldn't patrol her entire estate. She couldn't even patrol her henhouse. How was she to stop vandalism? How was she to prove it? If it was Martin behind this, he had the resources to stay a step ahead of her.

By the time she reached the cellars late that evening, a jug of hot coffee and another poultice in hand, she was distracted and impatient and long past exhausted. She shouldn't be spending all this time with Ian. She should be protecting her little farm.

One look at him, sitting hunched on the side of his cot, made her feel guilty even for thinking of it. Pale as a specter, he looked even more exhausted than she. She thought he had lost another stone in weight, which carved hollows out of his bristly cheeks. It should have diminished him, sapped his power. Somehow, even shivering and weak, it did nothing of the kind. Sarah was hit by the force of him even before he spoke.

"Has a letter arrived?" he asked, just as he did every time she came down.

She set down her supplies. "And here I thought you were anxious to see me because of my clever badinage."

His grin was macabre. "Och, lass, how can ye question it?" Straightening, he pulled up his shirt so she could check the wound. "How many days has it been?"

She poured him a cup of coffee and passed it over, brushing against his hand for its unintended warmth. "Four. I don't think it's enough time for a letter."

"Probably not." He cradled the mug in his hand. "Thank you. Still . . ."

She peeked beneath the bandage to find improvement.

"I need to return to Lyme Regis in a few more days. Mother Clarke's mummy will be arriving."

Ian swung his head toward her. "Her what?"

Sarah found she could still smile. "Egyptian Mummy. A color in her palate for painting butterflies. The Lulworth Skipper, to be precise."

"And it's called Egyptian Mummy because?"

She grinned. "Because it is. Ground up, of course."

Ian just gave his head a mournful shake. "You live a far more interesting life than I do, Sarah Clarke. Any more visits from Stricker and his troop?"

"Yes," she said, working as she spoke. "They stopped by yesterday, but once I informed them they would be waking Lady Clarke, the visit was amazingly brief."

Ian managed a grin. "I think I'd like to meet your husband's mother," he said. "She sounds a formidable woman."

"You have no idea. She caught Willoughby sitting in Boswell's arbor today and almost turned him into slabs of bacon. I haven't heard that pig squeal so loudly since he got caught in the fence with the squire's mare on the other side."

"Boswell's arbor?"

She blinked, for some reason startled by his question. Surprised, somehow, that he didn't already know everything about Boswell. About her. As if all her time down in this cave holding onto him as he sweated and shouted had created an intimacy that didn't really exist.

Frozen, new linen clutched in her hand as she battled an incomprehensible need to make that intimacy real. To tell him not just of Boswell's arbor, but Boswell himself. Of Boswell and her. If anyone might understand, shouldn't it be this man? Might he not be able to grant both Boswell and her absolution?

Ian must have recognized her hesitation, because his head lifted, his sky blue eyes gentler than she'd ever seen. Gentle enough to kindle a flare of grief in her chest, of loneliness. Of guilt.

No, she thought, seeing the pall of illness weigh him down, the burden of old nightmares and new fears. *Not now. Not ever, no matter how much I want to.*

"You might have seen the arbor on your way in here the other day," she said, forcing her voice past the knot of regret in her throat. "A little garden at the top of the rise with a view of the ocean where my husband planted his prize roses."

He must have seen something in her expression. "You don't like roses?"

She could at least tell this truth. "The ocean. Too big and unpredictable."

"I assume your husband liked it to plant his roses there."

She shrugged. "He never actually said. But he did love to sit there for hours. I always asked him what he thought about for so long. He said he wasn't thinking at all. Just smelling roses."

"Sounds rather nice."

"He w . . . is." Giving her skirts a quick swipe, she made to stand.

"Tell me about him," Ian said, his hands still wrapped around the hot mug.

Sarah froze. "Who? Boswell?"

"What is he like?"

She couldn't breathe, so strongly did the urge resurrect

to tell him. She had no right. And yet she found herself sitting again, searching his eyes for something.

"Nice," she said, finally looking away. "Too nice. Too simple for the life he inherited. All he wanted to do was putter about." Wearing belcher ties and gleaming tasseled boots. Another costume that hadn't fit. "Raise roses, ride his horse."

"Harvey?"

"Oh, no." She smiled, knowing there was no humor in it. "Apollo, an old gray breakdown of the squire's." She shook her head. "Poor old thing. The day of Waterloo, he simply laid down in his stall and died. The locals took it as a portent. Lady Clarke called them ignorant savages."

"What do you think?"

"I think the horse's heart was broken. Boswell had never left him behind before. But he refused to take him into battle."

The rest of the memories rushed in and drove her to her feet. *Not here. Not him.*

But oh, she wanted to.

"You might as well get some more rest," she said, retrieving her mugs. "It is the best thing for you right now. Besides, there is nothing you can do until you hear from Lord Drake. Did you give him your direction?"

He nodded. "He is to contact me through Lyme post. As Tom Frane. Old George says he has frequent correspondence from London that comes addressed to that name."

"Yes. He has many grateful customers." And no one in the village would admit to recognizing the name if asked. It was a brilliant solution.

Gathering her things, Sarah took another close look at

Ian. The fever was beginning to soar again; his skin was dry and flushed, his hands trembling. Closing his eyes, he laid his head into his hands. She clenched the scissors in her hand; she wanted to reach out. To ease him. To stroke away the weariness and cool the heat. The knot of anxiety that had taken up residence in her chest thickened and hardened. She had begun to hate this time of day; she was helpless to stop his suffering, to banish his nightmares. And being away from him was even worse. She fretted and paced, her chest tight and her hands clenched to keep from reaching for the kitchen door. She would be so glad when he left. She would be able to rest then.

No, she thought, thinking how hard she ached for him. That wasn't true. She wouldn't be glad when he left. The pain would be worse. It would never end.

Even so, she reached out. "Ian?"

For a second he didn't answer. She knelt, as if it could help ease his distress. As if it could ease hers.

"I can't rest," he finally said, never looking up. "I can't face what waits."

She swore her heart twisted in her chest. Oh, God, she couldn't bear this. "If you don't try, you will never get past this fever." Gently she laid her hand on his knee. "I think we've begun to turn the tide. A day or two more. Please. I'll stay if you want."

"You can't keep stayin' here with me, lass. Won't someone miss you?"

She brushed his hair off his forehead. "Not after dinner. They're all too afraid I'll put them to work."

Finally he lifted his ravaged face; Sarah all but flinched at the stark despair in his eyes. "They wait in the dark," he whispered.

She didn't even realize she had dropped her supplies until she found herself already kneeling, holding his hands when she wanted to wrap her arms around him and singlehandedly fight the phantoms away. "Then I'll face them with you."

Ian's didn't even smile. "I don't even want to face them. How can you?"

Her heart seized. She felt the harsh burn of tears in the back of her throat. How could she? He didn't want to know.

"They're not my nightmares," she said instead. "Now, lie down." Reaching out, she cupped his ragged, weary face in her hands. "I will be here, Ian."

Her heart, so newly vulnerable, wept in grief. And then, because pragmatism was her best defense, she helped Ian rest back on the cot and spent the rest of the night futilely trying to keep his fever down.

Just as he had feared, that night was the worst. Sarah wasn't certain whether it was her fault or his, but by naming his ghosts, he called up the very worst. At first she wasn't certain what they were. It wasn't a battle, she knew. When he saw carnage before him, when his men died around him, he seemed to grow larger, harder, his pain a living, writhing thing. When he began to mutter this time, deep in the dark early hours, the lantern light illuminated eyes that widened in shock. Confusion. Growing terror.

"Nae here?" he rasped, reaching out. "Of course they're here. They must be."

She took hold of his hand, thinking to calm him. He grabbed it so hard she thought he would crush it. "I left them *here*," he snarled. "You know that. Where would

Fiona and Mairead go if they aren't here? They're only twelve!"

Oh, sweet God, she thought, holding on tight. *He is searching for his sisters.*

"They are," she said, wanting only to stop this nightmare. She didn't want to know what it had cost him to find them beneath that bridge. "They're just not here now."

He yanked on her hand, as if to punish her lie. "Nae! Nae, I left them here. They were...they were safe. I made sure they were safe, even if we lost our mam."

"They *are* safe, Ian. I promise you."

But he didn't hear her. He heard other voices. Saw other realities, his open eyes blind to all but the old scene playing out before him.

He argued and searched and called in Gaelic, the words spilling like a rill through the room. Tears rose in his eyes and spilled over. Sarah heard the raw anguish in his voice, the tearing guilt. The dogged determination to change the truth.

"Have you seen them?" he began asking. "Two girls, about twelve. Redheads, like me. *Please.* You must have come across them."

She could almost see him trudging through the raw damp of winter as he followed the trail deeper and deeper into the Edinburgh slums. She saw his heart fracture a little more each time he was told he was too late, and her heart crumbled alongside.

"Ian, please," she kept saying, wiping the tears from his gaunt cheeks. "They're safe. Fiona and Mairead are safe."

He never heard her.

Sarah had been able to bear the battle scenes, the loss of his men. This was different. Not merely because she knew even better than Ian what Fiona and Mairead had suffered in the fetid darkness under that bridge, two twelve-year-old girls abandoned by everyone but each other. It was worse because now Sarah knew Ian. Without meaning to, Ian had shattered the protective shell Sarah had constructed as if it had been thin ice, and she suddenly found herself, not in hell, but confoundingly enough, in a place teeming with life, with possibilities, with pain and joy and wonder. Trembling, terrified, exultant, alive. Perched atop a perilous height with no hold except Ian's hand.

She didn't know what to do, how to grasp this intimacy, how to force it into a familiar shape. It was too new, too terrifying. She wanted it gone, and yet she wanted to embrace it even more closely. It hurt too much, both the grief of it and the joy of it. She wanted to be the one Ian always came to in pain. She wanted to help him carry it.

"How can I stay with you?" she echoed his earlier question, her tears mingling with his, her answer only for herself. "How can I not? I love you."

Chapter 9

The earth didn't move. The stars didn't tremble. Ian didn't even notice that Sarah's life had convulsed around her. At least she prayed he didn't. Because loving him changed nothing. Except that she didn't know what to do with the maelstrom of feelings that swept through her.

She had never had the chance to really love someone before. Not like this, with a sweet, deep emotion. With joy and grief and the most alien sense of possession. She had never been allowed to. An orphan belonged to no one. Certainly not the father who refused to acknowledge his mistake. Not the staff at an overcrowded orphanage, or the couple who never let her forget that they had only taken her away out of Christian duty.

Even her friends had never quite belonged to her. She loved them, certainly. She thought they had loved her. But she had walked into that school knowing she had to protect herself from becoming too close.

And yet six days with Ian Ferguson and she was completely lost.

It didn't matter that he didn't love her; he couldn't, after all. He was too honorable to allow it. He was betrothed to someone else, his promise inviolate. But she loved him. She was connected to him, entwined with him. Suddenly without ever meaning to, he had invited her to join life. To participate. To belong.

To *belong*. To be part of something, of someone. To join hands and step into a dance she had, for so long, only watched. To recklessly, ruthlessly, fearlessly open herself to him and let him in.

She should run. Escape before she reached a place from which she couldn't retreat. Before the life she lived lost its worth.

And yet she stayed. She refused to flee from him. Instead she lay down beside him and wrapped him in her arms, as if she could cushion the blows he suffered. When he wept, sobbing his sisters' names, she wept with him. And when he crushed her to him, she burrowed her face against his neck and stroked his tangled hair. She felt him shudder in her arms and gathered him to her, closer than comfort, closer than friendship, closer than love. Which was how she truly lost her way. Because when she could think of no other way to comfort him, she lifted her face and she kissed him.

It was something she had done before, after all. She had never given her whole self to Boswell, but she had known how to comfort him. She had kissed her husband when he was at his most despairing, and she knew it had sometimes brought him peace.

This kiss began in the same way. With closeness. Companionship. Compassion.

It changed instantaneously. The first touch of his soft mouth against hers left her reeling. Lightning struck.

Lightning and smoke and sunlight, all caught in a simple touch. Life. Passion, madness, joy. She didn't know how it happened, but suddenly she was wrapped in his arms, both of them trembling, both seeking, mouth and tongue and teeth, desperate to get closer, as if they could climb inside each other. As if they would both die unless they could share this primal force. She tangled her hands in his hair to hold on. He ran his great, gentle hands down her body.

Contact. Communion, comfort. A maelstrom of need and heat and pain metamorphosed into light by a touch, a kiss, the entwining of two bodies. Her body glowed and glittered and hummed. Her breasts ached, suddenly tender and full. Her skin seemed to have a life of its own. She swore if she looked in a mirror, she would gleam like starshine.

And oh, was this what it was like to want? To feel a hunger deep inside you, to the core of your womb? His hands moved erratically, as if he could hardly imagine he swept them along her hip, her thigh, the edge of her ribs. His mouth burned her throat, her shoulder, the swell of her breast, and she suddenly wanted that mouth everywhere. She wanted him to brand her with his touch so that no one else could ever claim her.

She wanted to *belong* to him. She wanted a connection so deep that he would fight for her as hard as he had his sisters. She couldn't imagine that kind of loyalty, that kind of raw, simple faith in another human. She would have given everything to have one person in her life who would have searched for her. To have *this* person, this driven, imperfect, loyal man follow her to hell to find her. Even if she didn't belong to him.

That one stray thought restored her senses. From one second to the next she passed from delirium to cold, stark sense.

The minute they stepped out of this cellar, their paths would part. He would return to his sisters and his fiancée and his life, and he would do great things. Sometimes he would remember his sister's friend, the one who had sheltered him, and he would tell amusing stories about her pig and a little estate on the south coast. Sarah would love him, though, forever. She would carry this exquisite pain with her where she went. She would tuck the memories away somewhere safe like petals pressed in poetry, so that when life grew too hard, or too lonely, she could pull them out and refresh herself with their scent. Because she would be alone again, to make it through as best as she knew how.

Gently she disentangled herself from him. She held her breath, half afraid he would wake and wonder why she lay in his arms. He didn't. He was quiet again, his features relaxed in sleep. She ached to return to his arms, to fold herself against him, arm around arm, cheek to shoulder, heart hearing heart. It was to comfort him, she assured herself. To offer contact with someone who understood. To do a kindness.

She was lying and she knew it. Tears slid down her cheeks again, but this time not for him. They fell as she climbed off the camp bed and as she reclaimed her seat on a nearby crate. They continued to fall until the sun came up and the nightmares fled. And they fell as she picked herself up and crept alone back to the house.

* * *

London

At four o'clock in the afternoon, White's was thin of company. Only Alvanley and Poodle Byng occupied the bow window, quizzing glasses raised as they commented on the gentlemen passing up St. James Street. A few older members dozed over newspapers in the reading room, and a dozen or so men sat over various card games. None looked up when the front door opened. Bets were being laid, which was more important.

"You owe me a pony."

Four gentlemen looked up from their hand of whist. Only Marcus Drake saw sharp interest flaring in the eyes of his fellow Rakes as he handed off his hat to the footman and strolled grinning into the nearly deserted card room, twirling his Malacca cane.

"Well, you're looking like the cat who's cleaning feathers from his chin," Beau Drummond greeted him, his usually severe features amused.

"A bottle of claret," Drake told the hovering waiter, who immediately turned and left. "With what strength I have left, I am celebrating."

A few men at a table on the far side of the room briefly looked up from their cards and smiled. Drake dragged a chair over and placed it next to Knight.

"A small matter," he announced to the room at large as he settled into the seat with the elegance of a big cat. "A new and innovative use by my mistress of silk cords. These clodpoles said it couldn't be done. Well, I am here to tell the tale."

"Ah," one of men at another table sighed. "La Paloma.

Most creative practitioner in the demimonde. Once saw her make use of a swing and a piccolo . . ."

Glasses were lifted in the lady's honor before play resumed.

"Ian?" Alex Knight murmured as Drake seated himself.

"Alive and well."

"Begad," Chuffy Wilde laughed softly, and pulled off his glasses for a good wipe. "I'll gladly pay up. I counted him out this time. Man's got more lives than a ferret."

"Not a ferret, Chuff," Beau Drummond said behind a lazy smile. "A cat's the one with nine lives. I don't think ferrets have more than one."

"You sure, Beau?" Chuffy dispensed a particularly sweet frown. "Don't know why. Sly nasty things, cats. Like ferrets better. Like birds, come to that. Always chirpin' and flittin' about—'til a cat gets 'em, anyway. But then, like Ferguson best of all."

Drake smiled complacently, as if he would be happy to hear Chuffy rattle on all day rather than impart his news. The waiter returned and poured out a glass for each man before leaving the bottle and silently departing. Sips were taken with smug smiles and a loudly conveyed suggestion or two for other tricks Drake's mistress might try.

"How 'bout the noose trick?" Alex Knight asked, his voice lowered as he contemplated his cards. "Are we to be spared seeing Ian attempt it?"

"Not if we have anything to say to the matter." Frowning, Drake laid a hand on Knight's black-banded arm. "I thank you for running down to London, Knight. Can't have been easy."

All the other men nodded, acknowledging the death

five months earlier of Knight's wife of four years. Knight nodded back. "I'd rather be productive, if it's all the same to you. A friend in need is the perfect excuse."

"He didn't do it, of course," the gently rotund Chuffy insisted, shoving a guinea into the center of the table. "Ferguson. Silly idea."

Postures relaxing, the other four men gladly moved away from tragedy.

"Indeed, Chuff," Drake agreed, sitting back with glass in hand. "However, we still lack proof. Ian asks an audience to mount his defense. He did give us a name, though. Stricker. Anyone know him? Seems he was in possession of a certain flask."

That quickly the tension returned. "Flask?" Alex asked. "I thought Horse Guards had it."

Drake sighed. "*Had* being the operative word. After getting his missive, I checked out the matter, and found it to be mysteriously missing."

"Devil a bit," the fourth member of the group drawled, managing to look outraged and uninterested at once. Only Nate Adams's usually languid black eyes gave him away. "Know Stricker. Bright new face at Horse Guards. Some relation of Jersey's."

Drake's head came up. "Horse Guards, huh? Well now, doesn't this get cozy?"

Drake turned to Chuffy. "What do you say, Chuff?"

Chuffy laid down a card. "Stricker? Don't think I'm related to him." He sounded surprised, which was understandable. Chuffy was related to most of the *ton*.

Adams downed his glass in one swallow and poured another. "Better get Stricker in fast. You know how much his compatriots like their members to be found out."

"Where is our lost lamb?" Alex asked, plucking bills from his stack.

Drake sipped at his wine and observed the room. "Wouldn't say. South coast somewhere, I assume. I'm to send a reply at the Lyme post office to let him know arrangements for bringing him in."

"Lyme?" Chuffy asked, peering up from his cards. "Happy coincidence. Was just about to tell you. Been invited to a house party given in honor of our blessed Princess Charlotte. Down near Cerne Abbas. No more than a toad's leap from Lyme."

"Didn't think toads could jump that far," Nate Adams drawled.

"Prodigious jumpers," Chuffy assured him with another ineffectual push at his glasses, which kept sliding down his nose. "Once won a monkey on Toadkins. Pet, you know. Prodigious jumper."

Alex nodded his dark head. "I remember Toadkins. You kept him in your pocket during class. Bloody well gave the venerable Patricks a seizure when the old boy landed in his lunch."

Chuffy shook his head slowly. "Bit of a prig, Patricks," he said. "Preferred Stevens. Amphibian man, all the way. All that time in swamps, I imagine."

"Well, don't take the toad down to the weekend," Drake advised. "Women are notoriously unimpressed by things that eat flies. Might throw the princess off her food."

"A real stick is the princess," Chuffy defended her. "Met Toadkins. Called him delightful. Can't bring him anyway, you know. Dead. Buried in m' father's snuffbox in the back garden."

The three men broke out laughing. "Your father's snuffbox?"

Chuffy didn't so much as look up from his cards. "Mater didn't like it. Risky scenes painted on the inside. Naked ladies and all."

"I think that's risqué," Beau offered. "Not risky."

Chuffy gave him a look over his glasses. "Risky for m' father when my mother saw it. Better to bury a toad in it."

When they finally stopped laughing, Drake lifted his glass. "To the princess," he said. "Chuffy, who will you take along?"

"Alex?" Chuffy asked.

Alex Knight sighed. "I already have an invitation. My sister Pippin is good friends with the duke's sister Elizabeth."

"Good," Drake said. "We can kill two birds with one stone. Find our lost lamb and keep an eye on our princess. Keep me apprised."

"Should we speak with the princess?" Alex asked. "Put a flea in her ear?"

Drake didn't need to think on it. "Too soon. She might give away the game."

"She would, too," Chuffy said. "Not treated well by that family, but loyal to the bone. Would be out for blood."

The others nodded. "Well, see who has her ear."

"That's easy," Alex said. "Mercer Elphinstone. Thick as inkleweavers. I think she was the one talked the princess into that indiscretion with her cousin."

"See if you can learn anything new," Drake suggested. "Anyone...oh, you know what to look for. You've done this long enough."

Standing, he downed his wine with a wink to his friends. "Enough rest," he announced to the room at large. "A man doesn't keep La Paloma waiting for long. I'll expect your notes, gentlemen."

Alex gave a huge grin. "If you live through the week."

Drake left to applause, and the others got down to planning their trip.

* * *

A few blocks over on Bruton Street, a young man knocked on a library door and pulled it open. The young man did not particularly like these duties. He wasn't bred for sedition, no matter how good the cause. And he believed the cause good. England needed a change. She needed men like the self-proclaimed Lions who would not flinch before the hard tasks. And God knew this task was hard.

The secretary waited for the old man to lift his head from where he'd been perusing a folio of bird etchings. "You owe me a monkey, sir. He's alive."

The old man set down the glass and sat back. "Ferguson?"

"I told you he would be. Stricker was never up to his weight."

The old man gave a frustrated huff. "The information is good?"

"Right from a letter posted to the General Post Office account used by Horse Guards for emergencies." A ruby glinted from the young man's signet as he rubbed his nose. "After interception, it was sent on, hopefully to whoever has been directing these operations. I'm afraid

Ferguson did mention Stricker." Which satisfied the young man. He considered Stricker a buffoon. "Ferguson asked a reply be sent to Lyme Regis."

The old man sighed. "I expect he still has the flask. Make certain we reach him before his friends do. Alert Madame Ferrar. She can take care of Ferguson and Stricker at the same time. She should enjoy that."

The young man had witnessed some of Madame Ferrar's work. He swallowed hard, glad he would not need to supervise this time.

"And please," the old man said. "Make certain that anyone who might have had contact with our Colonel Ferguson regrets their charity."

The younger man paled.

"Well?" the old man barked.

His companion swallowed and bowed. "It will be done."

And God help Ian Ferguson. God help them all.

Chapter 10

Two days later Ian opened the cellar door and stepped out into the early darkness. He had been in this benighted cellar for eight days now. Well, mostly the cellar. Once the fever had passed, he'd taken to walking late at night. With only the moon and starlight to light his way, he had familiarized himself with nearby terrain and built up his endurance for the moment Drake answered his summons.

Then, this afternoon Old George had appeared with some unwelcome news. Ian still held the newspaper George had brought in his hands. The *Dorsetman*, stamped with yesterday's date and a damning headline.

Search Continues for Villainous Traitor

"She didn't want me to show you," George had said, hands in pockets. "But you need to know."

Wasn't it funny? Ian thought. Sitting in this blighted cellar, he'd all but forgotten how desperate his situation really was. He had actually begun to drift along on the current of Sarah's concern, the soft lilt of her voice. The narcotic of her company.

Old George had been right. He needed to remember who he was.

...vile traitor...Scot animal...dead or alive...

He'd read the article three times, as if the news would change and he was no longer a wanted man. A free man to enjoy...what? No matter what happened, he had to leave soon, before he came to depend even more on the sound of Sarah Clarke stepping through that cellar door. Before he completely forgot the commitments that waited for him out in the real world.

"George," he'd said, clenching the paper in his hand. "How would you like to help me plan an escape?"

He just had to tell Sarah when she came tonight. He just had to walk away from her, knowing that he would never see her again. Knowing he wouldn't have the right.

Eight days. He'd known her eight days, and already parting from her was torture, the price of knowing her higher than he ever could have imagined. In one week, she'd made him question the future he'd so carefully planned.

He had such lofty goals, such promises to keep, and he'd thought his bargain reasonable. After all, he would have the chance to give voice to the people who had populated his childhood. The starving, the homeless, the orphaned and abandoned. The soldiers who had been left to the street corners with their empty-limbed uniforms and begging bowls. He would finally speak for those two starving girls he had failed.

He owed it to them. He owed it to them all, and he had made a sacred vow to repay them. Was a comfortable wife and a privileged life too great a price to pay?

Until he'd found himself hiding behind Sarah Clarke's henhouse, he had never questioned it.

Henhouses. He lifted his head. What the devil? He could hear chickens. Panicked, flapping, squawking chickens. Pushing past the screening bushes that hid the cellar, he climbed up to the lip of the lawn.

It was fully dark, with the quarter moon riding low over the sea. The sky for once was clear, with the wind blowing from the east, which helped him hear the chickens. Of course, with the racket they were making, they ought to have been heard in London. Trying to stay out of sight of the house, Ian crept along the garden wall toward the coop. He could deal with a fox in the henhouse; he could not with discovery.

He needn't have bothered. He heard a door slam open and then Sarah's voice. "You stay here, Peg. This fox is all mine."

Ian had to grin. Incongruously clad in a pale dinner dress that glowed like a ghost in the gloom, she made an unlikely soldier as she strode through the kitchen garden. Ian heard the gun snap shut as she made for the henhouse. Yanking open the door with a screech, Sarah ducked into the little building. Instead of running up to join her, for once he waited, perfectly happy to be the audience.

A shot cracked through the silent darkness. Ian nodded. *Good girl.* The hens set up a distressed racket, and goats bleated. Ian considered moving closer. He wanted to see the triumph on Sarah's face when she came out of the coop.

But she didn't come. And then... Ian tilted his head. It sounded like a scuffle. The hair went up on the back of his neck. Something wasn't right. He didn't question his instincts. He ran.

He was still at least a couple of hundred yards from

the henhouse when he saw the door open. He stopped, relieved. He almost called out, praising Sarah's intrepid defense of her chickens. Then he saw her and dropped straight to the ground. She wasn't alone. A hand over her mouth, a man was dragging her out of the henhouse.

God and the Bruce. Ian froze where he was. It would do Sarah no good for him to fly off half-cocked. He went into battle mode, slowing his breathing, gathering calm. Focusing his attention on Sarah. She was fighting. He saw her stumble. Saw the man drag her across the cobbles like a sack of grain, even as she clawed at him, fists and feet and nails. Her pretty pale dress was ruined. Her assailant had pulled her hair loose. Ian figured distances, times, opportunities.

And then she whimpered. Sarah, who had faced surprises and soldiers and seditionists with aplomb, betrayed her terror. Rage hit Ian like a high tide. Battle madness swept through him. That squinty-eyed, cowardly little *mac na galla* wouldn't survive the night.

Gaining his feet, Ian crept closer, keeping into the deeper shadows along the stable wall. He saw the red of a uniform jacket.

Bloody hell. A soldier. Probably one of that half-starved lot he'd seen the other day. Sarah was struggling in the soldier's grip. Ian could hear an occasional grunt or curse as her elbow or foot made contact. *That's right, lassie,* he thought, the taste of fear rancid in his mouth. *Hold him off 'til I get there.*

He waited only long enough for them to reach the trees. Then, bending low, his steps silent as death, he sprinted after them. Moonlight glinted off the steel in the man's hand. A knife. Ian knew he was running out of time. There was a small clearing about a hundred yards on. Ian had the feeling the soldier was making for it, where he would have room and no witnesses. It would be better for Ian too. Give him more room to act. He changed direction and ran faster.

"It's not personal, miss," Ian heard the solder say, almost conversationally. "I'm delivering a message, that's all. The chickens was just to get y'r attention."

Sarah answered with a kick back at his shins. Keeping his focus on Sarah's panicked face, Ian wove through the trees like a red Indian.

Sarah must have anticipated that clearing as well. The closer they approached, the harder she fought, even as a line of blood trickled down her throat from the knifepoint. Ian could almost smell her terror.

The weasel-faced bastard who had her was smiling. "Go ahead and fight, girlie. I like my women sparky. Adds a bit of spice, it does."

Ian could hear his own heart in his ears; his palms were wet. He'd spent his life in battle. He couldn't remember being this afraid. He had seen what soldiers did when let loose. He couldn't allow that to happen to Sarah. He *would* not.

Then the bastard made a mistake. They had just reached the clearing. Ian had a few yards to go to reach them. Sarah kicked out again. This time the soldier grabbed her by the hair and pulled her right back against his body. Ian could see the whites of her eyes in the gloom.

"That's right," the soldier growled, running the flat of the knife down her cheek. "Mort's in charge here, my sweet little cunny. Make 'im happy, an' you can live."

Sarah answered him by cracking the back of her head into his nose. The man cursed. She kicked. He spun her around and backhanded her so hard she flew across the clearing to slam against a tree. She tried to scramble up, but the soldier was quicker. Grabbing her again, he threw her down and then threw himself atop her.

She tried to dig her fingers into his eyes. The soldier wrapped one hand around her throat and lifted the knife with the other, ready to score it down her face. Reaching the clearing at a dead run, Ian let loose a Highlander's yell.

Sarah shrieked. The soldier whipped around, his mouth gaping. Ian charged in like a bull elephant, leading with his shoulder. The soldier jumped up. Sarah rolled away just as Ian slammed into the man with a resounding crunch, sending them both hurtling.

"Like to terrorize women, do ya, little man?" Ian grated, punching at that chinless face. "Let's see how you do with me."

The soldier was no longer laughing. He fought like a street thug. He tried to gouge out Ian's eyes, to slice the tendons at Ian's elbows, at the backs of his knees. He even, finally, tried to run. Ian would allow none of it. He had fought on the same streets and was just as merciless, bloodying that face past recognition until the little man was lying on the ground beneath him begging for him to stop. But Ian couldn't. He couldn't remember such a feral need to batter a human in his life.

"Ian!" he heard behind him. "Enough!"

It wasn't. Not quite. Rearing to his feet, he dragged the soldier with him, the man's face unrecognizable and the fight gone out of him. Wrapping one hand around the man's skinny throat and the other around the knife hand, Ian lifted him completely off the ground, feet kicking, gaping pale eyes at level with his own. The soldier began to babble. Ian ignored him. He twisted the knife arm. His feet dangling well off the ground, the soldier screamed. There was the terrible snap of bone and the knife fell.

Ian didn't move. "Sarah," he said, his voice stone calm, even as the soldier sobbed. "Are ye all right, lass?"

She tried to scramble to her feet, but didn't make it. On her knees, she nodded, her hair tangled around her face. Her hands shook as she pushed it back to reveal her blood-stained dress. Ian wanted so desperately to go to her, pick her up, hold her in his arms until he knew she was safe. But he had to deal with this piece of vermin first.

"Now then, laddie," he murmured in a voice that should have terrified the man. "Ye and I have some talkin' to do."

Blinking at Ian, the man gaped like a fish. "You're the one."

"I might be," Ian agreed, then pulled the man close enough to smell the terror on him. "I'll tell ye what else I am. I'm the Scot who shot Englishmen at Badajoz for what they were doing to the Spanish women. Imagine how much more I'll enjoy killing ye, little man."

The soldier began to plead. Without letting go of him, Ian bent to gently help Sarah up. Her pretty dress was ripped and her face the color of paste. Silent tears rolled down her cheeks.

Setting her gently on her feet, Ian brushed the tears with his free thumb and turned back to the soldier, whom he still held up with one hand. "I dinna hae any real love for an English uniform," he said, the rage a living fire in his chest. "But still, it should nae be dishonored. You've just done that, laddie." He began to squeeze the man's throat. "Worse, ye've dishonored this lady."

"Ian."

He could barely hear her through the fury that choked him. "No, Sarah. If I let him go, he'll just hurt another woman."

"Ian, no." Her voice was trembling and high, which fed Ian's rage. "He said he was giving me a message. I need to know who the message was from."

Ian stopped. He turned when Sarah laid a hand on his arm.

"Please," she said with a watery smile. "Let me talk to him first. If you don't think his answers sufficient, strangle away. But I think he has information I need."

Ian almost dropped the soldier on his head. "Are you sure, lass?"

She gave a tremulous smile and pulled her dress back up over her shoulder with shaking hands. "Please."

The soldier's eyes were swiveling as if he were at a shuttlecock match. Ian pulled him nose to nose. "What do ye have to say tae the lady, lad?"

"He'll kill me," the soldier whined.

"So will I," Ian assured him. "I'll just do it sooner. And slower. And not bein' raised a gentleman, I'll make it far worse. Now then, let's begin again. What name should I put on your tombstone?"

If it was possible, the weasel-faced soldier paled even more. "Briggs. Mort Briggs. Corporal."

Ian shook his head. "Not anymore, I'd say. Was this ye're idea, or were ye even a greater coward and let some other bastard talk you into it?"

"Clarke . . ." His eyes swiveled to Sarah, and he crumpled. "Him what hired us. He asked me to...to scare her a bit. That was all."

Ian growled. "That was nae all and you know it, you whore's son." He was just about to start squeezing again, when a fact made it through the red haze. "Clarke?" Quickly he turned to a still-ashen Sarah. "That high-nosed skint who was threatening you the other day? Your husband's cousin?"

She gave a shaky nod. "I've suffered a series of losses. I had a notion who was behind them, but I couldn't prove it." She motioned to the soldier, who was still hanging from Ian's grip. "He will."

Ian shook with the effort to not strangle the little *cac*. "Are ye tellin' me I canna wring his worthless neck?"

This time he earned a pallid smile. "You cannot kill my proof, Ian."

He looked down at her earnest face. He looked at the ashen soldier. "Well, hell." He sighed. "I can break a few more things, though, can't I? He can still testify."

The soldier sobbed. "T-testify?"

Ian set him on his feet without letting go. "You can testify and go to Botany Bay, once-Corporal Mort Briggs, or ye can stay silent and suffer far worse from me. Now, laddie, 'til you make up my mind, I think we need to truss you up as a gift to the law."

Just then they heard a voice from the direction of the house. "Miss Sarah?" Turning to Ian, Sarah blanched. "Peg. Oh, I have to tell her something." Limping over to the trees, she stood in the deeper shadows. "I'm here, Peg. I'm just going to bury the fox!"

The answer sounded like a grumble. A moment later, a door shut and quiet fell.

Sarah didn't move, but stayed staring at the distant house. Ian marveled at her composure. Considering what had almost happened, she should have been hysterical.

That was when he noticed that she was rubbing at her forehead. "We can't," she said, turning back to him.

"Can't what?"

"Turn him in." She waved a trembling hand at the soldier. "If I take him to the authorities, he'll give you away."

The soldier shook his head. "No, I won't."

Ian shook him like a rat. "O' course ye will. Shut up now while I think, laddie."

In the end, they dragged the soldier back to the cellar with them. Sarah recovered her shotgun from the henhouse while Ian splinted the soldier's arm and tied him up with cords he stole from George's cache.

"Can you watch him here?" Sarah asked, setting the gun against the cave wall. "Just until you can safely get away."

"Longer," Ian corrected, binding the man's ankles. "'Til I prove my innocence, or they'll know you hid me. He could be down here weeks."

"I'll be missed," the soldier protested.

"No ye won't. Shut up."

"Maybe George would watch him for us." She sighed. "I'll contact him tomorrow. Right now, I need to get back to the house."

Ian knew he should tell her what he and George had already concocted. One look at her washed-out features dissuaded him. They had time to worry about his escape later.

She was picking at the ruined dress and making impatient little noises, which made Ian want to gather her to him and just hold her. Just shut out the sight of her struggle. She began to tidy herself, trembling hands reassembling her hair and plucking at the hang of her dress as she gave voice to various stories about battling a fox she could give Peg to explain her condition.

As she did, Ian finished trussing up the soldier so he couldn't so much as scratch his ass. He was just finishing tying the last knot when he heard a curious sound behind him, like chattering. He turned around to see Sarah suddenly white-faced and shaking like an ague victim. Shoving the soldier over onto the floor, he grabbed Sarah just as her eyes rolled back in her head.

"Oh, lass," he said, catching her in his arms. "You are not all right." Gathering her gently into his arms, he carried her to the cot. "Ye're cold as midnight on the moors."

Pulling a blanket up, he wrapped it around her and sat with her on his lap. It was her teeth he'd heard. They were clicking madly.

Her eyes fluttered open. "I'm…fine…really." She made a dismal attempt at a smile.

"O' course ye are." He tucked her tightly into his arms, desperate to give her some heat. Some comfort. He could feel her heart thrumming like a sparrow; the violence of her fear burned right through him.

"It's just…he . . ." She gasped, her voice wobbly. "He killed my chicken. He didn't have to do that, did he?"

Ian almost grinned. God, he could love this stalwart girl. "I'll break his other arm for ya, lass. Then I'll buy you a new chicken."

He heard another funny little sob. "Her name was... Rachel."

He nodded against her hair, suddenly full with wanting to give her anything to make her feel better, this girl who mourned a lost hen. When he felt another tear splash on his wrist, he thought his heart would shatter.

"I'm that sorry, ma'am," the soldier spoke up, his voice high and reedy.

"Shut up," Ian snapped. "If she didn't need you alive to protect her estate, I'd snap your neck without blinkin' an eye. I may yet."

"How did you know?" she asked him, her voice small, which tormented him.

"That something was wrong?" He smiled into her hair. "I'd know the sound of those hens anywhere."

Her chuckle was a bit strangled. Closing his eyes, Ian just held her. He couldn't think of a thing in his life that had ever felt more right. He could smell the clean rain scent of her hair. He felt the staccato of her pulse against his fingers and the silk of her skin against his cheek. She suddenly seemed so fragile. So vulnerable. He couldn't bear it. He wanted her here in his arms, where she could be safe. He wanted, for the first time in his life, to stay. He wanted, unforgivably, to stay with *her,* no matter what it cost him.

He knew better even as he thought it. Because he wouldn't be the one to suffer. She would.

* * *

Ian dreamed of her that night. The few minutes he'd held her in his arms hadn't been nearly enough. But he had no right to ask for more from a woman waiting for her husband to return. He had nothing to offer, a man whose own fiancée also waited.

He ached for the comfort he could give her, if it were only his right. The strong arms she needed, the laughter. The joy. She deserved a man to warm her bed. She deserved passion. And Ian was human enough to want to share it with her. He was enchanted enough that he wanted to offer it to her as a gift.

He knew her shape. He'd cushioned it in his arms, framed it with his hands. He knew her taste and her laugh and the calluses on her palms. He knew that her hair was soft as thistledown where it escaped from that horrible bun. He knew how her smile stole a man's strength, and he knew what the plump bounty of her breasts felt like pressed against his chest.

He knew this from the short moments she'd lost her way and shared that kiss, that embrace, that sharing of pain and loneliness and comfort. He knew all this, but when he dreamed, he dreamed more.

In his dream she was naked and smiling, welcoming him to her soft bed, her skin milky and sleek, her nipples dark pink and pebbled, her sunstreaked hair cast across the pillows like a gleaming river. He imagined winnowing his fingers through that hair, tormenting himself with the weight of it, the sleek satin of it. He saw himself set his hand to her soft skin, seeking out every crest and slope, tracing the line of every rib and dipping into the hollow of her belly. He imagined tracing his tongue along her throat, sweeping along to her shoulder and following the sure track of her collarbone. He swore he could taste the tang of her skin and hear her throaty chuckle as he crested the swell of those sweet, full breasts she camouflaged so well beneath her dreary clothing.

He would linger there, savoring their delicious ripeness, memorizing every curve and shiver, catching their weight in his hands and nibbling every delicious inch, top to bottom, side to side. And finally, after tormenting her with his hesitation, he would close his hand around one nipple, teasing it to a peak with finger and callused thumb, and close his mouth around the other. He could just hear the moans he would pull from her as he nipped at the tender skin, soothing it with his tongue, suckling hard enough to light that fire between her legs, there where she hid such treasure beneath a nest of dark gold curls.

He would lay his head on her belly and watch as he let his hand seek out that fire, his fingers dipping below those tawny curls to come away dripping with her want for him. He would return, finger, palm, and thumb, relentlessly stroking, circling, sweeping, until she could no longer hold still, until the shivers built up in her skin ahead of the pleasure that raced through her, and her body arched to his touch. Until she moaned, whimpered, begged. He would take her to the very edge, to the perfect moment just before she lost herself, and then, with one smooth movement, he would lift himself over her, he would spread her legs beneath him, never taking his eyes from hers, from those soft, earth-rich eyes that expressed so much if you knew how to look, and he would plunge home.

Home.

Ian bolted upright on the cot, the dream fragmented and fading. He still shook with need, his body rock hard and hurting. His heart thundered, and he couldn't seem to draw in a good breath. His chest felt as if it were collapsing.

Home? What was he thinking? Sarah wasn't his home. She couldn't be. Even in his dreams. *Especially* in his dreams.

Throwing his legs over the side of the cot, he laid his head in his hands. He had to get out. He had to breathe, and suddenly he couldn't do it in this cellar. He swore he could still smell Sarah on the air in here. He knew he could still hear the echoes of her climax, a climax he'd only dreamed.

Maybe he should just go now. Walk out of the cave and keep on going, without waiting for Drake or George or even daylight. If he left, he could avoid seeing Sarah again. And right now, with his body still taut as a bowstring, and the memory of her in his arms still far too clear, he thought that might be a good thing.

But he couldn't go. At least not until he spoke to Old George again. Otherwise, who would protect Sarah from her cousin after he'd gone?

Giving the soldier a quick look to make sure he was still asleep over by the stacked crates, Ian climbed to his feet. It was coming onto sunrise. He needed to see the sky and cool off. Grabbing his blanket, he stalked out the cellar entrance.

The chilly wind was a shock. The sky, still only a faint blush toward dawn, was star-scattered and deep, the moon lost beyond the horizon. Below the sea churned and chuckled in its peculiar way, and early morning birds had begun to chatter.

Ian had never been much of a one for the sea. But the

little arbor was a convenient place to think. And right now he needed that more than anything. Pulling his blanket around his shoulders, he turned to climb out of the hollow.

He stopped after no more than three steps. He swore he heard snuffling nearby.

A bhidse, he thought, ducking down. *Now what?*

He went very still. After what had happened the night before, he was expecting another of Clarke's soldiers to be lurking nearby, maybe that *cac* Clarke himself. Slowly, silently, Ian lifted his head just over the lip of the hollow.

He was right. There was a shadow up in the arbor. Ian could just see it, bent over the roses. Dropping the blanket, he crept closer. Abruptly the snuffling stopped.

Ian froze. The shadow grunted and returned to the roses. Ian laughed and stood up. He had steeled himself to meet a vandal. He'd gotten a pig. There, his nose back to the ground snuffling away like he was on the trail of a new love, was Willoughby.

"Och, now, laddie," Ian greeted him, stepping up. "I'm no' at all in the mood to be hauling you back home. I dinna suppose ye'd like to wander back to your pen on yer own. I hear there's a mighty fetching blanket waiting for you."

Willoughby looked up and snorted, and Ian smiled. "No. I suppose not. Freedom is much more enticing."

He approached, thinking to share the bench with the pig. The pig didn't even seem to notice him. He was pawing at something in the ground, shoving at it with his snout. If Ian wasn't mistaken, Sarah was about to have her rosebushes uprooted.

"Here now," he protested, shoving the pig with his

knee. "Is that any way to pay the lass back for feeding ya? Come awa', pig."

The pig didn't budge. The rosebush shuddered from the assault, and Ian began to worry. He hoped Sarah wasn't attached to the damn thing. Because if the pig got it up, it wouldn't do any good for Ian to replant it. Back at barracks, he had been called the black thumb. Even mold had died in his care.

Determined to stop the destruction, he grabbed the pig's rope, which was entangled in yet another rosebush. That bush went over as well, making an odd sucking sound. Willoughby whuffled into the resulting hole.

Ian took another tug on the rope. This time Willoughby looked up at him, as if surprised to see him there.

"Come along, then," Ian coaxed, pulling the pig away from the roses.

Amazingly, Willoughby followed. Tying him to a nearby tree, Ian returned and grabbed the rosebush. The least he could do was shove it back in. Maybe Sarah wouldn't notice.

Kneeling, he shoved his hand into the hole to widen it. Instead he hit something solid. Something soft and...oddly familiar. Ian yanked his hand back. What the blazes? His heart was suddenly pounding again, and his chest hurt.

"Willoughby," he murmured, back on his heels. "What have you found?"

Reaching down, he pushed aside more dirt, upending another rosebush. No wonder Willoughby wanted to dig. There was a blanket buried beneath the roses, and it was wrapped around something solid. Ian gave a good yank, and a corner pulled free. The stench that escaped sent him rearing back. He stopped. There was no question now. He knew that smell all too well.

Careful now, dreading what he would see, he went back to work, opening the hole wider. Beside him Willoughby squealed and tugged at the arbor. Ian looked into the hole and saw why. There was more wool down in that hole. Red wool. Crimson wool with orange facings. A uniform jacket from the 35th Foot.

Chapter 11

Sarah found herself standing in front of a hat shop, looking at nothing. She couldn't seem to focus on anything, still too overwhelmed and upended for sense. It had been more than twelve hours since Corporal Briggs had attempted to...attempted...Lord, she couldn't even think the word. She swore she could still smell the sour stench on him, still feel the sharp edge of that knife against her throat. She hadn't slept more than moments since without startling awake, swearing she heard his voice in the corners of her room.

But the attack alone wasn't what was still provoking the shivery, liquid feeling that beset her. The rescue was. She couldn't remember ever experiencing such an intense rush of terror, relief, and gratitude in her life. Nothing could compare with the feel of Ian's arms around her, of his gentle comfort. She wasn't used to being held. No one had ever thought to do it. No one but Ian had ever offered her safe haven.

He had been so caring, so calm, that only when she sat with her ear pressed tightly against his chest had she realized how hard his heart was beating. Only by closing her eyes and being very still had she felt the tremors in his arms. He had hugged her, and he'd hugged hard. And Sarah had never, ever, felt so safe.

She wasn't, though; that feeling of safety, of protection, was an illusion.

Oh, what was she to do? She couldn't bear the sweet, sharp flood of yearning that swept her. She *wanted.* She wanted Ian's arms around her. She wanted to hear his voice and catch the substance of him in her hands. She wanted to share secrets and laughter and the comfort of embraces. She wanted to etch the memory of herself on Ian's soul.

But that was something she would never do. He had an entirely different future to follow. He had a fiancée, who would stride with him through the world with purpose and do great things. As for Sarah, she would wait here, hoping for occasional word from Fiona about how he was doing.

"Sarah, for heaven's sake," she heard next to her. "You have stared at that window for ages, and there is nothing in it but a perfectly hideous bonnet you wouldn't buy anyway. At least I hope not, because I would never be seen with you in it."

Blinking, Sarah turned to find Artemesia glaring at her. They were standing in front of Mrs. Ames' Milliners on Broad Street in Lyme Regis.

"Oh, I don't know, Artie," she said, tilting her head at the immense concoction of silk, lace, feathers, and fruit. "Don't you think that would look fetching on Elinor?"

Artie giggled at the image of feathers on a pig.

"A relative, ma'am?" Sarah looked up to see Mrs. Wilks step into her doorway.

Sarah kept her countenance with some difficulty. "A very dear friend."

Artie's giggle was more carefree than Sarah had heard it in a while. "Oh, no, Sarah. I don't believe it suits her coloring at all."

Sarah shared sly glances. "True. I also suspect she lacks the height to carry the look."

"Well, my bonnets are all beautiful," Mrs. Wilks offered. "But very dear."

The tone was speaking, the look even more so. Ah, Sarah thought, seeing it. So the word had spread. Sarah had heard a similar refrain from the butcher, the coal merchant, and the cobbler. The Clarke ladies' security was suspect. It made her wonder just what rumors Martin had been spreading.

Artie had greeted the gentle snubs with growing silence. This time she smiled. "Indeed, Mrs. Wilks," she said. "Perhaps another time."

Sarah slipped her arm through Artie's, relieved and proud of the girl. "Well done."

They progressed down the hill toward the sea, nodding to an acquaintance or two, chatting about the offerings they saw in shop windows.

Lyme Regis was a classic South Coast resort town, built for and supported by the summer months, when tourists flocked in for the sea bathing and atmosphere. Now, as winter approached, the shop fronts looked a bit worn and the atmosphere a touch tawdry, like an aging courtesan in daylight. Only fossil hunters remained, hardy souls like Rosie, who instead of painting, happily tromped the windswept coast for a chance to find a rock imprinted with ghosts of a distant past.

Actually, Sarah wouldn't have minded spending a day following Rosie around, or Rosie's friend Mary Anning, learning about their theories, considering a world where great fish swam that were no longer seen. Contemplating a God who, by Mary's own discovery, had made mistakes. Sarah had seen the creatures Mary had dug out of the blue Lias clay; exotic, unrecognizable things with paddles for hands and thin, long snouts. Creatures God had created. And then what, destroyed? Forgotten? Changed?

Wouldn't it be lovely to have the comfort to sit somewhere and just think of these things? To have a companion who wished to discuss them? A man who wouldn't be irritated by a woman's need for knowledge. A man . . .

"Sarah, you're wandering again."

Sarah looked over at the girl with a sheepish smile. "Merely woolgathering."

Again she thought of sharing her thoughts with Ian. Again she wished she had the right to do so; the leisure, the security, the unspoken understanding that no matter what, each could carry their joys, their worries, their sorrows to the other, knowing that they would be safely received and kept.

Sarah scowled at her own whimsy. By now she should know better. Briskly, she picked up her pace. They passed the Anning's fossil shop and waved to Mary out at the table. The sea wind whipped up the steep streets, sending bits of paper skittering before it and tugging at skirts and bonnets. Sarah and Artie turned up Coombe Street.

"Sarah?" Artie said, her head down.

"Hmmm?"

"*Is* Boswell coming home?"

Sarah came to a halt. She wished people would stop blindsiding her. "What?"

Artie shook her head. "*Maman* and Rosie refuse to ask. They don't want to know. They're too afraid. But I must. I need to prepare."

The girl looked so frightened suddenly. Sarah wondered how long she had been wanting to ask this one very important question. Sarah's heart went out to her. Even though Artie could be difficult, she was still a child who had suddenly had her comfortable future exploded on her. And if anyone understood that, it was Sarah.

She wanted to sigh. She would gladly give the responsibility to someone else.

Except, as always, there was no one else. She took Artie's hand. "I am already prepared."

Scowling, Artie pulled away. "Of course you are. You're leaving."

Sarah blinked. "I am?"

Artie's laugh sounded sadly like a sob. "Well, naturally. After all, why should you stay? You can go anywhere. Well, go. Nobody wants you here."

Spinning back around, Artie resumed walking.

It took Sarah a minute to follow her. "Artie," she said, bringing the girl to a stop. "I'm sorry you feel that way, but I have no plans to leave."

"Of course you do," the girl insisted, her voice thick with fear. "It is all *Maman* speaks of. How you'll desert us in our hour of need."

Sometimes Sarah would love to beat that old woman. What a job she had done dividing her own household with her drama. "I regret disappointing you, dear," Sarah said, brushing back Artie's hair. "But I am not going anywhere.

You may not consider me your family, but I consider you mine. And I would *never* desert my family."

She didn't mention the vow she had made to Boswell that last day that she would be more loyal to his family than he had ever been. The family that had never wanted her. Well, odd as it seemed, she wanted them. They were all she had.

Artie looked stunned. "But I was sure . . ."

Sarah smiled. "Well, don't be. You are stuck with me, missy."

"Even if Boswell . . . if Martin takes the estate?"

"Even then."

Tears welled in Artie's blue eyes. Her face trembled.

Her own heart swelling, Sarah pulled the girl into a hard hug. "We'll come about, Artie. I promise. Now—" She pulled back and smiled. "Rosie gave us a bit of money to spend. What do you think? After the post office, shall we have tea?"

Artie stopped in her tracks. "Truly? Tea? And scones that don't taste like . . ."

"Cricket balls?" Sarah chuckled. "And here I thought I was the only one fearing Peg's food."

"Oh, no. It's just that *Maman* and Rosie have a happy knack for not caring. And I am far too polite to hurt Peg's feelings."

This time they laughed together.

"Well, let us be off then," Sarah said, once again linking arms and turning uphill.

As if Sarah had pulled a stopper from an overfull bottle, suddenly Artie was chattering away about her friends, the people and stores around her. Sarah found herself really smiling for the first time in days.

Artie was in mid-sentence when she stopped right in the middle of the walk. "Oh, would you look at her," she sighed. "Isn't she the loveliest woman you've ever seen?"

Sarah looked up, expecting to see a fashionable fossil hunter. What she saw stopped her breath in her chest. Artie was right. Standing in front of the post office talking with, all people, Mr. Stricker, was the loveliest woman she had ever seen. Vibrant, graceful, lush, with cornsilk hair and a figure to make angels weep. Unforgettable. Which was why Sarah could never have mistaken her for anyone else. It was the woman on the miniature in Ian's pocket flask.

In the painting she had worn a low-necked dress of silver that offset the wheaten hue of her hair. She had been deftly painted and rouged, with the shadow of her nipples showing through the lawn of her chemisette. Standing on Coombe Street, she was clad in unrelieved black, even to the handkerchief she held to her cheek. The question was, why was she here? And why was she introducing herself to Horace Stricker?

"My dear husband . . ." they could hear over the wind. "Seaside air . . . recovery . . ."

Artie huffed a bit. "Only if she enjoys winter gales. I would think she'd rather go to Brighton. Or Italy."

Indeed.

What had Ian said? Sarah tried to pull the memory out of her suddenly whirling mind. An assassin. A clever, deadly assassin named Minette Ferrar. Standing right outside the post office where Ian expected to receive his answer from Drake.

There could only be one reason that woman could be here. Ian had been betrayed.

Surreptitiously Sarah looked around. If that woman was here, others might be as well, watching to see who picked up mail. Sarah's brain froze; her heart faltered badly. She could not walk into that post office. She was suddenly terrified Minette Ferrar would know exactly what she was there for.

"Sarah?"

Sarah shook her head. "My," she said, praying her voice sounded natural. "You're quite correct. She is lovely. Lyme seems to be attracting a better class of people entirely. I hope she doesn't put us completely in the shade."

Artie evidently didn't hear any panic in Sarah's voice. "Perhaps we should go back and get that bonnet," she suggested slyly. "At least we'd be noticed."

Sarah chuckled, as if nothing had changed. Minette Ferrar must have heard her, because she turned. Obviously seeing the astonished admiration in Artie's eyes, she flashed them a smile that was a masterpiece of etiquette, polish, and lingering sorrow.

Sarah had no choice, of course. She had to get her mail or explain to Artie why she didn't. Exchanging nods with the woman and Mr. Stricker, Sarah led Artie into the post office.

"Good day, Lady Clarke," the postmistress greeted her from behind the counter. "Got somethin' special for you today, don't I?"

Sarah swore she felt Madame Ferrar's attention. It was all she could do to focus on her task. On getting Artie safely home so she could warn Ian.

"I'm hoping you have the dowager's paints, Mrs. Pope," she said, wondering if she sounded too strident. "If not, I'm afraid there will be no Lulworth Skipper in Lady Clarke's portfolio."

The comfortably plump woman handed over a small package wrapped in brown paper along with several franked envelopes, most addressed to Artie. "Well, it's from that shop in London she likes, that's for sure. What color is it today, dear?"

Any other time, Sarah would have been delighted in entertaining Mrs. Pope with the tale of a color called Egyptian Mummy. Today it was all she could do to breathe.

"Oh, some brown," she said. "I fear the only thing I know about brown is its resemblance to every color I attempt to paint."

She accepted the mail with a smile. "Oh, and Old George is over helping Mr. Hicks repair some walls. He asked if I would check for any mail for him."

Fortunately, Mrs. Pope would know to include any missive for Tom Frane without comment. But Mrs. Pope was shaking her head. "Not today. But the mail was held up by the rain up north this afternoon. It might be coming tomorrow. Have him check back."

Sarah thanked her and pocketed the letters. She had to hurry. She had to let Ian know about Minette Ferrar, to give him time to get away. But when she turned, it was to suffer another shock. Stepping through the door was none other than Martin Clarke.

Sarah knew she lost color. She felt as if she were swaying on her feet. She barely felt Artie slip a hand through her arm, as if the girl needed support as well.

"Mrs. Pope," Martin greeted the woman as he doffed his high-crowned beaver. "Miss Clarke. Sarah."

Sarah and Artie dipped a knee. Sarah wasn't breathing. Martin stepped right up to them, cutting off their escape, crowding them into a corner of the small room. She knew what he was here for, and there was no squire to deflect his venom.

"Sarah, I wonder if you can help me," he all but purred, which made Sarah's skin crawl. "One of my men is...unaccounted for. You met him. He helped rescue your...pig. Corporal Briggs. Could you have seen him?"

Panic closed Sarah's throat. Revulsion. Suddenly she could smell sour breath in her face. She could feel the harsh grip of vicious hands. "Briggs?" she managed to answer with an unconcerned shrug. "Why, no. I shouldn't be surprised that one of your employees isn't to be found, though, Martin. They struck me as rather unreliable."

Leaning in even closer, Martin raised a gloved finger to Sarah's cheek. "Is that a bruise rising, cousin? I believe Fairbourne is becoming a dangerous place."

Sarah saw Artie whip around and peer at her. Mrs. Pope leaned over a bit.

"You must not be involved much in the day-to-day operations of your estate, cousin," Sarah responded. "Farmwork is often hard. But dangerous?" She deliberately shook her head. "Nothing I am unable to handle, I assure you."

It was his color that rose. He glared at her, stymied by the public arena he had chosen in which to confront her. "If I don't find my employee," he warned, "I will feel free to do anything to ensure his safety."

"You do admit that he is your employee, then?" she asked, unable to believe her own bravado.

She knew he couldn't answer. He looked rather as if

he would explode. Without another word, he slammed his hat on his head and stalked back out the door. Sarah wasn't certain how she kept her legs under her. She swore all the blood in her head drained out, leaving black spots in front of her eyes.

"Sarah," Artie whispered in shocked tones. "You *do* have a bruise."

It took every ounce of strength in her, but Sarah smiled. "I forgot to bring Harvey his scone. Now," she said briskly. "Shall we go? I am perishing for a cup of tea."

She was perishing for a seat. If she stood any longer, she might simply collapse.

*   *   *

Even though it was still broad daylight, Sarah took the chance of discovery. The ladies were still out along the undercliff somewhere, and Artie inside practicing Scarlatti. Making very certain that she had no witness but Willoughby, Sarah made her way down to the cellar door. She noticed on her way past Boswell's arbor that for a change, his rosebushes looked good. She was glad. Boswell loved those roses.

Slipping down into the hollow, she pushed past the screening bush. Since she'd never been to the cellar during the afternoon, she didn't know what to expect. She dreaded seeing Corporal Briggs. Just the thought crawled through her like worms. She would not betray her fear, though. She would not give him the satisfaction.

The first thing she saw was Ian standing by his cot, hands behind his back as if at military revue, his stance rigid. Sarah thought it odd, but she was more interested in her news. She looked around to make sure Briggs was out of earshot.

He wasn't there at all. "The corporal . . ."

"George came and got him. You won't have to worry about him anymore."

Her attention caught by the blanket that remained on the floor by the crates, Sarah nodded absently. "Good. That will make this much easier."

If she were a better person, she would hope that George didn't treat the man too harshly. She hoped George broke his other arm.

Sucking in a breath, she turned back to Ian. "Your letter did not come in yet," she said without preamble. "But there is something much more important."

Seeing the flask sitting on the cot, she picked it up and opened it. "I saw her," she said, pointing to those laughing blue eyes inside. "She's here, Ian. At Lyme Regis. Someone betrayed you and sent for her. We have to do something."

Oddly, he didn't react. Sarah couldn't understand it. "Did you hear me?"

Silence. Finally, "I did."

"Then talk to me. Tell me what to do."

"Oh, I don't know Sarah," he said, his voice very quiet. For some reason, the tone sent *frissons* slithering down her back. "I think you need to tell me what to do first."

She frowned, completely disoriented. "About what?"

"About the body buried under your rosebushes."

Even then she didn't react, sure he meant something else. But he didn't.

"Your husband isn't coming home, is he, Sarah?" Ian demanded. "He isn't coming home, because he's already here, where you buried him."

Chapter 12

Did you not hear me?" she demanded as if he hadn't spoken. "Minette Ferrar is here."

"Didn't you hear *me*?" he countered. "I found your husband's body."

Perhaps she had simply had too many surprises, too many traumas packed into too little time. She wasn't certain. But for the longest moment she could do nothing but stand there staring at the man she loved.

"You've been lying to everyone," he accused. "Making them all believe he's alive and coming home. But he isn't, is he? Because you buried him under his own goddamn roses!"

Well, that she understood.

"Yes," she finally said, suddenly cold. "I did that. I buried him in his favorite place in the world and lied about his returning."

It had taken all night, in the absolute darkness, with the smell of wet earth and blood in her nostrils.

"For God's sake, Sarah," Ian retorted. "What happened? Did he come home at the wrong moment? Did he catch you in a lie, or cooking the books or conspiring with your good friend George?"

Another blow to her fragile equilibrium. "What?"

"Did you kill him?"

She didn't even remember lifting her hand. She only realized she had slapped him when she heard the resounding crack echo through the cellar and felt the hard sting of contact in her palm.

How could he think she could kill anyone? Hadn't he learned anything about her in the last days? Didn't he at least want to believe in her a little? And if he thought so little of her, why answer at all?

He didn't so much as flinch. "Answer me, Sarah."

That hurt even worse. "No," she said, "I don't think I will. I believe you have this all figured out for yourself. Well, if you believe I am guilty, feel free to contact the authorities. I have too much work to do to wait here to be insulted. I am late today, you see. I was in town doing a favor for a friend."

Before she could turn, he grabbed her by the arm. "You're not going anywhere until you explain yourself."

"Explain myself?" she countered, rearing back. "*Explain* myself? Who do you think you are?"

He was all set to shout back at her when suddenly his hand dropped. He stepped away and raked his hand through his hair. "Tell me," he begged. "Please. What happened? How did he die? Why haven't you told anyone?"

She was so angry. So disappointed. Undoubtedly she shouldn't be. The evidence was against her. And no matter what she felt for Ian, he had no reason to suddenly trust her. Except for the fact that she hadn't turned him in.

She hadn't turned him out. She had stood by him, when the consequences could still be fatal.

She kept shaking her head, as if it could help her clear out all the anguish, the frustration, the confusion. "I cannot talk down here," she finally said. "Follow me."

Turning around, she strode from the cellar. She didn't stop until she was in view of the arbor. Haloed by the late afternoon light, it looked so peaceful. A place for contemplation and calm. For meditation. Not suicide.

She didn't need to turn to know that Ian had followed her. She could sense him. She could smell the clean scent of him, feel that odd humming energy that seemed to surround him. That seemed to draw her inexorably to him.

"Sarah," he said, laying his hand on her arm. "I'm sorry. It's just…so much has happened." He looked around. "Here, lass, sit down a moment. Talk to me."

She yanked her arm free. He gestured to the stone bench at the corner of the garden, where they could not be seen from the house. Well, Sarah thought, sitting down. At least they weren't to sit in Boswell's arbor.

Seating himself a careful distance from her, Ian reached out a hand. She ignored it and folded her hands in her lap.

"What happened to him, Sarah?" he asked.

She looked up only to see the sea. Boswell's favorite view. The one that made her shudder, because she could still see him standing there silhouetted against it sun-reflected sheen. "Did you leave him where he was?" she asked.

"What else was I going to do with him?"

She shrugged. "Oh, I don't know. Take him up to the house and destroy his mother."

He actually looked hurt. "You can't think I would do that."

She looked over at him. "I can't?" She laughed. "Why? You have already accused me of murder."

"I'm sorry. I should have thought. I was just so . . ."

"Angry? Yes, I know how you feel. I have been angry now for a long time. Did you happen to look at Boswell's wound?"

"Of course I did. A single gunshot to the head."

It was safer to look at her hands, clenched in her lap. "Mmmm, yes. Pressed right up against his forehead. His hands were shaking so badly, I'm still amazed he actually hit what he was aiming at."

She hadn't reacted soon enough. She hadn't believed him. He had always recovered before, crawled out of the black depressions that had plagued him since childhood. She had always had another chance to make it better.

Not this time. He'd waited until he convinced her that if he could just sit on that little bench to watch the sea, he would feel well enough to face his family. She had turned away. And then she had heard the unmistakable sound of a gun cocking.

"You're telling me he killed himself?" Ian asked. "Why?"

She spread her fingers, as if she could still see the blood splashed on them. "Because going to war was merely another mistake for him. Boswell was not made for it. He couldn't bear the burden." She looked out to sea. "He was so excited. He was going to be a hero. He would ride a grand horse into the greatest battle the world would ever see." She shrugged. "Reality is a hard lesson. Boswell was not prepared for it."

Especially the reality that sends an unprepared man into hell. Poor Boswell. She hadn't known that he had failed until she read the note he'd left in his rucksack. He had run from the battle, and kept running. He had run all the way home.

"You mean he came all the way back here only to shoot himself?" Ian asked.

"In his arbor. Where the ocean could be the last thing he saw."

"I canna believe it."

She turned on him. "It is easier to believe I shot him?" she demanded.

He was on his feet. The pain she could see in his eyes should have satisfied her. "No...no. Of course I've seen men give into despair. But to come all the way home. To kill himself with his family nearby."

"Oh, that he did not do. They never knew he was here." She laughed, a dry huff. "I think he must have been living in that cellar for a week. He just showed up one day when his family was staying away overnight. It was only me. He did not want his mother to know what he'd done. So he begged me to let her assume he had died on the battlefield. And then before I could reach him, he put a gun to his head."

Not looking on her as his last memory, or his home or the sky. The sea. He had looked at the sea.

"Why didn't you tell me, lass?" Ian asked, his voice gentler, as if he could see the memory in her head.

She blinked up at him. "Tell you? Why should I tell you? You were supposed to move on as quickly as possible. Your stay here is temporary, Ian. Mine is not. Therefore it is my problem to handle."

He looked as if she'd struck him. "You think that even now?"

Somehow she was on her feet too. "I think that especially now. You have problems enough of your own. Leave me to mine."

He dragged a hand through his hair. "But I canna."

They stood faced off like that for the longest time, the world dimming toward night, the lights winking on in the house. Finally, Ian shook his head. "Oh, Sarah," he murmured. And then, before she could stop him, he gathered her into his arms.

"Oh, lass," he whispered against her hair. "I'm so sorry. Not just for Boswell. For me and my ridiculous suspicions. I'm a muckle fool."

"Yes," Sarah agreed, nestling against his shoulder. "You are."

"I was just so surprised. Will you forgive me? It's more than I deserve."

That answer took her a bit longer. She was too busy cherishing this brief moment of comfort, of support. She was savoring the strength of Ian's arms around her.

Could she forgive him? Not yet. His assumption stung. But honesty would do nothing to get Ian on his way. Which he had to do.

"Yes," she finally said, her voice muffled against his chest, her eyes closed. "I suppose I do."

Ian tucked a loose strand of hair behind her ear. "Were you ever going to tell his family where Boswell was?"

Sighing, she looked up at him. "Truly? I can't say. I believe his mother would be happier if I did not. That way she can still think of Boswell as safely in Belgium waiting to come home. The only one who is anxious for resolution is

Martin." She shrugged. "He will eventually get the estate. But I need enough time to protect Boswell's family."

For a long time, they just stood there, wrapped in each other's arms watching the leaves skitter across the lawn and clouds dapple the sea. It was quiet here for a change, the animals still. Sarah wished with all her heart it could just stay this way, suspended in time like a soul in limbo, like Lady Clarke's memory of Boswell.

It couldn't, of course. Just as always, reality intruded. So no matter what she wished, she lifted her head and stepped out of his arms.

"I'm not certain if you heard me earlier," she said. "But time for you has run out. We can no longer wait for your friends to contact you."

"I heard you." He led her back to the bench and seated them both. "You're sure it was Minette you saw?" he asked, reaching once again for her hand.

"Hers is not a face you can forget." Sarah's smile was weary. "I am no longer surprised she caused such havoc among your friends."

"She did, that." He sighed. "And now she's here. I wonder who peached on me."

"Someone obviously intercepted your letter. She was standing by the postal office speaking with Mr. Stricker as if they were chance met. She is posing as a new widow. Very affecting."

Ian's head abruptly came up. "Stricker? You'd think he'd be more careful."

"Perhaps they think his presence will draw you out."

"Perhaps." He reached down and ran a gentle finger down her cheek. "My brave lass. I have imposed on you quite enough already."

She lost a moment thinking of what it would be like when he left again, and struggled to ignore the gaping hole he would leave behind.

Suddenly Ian turned to her. "Come with me," he said.

Sarah whipped her head around. "What?"

"I need some kind of guide. I haven't been able to wander far enough to know the area well." He motioned to the house. "You could show me the way past the soldiers. And people are looking for one tall redhead. Not a couple. We'd be a grand team."

She was already shaking her head, the brief, heady temptation of adventure vanishing. "How could I explain my disappearance? How could I defend the women against Martin, or keep the estate going?"

How would I survive one more day with you?

"Let George do it."

She huffed. "I think even you know better."

He needed to get away before he was caught, before she was lost. She could never tell him how close she had just come to saying yes.

Suddenly he grabbed her hand. "Sarah," he said, his voice urgent. "I mean it. Come with me. Not just to see me through. To get away from here yourself."

She turned, a sharp rejoinder on her tongue. It was a very unfunny joke, after all. But the light in his eyes was bright; it was intense; it was perfectly sincere.

Pulling her hand away, she stepped back. "Are you mad? I can't leave here."

Ian didn't move. "Yes, lass," he said, lifting his hands. "You can. What do you have here? A life of drudgery without relief or support. George told me the old woman won't even address you by your proper name."

Did everyone need to remind her of how unwanted she was? "What does that have to do with anything? This is the only real home I have ever had, Ian. I won't give it up. "

"I can give you a new home. Change your name, find a little place for you to live, so that if Boswell is found, no one will hurt you. I owe you that at least."

Owed her what? Another life of loneliness? The chance to be close to him but never his? How could he be so cruel?

She refused to let him see the pain he was inflicting. "You want me to simply walk away."

"Why not? Wouldn't you like your own little place?" He stepped up before she knew it and claimed her hand. "I could make sure you're comfortable. Not scraping by. You deserve better, Sarah."

"I see. And where would you be in this equation?"

He shrugged. "Anywhere you wanted."

Maybe she was tarring him with the same brush as other men. But the sound of this offer was too familiar. *You could have a small cottage, a townhouse, a carriage.* After all, what could she expect, a by-blow and all. She certainly wouldn't be lucky enough to nab another baronet. How could she ever believe she could expect more?

Poor, deluded her. She couldn't expect more. All the same, she had wanted it.

"I'm sure the offer is generous," she said, her voice as icy as her heart. "But I'll have to decline it all the same."

"Why?" he demanded. "What holds you here?"

Self-respect. Pride. The only wholly owned treasure of a bastard child. The only possessions she would never give away.

Stepping back, she wrapped her arms around her waist. Could she grieve for the fact that he was as human as the next man, wanting to have everything with no cost to himself? Did he even realize yet what he was asking? She wasn't really certain.

"When you think on it a bit, Ian," she said, struggling to keep her voice even, "you'll come up with the answer. Until then, you would be better served finding a way to get to your friends."

"I *have* a way to get to my friends."

She nodded. "Good. Because your enemies are closing in fast."

And then, before she could humiliate herself further, she turned away.

He didn't let her. Before she could get two feet, he caught her by the arms and was turning her back to him. "Come for this," he growled, and pulled her into his arms.

And then he was kissing her.

She should have fought. Later she swore she would have if she hadn't been so surprised. She would have slapped him, stepped on his foot, lifted a knee into his groin.

She didn't, though. She *was* surprised. For two or three seconds. And then she was overwhelmed, devastated. Compelled, consumed by a fire that swept through her as if she were nothing more than dry kindling. It wasn't the power of his arms around her, although it was. They were a fortress, a bastion, protection and prison, enclosing her so tightly she could feel the buttons of his jacket imprint on her suddenly tender breasts.

It wasn't his height, or his rock-solid stance, a warrior's stance, a fierce protector and fiercer destroyer. It wasn't even the kiss itself, a consuming, ravishing kiss that seemed to sap the strength from her and light up her heart.

It was his mouth. His soft, seeking sensible mouth, his lips so mobile, so hungry, so delicious that she found herself opening to him without coercion. She felt her arms lift to him as if of their own accord, doing their best to bring those strong, wide shoulders closer, woefully inadequate to encompass him, to even reach that fire-limned hair that curled at his neck.

Suddenly she wanted to wrap herself around him like a vine, climb him like a rampant weed. She wanted the taste of him on her, the scent of him, the scratch of his beard and the brush of his thumbs. She wanted fire. She wanted sweeping, swirling cataclysms so strong they left nothing behind but cinders.

Oh, sweet lord, she thought, coming up on her toes to get closer. He was so fierce, so gentle, so hungry, and it woke the same in her. She nipped at his mouth, brushed it, molded it, explored it like a dream she had just woken to find real. And it was warm and soft and pliant, that mouth, dipping, seeking, sipping, fitting more closely as he tilted his head, as he tilted her head in his hand to meet him more fully, to open to him, to invite him in. And she did, sliding her tongue along his lower lip, running it against his surprisingly straight teeth, tentatively tasting the rough pleasure of his tongue.

His tongue. His clever, darting tongue, dancing with hers, spearing her, seeking the deepest recesses of her mouth and taunting her with the faint taste of whiskey and smoke, which she knew she would wonder about later. Later when he took his broad shoulders away, his powerful hands and his clever mouth. Later.

As abruptly as he grabbed her, he pulled away. Panting, his forehead resting against hers, his arms still wrapped so tightly she could feel the thunder of his great heart and the jut of his erection against her belly.

"*That* is why I want you to come with me," he growled, rubbing his cheek against her hair, his fingers tangled in her sensible bun.

She was trying to catch her breath, to drag her body back under control, when it was the last thing it wanted. She was swollen and pliant, hot and hungry and impatient. Her breasts ached and her womb wept, and she wanted nothing more than to pretend that she never again had to move from this place of safety that wasn't safe at all.

Her heart sang with surprise at his hunger. At her own. How could she have known? How would she survive it? Suddenly the world was painted in more vivid hues, the colors of conflagration, and she didn't know if she could bear to return to the grays that made up her life.

"That is why I will not," she said into his jacket.

He held her close, stroking her hair as she clutched his coat, her body still shaking with the force of her desire. "I didn't mean . . ."

She pulled back so she could see him. "Yes," she said baldly. "You did."

Fresh guilt darkened his eyes. "I think," he said, his voice raspy, "maybe I did. I'm sorry, lass. I wasn't being fair." He shook his head. "I'm an honorable man. But all I've wanted since I first saw you is you in my arms, you in my bed. I'm dying for it."

She wanted to weep. "Oh, Ian," she whispered. "Don't do this."

She stepped back and wrapped her arms again around her waist, suddenly so cold without his arms to shield her. Wobbly at the loss of his solid support. Achingly, surprisingly alone without the feel of his body around hers. Oh, lord, and she had only been in his arms for minutes. How hard would it be if he stayed, even a while longer?

"I'll rescind the offer that offends," he said. "But I won't change my mind about the other. You've put yourself in harm's way for me. I canna leave you here to face the consequences alone."

"You cannot force me to come with you either. You must get to Wellington. I must stay here so no one knows you enjoyed our hospitality."

He reached out for her again. "I won't let you."

She evaded him, shoving her hands in her pockets. "You have no choice."

* * *

"Ah, *mon cher,* how you excite me."

Stricker was so excited he could hardly see her. She was beautiful. She was lush and smiling and wrapped tightly around him, her hand down his pants. She was in the rooms he'd taken over the green grocer, and she was naked as dawn. And he was going to have her. "You make me very happy, Minette," he said.

Her smile was as old as sin. "As you make me, *cher.* And you will make me even happier very soon."

He smiled at her and took hold of her breast. He wasn't suave about it. He was too bloody hungry. He wanted to take her up against the wall. He wanted to have her on the ground, driving into her like a stallion. He wanted her bent over a chair, her pretty round derriere pushed against his groin as he pounded into her.

He was so busy imagining what he was going to do that he could barely get his placket unbuttoned. She was chuckling, her voice earthy and sensual. Her cloud of thick, curling blond hair cascaded over her shoulders. She held her hands behind her back, which just thrust her breasts forward even more. Stricker could barely contain himself.

He probably should have. Because his distraction was so great as he focused on his shaking hands that he failed to hear the *snick* of Minette's knife. He never did get his buttons open. Instead he ended up twitching on the floor, his throat slit and pulsing blood all over the hooked rug as Minette watched.

She bent over him, her knife still dripping, her exquisite face pursed in a *moue* of disappointment. "Aaaah," she sighed, bending to wipe the blade on Stricker's pants. "Too slow. Too slow. Minette, she is not allowed to enjoy her work."

It had been quite an argument with the old man, but Minette had finally agreed that if she left her usual calling cards on Stricker, they could never blame the murder on Ferguson. So no pretty designs on the little man's face, no souvenirs taken. Just a workmanlike slit of the throat. She sighed again, thinking about how much of Ferguson there was upon which to practice her art. That was what finally brought a smile.

Stepping around the congealing pools of blood, she slipped back into her clothing and opened the door to be met by two working men.

"Check him for any inconvenient papers," she purred,

exchanging places. "Then make sure this is cleaned up and he is found down by the Cobb so they think the Scottish brute killed him."

The room door closed, and she stepped up to the cracked, tarnished hallway mirror. Winding up her hair, she inserted a pair of improbably sharp hairpins before strolling down the stairs, humming to herself.

* * *

Sarah spent dinner in a daze, so overwhelmed by what happened that day that she missed most of the conversation and all of the food. When the ladies rose, she followed by rote. She knew she should escape to her book room to work on accounts. Heaven knew she hadn't had much time for them in the last few days. But her roiling emotions so battered her, she couldn't concentrate on anything except the urgent need to get Ian away from Fairbourne.

There was no more time to wait on his friend. He would have to leave the next night during the dark of the moon before either Martin or Madame Ferrar could find him on her land.

She was restless and fractious. She needed to draw a decent map for Ian to take with him. She needed to pack a rucksack with staples to keep him from stealing from any more henhouses. She needed to get hold of George to help ease his way. She could do nothing until the women were asleep. So when they retreated to the Oriental sitting room, she settled by the fireplace and took out her mending.

A red-papered room with a surfeit of Oriental screens,

black lacquer chairs, and a gold settee, the Oriental sitting room was the last room redecorated before the money ran out. The jade was real, the Japanese artwork a clever copy from memory by Lady Clarke. Sarah had always liked the room, a true reflection of Lady Clarke's taste.

The dowager was seated at a card table with Miss Fitchwater, perusing a portfolio of the dowager's artwork they had spread across the table. Red and black cinnabar moths and peacock butterflies danced across the papers, dog orchids, cowslips, curling ferns, foxglove. And there, at the top, the dull brown Lulworth Skipper butterfly.

Sarah could usually ignore the watercolors. Tonight they filled her with frustration. Life could have been so much easier the last four years if only Lady Clarke had sold some of her paintings.

Sarah had slipped one of the watercolors out of the house once to see if Lady Clarke was the artist she suspected. Better, Mr. Yardson at the bookshop had told her, comparing the drawing to the folios they already had. Brilliant.

"This work compares with the great Adenson," he enthused, setting the dowager's painting beside a large folio of similar works with shaking hands. "The color, the setting. Exquisite." He lifted the delicate rendering of a sulfur yellow brimstone butterfly as it emerged from its chrysalis. "Just this painting could see you a profit of twenty guineas. And think of the money we could garner from prints. If we gather them into a folio, your artist could well be the first great British natural artist. When can I see more?"

She had hated to burst his bubble. She hated even more returning home with a painting she knew the dowager would miss. These were her children, and she cared for them with a gentleness never afforded her real children.

Sarah had attempted to convince Lady Clarke to put up even a fifth of her collection. The older woman had been outraged even at the thought of selling her artwork. It had smelled of the shop, after all. Miss Fitchwater had smiled at Sarah in commiseration, but she would never think to contradict her dear Winnifred.

Perhaps, Sarah thought, she should suggest the idea to them again. After all, if she were taken up for aiding Ian, they would need another source of income.

Ian. Sarah briefly closed her eyes at the thought of him. Her body still seemed to thrum with residual energy. She felt restless and a bit giddy, as if she'd stood next to a lightning strike, and had trouble following the simplest conversation. She wanted to be back in that cellar. She wanted to be back in his arms. She wanted, God help her, to meet him skin to skin and discover every inch of his broad, strong body with her hands, her mouth. Her tongue. She wanted to understand the current that seemed to run so strongly between them.

She was a grown woman. A widow. And yet she had never experienced the like in her life. She didn't know how to set it aside or ignore it. She didn't know how *not* to want it.

It was a good thing he was leaving, she thought. She didn't need any more trouble. She certainly didn't need a man who failed to trust her at the first turn. A man whose offer of help was nothing more than *carte blanche.*

Sarah pressed her hand to her chest, where the pain still twisted in her. How could he have even made the suggestion? Was that all he thought of her?

"Sarah, are you listening?"

Sarah blinked and turned to see Artie standing behind her, bouncing on her feet.

Sarah snapped back to attention. "Yes, Artie," she said, returning to her work.

Her features cast in a suspiciously innocent expression, Artie handed over a letter. "I found this on the hall floor when I went by your office. I thought you might want it."

For a second Sarah stared uncomprehendingly at the paper. It was a letter from Lizzie. Sarah's heart stumbled. She had asked Lizzie not to respond, hadn't she?

"I think it was in with the mail that you put on your desk," Sarah reminded her. "I only went in because I thought there might be a letter for me. And there was. There were two, which you should have given me right away, you know."

Sarah put aside her sewing. "Yes," she said absently, turning the letter over in her hands. "I'm sorry. You say you already got your letters?"

"Yes, I was about to read them." Artie pointed an accusing finger at the frank on Lizzie's letter. "That is the Duke of Dorchester's frank," she said. "I know, because he franked Cecily's letter."

Sarah nodded. "Mmmmm."

She wishing Artie would go away. Instead Artie sat right next to her. "You mean you are in correspondence with a relative of the Duke of Dorchester?"

"Not really. Certainly not enough to get us invited to the house party."

Artie pointed at the paper as if it were a bloody knife. "But you never told us!"

Sarah smiled. "You have never wanted to know about my friends, Artie. Besides, Lady Elizabeth was never a close friend. An acquaintance, merely."

It was all Artie needed to know. All anyone needed to know.

"But what could she want?" the girl asked, leaning close.

Knowing she could put it off no longer, Sarah broke the red wax seal, only to have a slim packet slide into her lap. She froze. Oh, heavens. *Please,* she thought. *Let it be anything but what I think it is.*

Even without opening it, she knew better. Someone had decided to bypass the route Ian had suggested for his message and sent Ian's reply through Lizzie. Sarah's heart galloped. She could feel her palms go damp. Could that be why an assassin was here? Had Lizzie said something? Could Minette Ferrar know about the Clarkes?

Sarah had to get to Ian. She had to warn him. She had to get him away.

"What is that?" Artie asked, reaching for the packet.

Before Artie could reach the neat, sealed square, Sarah slipped it into her pocket. Glancing at the cover letter, she smiled. "Lizzie says it is the recipe for the Ripton chef's Chantilly cream I asked for."

Artie's eyebrow soared. "Chantilly cream?"

Sarah smiled up at her. "We may not have much, Artie. We do have a surfeit of cream. Why not enjoy it?"

Artie giggled. "Because Peg would be cooking it. That's why."

Sarah couldn't help answering with a rather comical frown. "Good point. Perhaps we can convince her that I wish to train in the kitchen arts."

Artie pointed to the letter again. "Does your friend mention her guests? At least tell me if she mentions my particular friends."

"I fear not. Simply that she is happy to hear from me, and glad to share the recipe. Other than wishing us well, I fear that is all."

To prove her statement, she handed off the letter. Artie took it and threw herself onto the settee. "She is not much of a correspondent, is she?"

She was, of course. Just not with Sarah.

Which meant that the inside note was important. "Artie," she said, picking up her needlework, "I would love to hear the new Scarlatti you have been working on."

Artie cast a quick look over to the table where the dowager and Rosie sat over the watercolors. "You know Mother doesn't like to be distracted."

It was true, of course, especially when Lady Clarke was perusing her paintings.

"A quieter piece then," Sarah suggested, anything to distract the girl.

"I'm afraid she won't have time to play anything," came a voice from the doorway.

Sarah gasped, on her feet. Artie shrieked and fell against the settee. Lady Clarke waited a heartbeat and then clutched her heart with a pathetic little cry. It was up to Sarah to face the wild man standing in her doorway, a gun in each hand.

Evidently Ian had decided to take matters into his own hands.

Chapter 13

Ian saw Sarah go deathly pale and hated what he had to do. He wished he could have warned her. But he and George had agreed that to keep Sarah safe from Martin Clarke and the law both, Ian had to take her with him. And the only way to do that was to surprise her. Unimpeachable witnesses must swear that she was as shocked as her kinswomen to see him walk in the door.

Judging by her color, she certainly was that.

"What the devil is going on?" she demanded as she helped the girl up.

"We're going to die!" the woman Ian assumed was Lady Clarke cried in fading tones, her hands in the air, posed like a tragedian in Act III. "Oh, Rosamunde!"

Ian noticed she poised herself over a pile of watercolors, as if that were the child she would save. Next to her, a storklike lady in gray was rummaging through a reticule. He knew how wild he looked, with three weeks growth of beard and his hair as snarled as a skein of red wool. Clad in his homespun clothing, and carrying a Manton dueling pistol in each hand, all he needed was an eye patch and a parrot to play pirate. He gave them all a big, mad grin to cement the image.

The old dame fluttered and screeched about her heart. No one but the stork paid attention.

"Dinna fesh y'rself, ma'am," he said in his broadest brogue. "I willna be long. It's just that I'm in a great need of victuals and weapons." He lifted the guns for her perusal. "And a finer pair I canna remember seein'."

Now the old lady went pale. "Those are my son's. How did you get them?"

He'd been afraid of that. If the stark pain in Sarah's eyes was any indication, they must have been the guns the old lady's son had used to kill himself.

"Ach, woman. Ye dinna store fine weapons like this in a safe. Somebody lookin' for a bit o' loose change might know how tae get in."

"Not much loose change," Sarah muttered.

He laughed. "Enough tae get me down the road, lass. I'll pay ye back, both cash and poppers, on my honor."

"Honor," Lady Clarke spat. "What honor is there in terrorizing helpless women?"

Ian couldn't help it. He laughed. "Wheesht, woman, if ye're nae a treat. If there was e'er a female who was nae helpless, it's ye."

The old lady glared at him. Now that he'd blown her disguise, she seemed to grow in her seat, her back ramrod straight.

"Where is our butler?" Sarah demanded, her eyes flashing at him. She never reacted to the dowager's change of attitude. She must be used to it.

God and the Bruce, the girl was magnificent. The woman he'd thought plain absolutely shone when she was in a rage. So taken was Ian by the flash of her earthy eyes and the high color in her cheeks, he almost forgot to answer.

"I have nae quarrel with old men, lass. He is safe, along with your cook and scullery."

"You will address *me*," the old bat demanded. "It is my house you have invaded."

If Ian hadn't seen the frank terror lick the older woman's eyes, he would have laughed again. No wonder Sarah didn't get along with her. Nothing worse than two queens in the same beehive. Sliding one of the guns into his waist, he stepped back and bent for the loops of rope he'd left on the footman's chair in the corridor.

"All right then," he said instead with another small bow. "Much as I'd love tae linger, you'll be glad to know I canna. Which of ye is good at tying knots?"

"Tying knots?" Lady Clarke echoed, straightening even more. "Don't be absurd. We are ladies, not stevedores. Tie your own knots."

"Ah, now, that I canna do, not and hold this wee popper."

"If it will get you on your way," Sarah offered, letting go of the girl, "I'll do it."

"You will not," Lady Clarke retorted. "Not one of us will cooperate with this dastard. After all, what can he do but leave?"

Damn the woman. "Aye well, ya have me there." He deliberately turned the gun on the wide-eyed blond girl. "But I'd have to leave with the young lass here, if I did. And who knows if I could return her as easy as the popper?"

He would do nothing of the sort, of course. He tried to

make it a point never to terrify children. But sadly, he suspected a threat to Sarah wouldn't produce cooperation.

When the blond girl's eyes rolled back in her head, he almost gave the game away by dropping everything to catch her. Fortunately, Sarah was there ahead of him, easing the girl to the floor. The tartar gave a small cry and dropped to catch the girl's head in her lap. If the surprise on Sarah's face was any indication, not a normal reaction.

"Oh, now, Artemesia," the woman commanded in a suspiciously thin voice as she briskly patted the girl's pasty cheek. "Fainting is so overdramatic. You will have this beast convinced that we are poor Janes indeed. Besides—" Even Sarah looked surprised when the older woman looked up at her. "Sarah will take care of everything, won't she?"

"I will," Sarah said, turning to Ian. "And no one is taking my sister anywhere." He was surprised his hair didn't catch fire at her glare. "Such a brave man," she sneered.

"If my mission were nae more important than just the four of us, lass, I'd nae terrify anyone. But I dinna have a choice. The Duke of Wellington himself is in danger, and I'd be a muckle fool tae keep the news from him."

"You're the one who tried to shoot him," the stork protested, on her knees next to the mother, her arm around her shoulder. "I recognize you from the posters."

He smiled. "A small misunderstanding, don't ye ken. Which is why I need a wee bit o' help getting' tae the duke."

Sighing as if she were at the end of her patience, Sarah held out her hand. "Give me the rope, then. The sooner it's done, the sooner you will leave us alone."

He didn't smile for her. "Ye'll need to tie them good, lass. So they can't get out too soon and stop me."

She didn't budge. But Ian would never lose the memory of the disdain in her eyes. "Fine."

The young girl whimpered and turned her head. Her mother looked up. "You cannot do that," she protested. "We are isolated here. No one will find us."

And he couldn't tell her that Old George had their rescue timed to the minute.

Sarah accepted the rope and stepped back. "Don't worry, Mother Clarke. Between you and me, we'll manage."

"Ah, well now," Ian disagreed with every evidence of reluctance. "I fear the others will have tae manage by themselves. I've decided that ye'll be the one to have the pleasure of my company. Yon child is a wee bit too delicate for the trip, I'm thinkin'."

In the process of tying the stork's hands behind her back, Sarah froze. "I what?"

He almost smiled again, entranced by her eyes. "Ye need nae fear me, lass. I'll nae harm ye. But if I'm tae get as far as the duke, I'll need a guide."

She stood there, the rope dangling from her fingers. "A guide? Where?"

She couldn't have played it better if he'd given her a script.

"Back down tae the coast, I thought. The land has nae worked so well for me, so maybe I can catch a wee boat to London."

Sarah scowled and pointed. "The coast is right over that cliff. Be my guest."

He could truly love her. "No boats there. I looked.

Weymouth is just up the road, though. Sure they have a few extra boats that willna be missed."

She turned back to finish securing knots. "You'll be recognized and shot."

"Not if I have a . . . guest."

She straightened slowly. "Hostage, you mean."

He shrugged.

She stood perfectly still, hands on hips. "No."

He pointed the pistol back at the blond girl, who whimpered. He swore Sarah growled. She went back to her knots, though. She had just moved to the woman she'd called Mother Clarke when that woman abruptly reared to her feet.

"No," she said, standing there like a saint set for martyrdom. "You don't need Sarah. She will do you no good. She is not as familiar with the area as I. Besides, if we are followed, the militia would not dare shoot a Clarke of Fairbourne."

"Oh, Winnifred, no!" the stork protested, pulling on her bonds. "Your heart!"

The older woman didn't precisely smile. "I cannot run the estate," she said, not looking away from Ian. "I cannot even sell eggs. But I am an excellent walker. I might as well be useful for something."

Was that what an apology sounded like from her? Ian would have to ask Sarah.

"You'll go nowhere without me, Winnifred," the stork protested, jumping up.

Lady Clarke patted the woman's shoulder.

"I canna say I've ever heard such a grand offer," Ian said, and then gave another small bow. "Still, my decision stands. Come now, lassie, keep tying."

Sarah tied. She made sure all three women were as comfortably situated as she could make them on the settees, and Ian checked to make sure her knots were real.

"Now," he said amiably, showing Sarah an empty bag he'd found in the stables. "If ye'd fill this with a bit of food, we'll be off. And remember." He lifted the gun. "If you do anything I dinna like, I have a surfeit of hostages. One less willna matter at all."

Sarah's glare could have shattered glass. Even so, she snatched the bag from Ian's hand and marched from the room. When she reached the kitchen, he hoped she would be a bit mollified.

"Well noo, ladies," he said, settling into one of the lacquer chairs and crossing one leg over the other. "How can we pass the time? Would ye like to hear a wee bit o' Scottish verse?"

The three of them turned their heads from him in a unified motion that almost made Ian laugh. Imagine. Being given the cut direct by his own hostages. He couldn't wait to share that with Sarah.

*   *   *

Sarah walked into the kitchen and gasped. "You aren't even tied up," she protested.

In fact, Peg and Parker were comfortably seated at the staff table, enjoying a mug of tea. The minute they saw her, they were on their feet.

"Are you well, Miss Sarah?" Peg demanded. "That blue-eyed devil hasn't upset you too much?"

Sarah gaped at them. "But . . ."

Peg chuckled and came around to relieve Sarah of the

bag. "Wasn't he the very gentleman when he showed up in the kitchen, Mr. Boswell's guns in his hands. 'I don't mean to bother you all,' says he, as if we're in a sitting room. 'But I need help getting away.' It came to me then as how we'd been losing eggs and you'd been losing sleep. Well, says I to Mary Sunday, If Miss Sarah takes his side, then he must be all right."

"What made you think I'd taken his side?"

Busy stuffing apples into the bag, Peg cocked her head. "Haven't you been feedin' him, then?"

Sarah knew her face went crimson. "I might have. But this is different."

Peg's eyes twinkled. "A fine strapping man, isn't he? 'Tis a pleasure to help him."

Sarah stared at her cook. "You believed him because he's handsome?"

"Course not. Old George came in with him."

Sarah plopped down on one of the chairs. "Of course he did," she moaned, her head in her hands. "They could have told me."

"Oh, no, Lady Clarke," Parker wheezed as he helped Peg stuff the bag with food. "You had to be surprised, didn't you? They told us that. You couldn't stay here, they said. You were in danger from Mr. Clarke. But you couldn't be seen willingly helping Colonel Ferguson. That is why he surprised you."

"That's right," Peg said, intent on her work. "Now, once you have your supplies, you have to go quickly. Parker's rheumatiz is predicting rain, so you'll need to bundle up. And don't worry about us or the three out there. We have it all worked out."

"I'm not worried about you all," she said with a wry

smile. "I'm worried about the animals. Who will see to them?"

"Ole George, o' course," Peg said. "Colonel Ferguson made him promise. Said as how you'd never forgive him if ought happened to yon pig."

Still Sarah didn't move. She had the most awful feeling that if she stepped out the door with Ian, she would never return to Fairbourne. Never again match wits with Willoughby or feed scones to Harvey. Never see the ladies who had shared her life for the last five years. And suddenly she couldn't bear it.

Fairbourne was more hers than it had ever been Boswell's. She had been the one to fight for it, to scrape her hands raw and wear her feet out as she hauled and herded and mended. She had been the one to squeeze pennies until they shrieked. She had turned dresses for Artie and housed Rosie and kept Lady Clarke in watercolors. *She* had. And if she walked away this night, she would be surrendering everything she had struggled to achieve. She would desert the only real home she had ever known.

She couldn't do it. She wasn't that brave. She couldn't simply close her eyes and step out over a chasm with no more than the hope she could find the other side.

It was irrational, she was sure. Certainly Ian and George would have planned a way to protect her. They had set up this little farce for her to play out, hadn't they? They must have a way for her to slip back into her old life without a hiccup.

Still, she sat there, her gaze on the green baize door that separated the servants' quarters from the main house, keeping one world apart from the other, and all she could see was that it separated her safe, tedious life from the unknown. That one step through that door would carry her irrevocably away from all she knew.

That unknown frightened her. Especially the unknown with Ian.

"Miss Sarah?"

She nodded, not moving. She had to make a decision. So far she had helped Ian almost by accident, her intent to get him better and away, so she could protect her home. This, though, was different. If she walked through that door, she would be casting her lot with him. She would be hazarding everything she had struggled to achieve on the chance that he could prove his innocence. That he *was* innocent. A man who had made no honest offer for her. Who planned a life that had no place in it for her.

"Miss Sarah, come along. The colonel needs to be down the road before Old George brings the militia back. You need to help him clear his name."

Sarah looked up at her dear Peg. She made no declaration. She felt no great sweep of emotion, no urge to laugh or cry. She simply got to her feet and held out her hand for the food bag.

Peg shook her head. "You need to change first. Don't want you catching the ague."

There was nothing Sarah could do about her gray dinner dress, although thankfully it had a high neck. Quickly changing her slippers for half-boots, she plucked her hooded cape from the hook by the back door and returned.

"Thank you, Peg," she said, suddenly afraid that this was good-bye.

Peg did something she hadn't done since Sarah had

been married. She pulled Sarah into a hard, tight hug. "You keep yourself safe out there, Miss Sarah, you hear?"

Sarah hugged her back, inhaling the scent of wood smoke and cinnamon to take with her.

"Stay off the road if you can," Parker added, too inured to his rigid propriety to follow Peg's example. "We couldn't find a hat big enough to cover that red hair of his."

Sarah saw the concern in his rheumy old eyes, though, and reached up to kiss his papery cheek. "We will. Keep the ladies safe 'til I get back." She pulled away with a wry grin. "And make certain you give Lady Clarke a bit of extra cosseting. She has earned it tonight. Thank you both."

"Now," Peg said, holding up more lengths of rope. "We'd appreciate it if you'd tie us up too. Nice 'n tight, now. We don't want to be suspicious."

Sarah quickly tied them both to their chairs. Then, giving them each one last quick hug, she picked up the bag and turned for that green baize door.

"Don't cook up my pig while I'm gone," she warned with a hard-won grin, and pushed the door open into the dining room.

"Och, there you are, lassie," Ian greeted her when she reached the parlor. He had been lounging in one of the lacquer chairs, his frame overwhelming its delicate bones. "I was running out of old poems to entertain y'r ladies."

"Entertain?" Lady Clarke retorted. "It is not entertaining when a person cannot understand a word."

Ian gave her a big grin as he unfolded himself from the chair. "Ah, but isn't the Gaelic a fine language? Pure poetry itself. Would that I could stay and share more."

She huffed. "Sounded like you were swallowing marbles."

He turned his grin on Sarah. "Ah, lass, aren't you lucky to have such a grand one for a mother?"

"In law," both Sarah and Lady Clarke objected at the same time.

Ian laughed as he bestowed a sweeping bow to the women who sat tied up on the good furniture. "Alas, I must be off. I thank ye f'r y'r grand hospitality, and hope one day to repay the generosity."

His answer was a snort from Lady Clarke and a breathy giggle from Artie. Well, Sarah thought, at least the girl was recovering. Sarah checked to see that the women looked fine. In fact, Lady Clarke looked more lively than Sarah had ever seen her.

"May we be off?" Sarah asked, sounding strained even to herself.

"In just a second," Ian said. Then, before Sarah knew what he was going to do, he had another length of rope in his hand. She instinctively stepped back. He caught her and dropped a loop of the rope around her wrist, pulling it tight. "So I don't lose ye in the dark, lass. I'd hate to have you fall down a badger hole."

She flushed. "I swear you'll pay for this."

His smile was darker than before. "I have no doubt, lass. No doubt at all. Now give your good-byes, and we'll be on our way."

Sarah was even more surprised to realize that tears burned the back of her throat. Even more shocking, she saw tears glint in the older woman's eyes. "You will be all right?" she asked Lady Clarke.

"Of course we will," the older woman declared primly.

"Do you think I would let one Scottish traitor discommode me? Be off, Sarah. Sooner gone, sooner returned."

Sarah nodded. "I will be back as soon as I may. I promise."

It seemed there was nothing else to say. Lifting the bag of supplies, she followed Ian out into the darkness to find Harvey tied up to the railing.

"I see you thought of everything," she said, giving the horse a pat. "I hope he bites you."

"He tried," Ian admitted, and offered the great horse a scone.

Harvey gave the lumpy pastry a glare, then lipped it. Lifting Sarah onto the horse's back, Ian swung up behind her. Sarah pulled at the rope around her wrist.

"Leave the rope on," he ordered, reaching around her to wrap the rope around his fist and settle the reins. "Appearances are everything," he said, clucking Harvey into motion. "And you have to appear to be participating in this little adventure through no fault of your own."

"I *am* participating through no fault of my own."

Pulling Harvey's head around, Ian urged him into a trot down the lane. Sarah shivered, not from the cold, but from the solid wall of heat at her back. From the feeling of upheaval and incipient madness. She had been right when she'd stood at the green baize door. She had stepped through a door and suddenly the world no longer looked familiar. And it terrified her. It exhilarated her.

"Are you all right, lass?" he asked, his voice rumbling in his chest, his breath brushing against her sensitive ear.

She almost laughed out loud. Of course she wasn't all right. She might never be all right again. "You should have warned me," she said, her voice sounding strained.

"I couldn't." He did sound apologetic. She didn't trust him. "I didn't have time. Not with all the interest here suddenly. Not with . . ."

She turned in the saddle. "What?"

He looked away for a moment. "After you left today, Old George brought me news. Stricker's been found. He's dead."

Her heart skidded. "Then you cannot prove he is the culprit."

"Worse. They caught one of the men dumping the body. He blamed me."

She looked back at him. "We will simply prove you couldn't have been there."

"I'd rather not bring you into this if I can." He shrugged. "I'm hoping I can get one of my friends to investigate."

Sarah felt herself pale. "How did he die?"

"His throat was slit."

Sarah squeezed her eyes shut against sudden nausea. This new world she had stumbled into wasn't merely unfamiliar, it was violent and unpredictable. And Ian seemed to move through it far too easily.

He focused on guiding Harvey out onto Pinhay Road and east. Harvey escalated into a long, ground-eating trot, the rhythmic staccato of his hoofs almost mesmerizing.

"You will never get as far as London now," Sarah said a few minutes later. "Everyone will be looking for you."

He bent his head as if studying her. "You don't think I'm making for Weymouth?"

"Don't be daft. That wasn't even a particularly clever

feign. The problem is, if this assassin is as smart as you say, she will also know you won't head for the coast."

"Of course not. But she doesn't know I'm not headed for London either."

Sarah looked back at him. "Then where?"

"One of the Rakes has an estate in Sussex. I'll make for there."

"You can trust him?"

Ian nodded. "Oh yes. He and his wife were the first ones to run into our friends the Lions." He slowed Harvey to a walk. "You'll like them."

"I am not going to Sussex," she informed him. "I will point you in the right direction, but that is all."

He shook his head. "I don't think so, lass. I think you'll be coming with me."

She wouldn't, though. She couldn't. The farther she went with him the harder it would be to step away from him again. Even now it was too late to return to what she was. How safe she had been. Her isolation might have been hard. It might have been a life she could live by rote. But now, suddenly, Ian had torn her from it, leaving her certain of nothing but the fact that when this was over, she would be left alone with nothing but fractured, half-thought dreams.

Don't make me go with you, she thought, her eyes closed against the exquisite pain radiating through her from his proximity. From the unfamiliar sense of belonging incited by nothing more than a pair of strong arms around her. *Let me stay behind where I'm safe. Not from enemies or from assassins. From you. From me.*

"Ian . . ."

She knew he heard the plea in her voice, because he

cut her off. "Until I hear from London, I can't risk anyone questioning you."

"But you . . ." She gasped and wrenched around. "Oh, dear lord. The letter."

He tightened his hold. "Stop squirming. What letter?"

"*The* letter." Frantically she twisted until she could reach into her pocket. "The one from London. It came. I was going to bring it down to you tonight."

He yanked the horse to a shuddering halt. "What does it say?"

"I haven't read it yet. A madman burst into the drawing room and distracted me."

Ian hopped off the horse and held up his hands to help her down. "Well, let's have it then. We dinna have time to be lounging about out here."

Sarah leaned into him, her hands against his chest as he set her on the ground. For just a moment, she wanted to stand right there, leaning against his too-solid frame. Warming herself on him.

She stepped away, her movements abrupt, and pulled out the letter. "Here."

He crouched down. He must have pulled out a tinderbox, because suddenly there were sparks, and then a small flame. When he'd lit a small fire among the leaves, she heard paper crinkle.

"Well," he muttered, as he tilted the unfolded page toward the uncertain light. "The handwriting is definitely Drake's. It's execrable…He says that they're searching for our subject. Stricker, I'd say. Much good it'll do them. He says to use extreme caution and to hurry." He laughed, a dry huff. "He doesn't know the half of it. And . . ." He peered more closely to the letter, softly cursing. "Fairy steps? What is he talking about? And who the hell is Jack Absolute?"

Sarah spun around. Jack Absolute? Before Ian could protest, she ripped the letter from his hand and crouched to the little fire to get a better look.

Jack Absolute says to meet us at the end of the Fairy Steps.

Suddenly Sarah couldn't breathe. She couldn't think. *Oh, God. Lizzie.*

Sarah swore that the world went silent. Even up on the hill the breeze stopped. A vast and absolute silence pressed against her ears. She pressed her hand against her mouth, as if it could hold in the emotions that were suddenly whirling around in her.

Ripton Hall. They wanted Sarah to take Ian to Ripton. *Lizzie* wanted her to come.

Oh, Lizzie. Tears burned her eyes. *You knew. You knew all along.*

"Sarah?" Ian asked, reaching a hand out to her. "Do you know what this is about?"

She lurched to her feet and looked out into the darkness. "Jack Absolute is a character in a play. The Rivals, by Sheridan. My—" She stopped, swallowed, started again. "My friend Lizzie Ripton managed to sneak a copy into school, and we used to do readings of it up in our dormer. We thought it quite salacious. And although she always wanted to play the part of Mrs. Malaprop, we made Lizzie play Jack Absolute. It just seemed so... appropriate. After all, Lizzie is the sister of a very proper duke." She drew another uncertain breath. "Lizzie is telling us to come to her home. To Ripton Hall, the estate of the Duke of Dorchester."

"And the fairies?"

She sucked in an unsteady breath. "The Fairy Steps are a secret way into the manor house."

"And you know where they are."

She closed her eyes. "I do." And Lizzie had known it. "I will take you that far. And then I am coming home."

Even saying that hurt, now worse than ever. There was a long silence, punctuated by rustling leaves, the faint bite of dissipating smoke, a dog barking in the distance. The stars were out now, throwing the earth into deeper shadow. Sarah could see a faint gleam wash the color from Ian's hair. She still couldn't see his expression, but she could almost hear him thinking. Reformulating his plans.

"I'm afraid I canna let you go home, Sarah," he said.

"You have no choice," she said, steeling herself against herself. "I helped you. I hid you. I will lead you to your friends. That is all you can ask of me."

"It's not for me," he protested. "It's for you. Don't you understand? I can't let you win this argument, lassie. Until I can clear my name, you run the risk of being arrested for helping me. Do you want your family to suffer the same thing? You'll be much safer with me, and the others will be much safer without you. I'm sorry. Ye'll stay with me wherever I go."

"No," she insisted, feeling the panic ignite in her chest. "I cannot. I am not being difficult, Ian. I swear. But it is impossible for me to go farther than the entrance to the Fairy Steps."

"I willna argue with you, lass." He was furious. She could feel it pulsing off him.

"You're not thinking," she insisted, trying any argument but the truth. "If you keep me away from my home, no matter the reason, what reputation I have will be lost, and that will reflect on the rest of the house. It will ruin Artie's chances."

"Even if you're invited to stay with the Duke of Dorchester?"

His arrogance took her breath. "Do you always make such crackbrained assumptions?" she demanded. "How can you possibly think the Duke of bloody Dorchester is going to welcome a bastard into his home when Princess Charlotte is expected?"

It was the wrong thing to say. Ian's head snapped up. "The Princess?"

She felt as if she were smothering. "The reason your friends are at Ripton, I assume. The duke is holding a house party for her."

His grin was mad, his arms thrown wide. "Well, that settles it, doesn't it? How better can your reputation be protected? As for your presentability, if there are Rakes at that party, there is no question that you'll be welcome as long as we deem it necessary. Now, get on the horse or I'll throw you there myself."

She didn't even remember turning away from Ian or throwing the loop of rope onto the ground where it lay like a dead snake. Suddenly she was just stalking down the hill, tears of frustration and fury burning her throat. She couldn't go with him, and she couldn't explain. She might as well just go home.

She made it to the road before she heard Harvey's plodding steps behind her.

"Don't be a child, Sarah," Ian said, sounding unforgivably as if he were chastising an infant. "We don't have time for it."

If only she could get back to Fairbourne, she thought. She could simply walk west until she saw the ridiculously ornate posts the last baronet had topped with Italian marble. Turn in, walk up to the house, and resume her life. Regain her heart.

Except she was very afraid her heart no longer lay at Fairbourne.

"If you refuse to listen to me, " she said, "it is pointless for me to continue. Go on your own. Follow the signs to Beaminster and then to Cerne Abbas. The Hall is on that road. You cannot miss it."

"Sarah, stop it!" Ian snapped, grabbing her arm.

She tried to pull away. He wouldn't let her. Again, like in the cellar, he simply swept her into his arms and silenced her with a kiss. Again, thought and objection vanished. Her emotions raging, she grabbed him hard and kissed him back, open-mouthed and hungry, with tongue and teeth and every inch of her body pressed so tightly to his she was surprised she didn't push him back onto the ground.

Lightning struck. Blood surged and thickened, and her heart, struggling to keep up, thundered in her ears. She felt his great, hard hands wrap around her and hold her frozen, felt the pounding of his heart against her breast and the intrusion of his cock against her belly. Oh, sweet God, she wanted him. She wanted to simply disappear into him, needing nothing but this fire, this exquisite pain his kiss woke in her chest, her belly, the hollow inside her that had never been filled. She wanted to weep with it, to sing, to shriek like that fabled banshee, as if calling her own death.

She had no idea how she did it, but she pulled away.

He resisted, claiming her mouth, cupping her head against him so she couldn't move. But when she protested, pushing against his massive chest, he stopped. He was gasping for air, just as she was, and trembling like beech leaves in a high wind. Sarah shuddered at the strength of his passion. She closed her eyes against the need for him and laid her head against his still-heaving chest.

"You cannot...keep ending arguments like that," she protested weakly.

His surprised chuckle reverberated through her, like the hum of the earth itself. "Can you think of a nicer way?"

She smacked him with her open hand. "You don't have time for nice, Ian. You need to get on before you're caught."

"And you need to come with me."

"Ian . . ."

He pulled back, glaring down at her. "Do you think I *liked* terrifying your family? Do you even remotely believe that I consider this all a farce, or my decision to bring you with me to Ripton is a capricious whim? These are killers, Sarah. They are relentless, and they are merciless. And I will *not* leave you behind to face them. And even if I had ever thought to do so, how can I allow you to remain alone to face your cousin? He has shown his hand. He doesn't have the nerve to hurt the other women. But you are a different matter altogether. Now be a good girl and resign yourself to your fate."

Tears welled in her eyes. She lifted her hand to his whiskery cheek. "And don't you think I would go willingly if it was better to do so? I *cannot.* I cannot show my face at Ripton Hall, and all the Rakes in the world will not change that."

"Why the hell not?" he demanded, peering down on her. "Why are you in such a fidge over having the Duke of Ripton invite you to stay for the weekend?"

Suddenly so weary she struggled for her next breath, she scrubbed at her face. "Ian," she said. "The Duke of Ripton will never allow me inside his home, and if you ask it, you will only make things worse. If you force the issue, I will find a way to stop you. And your insisting that I go changes nothing."

"Why?" Ian asked, his voice sharp with impatience, holding her by the arms. "Do you think they'll eat you?"

She sighed, bile burning her throat. "I think he will turn me away, just as he has the last two times I breached the walls. Or he will have me arrested, just as he's threatened."

"But why?" Sincerely bemused. Seriously concerned.

She sighed, out of options. "Because, you nodcock. He's my brother."

Chapter 14

Ian looked as if she'd struck him. "He's what?"

"Ian, it is not complicated." She stepped away again, praying for a bit of reason, not sure whether she was hurt by his confusion or amused by it. "The duke is . . ."

She never got the chance to finish. Suddenly Harvey lifted his head and whuffled. Sarah and Ian turned in the same direction, dead silent, waiting.

There. Horses. A herd of them, it seemed, racing along Uplime Road from Lyme.

"Oh, no," Sarah breathed, frozen. "What are they doing here?"

Ian didn't answer. He just grabbed her around the waist and threw her onto Harvey's back. Swinging up behind her, he kicked the horse into motion and turned up the hill. Below, a troop of soldiers thundered past without pause, and it looked as if riding right alongside the lieutenant, was Old George.

"You arranged this?" she asked Ian.

He shrugged. "I think George was a bit early. It means we must be off, lassie."

She couldn't seem to turn away from the direction of Fairbourne, as if she could help the women simply with her worry. Harvey crested the hill and Ian again pulled him up. "You said you would get me to the Fairy Steps," Ian said. "Will you do that?"

For a long moment, still facing west, she held her silence. She wanted to tell him no. She wanted to tell him to go to hell. She wanted to wrap her arms around his waist and sob into his shirt front, because he didn't understand, and she couldn't explain.

Was there any place on earth she craved more than Ripton Hall? Was there any place that gave her more pain? Maybe someday she would be allowed to walk back in the front door without footmen chasing her down. Maybe she could embrace her sister without fear of punishment. Her sister, Lizzie, who, it seemed, had known all along of their relationship. Maybe...someday.

"Yes," she finally conceded. "I will take you as far as the Fairy Steps. Beyond that, I would not be welcome and no help to you."

"We'll figure it out as we go, Sarah," he said.

Before she had a chance to argue, Ian gathered the reins, gave Harvey a nudge, and set him to an easy trot east across the rolling farmland. They reached another coppice, the trees only identifiable as even darker shadows. His one arm tight against Sarah's waist, Ian walked Harvey through the thick darkness as if he could see.

"Tell me about the Fairy Steps," he said, his breath a warm breeze in her hair.

A delicious chill chased down her body, briefly stealing her attention. She shuddered with the pleasure of it. It took her a moment to recover her senses.

"There is a secret way into Ripton Hall," she finally said. "Caves. No one is sure who did it, but steps have been carved, tunnels expanded. The dukes have been using them since at least Elizabeth to sneak out for a bit of fun and religious rebellion."

"How did you learn about them? You didn't live there, did you?"

"No. I was adopted by the Reverend and Mrs. Tregallan, distant relations. He held one of the duke's livings in a nearby village."

It had been the duchess who had found Sarah in that orphanage. Her real father's wife. Sarah had only been three, but how could a child forget such a vision of elegance? A tall lady with soft hands, such gentle eyes, and a stern voice when turned on adults. One of Sarah's most precious memories was holding the duchess's hand as they walked out of that fetid, stinking place. She had been fascinated by kid gloves ever since.

"Sarah?"

Startled, she realized she had been silent for a while. "I believe I told you before that when I was a little girl, the Tregallans would take me up to visit the duke's house. I don't remember ever meeting the duke or my brother. The duchess, however, was kind."

Amazingly so, considering the fact that Sarah had been born only a month before Lizzie. Sarah remembered Lizzie from the visits. Two or three times the vicar had misjudged his timing, and the duchess had still been with her little girl, a tiny, plump thing with the same ruffled dresses and shining blond hair as her baby doll. Sarah remembered that particularly, because she had thought them something magical.

She had once even tried to talk to the little girl. Mrs. Tregallan had lectured her for days on her presumption. Bad girls didn't deserve to make friends with the daughter of a duke. Sarah almost smiled. A bad girl *had* made friends with the daughter of a duke, though. Good friends.

"Was that when you heard about the tunnel?" Ian asked, his voice soothing in the dark. "When you were taken on your visits?"

"We used to leave by the Fairy Steps to sneak out when we overstayed our visit."

She had been so frightened of that dark, dank tunnel with the wan lantern light that shuddered over the walls, and the chitter of bats following them into sunlight. She had sworn never to step inside again.

"When did you find out?" Ian asked. "About your father."

"When I was at the academy. I always knew I was someone's by-blow. I never thought to ask whose. But when I was admitted to school, the Tregallans made sure to impress on me the difference between myself and the other girls. Especially Lizzie."

Do not ever presume to bring yourself to her attention, Mrs. Tregallan had ordered, thin lips taut. *You are only able to attend at the sufferance of the duchess, and she will not want her husband's by-blow to sully her daughter's good name.*

But Mrs. Tregallan had been wrong. Lizzie *had* acknowledged her. Dear, solemn Lizzie, to whom she had never been able to say good-bye.

Sarah had never thought that Lizzie knew the truth about her. But she must have. She must have remembered Sarah's visits, or she wouldn't assume Sarah knew about the steps. Sarah's heart squeezed at the thought they might have shared that memory. That they might have reached out to each other as more than friends.

"What about the new duke?" Ian asked. "Is he the one keeping you away?"

Scrubbing at her tired face, Sarah nodded. "I don't blame him really. Who wants his father's saintly image tarnished by such scandal? If you knew the old duke, you would understand. He might have gone mad later in life, but it was more visions and miracles, not the chase-the-chambermaids-in-his-drawers kind of thing. Ronald is definitely not interested in people learning that the duke had an extra daughter."

"Why should anyone know simply because you came to Ripton Hall?"

Sarah laughed. "You've obviously not met the duke or his siblings. The Riptons are all butter stamps of the old duke. I might not be as identical as the others, but a discerning eye would be quick to identify me. Ronald lives in dread of discerning eyes."

"But you said your sister was a friend from school."

"Yes, well, Ronald had no notion of my pedigree until his father died. Within two weeks of that, I was married, my silence secured and my sisters' names protected. No one knows about me. No one ever can know. It was the price of my dowry."

Since there really wasn't much else to say, Ian kept his silence. Sarah did her best to keep her posture. She was far too vulnerable right now, too susceptible to the comfort of him. The hard, broad expanse of his warrior's body, the great warmth of his heart. She wanted nothing more than to curl up in his arms and close her eyes. To listen to that heart steadily beat, a reminder that there was honor and strength in the world. That there were others who offered to carry burdens.

"When will I go home?" she asked, eyes closed.

Moments passed, broken only by the rhythmic crunch of Harvey's hooves through the underbrush. Again Sarah held her breath, not sure exactly what she was awaiting.

"I don't know," Ian finally admitted. "Everything depends on whether I am cleared of charges. If so, you could return as early as next week. If not . . ."

Sarah wondered if she would ever be able to breathe again. She thought briefly of how impatient her life had been making her. Was it too much of a cliché to wish every slogging, wearying moment back? She detested the unknown.

"If you don't mind," Ian said a few moments later, "we need to cover ground. It's beginning to cloud up, and I don't want to be out in the rain. Where away then, lass?"

She took a look around. She thought they might have been on Denhay Road near Broadoak. "I fear I am not as familiar with this area, but I believe we should follow this road 'til we reach a road sign. At this point, we are looking for Netherbury."

Behind her he chuckled. "You seem awfully good at this. You haven't done it before, have you?"

She shuddered. "Not even in my dreams." Actually, her nightmares. There was no worse possibility to an orphan than finding herself out on a road with nowhere to go and no idea how to get there. Which just made her wonder how she had allowed herself to end up in that precise position.

"Speaking of unpleasant situations," she said. "You

should know that if we take the most direct route to Rip-ton Hall, we will pass through Cousin Martin's estate."

"We'll have to take a chance," Ian answered. "We have no time to waste."

She nodded against his chest. "Try not to attract atten-tion, then, if you will."

She could hear a smile in his voice. "Believe it or not," he answered, "I am quite good at going unnoticed. Of course, a hat would have helped."

She couldn't help smiling. "I shall keep an eye out for clotheslines."

They took the small lanes north and east, from Woot-ten Fitzpaine to Monkwood, passing darkened hamlets one after another on Harvey's strong back. Sarah kept an eye out for road signs, and an ear out for other hoofbeats.

"I had no idea the dark was quite *this* dark," she said at one point as she attempted to read a crossroad sign in the Stygian gloom. "I cannot see a thing. I will be amazed if we don't end up in Wales."

Mostly they kept their silence. In contrast to the har-ried, anxious pace of the last few weeks, suddenly time stretched and slowed, the night so silent Sarah could hear herself breathe. The exhaustion she had been fighting off caught up with her, and the cold had time to collect in each bone and sinew.

It should have been soothing. Sarah liked silence. She liked the dark. But that was because it usually meant a temporary surcease from responsibility and recrimina-tion. This time the silence seemed not restful, but dis-turbingly empty. A void that inevitably began to fill with emotions, like a caldera that began to bubble in her chest.

It began quietly enough. The cold began to creep in.

When Sarah shivered, Ian opened his oversized coat and buttoned it around both of them. Pulling her more closely against his chest, he bent his head over her, providing a cocoon against the night.

His heat quickly surrounded her. His scent, his strength, his protection. And most disturbing of all, the very obvious evidence of his arousal against her bottom. Her own body, so unacquainted with real desire, flared like a rocket at the feel of him, the horse and leather scent of him. She felt hot and cold and oddly liquid, as if all her strength, all her determination was melting within her from no more than the wash of Ian's breath against her neck. She wanted nothing more than never to move from where she rested against him, his massive arms pulling her into the solace of his embrace. To lift her face to his and once again meld her mouth with his. She wanted his kiss, his touch, his fire. She wanted those large powerful hands on her body; she wanted him inside her.

It was a noisy feeling, all maelstrom and uncertainty. Wanting and fearing and wishing, all tumbling about in her until she thought the cacophony of it should wake every bird in Dorset.

If she could have, she would have simply sunk into that storm without a trace. She would have smiled into the darkness and snuggled closer to Ian.

But it was not that simple. Alone, those feelings could have been withstood. But sometime deep in the night, as they plodded along across the rolling farmland, illuminated only by blurring starlight, something more insidious crept over her. Something even more unsettling to her frayed peace of mind. Something that spread like ground fog in the morning, low and uncertain and unnerving, that mixed inexorably with the very real need for warmth and comfort and closeness.

She sat the horse with Ian's arms around her, his head tucked over hers, his breath warming her neck, and into the thick silence of the night, a memory crystallized. She had been at school, tucked away with her friends in the grim little dormer with its mold-stained ceiling and gray-blanketed beds. Lying on one of the beds atop the bright yellow afghan her mother had sent, Pippin was saying how it wasn't until she walked into the family library that she felt truly at home. The smell of leather and old paper, the late afternoon light slanting in through the mullioned windows and glancing off the dancing dust motes, the hush of thick Turkish carpets and the warm, honey-colored oak of the wainscoting. That, she said, was the feeling of home. The timeless sense of belonging, of comfort, of stability. As much a hug as her mother's arms.

Oh, no, said Lizzie, sitting at her desk working on a sampler for her sister's birthday. Her mother's garden. Stepping out the parlor doors to see the precisely trimmed geometrics constructed of boxwoods and pansies, breathing in the heady scent of evergreens, a hundred different kinds of roses, honeysuckle and lilies and iris. Watching the larks tumble in the air over the glittering little ornamental pond. The sun-warmed stone wall she sat against as she sketched the scene. That, she said, was home. It was safety and understanding and acceptance.

No, Fiona disagreed, worrying an old silver penannular brooch in her hands. The smell of peat smoke and heather and wool. The sharp white of a whitewashed stone cottage with thatch over your head and a fire always lit. Bannocks and the familiar drape of a plaid and her mother humming as she cooked. Affection and support and the knowledge that at least in that place she could be brave.

They had turned to Sarah then, where she sat against her plain headboard, her hands empty and her feet curled under her so they couldn't see her darned stockings.

"What about you?" Pippin asked, not realizing what an idyll her life had been.

Sarah could still remember how lost she had felt trying to answer the question. How could she explain that she had nothing to compare? That this notion of home seemed an exotic land to which she would never be invited. That she ached with black, thick envy at the pictures they painted, because she simply didn't understand.

No one in her right mind would say such things about the vicarage, with its grim décor, unrelieved gloom, and rigid rituals. Prayers on rising, prayers at meals, prayers while she was being chastised for some infraction or other. And even if the vicarage had been warmer, or brighter or smelled of comforting food, she had never been invited to consider it home. She had only ever been a tenant paid for by her father's stipend.

Now she called Fairbourne home. She had fought for the right to call it so. But in truth, it wasn't. She loved the old house. She had tried to love Boswell and his family. But as she traveled away, she finally admitted that Fairbourne had been no more a home than the vicarage.

What was beginning to frighten her was that plodding through the unending darkness, she finally began to understand what it was her friends had felt. The sense of it had sparked the minute Ian wrapped himself around her, and over the hours it kept growing. Warmth, deep in her soul; comfort, a sense of unshakable stability and certainty, as if instead of Ian's coat she was tucked inside the time-soothed stones of an old house that had withstood centuries of storms. She recognized every one of the emotions her friends had named: comfort, safety, affection, acceptance, stability.

She had spent her life looking for a home. And all along it had been waiting in this man's arms.

Sarah was not given to weeping. But as she rode along, she could feel tears well up and spill. Wasn't it hard enough she loved a man she couldn't have? How could God finally show her what a home was, only to show her how it could never be hers?

It wasn't fair. She had always believed that she didn't belong anywhere, that loneliness would be a normal part of her life. She had accepted it. She had gone on anyway, knowing she had no choice.

She did belong somewhere, though. She simply had no right to live there.

"Are you all right?" Ian asked.

Sarah prayed he didn't hear the hitch in her breathing. "Of course. You?"

"I *am* sorry, Sarah," he said in a tone that told her he'd been thinking of it for quite a while. "I swear if I could have done it any other way . . ."

"I know." She kept thinking of Fiona's whitewashed house with the thatch. She wouldn't have minded living there, eating bannocks, draping Ian in his plaid. "I am only worried for the women and the estate."

A lie. She hadn't thought about them for an hour. She had thought about herself, and how she would finish this trip back where she started, stripped of even the lie that she was content.

Chapter 15

Resettling his arms around Sarah, Ian desperately tried to ignore her soft weight on his groin. He didn't know how much more of this he could take. He was in agony.

God, what was he to do about her? How long had he known her? Two weeks? Three? In that time he had gone from respecting her to needing her like the next breath he took. His cock hadn't rested since waking up in her barn. His raging, anxious, impatient, *hungry* cock. The rest of him just wanted to be with her.

And when that piece of offal Briggs had attacked her, he'd sworn his heart tore loose. Just the memory sent the red rage coursing back through him. He'd come so close to killing the *riataiche*. To pummeling him until there was nothing left but bruises and bones. The only thing that had prevented him had been Sarah's small hand on his arm. It had been in that moment that he'd first suspected that he had forfeited his sanity.

He was so afraid he was falling in love with her, and he wasn't even sure what that meant. He'd never allowed himself that kind of self-indulgence. He loved his mam and the girls, of course. But this was different. This was...primal. Visceral. He felt as if he would kill to protect her, as if he would give away every penny to see her secure. He wanted nothing more than to see her laugh, watch her sleep, wake her in the morning. He couldn't think of a place he wanted to be more than here, wrapped around her, warming her in the cold, holding away danger. Wishing there was a better reason to have her in his arms.

And he had no right. He would never have the right, and he had needed her to remind him. He still couldn't think of that moment without flinching. He had asked her to come away with him. Just that, as if the details didn't matter. He wanted her. He wanted to be with her. The rest could be worked out later.

The invitation had been barely out of his mouth before he'd realized his mistake. Details, he realized, were very important. He could not marry her. He had already made that commitment, and even if he changed his mind tomorrow and decided that he had no desire to help anyone, he could not dishonor his pledge to Ardeth. Nor could he carry on a liaison behind her back. He wouldn't do that to any friend.

And even if Ardeth walked away, with every good will in the world, he could never accomplish what he needed if he married Sarah, either for him, for his people, or for her. He could never expose her to the world of politics, a bastard of an unknown peer. The women would excoriate her, their tongues far more deadly weapons than any knife. They would forbid their husbands his association, as if Sarah could personally stain a worthy cause, and isolate Sarah's children as pariahs. He would see her shrivel, hour by hour, day by day, until his strong, witty Sarah was no more. He had no right to do that to her, no matter how much he needed her.

Nor could he give in to the basest temptation and set her up as his mistress. It didn't matter that she had been born on the wrong side of the blanket, or that she'd been married and was supposed to know the rules of the game. It didn't matter that she must know that any real relationship between the two of them was impossible. She was a lady to the marrow, and a gentleman did not make that kind of offer to a lady.

He would finish this mission and send Sarah back to her family. And then he would marry Ardeth—funny, committed, sensible Ardeth—and, just as he'd planned, he would change the world. Only three weeks earlier, he had seen their future together as productive, powerful. They would be friends, and they would be partners, and that had been enough. Three weeks ago. Before he met Sarah.

Which meant he had to keep his head about him and his prick in his pants. Even if he could smell the soap and fresh wind in her hair, the lush weight of her breast against his arm, and the elegant sweep of her bottom on his thighs.

They had at least another day of travel ahead of them. He wasn't sure he was going to make it.

And then the rain started. First a mist, enough to bead up in Sarah's hair and slide down his neck. "*A bhidse,*" he snarled, bending lower to shield her.

"I assume that doesn't mean, 'oh look, rain.'" Somehow Sarah sounded amused.

"It was more an opinion."

She huffed. "A little rain won't melt us."

It seemed nature considered that a dare. Suddenly the skies opened. There was no wind, no noise except the steady, soaking torrent of rain that even trees couldn't break.

"You had to say something," Ian said, ineffectually wiping his face.

She chuckled. "I thought things were going too well. Which reminds me. You should know that we have been on Martin Clark's land for about the last two miles."

Ian sighed. "It only wanted that. Well, we have to find shelter."

"I believe we're well south of the manor," she offered.

Ian did his best to see through the darkness and rain, hoping to see shelter before he saw enemies. Even so, Sarah saw it first.

"Ah, good," she said, pointing. "I thought so. There's a barn down there."

And there it was at the bottom of the hill, an untidy lump of a stone building that would have won no awards for beauty. It had a roof, though, which was all that mattered. Pulling Sarah more securely against him, Ian kicked Harvey into a trot.

By the time they reached the building, they were both soaked to the skin. Ian swung off Harvey and helped Sarah down. She unlatched the door and swung it open. For being so worn, the barn door was well oiled and opened easily, revealing a surprisingly neat interior filled with stored hay and two disinterested plow horses. It wasn't fancy, but it was warm and clean, and boasted a ladder to a very tempting loft.

Ian led Harvey inside and began to untie the supplies.

He should have been feeling better to have Sarah off his lap. At least his cock should have been relieved. Instead he felt oddly bereft, as if she had left him alone out in the dark.

He should have been used to the feeling. He had been left alone enough times in his life. But he couldn't remember such an acute feeling of abandonment. He wanted to grab her, pull her back into his arms, bury his face into her neck so he could smell the warm, female scent of her.

"Would you like me to clean out the stall?" she asked, startling him.

He realized he had been standing in the middle of the barn with the rolled bundle in his hands staring at her.

They didn't have time for this. They had to get warm and dry and decide what to do next. He sucked in a steadying breath and wished his cock understood. But his cock was saluting the surprising curl of Sarah's wet hair, the shape betrayed by her soaking gown. Soft, comfortable breasts, narrow waist that swept out to lovely rounded hips. He knew without a doubt that if she turned about, he would be privileged to see the sweetest bottom in Dorset, and it struck him hard in groin and brain and heart.

"Uh, no," he said, struggling to regain control over his body. "You need to get out of those wet clothes."

She frowned.

"We can't have a fire, Sarah," he said. "And you're soaked. Your woman sent along an extra dress." Finally remembering the bundle, he shook the water off and handed it over to her. "It's in the roll. I'll see to Harvey while you change."

She looked between him and the horse, as if for an explanation. "I still don't understand how you made friends with him."

He flashed a grin. "We understand each other. And Peg gave me plenty of scones."

She managed a return grin. "He does love scones."

It took her another minute of hesitation, but finally she accepted the bundle and stepped into the adjoining stall, closing the door behind her.

"All of your clothes, Sarah," Ian said in what he hoped was a disinterested voice.

She would have caught him out if she'd seen him. He was so distracted by the idea of her disrobing that his hands shook. He gritted his teeth against the pain of anticipation. Against the greater, more demoralizing ache of honor. It wouldn't be fair to take her. It wouldn't be right.

His body didn't give a damn.

"I think we are more than halfway to Ripton Hall," she was saying, her voice muffled by the dress she was shucking. "If we start soon, we should make it tonight."

"We'll wait here today," he said.

"We cannot. The grooms will be here soon to check on the horses."

"They'd have no reason to climb into the loft." He finally took the time to give the barn a serious look. For such a tumbledown place, it really was surprisingly tidy. "How far away is the manor, do you think?"

The *shush* of sliding material almost took Ian's breath. "Not close," Sarah finally said. "If I remember correctly, about a mile."

Ian tilted his head, the hair on the back of his neck

rising. No farmer kept his animals this far away from supervision. Just what were these horses for?

"I changed my mind," he said, leading Harvey into an empty stall. "As soon as this rain lets up, we'll get back on the road."

Sarah peeked over the wood partition. "What changed your mind?"

Ian busied himself removing the saddle and wiping Harvey down with straw. "I'm not sure. It just doesn't feel right."

He was sure. He just didn't want to force another burden on her right now.

He should have known better. She took her own look. "It's too far away, isn't it? Um, did I remember to tell you that Martin is undoubtedly involved in smuggling?"

He made the mistake of turning to answer. Oh, Christ. Her shoulders were bare. All he'd have to do is take two steps . . .

"Get dressed, Sarah," he barked, turning away. "Use the blanket to dry yourself."

Her face disappeared. "You mean I shouldn't rub myself with hay?"

His heart seized. He knew she hadn't meant to make a double entendre. One look in her eyes told him she recognized it.

Christ.

He was so distracted that he almost missed the voices.

"Well, Sarge, at least we'll be out of the rain a while," a deep voice said outside.

"Bloody hell," Ian snapped.

"Militia," Sarah whispered, frozen, the blanket held against her chest.

Ian looked desperately around. The stalls were too open for cover. The ladder was the obvious choice, but the loft would be the first place a searcher would look. There was no place to hide.

Harvey bumped against Ian, and inspiration struck. Before he could second-guess his decision, he ran for Sarah. "Come along."

And before she could protest, he scooped her up along with the blanket and her loose clothes and swept them all back into Harvey's stall.

Sarah squeaked in surprise. "What . . . ?"

"*Sssh.* Harvey looks like he belongs here. Excellent camouflage."

He hoped to hell the soldiers wouldn't look in the stall. Relying on instinct, Ian closed the door and latched it. Then, burying the supplies beneath the feed trough, he dropped down with Sarah right against the stall door just as he heard the barn door open. It was only when he laid down against her and covered them both with the dun-colored blanket that he realized just how big a mistake he'd made.

She was naked. Day-she-was-born naked. Every-fantasy-he-could-name naked. Pressed-right-up-to-his-frustrated-body naked.

Christ.

"Ian, I can't—" Her whisper was thin and breathy.

"Quiet."

His cock had just begun to settle down. It went rock hard again, and his balls clenched. Damn it, what had he been thinking? She was too soft, far too warm. He could feel every inch of her skin against his screaming body. Oh, God, her nipples were tight little pebbles from the cold, and they were pressed against his chest. His hand was perilously close to them, and the urge to take advantage was stealing his breath.

Pay attention.

The door closed. Ian could hear the rain and the rattle of horses' tack. Disaster was no more than ten feet away, and there was nothing he could do to prevent it.

Not only that, he was lying atop a naked woman. How could any sane man focus on danger when he was wrapped around a fantasy? He wasn't sure whether the situation was terrifying or ludicrous.

"This better be a good tip," somebody groused, shaking out a coat.

"Well," another man said, "at least we're inside. I don't fancy drownin'."

"That's enough," came a brisk voice. "Miller, check the loft. Thompson the stalls and storage area. Parsons, you and I will look for this trap door."

Ian was so distracted by the feel of Sarah beneath him that he almost missed the import of the words. Trap door? He hoped like hell he hadn't mistaken his strategy.

He hadn't. He could hear Thompson approaching, shoving open every stall hard enough that doors banged as he passed. Ian held his breath. Next to Ian, Harvey shifted. A perfectly innocuous movement. But then Thompson reached their stall. He must have reached for the latch. Suddenly Harvey exploded into motion. Trumpeting a challenge, the big horse lunged over the stall, great teeth snapping.

"Yow!" Thompson screamed, stumbling back and thudding to the ground. "Bastard bit me!"

"Try again," somebody said.

"*You* try."

The other man did, only to suffer the same indignity. Ian couldn't help but grin, and he could feel Sarah's shoulders shake. Oh, for the love of God, he thought, gritting his teeth. Don't move now.

"Nobody in there, Sarge," Thompson groused. "Let me look for the trap door."

"What if the trap door's in there?" the sergeant demanded.

"It isn't!" Parsons called from the other side of the barn. "It's here."

Ian damn near lifted his head. He stopped breathing.

"The shipment has to be in here," the sergeant said. "This barn is just too convenient."

Shipment? Ian almost laughed out loud. The soldiers weren't looking for him. They were looking for contraband. On Martin Clarke's land. So Sarah was right.

Beside him, Sarah stirred. He bent right up to her ear and shushed her. He could feel a shudder go through her at the action. Fear? Distaste?

Pleasure?

His cock went even harder and his hands began to shake. What a bloody foolish time to be courting disaster. He couldn't help it. He kept his head where it was, so his face was against the angle of her neck, where he could taste the warmth of her skin and smell the woman on her. He kept his hands where they were, taunting himself with the sleek landscape of her waist. He felt the thrum of her heart beneath his hand and knew that she was as disturbed as he was. He felt her hands clench on either side of her waist.

He knew he should be ashamed. Hadn't he just decided

that taking her would be dishonorable? Hadn't he planned to kiss her hand and send her on her way?

Well, as his old friend Bobby Burns was wont to say, the best laid plans o' mice an' men, gang aft agley.

"Goddamn it!" the sergeant suddenly barked, his voice muffled. He must have been down the hole. "He must have just moved it! I can still smell the damn brandy!"

There was general stomping around. "What do we do?" one of the men asked.

The door slammed. "Wait out the storm and go home."

Wait out the storm? Ian almost groaned out loud. If he didn't move soon, he would simply explode. If he didn't ravage Sarah's soft mouth and feast on her lush breasts. If he didn't drive into her until both of them were spent, shaking and smiling.

"We know he holds it here," the Sergeant was saying. "We'll be waiting the next time the moon is dark. Now, tend to your animals and get comfortable. We don't know how long we'll be here."

This time it was Sarah who reacted, grabbing hold of Ian's shoulder, as if holding on. Ian knew how she felt. His body was in torment, and the soldiers were settling in not twenty feet away. Soldiers who would be more than happy to take him as consolation prize. He didn't even want to think what would happen to Sarah.

She was trembling, her breathing quick and shallow. His own wasn't much deeper. He should be listening to every sound on the other side of the wall. He was too distracted by the warm satin of her skin.

A kiss, he thought. Surely they could kiss quietly. They wouldn't be moving around. Just…kissing.

The minute he touched his lips to hers, he knew there

would be no just about this kiss. Lightning shot through him. His breath seized in his chest, and he swore the world dimmed. Sarah stiffened, and Ian braced for a slap and discovery. It wouldn't matter. He couldn't have pulled away if one of the soldiers had put a gun to his head.

He could barely see her beneath the blanket, but he knew her eyes were open. Her fingers were dug into him like clamps. Time froze as he waited for her response.

He couldn't believe it. Her lips softened against his. He could feel her sigh into his mouth, and it almost destroyed him. He thought she might be smiling. Very carefully, he lifted his hand to her face and rested his fingers against the soft curve of her cheek. He nibbled at her lower lip, sucked on it, relishing it like a sweet, plump plum. Straining to hold still, he coaxed her lips open, stroked them with his tongue, traced the sleek line of her teeth.

Gently he pressed his tongue against her teeth, begging entry. She hesitated, as if she considered acquiescence to be a commitment. Ian knew that if she accepted his tongue, she would accept the rest of him. And that the minute those soldiers left, he would make good this promise. His body screamed for release. His brain screamed just as loudly for patience. Discretion. Control.

Just when he thought he would fail, she surrendered. Opening her mouth, she greeted him with her tongue. He almost crowed with delight, with triumph, with the primal victory of a conqueror. And sweet God, was she delicious. Dark, warm, tasting of coffee and just a touch of cinnamon. Luscious tastes, the seductive texture of silk. He couldn't get enough. He wasn't sure he would ever be able to get enough.

His heart was thundering, and his cock was straining

against her bare belly. His skin seemed to have been lit, suddenly too sensitive for his clothes. He wanted to be naked against her; he needed to be skin to skin, her lush breasts pressed against his chest. Against his heart, that was beating even harder. Almost as hard as hers, which felt like a lark's against his hand.

He wanted to kiss her eyes, her ears, her throat, to slide his tongue along the enticing ridge of her collarbone. He couldn't. He knew too well if he lifted his mouth from hers, one of them would give the game away. The sighs and gasps that were received by the other would be set loose and catch the wrong attention.

Even Harvey conspired against them, dipping his great head to nibble at the blanket. Ian wanted to laugh. If that horse exposed them, he would personally turn it into dog meat. Ian could only afford the beast a moment's notice, though, as Sarah managed to tilt her head in just a way to settle her mouth more intimately against his.

Ian couldn't stop. Slowly, so she wouldn't be surprised, he drew his hand down from her cheek, along her jaw, her throat, the hard plane of her sternum. She froze for a moment, her mouth going still against his. Her eyes grew impossibly wider, and her breath caught. But she did nothing to stop him, and her hands were right there. He considered it permission. And then he felt her body arch, just a bit, lifting her breasts closer to him, closer to his touch. And he knew he'd been right.

"I don't think this is going to stop today, Sarge," a voice said, from too nearby.

Ian was now the one who froze.

"Then we'll sleep here," the sergeant answered. "There's plenty of hay."

Ian closed his eyes, perfectly still, his mouth molded against Sarah's, his hand a scant inch from her breast, his breath caught hard in his chest. How could he have let himself get out of hand? He'd actually forgotten the soldiers. This had to stop.

"But won't somebody be comin' soon to feed the horses?" somebody else asked. "You don't want nobody knowin' we been here."

"You want to get back so badly?" the sergeant asked.

"If we're found here, we'll lose the surprise. The bastard'll just move his stash."

Come on, Ian thought. *Make up your minds.*

"Parsons also got a pretty barmaid down at the Half Moon who's waitin' on him," came an amused voice. "But I wouldn't mind me own bed, neither."

Say yes, Ian prayed behind closed eyelids, not sure his heart could take this. *For the love of God, man; say yes.*

The pause seemed to stretch forever, pulling Ian to the limit. He could feel Sarah trembling against him and knew she was just as distressed.

"I think the rain's lettin' up a bit, Sarge," said somebody.

"Fine!" the sergeant snapped. "Let's be off, then, before you lot drive me mad."

Ian almost gave himself away with a shout of joy. It was the last thing he wanted to do, but he lifted his mouth from Sarah's and his hand from her breast, resting it on the other side of her waist, where he could still feel her but would be farther from trouble.

The minute air reached his dampened mouth, sense rushed in. What the hell did he think he was doing? One wrong move, one moan, and it would be disaster. He looked down to see that Sarah's eyes were wide, her expression, incongruously, amused. He had to look away. Just the sight of those sparkling eyes drove the sense right out of him, and he wanted to ravish her. But with the interruption came some sense. He had no right to do this. Not to Sarah. Not here in a barn as if she'd been a trull on a street.

He shut his eyes, as if that could remove the temptation. As if it could douse the fires that swept him. He was shaking like an ague victim. His balls felt as if they'd been kicked, and his head swirled with her scent. Her warm, womanly scent that made him think of lazy morning lovemaking and cinnamon buns to celebrate.

The door barely made a sound, but Ian knew the moment it clicked closed. He waited exactly three more minutes. Then he jumped up as if he'd been spring-loaded, carrying the blanket with him. For the briefest moment he got a full, unobstructed view of Sarah's body: her peach-soft skin, her swollen breasts, the thatch of gold curls at the apex of her thighs. His mouth went dry. His hands shook. He dropped the cover onto her before he could change his mind.

"Move, Harvey," he snapped, pushing at the horse.

The horse, startled by all the sudden movement, tried to snap back at him. Ian smacked him and pushed past.

Sarah jumped to her feet, the blanket held casually before her. "Just what are you trying to do?" she demanded, her usually tidy hair tumbling about her sleek, bare shoulders.

Ian's mouth went dry. "Get dressed, Sarah," he said, turning away. "We should be on the road before we're caught by your cousin's men, or worse, your cousin."

He could hear the strain in his voice. It was hell being noble, he thought blackly as he bent to unearth Sarah's clothing.

"Are you mad?" she asked, reaching for his shoulder. "You can't kiss a girl like that and just walk off!"

He shrugged, unable to look at her. "Ride, actually."

"And how do you think that's going to go, Ian? You're hard as Martin's heart right now."

Ian winced. "I'd appreciate it if you didn't compare any part of me to that scoundrel. You realize those soldiers were looking for smuggled goods on his land."

"Of course I do. And right now, I don't care. What I do care about is that you spent the last ten minutes ravaging me, and now you act as if it never happened."

He spun around on her, sharp with frustration. "Just what do you want me to do?"

And damn if she didn't drop that blanket into the hay. "I want you to make love to me."

Chapter 16

Ian froze like a sinner in a sanctuary. His lungs seized up completely and his brain melted. What the hell was she doing to him, standing there naked and sleek and sweetly rounded in all the right places? Her hair, usually ruthlessly scraped back, had broken free and tumbled down well past her shoulders in damp waves of caramel and sunlight. Her breasts stood up proud and firm, with luscious pink nipples that just begged for a man's mouth. Her legs were strong and slender, all the way up to that lovely triangle of light brown hair at their juncture. And she had freckles. Ian couldn't help but smile. She had freckles on her shoulders.

He shuddered with the lust that raged through his body. "I'm trying to be noble here and walk away," he protested, hands clenched to keep them from getting into mischief. Into that lovely triangle of mischief.

Damn her again. She smiled back at him, but it was a smile like none he'd ever seen on her. It was the smile of Eve, of Delilah and Lucrezia Borgia, enticing him to his doom. "Ian," she said, her voice oddly breathy, "I have never in my life been absolutely selfish. To be foolish and giddy and mad. I have never done anything just because I wanted to, and do you know what? I think I've been wrong."

She was destroying him. "Sarah . . ."

"I want you. You want me. We both know this can mean nothing, because you cannot marry me and I will not be your mistress. But just for now, just for here, cannot we share a bit of warmth? Can't we take this moment for ourselves? Just once in my life I want to know what it feels like to make love."

Her words were like a spark to black powder. Ian pulled her roughly into his arms and kissed her. It wasn't a kiss of exploration like before. It was desperation and demand, raw hunger and stark need. He didn't coax her mouth open, he forced it, cupping her head to his so he could hold her still against him, so he could plunder her sweet mouth and surround her soft, warm body with his. And she answered on her toes, hands around his neck, breasts flattened against his chest, her mouth open, her tongue as ruthless and bold as his. She tangled her fingers in his hair as he did hers, so neither could escape.

It was a duel, a dance, played out with only their mouths. It was complex and humbling, smoke and sunlight and raw need. This need had been building, layer by layer, honed like Damascene steel into something so sharp and strong it could destroy them both, and they two knew it.

It was Harvey who brought them back. Obviously impatient with the humans in his stall, he butted Ian hard in the back, sending both of them bounding from the wall.

Sarah laughed, sounding surprisingly young.

"The loft," Ian growled, pulling away just enough to speak. "I'd carry you, but on that ladder we'd both end up ass over teakettle."

Sweet God in heaven, she climbed in front of him, still as naked as the day she was born, the bag of food caught in her hand. Her dainty feet were pale and arched on the steps, and he'd been right. She did have the sweetest bum in Devonshire, beautifully rounded and taut from her hard work, making him itch to reach up and give her a boost, just to cup it, to measure it with his impatient fingers. And every time she lifted a knee, he was taunted with just a fleeting glimpse of those decadent wet netherlips. He groaned out loud and earned a throaty chuckle.

"I'm not sure I can be gentle, lass," he warned, and heard terrible need in his voice.

She turned a smile over her shoulder. "I'm not sure I want you to be, laddie."

He barely made it up to the loft, where they found a lovely space full of hay, just made for sport. Ian laid out the blanket and reached for his buttons. Before he could get the first one opened, though, Sarah batted his hands away.

"I have been wanting to do this for the longest time. I want to touch your chest."

Her fingers were torture against his raw skin. "But you have touched my chest, lass. When I was sick, dinna ya remember?"

She smiled again and Ian almost lost the strength in his knees. "Ah, but I didn't get to enjoy it."

Impatiently she tugged his wet muslin shirt from his pants and pulled it up as far as she could. Ian felt the cool air wash his belly and heard her sharp intake of air. He

was yanking the shirt the rest of the way off when he felt
fingers at his waistband.

"Now, wait..."

She chuckled again. "I think I have waited long
enough."

And he had to stand there while she reached down and
slowly unbuttoned each button on his placket, his penis
straining against her fingers. The material parted, and she
reached inside to collect him with her hands.

"Mmm," she hummed in her throat, driving him mad.
"The answer to a girl's dream."

No less a man's dream, he thought, his knees almost
buckling with the bold grip she had on him. Gently ex-
tricating himself, he barely got the rest of his clothes off
before he collapsed with her onto the blanket, his arms
tight around her, his body humming like a bowstring. He
was gasping for air, his heart hammering against his ribs.
He wanted to slow down, to savor every second of her
body, her smile, her voice. But he couldn't. He was desperate.

She seemed to feel the same. Her small hands were
all over him, her touch sure and clever, inciting riots
along his nerves, inciting a consuming hunger. It would
have been enough to send him over the edge, especially
when she took his aching, distended cock into her hand
and tormented it. But it was her body that sent him over
the edge.

Her skin was just as soft as he'd hoped, her curves
just as delicious, her breasts even more luscious. He explored her like a foreign land, his hands big enough to
cup her breasts, to sweep over her bottom and span her
belly. Her breasts were taut and hot, silk against his fin-

gers, exotic to his tongue. He went from one to the other, teasing, touching, circling, suckling until she whimpered, her back bowed off the floor, her hands tangled in his hair, her eyes wide and glassy. He did his own tormenting, parting that delicious curling hair with his fingers and exploring a truly foreign land. She was hot and wet and swollen, and he sated himself on her. He plunged his finger deep as he teased her with the rough pad of his thumb, pinching, stroking, seducing her to madness.

He could have been happy to stay there forever, just feasting on her like a banquet, but his own body was clamoring for release. His own heart, truly lost, demanded union.

"Are you sure?" he managed to ask, even as he spread her thighs and settled between them.

"Don't ask...silly questions," she gasped, and brought her hands around to grasp his buttocks and pull.

He happily cooperated. Bending down to take her mouth, his tongue plunging deep, he settled himself right against her slick opening, taunting her, torturing himself. And then, surrendering, he drove into her, and the world was lost.

She arched against him, taking him deep. Her hands scrabbled at his shoulders. She met him thrust for thrust with a fury that matched his own, their bodies slamming into each other, his cock drenching in her juices as he plunged in again and again. Harder, faster, driving deep because he couldn't stop, he couldn't hold himself back. He took her the way a starving man would consume his first meal, greedily, in great gulps. And she did the same, her high, thin cries swallowed in his kisses.

They rode the maelstrom together, sweat-sheened and

gasping, bodies fused, hearts ready to explode until with his last desperate thrusts, Ian felt her body seize against him, squeezing him until he wanted to scream, until she screamed into his mouth, until she ignited his own orgasm and he pumped himself dry into her, into the core of her, the heart of her, the hot, sweet center of her. Until he could feel his very life pouring into her, and hers accepting and cushioning his. Until he collapsed, spent and satiated and smiling into her arms.

* * *

Sarah wasn't sure Vicar Tregallan would have approved the prayer she was uttering. Was it a sin to thank the Lord for illicit sex? She had no idea, but she thanked him anyway. She thanked him for Ian Ferguson, who seemed to have as vast a passion for her as she had for him. Who accepted a girl's word and ravaged her like a berserker.

She smiled into the sleek muscle of his chest. A berserker. Yes, she thought, the word was indeed appropriate. She could easily see him in battle, swinging a claymore over his head, roaring out a challenge as he ran. Kilted, of course, with the plaid swinging at his knees and his shirt open to bare a hint of that magnificent chest. She could see him returning to her, battered and weary, and taking her exactly as he just had, overwhelming her with sensation and sweetness.

She sighed, snuggling more closely beneath his arm. More than anything in her life, she wished she could stay right here, safely tucked away in a world only she and Ian inhabited. A world of comfort and safety and acceptance.

Acceptance. Her smile turned sour. Ah well, that was

one dream too many. She would stick to the dreams she could believe.

"Ian?"

He didn't stop playing with her hair. "What, *mo gràdh*?"

"Make love to me again."

This time he paused for a moment. "Are you sure, after that, you want to?"

"After what?"

He gave a small wave of his hand. "I wasn't... patient. It's not fair."

"You were a berserker. I find I like that in a man."

She evidently stunned him so much that he sat up, bringing her with him. "Berserker? Just what do you know about berserkers?"

"What your sisters taught me. They said you reminded them of one."

His face looked a bit thunderous. "I remind them of a man who lays waste to villages and ravages maidens?"

She felt a giggle bubbling up inside her chest, and it was so unfamiliar she almost stopped right there just to enjoy it. "Well, I cannot speak for the villages, but as one of the maidens—well, an ex-maiden, anyway—I think you ravage quite well."

She saw his reluctant grin and knew she would get her wish. "You find this all amusing?" he asked.

She gave him a bright smile. "Why, yes. I believe I do."

"Well . . ." He lifted a hand and cupped her face in his palm. "We do have to wait out the rain, lass. Don't we?"

She shivered with desire. "We do."

Turning, she kissed his callused thumb. She caught the scent of herself on him, and found it immeasurably exciting. She wanted that thumb to reclaim that sensitive territory, tormenting it 'til she screamed. She wanted it against the delicate skin of her breast, the inside of her thigh, the back of her knee.

Stupid, she thought with a gasp of laughter. Why waste your time thinking about what you want him to do? Make sure he does.

Rising up on her knees, she lifted her own hands to his bearded face. It was so dear to her, that face. She could feast forever on those startling eyes, the strong line of his jaw and that once-broken nose. But it was the little things that truly captured her. The scruff of his auburn beard and the way his hair curled at the base of his neck. The nicks in his skin that betrayed his past. The fan of laugh lines that spread from the corners of his eyes. The mad twinkle in his eyes and the freckles that didn't belong on a berserker.

And there, high on his left arm, a tattoo. She stopped, surprised by it. Amazed that she'd forgotten. A thistle wrapped around the shaft of a knife. The *sgian dubh*. A perfect symbol for Ian, who was both fearsome and gentle. Sentimental and strong.

Smiling to herself, she ran her finger along the blue lines. "Rather barbaric," she said, feeling giddy, "don't you think?"

"I thought so," he answered, his eyes the color of hottest fire, "'til I met you. Ah, lass, ye're gonna be the death of me."

She smiled against his mouth. "Ah, but can you think of a better way to die?"

He laughed as he swept her into his arms, tilting her head back. For the longest moment watching. Just watching as she watched back, memorizing the angles and planes of him for when he was gone.

She wanted to kiss every inch of him. He evidently had the same idea, because before she could move, he was kissing her eyes and nibbling on her ears and sliding his tongue along her throat until she could barely even kneel. She cocked her head as far to the side as she could to give him better access. She ran her own hands up his chest and delighted all over again in the soft curl of the fine gold-red hair there. The damp skin and solid muscles that bunched and eased as he stroked her.

It was a slower lovemaking this time, thoughtful, gentle. He didn't devour, he worshiped, with his hands and mouth and breath. His touch, butterfly soft, was surprisingly gentle. He touched her the way a child might a dreamed-of gift, as if it had been so longed for he couldn't quite trust that it was real.

And as he pleasured her, he welcomed her touch with a wondering smile. Sarah found that she loved touching him. There was something almost symphonic about the way his body was put together, art and music and balance. Broad, hard shoulders, soft throat, iron hard chest, and a belly that rippled with her touch. Warm, sleek, only a few battle scars shy of perfect. He had the thighs of a horseman and the arms of an athlete. She loved the different textures of him, the whimsy and purpose of him.

She didn't know how to contain the feelings she was setting loose. Joy, hunger, grief, all roiling around so violently they stole her breath. Desire she was beginning to understand. But what did one do with anticipation? She had never had anything to anticipate in her life.

But even as she reveled in his touch, his scent and security, she knew she had made a mistake asking him to love her again. It only tore harder at her heart. A woman made love to stake claim. She swept her fingers across his belly, along his hip, down his thigh, all the way to the bare soles of his feet and back up to proclaim ownership. He was *hers* to enjoy. To pleasure. To cherish. Every bone and sinew, every vulnerable place inside thighs and behind knees and the little hollow of the throat belonged to her and no one else. She staked her claim, just as surely as every other woman before her had claimed her man. She left a bit of herself with him, even though another woman would finally claim him. Because when that next woman ran her hands down Ian's thighs, she would pass through a faint trace of Sarah, who had come before. She wouldn't understand that Sarah had poured every part of her into that touch. Promise and passion and pride. Tears and laughter and the sighs of wonderment. But Sarah would. Because Sarah would remember.

"Lassie," Ian murmured, going still. "Are those tears?"

She squeezed her eyes shut for a moment. "Beauty always makes me weep." Beauty and loss.

She felt a rumble of laughter in his chest. "Och, lassie, ye're needin' to get your eyes checked."

"No I don't," she whispered, and bent to taste the ridge along his sternum. "I am discovering it by feel."

She had no time for sadness, she decided. Loss would come tomorrow. Today she would savor every second. This time she was the one to lay him down.

"And just what do ye think ye're doin' the noo?"

"You shouldn't have to do all the work," she said, and climbed up on top of him.

His hips were so wide, she could barely straddle him,

but she managed, sweeping her hair forward so it cascaded over his chest and belly and brushed the quivering end of his penis. His groan was harsh. It grew harsher when she took him in her hand.

"I am glad I already know we can fit," she murmured with a saucy grin, "or I would not be quite so sanguine about welcoming you."

His smile was strained. "There's gonna be no fittin' if you don't get on with it. Much more of this and I'll embarrass myself like a wee lad."

She laughed, delight sparkling in her. "Ian," she said, bending to drop a quick kiss on his mouth. "There is nothing wee about you at all."

His answering smile was smug, and she laughed harder. Humming, she watched as she slid a finger up his shaft. With her other hand, she cupped his balls, making him jerk and sweat break out on his chest. She shouldn't enjoy this so much, she was sure. But she did. She adored the amazing conundrum of how something could be so soft and yet so hard. She relished the fact that she was the one doing this to him. She was the one causing that look of exquisite pain on his face. She was the one who would ease it. It was a new experience, play. A new color she had never seen on her palette.

Ian had run out of patience. Sarah wished to play a while longer. Ian forestalled that by simply lifting her up and holding her over him in the air.

"Make up your mind, lass, or you'll never get down."

She chuckled. "Ah, well. The rest of my explorations will have to wait 'til later."

And positioning herself on him, she slid all the way down.

Oh, sweet lord, she had made a mistake. She was going to split in two. He was too big after all. She would never survive this tearing fullness.

And then he moved. Just a little, lifting his hips and then setting them down. And the fullness sparked a delicious heat inside her.

"Oh . . ."

She laid her hands on his chest and leaned over to kiss him. He took hold of her breasts, tormenting them with his cunning fingers as he rocked back and forth, back and forth, until she got the hang of it and began to move on her own. Up. Down. Up down, just a bit, then a bit more, then all the way, hard, squeezing a gasp out of him. She focused on the rhythm, on the sharp threads of pleasure that were unwinding from that friction and spreading throughout her.

"Open your eyes," he commanded, setting his hand on her hips.

She hadn't realized she'd closed them. She was too consumed by what was happening in her body, in the scent of sex and warm male and hay, the soft syncopated sighs and hums as they both courted the pleasure. She opened her eyes and looked down to see Ian's gaze on her, bright blue, just that, and it tightened her body. Just his hands driving her on, his cock driving into her, the beads of sweat that were beginning to slide down her back in the cold barn. The scratch of the blanket against her knees and the throb of her pulse in her ears.

An urgency was building in her, painful and sweet and sharp, pouring out from her core, spinning, tightening, harshening, until she couldn't stay still with it, she had to move, she had to open her mouth and gasp for air, her gaze still impaled on his, her body impaled on his, on and

on and on until she had to scream, until she wanted to beat
him with her hands to make it stop, except he was holding
her to him and watching her, watching the madness build
in her eyes.

"I…can't . . ." she gasped, batting at him.

"You can," he assured her, smiling. That quickly she
tumbled over that smile and shattered, and suddenly like
the hiss and bang of fireworks, she exploded into sound
and colors and the smell of summer. Fracturing her,
showers of light setting off in every muscle and bone in
her body until she screamed with it.

And seconds later, his head thrown back, letting go a
guttural cry, Ian followed, pumping so hard into her she
thought she would split for sure. Wringing every sensation out of her, every thought, every hope and regret and
belief, until she was left boneless and panting against his
damp chest.

* * *

She must have slept. The next thing she knew, Ian was
gently shaking her shoulder. His greatcoat, still a bit
damp, covered them both, and weak predawn light was
creeping through the badly joined boards.

For a moment she didn't move. She still felt replete,
her body humming gently with waning arousal. She
wanted for just those few minutes to pretend that Ian and
she would never leave this loft; that nothing mattered but
their delight in each other.

And then Ian ruined it.

"I want to make love again," he murmured, running his
fingers down her hair.

"*Mmmm.*" She closed her eyes again, as if that would hold off the world a little longer. Her body was reacting predictably to Ian's words, softening, warming, wanting.

Kissing the top of her head, he held her close. "I want to make love every morning when we wake and every night when we go to bed. And a few times in between."

She smiled, even as tears burned the back of her throat. "I am already exhausted. That would do me in completely."

Silence fell, filled with the comfortable sounds of the horses moving about in their stalls and the music of morning birds.

"Sarah."

"*Mmmm?*"

"Marry me."

And that quickly, her perfect little world disintegrated, and she was cold.

Chapter 17

Even as Ian reached out to her, she pulled away. It only made the turmoil in her heart worse, because she could see him, his hair tousled and his sky blue eyes sleepy and warm. He looked comfortable as an old pillow, as sheltering and safe as a stone wall. And he was smiling as if his own question wouldn't destroy him.

She half expected him to grab for her. He didn't move, which told her more than anything that he'd known even before he asked the question that he was wrong.

"I mean it," he insisted anyway, finally sitting up, the thick gray coat pooling in his lap, which left his chest bare. "I love you. I need you."

Which took Sarah's breath and broke her heart. She so loved that chest. She loved the unexpected vulnerability in his eyes. She loved the ridges that deepened between his brows as he watched her, and the way he waited as patiently as night for her answer.

She could see the arousal rising in him and reached for her clothing. "No you don't. You don't mean it. You only wish it."

On went the much-darned chemise, her hands trembling, her baser side screaming in protest. *Yes, damn it! Answer yes before he changes his mind. You can work it out if you only say yes!*

But she couldn't lie to herself either.

"Sarah," he said, his eyes brittle with hunger. "I made you an offer before. I never should have. I knew it the minute I made it. But, please, Sarah. I have to have you with me. And marriage is the only way that can happen. Please, lass. Marry me."

She waited until she had slipped on her dress before reaching for his hand. "Thank you," she said, wanting to weep with sorrow. "Thank you for respecting me so much that you would make such a sacrifice. But even if you don't understand what would happen, I do. I know what you would suffer if you broke your engagement. I know how fruitless your campaigns would be to help all those people if the wife you forced on the world was a nameless bastard. I know that Fiona and Mairead would lose their future. You don't want to admit it, but you know it too. The world will not change merely because you want it to."

He rose to his feet so fast she didn't have a chance to step away. And before she could say no, he dragged her to him, all but crushing her in his arms. "It can," he insisted. "I say it can. Don't you understand? I've never felt this way about another person in my life. *Any* person. You're brave enough, Sarah. You could do it."

She squeezed her eyes closed and inhaled his scent, and knew what it felt to die inside. "No, Ian," she said, pulling away, knowing he would never force her to stay, because he was a good man. "I'm not, actually. I am the perfect size for Fairbourne, where I only have to deal with local farmers and spinster women, and my birth can usually be overlooked. I was never meant for greater things. I was never raised to it."

"I wasn't either," he protested. For an eternity, he only looked down at her, his hands on her shoulders, his eyes fierce. "I could make you."

She couldn't help it. Smiling, she lifted a hand to his face. "You might," she said. "But you won't. You are meant for great things, Ian Ferguson. I would destroy that, and we both know it."

"I'll give it up."

She reared back, breaking contact. "You will not. You will live up to the vow you made and help those people. You know what it is like to be friendless and alone, Ian. You cannot desert others in the same position. And you will *not* shame your Ardeth. She does not deserve it."

The pain on his features was exquisite. "But you could help me so much."

Her temper snapped. "And how would I do that? Ian, the last time I saw my brother the duke, he warned me that if I showed my face in public again, he would have me arrested and transported for attempted extortion. And anyone who came with me. The *duke*, Ian, who will have been duke long before you will be a marquess. Who will, as a matter of pride, see you ruined for taking my side. How exactly will that help you?"

She saw the torment in his eyes, his instinctive urge to contradict her. The hard realization that he couldn't. Finally he lifted his hand to her face, his callused fingers unbearably soft. "But what of you?"

Grief impaled her like shards of ice. She forced herself

to smile. "Why, I will match wits with the wiliest pig in England and save my pennies to give Artie a season. And I will watch for your name in the papers as you cut your swath through parliament."

"It's not enough, Sarah."

"It is, Ian. As long as I know you are all right, it will be."

Once again he held her, but this time gently, his head bent over hers, his heart thundering beneath her ear. "Oh, lass," he whispered. "I'm afraid this will kill me."

"No it won't," she assured him, her hand to his heart, her face up to his. "No berserker dies of disappointment."

"He might of a broken heart, though."

Yes, she thought, fighting a tide of despair. A person might well die of a broken heart.

* * *

He couldn't breathe. He couldn't think. He had survived loss, injury, betrayal, and battle, and he had never felt like this, as if he were shattering to dust. As if the future yawned away before him like a lightless hell.

He loved her. He *loved* her, with a fierce hunger that ate through his chest and stole his sense. After hearing her story, he loved her even more. She wasn't merely pretty and kind and strong. She was unspeakably brave. He loved her and he couldn't think of any way to have her.

She was right. He could never shame Ardeth. He couldn't ruin Fiona and Mairead or desert the people who needed his voice: soldiers, widows, crofters, children. It would be unforgivably selfish to choose his own happiness over theirs. It would be dishonorable. But God, he wasn't sure he could survive it.

As matter-of-factly as he could, he finished tying the bundle to the back of Harvey's saddle and lifted Sarah up. She looked no better than he felt, which made him hurt even worse. He hadn't been fair to her. He should never have taken her. He should never have pushed her with his proposal, knowing what she would say, because she had more honor than he did.

Putting his foot in the stirrup, he swung up behind her. His cock went hard in an instant. He paid no attention. Arousal he could ignore. It was the unbearable memory of her lying in his arms that threatened to destroy him. Her warmth, her bright laughter, her generosity. Her unshakable sense. He wrapped his arms about her and fought the urge to ride south for the coast. For anonymity and freedom. He turned the horse east and clucked him into a canter.

Sarah cleared her throat, as if she hadn't spoken in decades. "Um, that road there," she said, pointing toward north of dawn. "I think it will bring us out near Powerstock."

He nodded, not trusting his own voice. The light was growing stronger, and he could see more clearly. Cowbells clanged in the distance, and a farm cart was traveling on a road that intersected the one they followed. Seeing it, he felt a familiar prickling on the back of his neck. They were too exposed. He looked around, and saw that a coppice paralleled the road just to the north. He made for it.

"We might have to pull up for a bit," he warned, scanning the area more thoroughly. "We are much too distinctive to forget."

"No," she said, her voice small. "We must get you to safety as soon as we can."

And away from me. He could almost hear it. He didn't blame her in the least.

"We will," he said. "I promise."

But they couldn't. Even before they reached the coppice, Ian heard the rumble of horses over the ridge and had to kick Harvey into a gallop. They just made it into the trees before a group of horsemen approached within fifty yards, headed north.

"Martin," Sarah said, her voice heavy with disdain when she recognized the leader. "And he's obviously found more out-of-work soldiers."

"Those look even more disreputable than the last lot."

It was nerve-wracking enough when she saw Martin set to pass them by. Then, with a lift of his hand, he stopped his troop at the crossroads. "I doubt she's made it this far," Martin said, shocking Sarah. "You four, go on east. If you don't see anything, go ahead and make the delivery. I'll take you five with me back toward Fairbourne."

"And if we find her?"

Martin laughed. "We see that she is hung for aiding a traitor."

"But 'e kidnapped 'er," Private Greggins protested. "All 'ave said so."

"And I say he didn't. If we find her, we'll find him. And since I am magistrate here, I'm the one who can lock her in the roundhouse, aren't I?" Even from where she sat Sarah could feel his malice. "I have a feeling a little gaol time will help us find out what happened to Briggs. He didn't simply vanish off the face of the earth."

"I would," Sarah heard distinctly. Obviously Martin

didn't, because in the next moment, the troop was off, split into different directions.

She shuddered in Ian's arms, and he hugged her. "There's no question of your goin' back now, lassie. If we want to give Briggs and Clarke their just rewards, you'll have tae come with me."

"First things first," she said, not ready to address that problem. "We need to avoid Martin's men to get to your friends. I think we should go south for a bit."

They did, weaving in and out of one small lane after another. They had to pull up twice more within the hour to avoid bands of militia.

"You would think they would have given up by now," Sarah protested as they watched the latest band of riders canter north.

"Not with Martin Clarke on a tear." Leaning around, he lifted the burlap bag Sarah had filled in the kitchens. "Why don't we eat? I'm fair gut-foundered."

They sat for a while as the sun rose higher and thin clouds crept over the horizon, crunching old apples and fresh bread topped with cheese.

"Ian," Sarah said. "What will you do if you cannot prove your innocence?"

"Marry you and run away to America."

"No, you won't. You would never desert your sisters like that."

"We'll bring them along."

She shook her head. "Mairead has been uprooted enough. She would not be able to acclimate."

"Oh, she's sturdier than that."

Sarah looked up at him, perfectly serious. "No, Ian. She's not."

Ian looked down at her. Stupidly, he was surprised by an odd flash of resentment. Envy. She knew his sisters better than he did.

"Tell me why," he said.

She looked up, briefly meeting his eyes before returning to her meal. "She needs to feel safe. To know what to expect. It was why school was such a disaster. Her routine was upended, and she never knew what to expect. And she couldn't really communicate with the other girls. It wasn't even enough that Fiona was there with her." She seemed to think for a minute, staring at her apple. "I hope the two of them are all right. They must have heard the accusations against you by now."

He looked up, struck. "They probably think I'm dead. Christ, they must think I left them alone with that bastard."

She gave a small huff. "There are many things you can say about the marquess, Ian. I fear bastard is not one of them."

He gave her a brief smile in return. "Spiritually, emotionally, morally."

She nodded and tossed her apple. "In that case...I wish I could go to them."

"As do I. But not until we know you're safe. I want you to promise that you'll wait right there at Fairy Steps until I send one of my friends to you."

"Ian . . ."

He cupped her face in his hand and turned it to him. "Promise. If I cannot bring you in with me, at least let me send my friends to you."

"Which friends? You never told me. And how do you know these friends are not the traitors? Minette was obviously told where you were, and only your friends knew."

He frowned. She was right. No matter how much he hated the idea, it was possible. "It had better not be any of them," he threatened. "I call no more than eleven Englishmen friend. I don't know what I'd do if one of them betrayed me."

She offered a faint grin. "You could spend the rest of your life saying how you'd been right about the English all along."

"No," he said, perfectly serious. "I canna. Not since I met you."

She flushed and ducked her head.

"Promise me, Sarah. You'll wait at the steps until Chuffy Wilde comes to get you."

Her head came up. "I'm to call him Chuffy?"

He couldn't help but grin. "His name is Charles, actually. But you'll never be able to think of him as anything but Chuffy. You will know the minute you meet him that he cannot possibly be the traitor. He looks like a bespectacled bear cub."

She didn't answer. Bread in hand, she looked out over the wakening landscape. Ian had a strong suspicion she was trying to think of alternatives.

Ian refused to look away. "Promise."

Finally she faced him, and Ian could see the cost of his request. He said no more.

Looking away again, she sighed. "I promise."

He dropped a tender kiss on her forehead. "Thank you. You have just made it easier to do my job."

She scowled at him. "There is no need to resort to clichés to get me to see sense."

He flashed her the brightest smile he had. "Lassie, I would have resorted to rope and a ring bolt if necessary."

When she actually laughed, he knew for certain; he was in love. Irrevocably, impossibly, immeasurably. It made no difference, except to the weight of his heart.

"Time to go," he said, and tossed his apple core into the trees.

Gathering the reins, he set them off once again to the east. They didn't talk, except to discuss directions. Ian assured himself it was to keep a better ear out for pursuers. It was a lie and he knew it. He was silent because he was afraid of what he might blurt out.

Sarah had been right, of course. If the Lions knew where he was to receive his missive, they might very well know about Ripton Hall. He could be riding straight into a trap. He wished there was another way to approach it, but the directions had been clear. One of his friends would meet him at the end of the Fairy Steps.

That was if he got there. Twice more they were forced off the road by patrols and traffic. Ian wished like hell he could lay low during sunlight. But he had a growing suspicion that the manhunt for him would only get worse.

* * *

Dusk was gathering fast as Ian pulled Harvey to a stop in among the thick stand of oak called Strawberry Wood that held the opening to the Fairy Steps. Leaves muffled noise, but Sarah could hear the rustlings of small animals, and a sleepy nuthatch called to its mate. She didn't wait for Ian to help her down. She slid off onto the spongy ground and stepped away. It was too soon, she kept thinking. She wasn't ready for her adventure to be over. She didn't want to give Ian back to his world.

Dismounting, Ian handed her Harvey's reins. He strode to the north edge of the wood. Sarah decided not to join him. She knew what the view was. She had stood in this very coppice with Boswell watching the setting sun glint off a hundred windows and warm the copper cupola across the glen. A mishmash of architecture, Ripton Hall had originally been a Cistercian monastery given to the Ripton family by Henry VIII for evicting the monks. Grown to a rambling monstrosity, it had been added to willy-nilly over the years, each succeeding duke wanting to put his own stamp on it, until the house itself showed far more character than its inhabitants. It was another old house Sarah loved, another she could never call her own.

"I didn't realize the dukes of Ripton had so much whimsy," Ian mused, obviously noting the gargoyles and crenellated turrets on corners that had never needed a defense.

"They don't," Sarah said, looking the other way. "The architects they hired did."

The sun had set, and the shadows were lengthening fast. Out in the fields cattle were wandering back to their barns, and sheep bent to their dinner.

Ian turned back to her. "You know a lot about the place."

She shrugged. "The lure of forbidden fruit, I imagine. It was a convenient setting for the fairy tales I told myself when I was young. Even though the tunnel frightened me, the exit into these woods always seemed . . . magical."

"When did you last go through the Fairy Steps?"

She looked up, but couldn't see his expression in the deep shadows. "Oh, the vicar stopped bringing me when it became obvious that I looked so much like a Ripton. When I was about four, I think."

He looked back to the house. "Then there can't be much you can tell me about the layout of the house."

Her smile was sore. "Oh, there is. I can show you how the ground and first floors are laid out. At least the main block, where visitors might wait." Briefly.

"A lot to remember for a four-year-old."

She couldn't look at him. Instead she turned to stroke Harvey's great neck. "Oh, I was twice here as an adult. Boswell brought me. He came to ask the current duke for financial help. Since his family had taken me off the duke's hands and all."

He looked down at her. "Was that when the duke threatened you?"

After having her dragged through the main hall the second time and thrown down the great steps. As if the visit had been her idea. As if she would ever beg her brother for anything but to leave her alone. "Yes."

For a moment, there was silence. Harvey nibbled at Sarah's hair, and she leaned her cheek against his.

"I'm sorry," Ian said, and Sarah had to squeeze her eyes shut against the pain.

"Not nearly as sorry as Boswell, I assure you."

"Can you tell me where the tunnel enters the house?"

"The duke's library on the ground floor. Behind a bookcase."

"And the entrance here?"

She pointed to a dip in the ground to the west covered by shrubs. Turning in a complete circle, Ian frowned.

"I don't like this," he said. "I canna leave you here, lass. You'll be too vulnerable. If my enemies know about the Fairy Steps, they'll find you. Besides, rain is coming on."

She looked up to see that clouds scudded low and fast before a freshening wind. He was right. Within a few hours, she would once again be soaked.

Hands on hips, he scanned the valley. "Where can you hide?"

"At Fairbourne."

He ignored her. "What is that?" he suddenly demanded, pointing toward a small stone building just visible to the east of the manor house.

Sarah followed his guide and shook her head. "No."

He faced her. "Why not? Will someone be using it?"

Her laugh was brisk. "The chapel? Unless the duke has been struck by lightning while seated atop a donkey, I sincerely doubt it."

"Can you get to the thing through the tunnel?"

She hated to even answer. "Yes."

He turned around. "You've been inside?"

"Yes." He didn't need to know that story, though, of how easily a wandering child could get locked in a chapel with no company but dust and the remains of dead dukes. She hated that chapel.

"Then it's perfect. You can guide me to the turnoff and wait for me in the chapel."

She turned away. "I would rather not have to go in at all."

"Neither would I," Ian said. "But when needs must…" Turning, he untied the bundle and pulled it off Harvey's saddle. Then, taking the reins from Sarah's hands, he turned the horse back the way they'd come and gave him a great swat on the rump. Harvey took off down the hill as if wolves were after him.

"What are you doing?" Sarah demanded, taking a step after him.

Ian caught her by the arm. "The farther he is from me, the better the chance I can convince anyone that you weren't with me when I got here. It will protect you."

She couldn't look away from where she could hear her horse galloping down the road. "It won't protect Harvey."

Ian hugged her, quick and hard. "We'll find him later, lass. I promise."

She squeezed her eyes shut, just for a moment. Otherwise she might tell him what he already knew, that he couldn't make promises like that.

"Come, lass," he said, taking her hand. "Let's get ourselves comfortable for a bit. We don't want to be sneakin' into a house when the inhabitants are still up."

Unpacking again, he unrolled the blanket and set it out on the ground. The shadows were collecting fast, the birds chattering in one last effort to beat the night. Dry leaves rustled in the breeze, and some fell, a sere storm around them. Sarah settled herself on the blanket because there was nothing else she could do.

"Now then," Ian said, dropping down next to her. "How shall we pass the time?"

The tone of his voice jerked her head up to see a wicked intensity in his eyes that shook her to her core. She immediately thought of those hours in the barn, curled up into the heat of him, claiming ownership of him, as if she had had the right. She could almost feel the rasp of his beard against her cheek, the hard angles and planes of his body protecting hers. She almost wept with wanting him.

"Oh, no you don't," she said instead, holding her hand out as if to ward him off. "I am not taking one piece of clothing off in this cold."

His grin grew mischievous. "Lass, you underestimate me. I don't need you to take off *any* of your clothes."

Well, at least the blush warmed her cheeks. She turned away, focusing on the lights that winked on in the great house rather than the light that was already glowing in Ian's eyes. "Don't be absurd. We cannot drop our vigilance like that. What if someone sees us? Or hears us?"

He tilted his head considering. "True. You are a wee bit noisy."

Her mouth dropped in outrage. Even knowing he was trying to distract her, she was mortified. She smacked him hard and came away with no more than sore fingers.

"What if no one comes for me?" she said, her gaze back on the house, which had lost all of the light now and faded into vague grays.

He spent a moment considering the same scene. "You know your way about the house. Find Chuffy Wilde. He'll be there. Speak only to him. And Sarah—" He took hold of her hands, his grip broadcasting his fear. "These people are deadly. I can't emphasize this enough. You *must* use all caution. Trust no one but Chuffy."

Sarah's heart skidded in her chest. She didn't want to take another step. When Ian kissed her, though, a soft, tender parting, she knew she had no choice.

By the time Ian finally led Sarah through the brush to the mouth of the tunnel, she was sick with dread. She couldn't go into that house. She couldn't risk her brother's ire. Anyone else might believe his threats to be unfounded. She knew better. Nothing was more important to Ronald than the sanctity of the Ripton name. But worse, what if Ian's enemies waited for him? How could she convince her brother to help him?

The cave was just as dark and damp as she remembered, even with the little torch that was waiting for them by the door. She shivered.

"See?" Ian asked, lifting the torch for her to see. "Someone is thinking of us."

She didn't bother to answer. The roof seemed a lot lower, the light fainter where it slithered over moss and jagged rock. Ian had to pass much of the way bent over to keep from doing himself injury. Sarah wanted to close her eyes to block out the too-familiar path. She wanted to never have to remember those clandestine flights again, when the vicar had dragged her along like an inconvenient parcel.

"Are you all right?" Ian whispered, his free hand holding tightly onto hers.

"Yes."

Still walking, he turned his head. "You don't sound all right." The uncertain light shuddered over his features, making him look barbaric. Sarah shivered again.

"I'm all right," Sarah insisted. "I am *not* happy."

He flashed her a wild grin. "Oh, well then. That's all right."

Sarah swore they had been walking forever, up and down the stairs carved into rock, before they reached the chapel turnoff. Ian stopped and let go of her hand.

"All right, then," he said, and held the torch out to her. "Go on. I'll wait."

She took a step back. "You have a longer way to go and more steps. Keep it." She assayed a weak smile. "Just make sure this Chuffy person knows where I am. I am not fond of waiting."

Her heart was stuttering; she wanted so badly to reach out to him, sure, suddenly, that he was walking into disaster.

"Please," she whispered, frozen in place. "Don't do anything stupid. Promise me."

She would forever remember the look on his face in that moment. His smile was so sad, painfully sweet. "I wish I could, lass," he said, his voice sore. "But that isn't how it works."

She closed her eyes, fighting hard against the urge to stop him, hold him here in the darkness where she could keep him safe. Even though she knew better. Ian would never hide from his enemies behind a woman's skirt.

"Just tell me this," he said, and stepped right up to her, forcing her eyes open, his hand cupping her face. "Do you love me, lass? Will I at least take that with me?"

She thought her heart would burst. Tears seared the back of her throat as she looked up into those sky blue eyes that seemed to suddenly carry more pain than a man should bear. "I must love you," she answered. "I can't think of anything else that would get me back into these tunnels."

His smile, when it came, was infinitely gentle, heartbreakingly sweet. The torch still held high above him, he wrapped his free arm about her and pulled her into his arms. And there he kissed her. And she opened to him, mouth-to-mouth, as if she could devour him, as if she could meld him inexorably to her, her heart racing and her throat clogged with want. It was only when he set her back and pushed her on her way that she realized that this had been their good-bye kiss.

She turned back to him, suddenly frightened. Lost. Empty. She should run to him, demand he stay, offer anything just to hold on to him here where they were both safe, both equal, both madly in love as if that were all that mattered.

She couldn't, and it all but destroyed her.

"Remember," he said. "Chuffy will find you."

Remember, she answered in her heart where it couldn't burden him. *I will love you my whole life.*

And with that, she walked into the darkness, her hand out against the rock, her head down. The darkness quickly enveloped her, reducing the world to touch and sound. She heard water dripping somewhere and the familiar chittering of bats. She prayed they would turn over and go back to sleep until she got through. Then she prayed that Ian would come himself to find her, no matter how hard that would be. She would give him up. She just didn't want to do it yet.

Fortune was with her for the moment at least. The door out of the caves was still there, and it opened without a sound into the back of the old confessional. Someone had been using it recently. Sarah stepped very carefully through into the wooden box in which priests had once sat to forgive Ripton transgressions. Fortunately the confessional walls were not solid, but carved in fretwork, so it might be seen that the booth was occupied, but not by whom. It also helped her see out without being seen. Closing the little panel behind her and making certain to lock it against further incursion, she stepped out onto the flagged floors and looked around.

The church smelled musty and unused. Kneelers had been pushed against the far wall, and the old statues that had so terrified her as a child removed. Only the stained glass windows remained to reflect the glory of God. At this time of night, though, they were ghostly and dark.

Two chairs remained on the denuded altar. Stepping out into the echoing nave, she grabbed hold of one, dragged it in front of the confessional, and sat down. And then, just as she was instructed to do, she waited.

* * *

On the other side of the entrance from the tunnel, the Ripton Hall library sat in shadow. A long rectangle of a room walled in filled bookcases and decorated in tones of deep green and gold, it boasted a coffered ceiling, rare Persian rugs, and the mismatched furniture of generations of dukes who had seen the library more as a statement of their wealth than a sanctuary of learning.

A desultory fire crackled in the Elizabethan hearth, and a candelabra spilled a small pool of light over a hunter green armchair in the corner where Alex Knight lounged, the black mourning ribbon still around his sleeve, a half-full glass of brandy in his hand, and Barnwell's translation of Aristotle's *Poetics* in his lap. He was paying less attention to the tome than the steady ticking of the Percier clock on the stone mantel. He was beginning to lose hope that Ian Ferguson would make his appearance tonight. Rain had begun to patter on the windows.

He had just turned back to his reading when there was a scratching on the door into the corridor.

He lifted his head. "Yes?"

The night porter opened the door. "A messenger has arrived, my lord," he announced in sepulchral tones that seemed to match the old pile.

Approaching on felt-silenced slippers, he bent over Alex with a salver that carried a simple folded note.

"Is a reply requested?" Alex asked, reaching for the paper.

"No, my lord. The messenger has already departed."

Having delivered the message, the man stood at attention. Not interested in nosy retainers, Alex flipped him a coin and waved him off before breaking open the wafer. *Something from his superiors?* he wondered. *Maybe Drake or Lord Thirsk?* Perhaps a change of plans. He was still waiting on any information about another operation going on up in London, a friend who was missing.

It wasn't from Drake. It wasn't from Thirsk. It was worse.

We believe you would want to know, the note read in precise, printed letters. *Your wife's letters have been found. We are holding them for you. There is a price, of course. You might wish to come to the center of the maze to wait for instructions.*

Alex found himself on his feet, the book forgotten on the floor. He suddenly couldn't catch his breath. His hand began to shake, making the paper rustle. There could be no question what the note meant. The Lions had reached him. They had found his one weakness, and they were about to take advantage of it. With a despairing look to the bookcase where he had been waiting for Ian Ferguson to appear, he walked out the French doors and ran down the lawn toward the maze.

Chapter 18

Sarah wasn't certain how long she waited in that relic of a church. She thought at least two or three hours. It seemed like years, each second weighing down the one before it until she felt caught in a morass of fear and loss. How dare Ian make her sit here alone in the dark with nothing but the memory of the last few hours to keep her company? How dare he not return to her, so she at least knew he was safe? So she could say a formal good-bye and escape before she made a fatal error. She swore she had never spent such agonizing hours in her life.

Only once did she think she had been discovered. She heard the secret panel rattle at the back of the confessional. Her heart seized, but the rattling stopped, and nothing else happened. She changed her position for one by the door, opening the warped, scarred wood a few inches into the old cloister and looking out into the darkness.

It only made her more anxious. She should have gone with Ian. She should have faced her brother, even if having her brother see her would do Ian no good.

Again, she shuddered. That was if Ian was still there.

She could see the east wing of the manor from the chapel, and no general alarm had gone out. No soldiers came thundering up the drive. The house remained dark and stubbornly silent.

She couldn't stand it. She had to get inside that house. She could only think of one reason Ian hadn't sent Chuffy out to her. And that was that Ian had never reached him. He was in trouble. She could feel the certainty of it thicken in her chest.

She had to find Chuffy Wilde. Chuffy would know where to look for Ian. It was the only thing she could think to do. She just had no idea how.

She couldn't use the tunnel. She had no idea what waited on the other side. No more could she walk in the front door. She was wrinkled and dusty and smelled of horse. No butler worth his salt would allow an unknown tatterdemalion across his threshold in the middle of the night, much less invite her to speak with the daughter of the house.

Sarah closed her eyes, trying to remember what Lizzie had said about her bedroom. A corner room. Sarah remembered because Lizzie had spoken of being able to see her mother's gardens on one side and the stone gazebo out the other. Which meant the back corner of the west wing. The duchess's gardens stretched from the parterre at the back of the house, and the gazebo graced the side knot garden. Sarah smiled. Now all she had to do was sneak over there and figure a way to climb three stories.

The grounds remained silent. Not even a guard dog or gamekeeper. Thankfully, the rain had passed, making her way easier. Sending a little prayer for luck, Sarah slipped out of the chapel and ran through the damp grass for the deeper shadow at the back of the house. Her palms were sweating and her mouth was dry. She thought her heart might just tumble out of her chest. She had spent more than one terrifying moment in her life. This, she decided, was the worst.

It took her ten minutes to circle the house, all the time alert for noises. At one point she almost changed her plans. There was a light on in the library. Her hands itched to open the window and peek in. Ian could be so close. He could be hurt, or need help.

No. She couldn't think of that. She had to move on. She had to get to Lizzie and pray she would help. Oh, lord, what she would give for an overgrown trellis.

Her prayers went unanswered. There was no trellis. No convenient vine meandering over the pale stones of the Ripton walls or trees growing branches that brushed the third floor windows. Not even a conveniently left ladder.

The lights in the corner bedroom were out, of course. They were out in all of the bedrooms. It was late even by London standards. Or early.

Sarah tilted her head, assessing her chances. There were no fortuitous vines, but there were balconies. They weren't directly above each other, but with luck they might be close enough to traverse. All she would have to do would be to climb onto the giant flower urns that bracketed the parterre to reach the first floor, then climb on top of that railing and reach up for the next. Pull herself up and repeat. So what if she would have to jump from the urns to reach that first balcony, and then leap again to the next without slipping on the wet stone and crashing to the ground? She could do this. She *had* to do this.

Finally, she thought with a rather frantic grin. *All of my tussling with Willoughby will pay off. I should have the strongest arms in Devonshire. Maybe when this is over, I shall hire myself out to a circus.*

She did waste a few moments contemplating the idea of tossing gravel at Lizzie's window. It seemed to work in gothic romances. If someone was in that lit library, though, they would hear it as easily as Lizzie.

Ah, well, nothing for it but to try. Wishing she had a bit of rope to tuck her skirts up, she wiped her hands along her dress and scrabbled atop the three-foot stone urn that graced the corner of the house. It took her a minute to gain her balance. Her half-boots insisted on slipping.

Praying nobody could hear the scuffling noise she was making, she reached up to find that the first floor balcony was just within reach. It opened from the green salon, if she remembered correctly, the site of more than one uncomfortable presentation. Taking a deep breath, she curled her hands around the balustrades. The stone was cold and rough and damp against her palms. Out in the woods, a small animal screamed, almost sending her over on her nose. Her heart would never recover from this.

Her feet swinging in the air, her dress belling out, her shoulders screaming with the strain, she pulled herself up hand over hand. She managed to get her shoulders above the railing and then strained to get a foothold. There. Narrow, but solid. She took a breath, recovered, then a lurch upright and over the railing to flop onto her back.

Lying there gasping, she stared at the lowering clouds for a bit. Willoughby, she decided, deserved a special treat. She never would have had the strength to get this far without her constant tug-of-war with him.

The next balcony was harder. She had to leap out into empty air to reach it. This time she was certain someone had to hear her as her knee connected with the stone wall with a crack and pain shot up her leg. She gritted her teeth and held on, knowing that if she slipped, she would definitely break something. Her fingers were cramping and her lungs were screaming for air. And her poor heart. It simply wouldn't survive. *Please, Lizzie,* she thought as she began the tortuous process of inching up the balcony. *Be in this room. And don't scream when you see me.*

Oh, and let the windows be open.

Not that it really mattered anymore. She would get those windows open if she had to smash them in with her head. She was taking too much time. The sky was beginning to pale to the east, and soon the staff would rise and catch her hanging off the balcony.

The thought must have distracted her, because suddenly she lost purchase. One hand slipped completely away. Instinctively, she shrieked and made a grab for the railing. She couldn't quite grasp it, and her other hand was weakening. She swung her feet hard, but she wasn't in a position to get a foothold. And she had too good a view of the patio she was about to fall onto. Her heart in her throat, she struggled to stay calm. She had a distinct image of herself lying broken on that stone.

"Don't . . . fall," she muttered, looking up.

She reached up again, throwing her whole body behind it. Success. She caught the balustrade and wrapped desperate fingers around it. For a moment, she just shut her eyes and held on, trying not to sob with relief. She wasn't completely successful. Oh, sweet lord, that had been close. She wanted to rest her head against her arms.

To take a moment before trying again. She didn't have the time. Focusing on her hands, she climbed. One hand. The other. Her leg, curled up beneath her, scrabbling for a hold.

With another ungainly lurch, she caught a foothold on Lizzie's balcony. She was sobbing with the effort, but she caught hold of the railing and threw herself over. And lay there, unable to do anything but gasp for air. She must have closed her eyes again. She was so shaken she wasn't sure. She just knew that it wasn't until she heard the window click open that she knew she had company.

She should jump to her feet. She should crouch in readiness. She should . . .

"Saint Swithin's sweet tooth. *Sarah?!*"

Sarah lay there like a lump staring up at the phantasm waving a large brass candlestick over her head. "*Pippin?*"

Sarah blinked. She blinked again. Lizzie. It should be Lizzie standing there.

Lowering the candlestick, Pippin crouched down next to her, her white cotton nightdress floating around her like a cloud. "My God!" she gasped. "It *is* you. What are you doing here?"

"Me?" Sarah retorted, still not moving. "What are *you* doing here? You're supposed to be in Ireland. And isn't this Lizzie's room?"

Pippin actually cast a quick look over her shoulder. "*Ssssh.* You don't want to give her away. I came to the house party, of course. Ireland had begun to pale."

Sarah blinked. She felt completely disoriented. She had to get up. She had to find help for Ian. But she couldn't comprehend what her other friend was doing here. As for Pip, she looked like a fairy child, her white-blond hair floating in a nimbus of curls around her piquant little face. She was smiling. But then, Pip was always smiling.

At least she was smiling until she took a look over the balcony.

"You *climbed* up here?" she demanded, her voice raising. "Are you mad?"

"Hush yourself. No one can know I'm here." Gathering her returning strength, Sarah pulled herself all the way up to her feet. "Where is Lizzie?" she asked, helping Pippin up as well. "I need to speak with her."

Gaining her own feet, which put her head at Sarah's shoulder, Pip took another look over her shoulder. "Well, in point of fact, I'm not *quite* sure. Can I help?"

Sarah shook her head, completely flummoxed. "What do you mean you're not sure? Pip, please. This is important. A life is at stake."

Pip shrugged. "She asked me to cover for her for a few hours. I decided I could do that better from her room. I have no idea where she is."

Sarah thought she might weep. What did she do now? "Do you know a man named Chuffy Wilde?"

Pip laughed. "Oh, everyone knows Chuffy. Come inside before you catch your death of cold. You're all damp."

"I need to reach him, Pip," Sarah said, following her inside and shutting the window behind her. "Do you think I can trust him?"

Pip turned from where she was lighting a spill in the embers of the fire. "Chuffy? Of course. After we get a bit of sleep, I'll introduce you."

"No. Now. Please, Pip. It is vital."

Instead of answering, Pip lit a lantern. Then, reaching up, she hugged Sarah hard. "I've missed you."

Sarah hugged back, suddenly desperate for her friends. "I have too, Pip."

Giving Sarah one last pat, Pippin picked up the lantern and led the way into a small sitting room, where she plopped down on a straw-colored settee. The room had to be Lizzie's, Sarah thought, distracted. Decorated in celandine and straw, it was restrained and elegant, deco-rated with simple lines and still lifes. Sarah was surprised by a wash of homesickness. Not for a place. For her friend.

Her *sister.*

"Now," Pip said, curling her feet up under her. "What brings you here in such dramatic fashion? You fright-ened five years of growth from me." Her grin was sudden and sweet. "And as we know, I can't waste a minute of that."

If it had been anyone else, Sarah would have hesitated. But this was Pippin, who had kept Sarah laughing all through the grim years of school. Pip who had organized forays with the younger girls into the countryside in search of fairies, who had painted the headmistress's room bright purple and convinced the local vicar that gruel was a worse punishment than the birch rod. She was the one who had saved the students at Last Chance Academy by finally getting someone to look beyond the facade of gentility to see the rot beneath. Because of Pip, Last Chance was now an excellent school.

Sarah wanted to curl up and lay her head in Pippin's lap. She wanted Pip to make her laugh. Instead, after di-vesting herself of her cape, she sat and gave Pippin as quick a recap as she could of recent events, ending with a plea for Ian's safety.

Pippin didn't close her mouth for five minutes. "*Fiona's* Ian? Really? Blessed Barbara's Bathwater. We thought he was...well . . ." She kept shaking her head. "My brother Alex is here. We'll get Alex."

"Ian said I had to find Chuffy," Sarah said. "He did not say Alex."

Jumping up, Pippin waved away her concern. "Don't be silly. Alex is perfect. Besides, I need him to wake Chuffy. If we're found in my brother's room at four in the morning, that's one thing. But if we're caught in a bachelor's quarters, Ian won't be the only one in trouble."

Sarah had to accept the logic. Besides, she needed all the help she could get. Surely she could trust Pippin's older brother.

Pulling open the door, Pippin snuck a peek into the darkened corridor. "Good thing nobody knows I'm here," she said.

The corridor was empty, the only light coming from a night candle at the stairway. "An adventure," Pippin whispered, and stepped out into the hall. "Excellent."

With another wave of her hand, she led Sarah down the hall all the way to the vaguely seen window, and then right through a portrait gallery Sarah had never seen. She wasted no more than a fleeting wish to see the family portraits before realizing that these people weren't her family. The portraits she should put in her own gallery would be of Pippin and Fiona and Lizzie. She didn't know if she would have the courage to include a painting of Ian. It would hurt too badly, she thought.

Ian. *Oh, where are you?*

Reaching another hallway, obviously the guest wing, Pippin tiptoed to the third door on the right and scratched on the door. There was no answer. Taking another look over her shoulder, she turned the knob and pushed the door open. Sarah wasn't surprised to see that she was grinning. Pippin adored high adventure.

"Huh," Pippin breathed, striding across the room to where a canopied bed rose before them. Empty. "Why, that sly dog. I wonder whose bedroom he *is* in?"

"There was a light in the library," Sarah suggested, staring at the tidy line of untouched bed linen.

"We don't have time," Pippin said. "We'll have to breach the defenses of Chuffy's sanctuary." She flashed another grin Sarah could barely see in the dark. "Gird your loins, Lady Clarke. We are about to do something quite scandalous."

Sarah scowled. "Pip, I have been kidnapped by a man wanted for treason, hidden with him in a barn, and climbed a wall in a dress. I think I left scandalous back at Fairbourne."

Only Pip would giggle.

Repeating the procedure of checking for witnesses, she slipped back into the corridor.

"You are having fun!" Sarah accused on a whisper.

Pippin shrugged. "I haven't been involved in a good clandestine activity since school. Of course I'm having fun."

"Pippin, this is deadly serious."

"You won't think so when you see Chuffy."

At first all they saw of Chuffy was a lump on the untidy bed. Navigating by the dull glow of a dying fire,

Sarah followed Pippin into his room. Pippin put her finger to her lips and climbed the stool by the bed.

"Chuffy," she whispered, shaking the lump. "Chuffy, wake up."

For a moment, Sarah thought they were going to fail. Nothing happened. Pippin repeated her command. She was just bending a third time when suddenly the bed seemed to explode in bedspreads and limbs and shrieking bear cubs.

It was the only way Sarah could think to describe Chuffy Wilde. A bear cub in a nightcap and bright yellow nightshirt.

"*Ssssh,*" Pippin commanded, her hand over the man's mouth. "Nobody can know we're here."

His eyes huge, Chuffy pulled her hand away. "You *can't* be here!! Ain't decent. Ain't decent at all, Pip. You could get me caught hard in parson's mousetrap, and I'd never forgive you. Don't want to marry. Not in the petticoat brigade. You know that."

"I do, Chuffy. This is something else. Were you told to meet Ian Ferguson?"

He not only reacted, he came right off the bed, all but knocking Pippin on her bottom. And there he stood, his skinny legs sticking out from beneath yards of yellow wool, his nightcap slipping over his ear, looking all around him as if enemies were approaching from the corners.

"You can't know about that." He waved his hands at her. "Shoo! Go away before somebody finds out. End up in prison *and* leg-shackled." He actually shuddered. "Don't know which would be worse."

"The leg shackle," Sarah said without thinking.

Chuffy jerked as if he hadn't seen her. "Who the devil is *that*?"

Pippin reached over to his bedside table and picked something up. "Here. Put these on. It will all make more sense."

He fit a pair of spectacles over his ears and peered through the darkness at Sarah. "Don't make a bit more sense. Don't know her. Don't want to marry her. Go away."

"We need your help, Mr. Wilde," Sarah said, immediately liking him.

"Baron Wilde, actually," he said with a drawing room bow. "And you are?"

"Not important."

"Is if I have to marry you."

"Well, you don't. You have to help Ian."

Again Chuffy jerked around, as if he'd back up against a galvanizing machine. "Stop saying that! Nobody can know."

"*I* know. I'm the one who has been hiding him. My name is Sarah Clarke."

Chuffy actually took another look around. "Where is he?"

Sarah's knees almost gave out on her, his words stealing her last hope. "You don't know? He was supposed to find you. He is here somewhere in the house."

"Can't be." He gave his glasses a quick shove and scratched his nose. "We met? I know an awful lot of people. Don't think I know you."

"Saint Simon's scissors," Pippin snapped. "This is a rescue, Chuffy. Not an at-home."

He shook his head. "No. Alex. He's in the rescue line. Not me. I'd muck it up."

Sarah was becoming frantic. "We tried to find him. He isn't in his room."

Chuffy nodded. "In the library waiting for Ferguson. His night. I take tomorrow. Why I'm sleeping."

"Can you go down and look?" Sarah asked. "Please. I led Ian through the Fairy Steps to the library at least three hours ago, and I have yet to hear from him. He said he would send you to me to let me know everything was all right." Tears welled, but she forced them back. "It can't be, can it? You don't know where he is."

Chuffy was frowning. "Not right," he said, considering. "Alex there. Must be."

"Ian would have fetched me," Sarah insisted, wanting to shake him. "I have been waiting for hours."

"She had to climb up the wall to my bedroom," Pippin said.

Chuffy gaped at Sarah. "No you didn't. Can't."

"Can," Pippin answered. "Did. Get dressed, will you? Go see if Ian is all right."

Chuffy started looking around again when somebody else knocked on the door. Sarah and Pippin spun around. Chuffy scowled. "Like Hyde Park around here. What?"

"You all right in there, old man? Heard you yell."

Sarah froze, her heart skidding. Dear God. She knew that voice. He couldn't find her here. She didn't realize she had grabbed Chuffy's arm until he patted her hand.

"Fine, Duke!" he called. "High bed. Fell out."

Sarah heard a chuckle. "You all right?" her brother asked.

"Bruised dignity. Prefer not to mention it."

"My lips are sealed, old boy. Good night."

"Was that the duke?" Pippin asked. "What is he doing in this wing?"

Chuffy gave her a look of disbelief. "House party. Could end up anywhere."

"Please, Lord Wilde," Sarah begged. "Check on Ian for me."

Chuffy went back to scratching his nose. "Need a reason to be down there . . ." His wide brown eyes lit. "Ah. Just the thing. Bruised nerves. Need brandy. Brilliant."

"You are," Pippin agreed, dropping a kiss on his cheek. "Now Sarah and I will turn our backs while you change."

Chuffy didn't precisely dress. He pulled on a pair of pantaloons and a chartreuse dressing gown and yanked off the nightcap, which only served to pull his hair into peaks, like a meringue. Pippin saw it and patted it down.

"Be careful," Sarah said, as Chuffy headed to the door.

"Don't worry. Never questioned." He flashed a winsome, sweet grin. "Benefit of lookin' dim. Worked since boyhood. Had nanny convinced m'brother was eatin' all the cakes." He shook his head. "One look at us woulda told the story. She never looked."

"What should we do?" Sarah asked.

"Go back to Pip's room. Safer."

And that quickly, he was out the door, his rolling gait making him look even more like a perambulating bear. Sarah took a breath, then another. It would be all right. She had reached Chuffy. He would take care of things.

She wished she believed that.

"Where do we go?" she asked, reaching for the door.

Pip ducked her head. "My room. End of the hall . . . oh, good lord. Now I'm talking like Chuffy. I have to retrieve my dressing gown from Lizzie's room." She pulled open the door. "Meet me there," she said, and pointed to the last door on the left.

Waiting to see Pippin tiptoe back toward the gallery, Sarah followed Chuffy toward the front of the house, where the stairway swept down across from Pip's room. It was so tempting. The house was quiet again. Surely Sarah could slip down the stairs and listen from the shadows. She only wanted to hear Ian's voice. To know that he was all right. To have the excuse to later soundly box his ears for frightening her so badly.

She reached the stairwell and took hold of the banister, a sleek line of mahogany she knew swept unbroken down three stories. She paused there, listening to a clock tick on the floor below and the house groaning a bit in protest as it settled. No voices. No outcry. Just the endless, precise passage of time.

She held on to her common sense and turned away, back to Pippin's room.

"What the blazes are you doing here?"

Gasping, she spun to face her worst nightmare. Ronald, fully dressed with a glass of brandy in hand, his neckcloth as mussed as his hair, was walking toward her.

"I asked you a question."

She didn't even hesitate. "I came to see my sister."

He sneered. "At four in the morning?"

"Would you have let me in at any other time?"

"I would not." Before she had the chance to move, he grabbed her wrist. "Why tonight?" he demanded. "Why now? You wouldn't have anything to do with my other surprise guest, would you?"

Her heart faltered. *Ian.* "Busy night, Ronald? I am sorry, but I came tonight because I have finally run out of money for the farm. Since I can make no other move until we know for certain whether my husband is alive, I thought to beg a loan from my sister. She has always been kind in the past."

She shrugged, as if it were that insignificant, when she knew he must hear the thunder of her heart. She could barely breathe past the panic that grew in her chest.

Fortunately, Ronald had too little imagination to distrust her. "Well…we'll just have to make sure. And then—" His smile was rapacious. "I will fulfill the promise I made to you."

"Which one, Ronald?"

"The one in which I told you that the next time I saw you in this house I would have you arrested for trespass and extortion."

She tried to pull away, but her brother was strong. Square and solid, with the blond Ripton features that had been so beautifully reproduced in Lizzie and less successfully on Sarah. The scar across his eyebrow was new, she thought. Not quite healed, like the slash of an epee. A fall over a fish knife, more like.

"Exactly how have I extorted you, brother?" she asked, knowing that it was the easiest way to distract him.

He smiled, which sharpened her fear. "Any way I decide."

She smiled right back. "You would actually have your own sister arrested?"

"I would have a thieving bastard arrested. Now, come along. Sadly, the town gaol isn't secure enough for anything more than the odd drunk. I think Ripton Hall can offer some lovely accommodations until the next assizes."

His hand like a vise around her wrist, he dragged her

down the stairs, the brandy still held in his free hand. Sarah tried desperately to think of a way to escape. Push him, trip him, punch him in the face. The problem was that each option would undoubtedly end up injuring her worse.

"There are benefits to being duke," he said absently, as if thinking. "If I cannot keep a trial and transportation quiet, I can simply make sure you leave and never come back. In fact, your husband's cousin is due here soon. He should be delighted to help."

Sarah shuddered. "You do business with Martin Clarke?"

"Who do you think introduced me to your precious Boswell? You can't imagine I would consort with a nonentity like him in the normal way of things."

She had always wondered how the marriage had been arranged. A month ago, she might have still cared.

"In fact," Ronald mused, "I imagine Martin will be most grateful if I get you out of his way. You have been a proper thorn in his side, you know."

"Don't be absurd, Ronald," she said. "You cannot simply make a woman vanish."

His smile frightened her all over again. "I admit I haven't tried yet. For now, though, it is enough that I have cause to accommodate you in the cellars."

She stumbled, sick at the thought. She had never seen the old dungeons. She had heard about them, though. An endless number of close, black, weeping cells constructed for the sole purpose of making their inhabitants lose hope.

They had almost reached the first story landing. Sarah knew that if Ronald got her to the cellars, she would lose.

She didn't think about it. She simply threw herself against him. He shouted as he lost his balance, the brandy glass flying from his hand and arcing into space. Sarah scrabbled for the banister as the glass shattered on marble two stories below, but Ronald refused to let go of her. End over end they tumbled, thudding like stones on the sleek, carpeted stairs, their momentum carrying them right past the first floor landing and all the way down to the marble foyer.

Bouncing badly, Sarah slammed into the floor. Almost instantaneously Ronald followed, his knee cracking into her nose and bouncing her head again. It was one insult too many. As her head cracked against marble, she saw a flash of brilliant light. She heard Roland screech like Willoughby caught in a fence. And then, nothing.

*   *   *

Closing the French door behind him, Alex Knight stepped back into the library and shook the water off his jacket. He was soaking and chilled. He was even more afraid. Afraid of what he would return to. Afraid of what he had missed. Afraid of what had sent him out to the garden in the first place.

There had been no one waiting in the maze, of course. No one anywhere on the lawn. Just a note, *Wait here,* sitting on the little stone bench that faced a fountain of Venus rising from the seashell. A Venus whose face he knew too well.

He had waited. He had waited for two hours, the weight of his cowardice bearing down on him. Finally he knew that it didn't matter if they came. It didn't matter if they brought every letter and freed him. He had to get back to the library.

Stepping over to his chair, he bent to pick up the book that still lay open on the floor. A quick look around the library made him feel exponentially worse. A casual observer would never have noticed, but several pieces of furniture had been moved. His brandy glass was missing from the table where he'd left it. He closed his eyes in despair.

"Were supposed to be here," he heard from one of the wing chairs, and felt even worse. He didn't even need to open his eyes to know who his accuser was. "Wait for Ian."

"I was called away," he said, his voice sounding flat even to his ears.

Chuffy shook his head. "Too bad," he said, and lifted what he had in his hand. A broken brandy snifter. "Think they got him."

Alex knew they had Ian. And it was his fault.

Chapter 19

Well, Ian thought, testing the ropes that held him to the chair, at least he'd been smart enough to hide the flask back in the tunnel. If only he knew where Sarah was. If only he knew she was safe.

Please, God, he thought, desperately seeking calm. *Let her have found Chuffy. Let her be well.* He could handle anything, as long as she was safe.

"I don't think you appreciate your situation, Colonel Ferguson," the silky voice insisted beside him. "We can do anything we want to you, and no one will care. When your body washes up on the beach in a few days, they will shake their heads and think how a traitor had met his just fate."

Ian laughed, even though it hurt. Hell, by this time, everything hurt. He could no longer see out of his right eye, his nose was broken again, and at least one tooth was loose. He didn't even want to think about his ribs.

"Wheesht now, lassie, if ye're trying to seduce me, ye'll have to do a better job. I'll wash up on that beach no matter what you or I do this evening."

He didn't even bother to look at her. He'd had his fill of the beautiful Minette, who had pulled up a chair and a glass of wine to watch her minion beat him into pudding. And that was before she had asked her first question.

"Too bad about your portrait," he said through his split lip. "It was a nice likeness. The crabs should be enjoyin' it."

At least he was able to put a crimp in her plans. It wasn't enough. He had to get out of here. He had to find out who had set him up. He needed to know why it had been these two thugs waiting on the other side of the library door instead of one of the Rakes.

And he had to know that Sarah had reached safety.

"You are saying that you lost my lovely miniature in the English Channel." The Frenchwoman didn't sound convinced.

He shrugged, his ribs grating. "Just like I did the last twenty times you asked."

"I do not believe you, me."

This time he grinned. He could at least win the little battles. "Paint another, lass. This one's gone."

She gave a little nod, and Ian braced for another blow. His ribs again, taking his breath and making the world dim. *Dia,* he was growing tired of this. If only he could get those ropes to loosen a bit.

"One of your friends betrayed you, Colonel," she purred as she rose sinuously to her feet, wineglass in hand.

She was licking her lips, as if she could taste his pain. Ian supposed he should have been repulsed. He wasn't. He didn't feel anything but impatience. He'd suffered worse than this at Salamanca when his horse rolled on him. At least this time he didn't have a musket ball in his shoulder.

There were quite a few people in this ill-lit cesspit: Minette, dressed in a low-cut red velvet gown and diamonds; four bully boys, lumpish ex-boxers with small eyes and big hands; and, most intriguing, an older gentleman who kept to the shadows, where his face couldn't be seen. Ian knew the man was older, because his hair gleamed in a silver nimbus in the lantern light. Thin, aristocratic, amazingly still. Ian would have given his claymore to know who it was.

"I realize you have a certain...rhythm to your work, Mimi," the man said in a soft, curiously sibilant voice. "But I really must insist on moving things along. I must go."

"Mimi?" Ian shook his head. "You're wrong. It's Minette." *Move into the light,* he thought, watching the man. *Let me know who employs this monster.*

It was Minette who answered. "Ah, but I am both, Colonel. I am...many things to many men." She sighed and sipped her wine. "And yes, *chéri,* Minette knows she must move along. She will hurry. First, though, the colonel needs to know that his so good friends turned on him. That he will never recover his name. He will always be called a traitor." Leaning close enough for Ian to smell the faint patchouli scent she wore, she reached out an elegantly manicured finger to wipe a bit of blood from his bottom lip. "That is, if he lives long enough to be shunned, *non?*"

Ian couldn't seem to turn away from her. She was looking at the dark red drop that slid down the pad of her finger, her pupils enlarged. Giving Ian another sultry smile, she put her finger up to her mouth and sucked. Then, as if experiencing sexual pleasure, she let her eyes slide closed. No one in the room so much as breathed.

"You know, don't you," she said, stroking his cheek with the damp finger, "that I am the one, me, who is the world's most proficient at the knife."

"I heard."

If nothing else, she was quick. Ian was still distracted by the smear of red on her full pink lips when he felt a sharp jab at the side of his neck. He hadn't even seen her unsheathe the bloody thing. She watched the knife pierce his skin. He held perfectly still. He wasn't about to give her more pleasure by flinching.

"It would be so easy to pluck out your eyes," she murmured, shivering. Ian knew damn well the shiver wasn't from disgust. The silver-haired man's was.

"I imagine it would," Ian agreed. "But then you don't need a knife to do that. I'd be happy to demonstrate on you."

She chuckled, and it was a sound of pure pleasure. "Ah, maybe another time, my colonel. Sadly, tonight for Minette must be of the business. She is not quite convinced of your story, you see. It is too convenient."

Again Ian shrugged. "Every once in a while—not often, mind you—things actually do go that way."

"Not this time, though, I think."

In the corner, the silver-haired man stood, careful to keep out of the light. "This is very edifying, Minette. But I have a schedule. Keep me informed, will you not?"

Minette never looked away from Ian. "Of course, *chéri*. It should not be long."

"Make certain of it." He walked out, his back to Ian, so

that all Ian could tell about him was that he was tall, thin, and wearing a signet with a ruby on his right hand.

Once the man was gone, Ian turned to Minette. He wanted to get back to the betrayal part. He was sure she was just goading him, wearing at his certainty. Even so. Could it be true?

Then she began running the flat of that damn knife right up his cheek.

"We will return to the flask, yes?" she said, sounding eminently reasonable, which sent sweat trickling down his back. "Let us spend a bit of time on who else knows of your…adventures. Who is this Tom Frane? Where did the letter go instead? To this Jack Absolute? I do not know this name. I thought I knew all your friends."

Letter. Oh, God, Ian thought, his heart plummeting. Sarah had been right. Someone must have seen the correspondence.

"Yes," Minette hummed. "A terrible thing, this, to have trust broken." Again she smiled. Ian felt a *frisson* of dread slither down his back. He had been interrogated by the best. Not one had unnerved him like this woman with just a smile.

Please God, he thought desperately. *Don't let Sarah ever have to meet this woman. Let me kill the bitch first.*

Just then the hinges creaked on the iron door, and another player entered the game. Even though he had never met him, Ian recognized him right away. Square, solid, and stolid, he had the obvious stamp of the Riptons about him. Blond, straight nose, high cheekbones, ears that made one think a bit of elves. So this was Sarah's brother.

"Ah, here you are at last," Minette cooed, not thinking to lift the knife away. When she saw that he limped, she tilted her head. "My dear duke, you are injured?"

He gave a wave of the hand. "Nothing important. An intruder."

Minette stilled. The bully boys all looked to her for direction. "An intruder is always important, *chéri*. Especially if it interrupts us. Tell Minette."

The duke actually ducked his head like a young girl. "It was nothing, I tell you. The old duke's by-blow looking for money. Stupid cow. As if the worthless slag thinks she can trespass on decent people."

Ian's heart stopped in his chest. Sweet Christ. *Sarah.*

Minette's expression became almost dreamy. "The old duke was your father, yes? So this must be your sister. What is her name?"

The duke scowled, shifted, as if he were uncomfortable sharing with Minette. Ian understood perfectly well. "Half-sister. Not worth speaking of. Her name is Sarah. Why?"

Minette was peering closely at Ian. The minute she began to smile he knew that somehow he had given himself away. "Sarah," she crooned, leaning close enough that Ian could see straight down her ample cleavage. "Is that not the name of the woman you kidnapped, my brave colonel? Can it be the same one?"

"Kidnapped?" the duke echoed, peering down at Ian. "What's this?"

"How interesting," Minette cooed, pointing the knife right at Ian's eye. "Minette, she says this name and his eye, it is of a darkness. Minette thinks he knows her, *chéri*. I think he *fears* for her, this *petite bâtarde*." She chuckled, finally lifting the knife away to consider it. "And Minette still cannot believe the handsome colonel here, he knows nothing. And is it not a lovely coincidence, this? That a woman named Sarah arrives just now. *Enfin,* something of interest."

The men in the room all waited in silence for her conclusion, Ian with dread.

Abruptly she nodded. "She is still here, my duke?"

Suddenly looking uneasy himself, the duke nodded.

"*Bon.*" She nodded and finished her wine. "It is good," she said, handing her glass to the second henchman. "Think of the enjoyment we can have with her tender flesh while we convince the colonel to share with us. Raul," she said, turning to one silent helper. "Would you enjoy entertaining this young lady the colonel worries over? Minette, she thinks the colonel would like to see you and I . . . *entertain* this lady."

Ian thought his heart would explode. It was all he could do not to erupt. He couldn't, though. Not yet. Not until he could get his hands free.

The duke took a step back. "Here, now," he protested. "Not the thing, ma'am. Not the thing at all."

Minette tilted her head. "You grow squeamish, duke? How so? You have helped us, have you not?"

He took another step back. "Smuggling," he said. "Brandy and laces. Not . . . *this.*"

"*This,*" she echoed, motioning to the room with her knife, "is part of what you have been involved in. It is far too late to be squeamish now, my duke. Besides, you say you hate this *bâtarde* of your family, who seeks to take advantage. Why protect her?"

"Because it isn't . . . *right.* She may be a by-blow, but

by heavens, she's a woman. I won't show you where
she is. And if I don't take you to her, you won't find
her."

While they argued, Ian worked on his wrists, tied behind him. At least the ropes were growing slippery, probably with blood. Another few minutes should do it.
Another few minutes would have to. He had to free himself before they could get to Sarah.

"You will not refuse, my duke," Minette assured him.
"You do not wish harm to your other sisters. Your mother.
Now, Raul and I will go see to this Sarah."

"No!" Ian blurted out, liquid with terror. "Nobody
knows anything but I. Leave everyone else out of it."

The words were barely out before he realized how big
a mistake he'd made. He felt sick. Minette's eyes had just
lit with triumph.

"You see?" she said. "The colonel, he will think while
I am gone about what he will do to save this *bâtarde* from
too much pain." Her smile grew rapacious. "But think,
Colonel. If you give Minette what she wants, I might keep
your little bird from any pain. Especially the harems of
Morocco." She smiled. "There are worse men out there
than Raul."

Holding the knife so that the faint lantern light slid
down the blade like warm water, she floated up to him,
an apparition in the faltering light, her eyes glittering
and cold. Lifting that obscene knife, she ran it down his
cheek, its touch whisper-soft, down along his neck, paus-
ing over the pulse in his throat. He was sweating freely
now. She knew just how to torture.

"It's pointless," he insisted, his voice raw and thick.
"I'm telling you that flask is at the bottom of the English

Channel. Tom Frane is nobody. It is a name for me. And Jack Absolute is a character in a play."

"*The Rivals*," the duke confirmed. "Why?"

"Another alias, Minette is thinking," Minette mused. "Good. It is a question we will put to this Sarah. Perhaps she knows."

Suddenly she sliced away Ian's sleeve, from shoulder to elbow. Then, still smiling, she took that knife and sliced Ian's arm, a four-inch cut that caused Ian to hiss in pain. She chuckled, her attention on the blood that immediately welled. He thought she might sip at that too. Instead she laid her knife in it, turning it back and forth until the blade was covered and dripping, as if she had perpetrated slaughter in this room.

"Now," Minette said, with a shooing motion of her hands. "Minette is impatient. Come, my duke. Come Raul," she said, floating out the door. "Let us be introduced to this Sarah. It will give our brave colonel here a little while to think on his answers."

"You truly won't stop this?" Ian demanded of the duke. "She is your *sister*."

The duke, his face a rictus, turned away. Minette, a hand on his arm, the knife still held carefully in the air, led him through the door, followed by one of the henchmen.

And then they were gone, and Ian was left behind with the rest. Fury surged in his chest. Terror. Guilt. He had brought Sarah to this place. He alone, because he was too selfish to leave her behind. And now she would suffer at the hands of the most sadistic assassin he had ever met.

He had to get out of these bonds, or heaven only knew what that beast would do to her. Sarah, who only wanted to keep her animals and her family safe. Whom he had dragged into this disaster without her permission. Sarah, who should never have to know that such evil existed.

He wanted to rip that door off its hinges. But Minette had left three henchmen behind with guns. "I don't know you," the tallest man said, his voice oddly petulant. "I got nothin' against you. But know this. Move a muscle, and I'll kill you."

"Worked for her long?" Ian asked, surreptitiously pulling at the ropes.

The small, mean eyes wandered toward the door. "A while."

"She doesn't let you share her prey with Raul?"

"The women? One day she will."

Ian shuddered at the thought. He shrugged. "Seems a bit unfair."

He could hear the man's teeth grind. Ian didn't even want to know what he was imagining. It was enough that he was distracted.

Ian worked his hands. Twist. Pull. Twist. Twist. Do it without moving his shoulders, so the men didn't notice. The ropes couldn't last much longer. Please God, they wouldn't last much longer. He had to get to Sarah before they hurt her.

Twist. Pull. Twist.

Snap!

Sarah had said she would like a berserker. If she saw him in that little room in that moment, Ian wasn't so sure she would feel the same. It was three against one, and the three never stood a chance. They just didn't know it until Ian erupted from that chair.

It wasn't easy. Each of his three opponents was at least

his size, and hired for their brawn. But Ian had been hired for his brawn *and* his brain. Grabbing the leader, Ian spun him right at the other two. The guns clattered to the ground. The men didn't. Ian smiled. When the first one bent to retrieve his gun, Ian slammed his knee into the *gàrlach*'s face. He heard the satisfying crunch of bone and spun again, landing a hard kick on the second man's knee. The third man charged, roaring.

After that, it was chaos.

It took longer than Ian had hoped and cost him another broken rib and a second blackened eye, but in the end the three henchmen found themselves hogtied on the floor, and Ian in possession of three guns, two knives, and a set of fine brass knuckles.

Grabbing the lantern from its hook on the wall, he strode to the door. He reached out and caught sight of the remnants of his right sleeve, soaked through with blood. What had that been for? he wondered.

He shouldn't have let himself get distracted. He was just reaching for the door when it slammed open right into him.

* * *

Ronald was going to pay for this, Sarah swore, struggling to keep the panic from swamping her. It was bad enough he had had one of his henchmen drag her down through the interminable cellars and dump her in this cobwebbed monstrosity. But just to make sure she knew how powerless she was, he had tied her to a chair and then walked out with the only light.

She was so cold. She hurt in a dozen places from that

ride down the staircase, and she was terrified to put her feet down. She didn't mind mice. Every barn in Christendom had mice. But the rustlings she heard in this lightless hell were not mice. They were rats. And Sarah hated rats. She had a memory of them crawling on her bed in the dark.

She wasn't certain if it was a true memory, but she knew that the orphanage the duke had placed her in had been a breeding ground for rats. She knew she had tiny scars on her toes from the three years she had survived before being adopted out. She *hated* rats. And Ronald said he was getting ready to put her on a ship to the Antipodes that was surely packed with more. Somehow she had to get away before he had the chance.

She was good at knots. She had to be. She could certainly untie these in the dark, she thought, even behind her back. And then, when she was free...what? The door was not just locked, but hidden behind a blank stone wall. All the better, Ronald had informed her while rubbing at his injured shoulder, to make sure she left without anyone knowing. Even if Pip and Chuffy Wilde asked where she was, all Ronald would have to say was that he had sent her on her way.

She would think about that when it came time to face it. First things first.

She had finally gotten purchase on the first knot when she heard the rattle of a key in the lock. She froze. Ronald had promised he wouldn't return until morning. Could it be someone had come to rescue her? Could Ian be looking for her?

Please. *Please.*

Not Ian. She battled tears. The door screeched open

to reveal three people standing in the hallway. Two of them held lanterns that cast a wild, sinister light over their faces: Ronald, looking oddly pasty and nervous; a behemoth with a hard smile and empty eyes. And a woman...oh, no. Oh, God. Sarah knew her. Gold hair that gleamed in the wavering light, and a voluptuous body straining a sleek red velvet gown.

Minette Ferrar.

Sarah realized then that terror had a taste.

"Ah, *madame*," Minette greeted her, stepping into the room. "I recognize you from the little village, *non*? You were there with the giggling girl. I remember, me."

She motioned to the big man with her, and he brought forward a chair. Holding her hand out in an oddly stiff fashion, the woman settled herself on it before Sarah and arranged her lovely red gown over her knees. "You do not greet your guest?"

"No," Sarah said thoughtfully, a snake of dread uncurling in her belly. "I don't believe I do."

She expected anger from the beautiful woman. Instead she got a brisk nod. "*Et bien*. There would have been no enjoyment with quick surrender. But I will have cooperation. I have promised that, me, and Minette does not lie."

Bringing her hand forward, she tilted it to show Sarah what she held. Sarah sucked in a breath. It was a knife. Long, thin, wicked-looking. Dripping in gore. Her stomach flipped with the sight. She could even smell its warm coppery tang.

"Beautiful, is it not?" Minette asked, her smile social as she tilted the blade this way and that to better show the congealing blood. "A tool for a master craftsman, *n'est-*

ce pas? I, Minette, am this craftsman. I create terrible beauty with my little friend. I created terrible beauty in your colonel just now."

Suddenly Sarah couldn't breathe. "My what?"

Minette actually giggled like a girl sharing secrets. "Ah, no, *madame,* do not dissemble. Not to Minette. She knows that you have a fondness for the colonel, *oui*? She knows you will miss him, which Minette regrets. I left him, you see, bleeding from a thousand cuts on my floor. He will not come for you, *madame.* Not anymore."

For a moment Sarah thought she might do what she never had in her life, and faint. Her vision went thick, and she was hot and cold. She battled a terrible sense of confusion. That was Ian's blood on that knife?

"I don't understand," she said, amazed at how calm she sounded. "What do you think I can do?" She turned to her brother, who was actually trembling. "Ronald? What part do you play in this? Isn't it bad enough you tie me up like a felon when all I wished was to see my sister? Do you think to terrify me with tawdry drama as well?"

Oddly, Minette leaned forward and inhaled, as if she were testing the air for smoke. "*Hmmm,* yes. You will, I think, provide much enjoyment. Go now, Duke. Your work is done here. You will be avenged."

Even more oddly, her brother paused, evidently torn about his actions. Sarah met his gaze and saw guilt, shame, anger. No redemption, though. He turned around and left, shutting the door after him.

Minette beamed, her knife held wide. "No one, you see, will save you, *bâtarde.* Not from Minette, and not from Raul. You see Raul here? Raul, do you think you will enjoy this tender flesh?"

"*Oui*, madame," he answered, stepping forward to finger Sarah's hair. "Raul prefers the yellow."

Sarah jerked her head back, struggling for composure. She had to think. She had to outsmart them and get away. She had to breathe past the terror that choked her.

If what Minette said was true, Sarah could not wait for Ian to come for her. Her heart lurched. Could this madwoman possibly be telling the truth? Could Ian be dead? Sarah couldn't think of anything but him, her great, courageous Scot, his life's blood seeping away in the dirt. Rage began to build in her chest. Despair.

"Now, madame?" Raul asked, catching Sarah's attention.

He stepped around, as if to untie Sarah. *Yes,* she thought, holding perfectly still. *Untie me. If I'm free, I will have a chance.*

Minette tilted her head. "Why, yes, Raul. In a moment."

The man nodded. "Will you mark her first, madame?"

Sarah's breath seized in her chest, and she swore her vital organs had liquefied.

Minette focused on Sarah. "Not on the face. It does not do to mar the merchandise. I know a man, though, who enjoys scars on a woman. Especially her breasts, *non*? You would enjoy marking her pretty breasts, I think, Raul. Is this so?"

His eyes grew black. "*Oui, madame.*"

She smiled. "Would you enjoy earning Raul's mark on your breast, *bâtarde*? Or will you tell Minette where your colonel has hidden his gift of the silver?"

Silver? What was she talking about? Sarah lost even that thought, when Minette slowly rose to her feet and bent to lift Sarah's skirt. Sarah froze. Minette smiled and proceeded to wipe the blood from her knife.

"The silver, *ma petite.* A flask of the most loveliness with a small painting inside."

The flask. Oh, dear God. What had Ian done with the flask?

Sarah frowned, as if she didn't understand. "Silver gift?" She shook her head. "I'm sorry. He bore no gift, silver or otherwise. I would know, after all. I had to undress him when he was injured."

Minette's smile grew coy. "It is not wise to disappoint Minette, *petite.*"

Sarah drew in a tremulous breath and shrugged. "It seems I have little choice."

Minette nodded absently and dropped Sarah's skirt. Sarah felt her breath whoosh out. She was just relaxing, even minutely, when Minette stepped right up to her. Eyes dilated, nostrils flared, the woman bent to nuzzle her face right into Sarah's neck. Sarah instinctively cringed. Minette chuckled and brought her arms around Sarah, as if she meant to embrace her. Slowly, sensuously, Minette inhaled. Sarah shuddered in revulsion, her body shrinking from the woman's touch.

"Ah," Minette breathed, running her tongue down Sarah's throat. "There is nothing as delicious as the taste of terror. It is of the greatest piquancy, *non*? Delectable."

Sarah could not stop trembling. She felt her stomach lurching and wondered if she would vomit on the woman.

She had almost reached a breaking point, when suddenly she felt that knife at her hands. Sarah gasped. Minette laughed. The knife tugged at the rope, and suddenly the knots were gone. Sarah was loose.

"You are free, *petite*," she whispered against Sarah's ear. "If you can reach the door, you can escape."

Minette straightened and backed away, never taking her gaze from Sarah's. Sarah fought another shudder. She wasn't fooled. Minette had no intention of letting Sarah go. Sarah didn't know how she knew this. Possibly the avid light in the woman's eyes. A hunter's eyes. A cat's eyes as he looked upon his helpless prey. Sarah hated her at that moment. Even so, she got to her feet.

"Oh, one more thing," Minette said with a huge smile.

Lightning quick, that knife flashed again and swept down the front of Sarah's dress, neatly slitting it down the middle and slicing a gash down her chest. So tidily was it done that Sarah only realized she had been cut when she felt blood slide down her belly.

Again she froze, suddenly confused, overwhelmed. Terror swamped her, the taste of it rancid in her mouth. Despair, dark as death, sucked the light from the room. From the world. She was bared to these two monsters, caught in an impossible game. And they were smiling, jackals perched at the edge of the light, waiting their moment.

She clutched her dress together. She would fight; she had no choice. But she would lose. This beast, even now unbuttoning the placket of his pantaloons, would take her up against the wall like a two-penny whore. He would slice her into obscenity, and the woman would watch, enjoying every whimper of pain and degradation.

Minette would expect Sarah to plead for mercy, to beg for release, ready to offer anything in exchange for her freedom. What Sarah suddenly realized as she considered the dark, thickening blood that stained her only evening dress, was that the game would be pointless. Sarah had nothing left to offer. Not hope, not honor, not truth. Ian was gone, taking with him any hope she might have had. Any light in a bleak world.

She would fight. She had to. She would never give this offal the satisfaction of seeing her beg. Pride, the only possession she still owned, demanded it. But if she did gain her freedom, it would make no difference. Nothing would.

Ian was gone.

"Now, *madame*?" Raul asked, his hand inside his pants.

Minette swept her hands out in acquiescence. "With my blessing, Raul."

Minette moved her chair to the wall and sat. Her avid expression made Sarah's stomach heave.

Oh, Ian.

She had one chance. Raul was distracted by the gaping dress. He approached relentlessly. It was no feat to look terrified. Sarah merely had to make him think she was frozen with it. Easy prey. She hated to move farther from the door, but as he approached, she backed up. She whimpered, one hand up. She watched Minette put away her knife and ease back on her chair as if she were settling for a night at the opera. Ian had been right, Sarah thought distractedly. The woman truly was a monster.

Too soon Sarah found herself backed against the cold, unyielding wall. She waited, sweating, even with the cold, dank air on her breasts, until the moment Raul stepped so close she was assaulted by the stench of him. Until he pulled his engorged member from his pants. Until he smiled, showing her the missing and rotten teeth in his mouth.

He took one step too many. Sarah rammed her knee straight up into his crotch. He screamed and fell forward. She clasped her hands and rammed them into his nose. Then when his head came up, she slammed the top of her head against that same appendage and heard the satisfying crunch of bone.

He screamed, a high, furious sound. She ran for the door. Minette was chuckling, as if she were watching a farce. She was also standing right in front of the door, her knife drawn. Sarah bunched her fist. She had no qualms about breaking Minette's nose too, knife or no knife.

But Sarah never reached the woman. Raul caught her. Grabbing her hair, he yanked her off her feet. He backhanded Sarah so hard, she slammed against the wall and crumpled to the ground in a senseless heap.

Her eyes were open. She could see him stride up to her. She felt him drag her into the middle of the floor. She couldn't seem to stop him. She couldn't seem to make her arms or legs move. She knew she would pay for her attempt to escape. She knew it was a game. How many times, she wondered, would they almost let her go? How many times would they punish her? She saw the blood pouring from his nose and was glad.

Minette must have given him a sign, because suddenly he backed away.

"You have injured him, *chéri,*" Minette purred from where she had reclaimed her chair. "Many fail. I shall reward you, me. You may try again. I will not intercede."

Sarah tried twice more. She failed, ending up back on the floor with her own nose bleeding.

"Tell Minette where the flask is," the woman said, "and Raul will let you go."

Sarah didn't bother to answer. Raul would do no such thing. Circling her throat with one hand, just as Ian had that awful Briggs, he lifted her against the wall.

Ian.

"You may punish her, Raul," Minette said from the corner in dulcet tones. "But do not forget. Only I may kill her."

Lights flashed at the periphery of Sarah's vision. Her feet didn't touch the floor. Again Raul's hand went down his pants. She only had seconds.

When Ian came, he came as a berserker. The door slammed in on its hinges so hard it bounced right off. Bodies poured into the room. Raul dropped Sarah. She collapsed to her knees, gulping air in great, ragged gasps, barely able to see.

Ian was all bloody, his eyes wild. And if that was the Highland battle cry, it was no wonder people ran from it. His roar ricocheted from the stone walls in a terrible wave as he barreled into Raul, who was even taller than he.

Sarah could barely see it, but she laughed. He was alive. He had come for her, just as he'd come for his sisters, not giving up 'til he found her. He would punish these terrible people. And then he would take her into his great arms, and she would be safe.

Someone dropped a coat over Sarah's shoulders and lifted her onto the chair by the door. Someone else shoved Minette out the door as the woman laughed.

"Stay where you are," Sarah heard, and nodded, never taking her eyes from Ian. Wild-eyed Ian. Battling, punishing Ian, who was beating the life out of Raul as inexorably as Raul had robbed the breath from Sarah's lungs.

She couldn't take her eyes from him. He had come.

"Chuffy," someone said. "Stop him before he kills the blighter. We need him alive for questioning."

Sarah turned to see Chuffy had indeed entered the room and stood alongside her, as if to protect her from the melee. "You tell him?" he asked her. "Turn me into talc."

She turned back to see Raul on the ground cringing beneath Ian's attack. Was she a terrible person that she felt such visceral satisfaction? Wiping the blood from her split lip, she shook her head.

Out in the hallway, there were new voices, thundering feet. Lights came and went. Sarah didn't move. She was waiting for Ian. When he was finished with Raul, he would come for her. He would warm her and chase away the terror.

"Ian!" Chuffy finally yelled. "Mrs. Clarke needs you!!"

Ian stopped so fast that Raul almost got in a lucky punch. "Sarah?" Ian asked.

"Give me the man, Ferguson," another man suggested, gingerly stepping forward to where Ian kept Raul upright by means of a hand around his massive throat. Sarah wanted to laugh. Raul was battered and whimpering from Ian's punishment. And his penis was still hanging out of his pants, now limp and ridiculous.

Ian let loose of him, and the man crumpled to the floor. Before Sarah realized Ian had moved, she was lifted and settled into a large lap, surrounded by the smell of rain and horse and lord, she swore she smelled heather.

"What is it you need, Sarah?" Ian asked against her ear, those wonderful arms cushioning her.

"Hold me," she begged. "Make me believe you're safe."

"*Me?*" he demanded, pulling her even closer with hands that shook as if he had the ague. "They couldn't hurt me. It's you who is hurt. Oh, my wee love, I'm so sorry."

Sarah looked up. He looked terrible, bleeding and bruised and torn. She had never seen anything more beautiful. She thought her heart might simply burst with joy.

"She told me you were dying," she whispered. "Her knife was so bloody."

He rested his forehead against hers. "Do you think I'd ever desert you, lass?"

That was then the tears came. Silent, steady, soaking her neck. "No," she said. "I believe I don't."

But she had. The tears grew to sobs.

He actually groaned as he stroked her back, stroked her hair, rocked her against him. "Oh, my lass," he whispered, and she could hear the torment in his voice. "I'm so sorry I wasn't here quicker. I died a thousand deaths when I opened that door."

"You didn't merely open the door, Ian," she said with an untidy sniff. "I believe you demolished it."

She could see tear tracks on his cheeks, which made her want to rock him in her arms, to soothe him with soft hands and murmured words.

"I had to save the woman I loved," he told her. "Did I get here in time?"

She quickly looked around to make sure no one heard. "Hush, Ian."

He gently rested his forehead against hers. "I love you. I loved you. I will always love you. You are the only one who will ever have my heart, *mo cridhe.*

He lifted a hand to cup her bruised face. She turned

into it and kissed his palm. "Yes, Ian," she said, knowing how much it meant to him. "You got here in time."

Something in him lightened. His eyes warmed, and he dropped a gentle kiss on her lips. "Come along, then, lass. We need to get you warmed up and decently dressed, and have that cut looked after."

"Yours as well," she said, letting him help her to her feet.

She was wobbly, but she stayed upright with his help. Someone handed her a blanket, and she wrapped herself in it. It was the first time she had a chance to see all who else was in the room. Chuffy was there, of course, and another man, handsome, lean, above middle height with dark curling hair. Sarah hadn't seen him in four years.

"Alex Knight," she said with a sore smile. "It is good to see you again."

"You know each other?" Ian asked, looking back and forth.

"Alex helped instigate an insurrection at Last Chance. His name is still sung among the litany of saints during Lent."

His expression oddly closed, Alex bowed. "Apologies that it took us so long to get to you, Lady Clarke."

Everyone else had already gone, she assumed. There had been a lot of noise in that room. Of course, with the cacophony her berserker had been making, she couldn't really assume he had much help. She wished she could just sit here holding onto him, making sure he was whole and well and safe.

"Will your name be cleared?" she asked, looking up at him.

His smile was wry. "I canna say yet, lass. The fact that I brought the flask back made a difference."

"You *did* have it then."

His eyes darkened. "I should have given the thing to her. I could have protected you."

Sarah didn't even need to answer. Both of them knew that nothing either of them had done would have swayed Minette Ferrar.

"Where is she?" Sarah asked.

"Safely tucked away. And Alex has the flask. When you're rested and warm and comfortable, we'll discuss it."

She clutched his arm. "Don't leave me."

She saw an entire universe of suffering in those bottomless blue eyes. "Not for a minute."

Not until his name was restored and he went home, anyway.

She refused to think that far. She had him now. Burrowing into his side, as if she could steal a bit of his strength, she followed him up out of the darkness.

Chapter 20

But of course, he did leave.

Sarah found out the next morning when she woke in a room at the end of Ripton Hall's family wing. Sunlight poured through leaf green curtains and skipped across a room decorated like a bower. The glossy hardwood floor was strewn in Aubusson carpets of pale yellows and blues, and gold gilt graced the white furniture. The walls were hung in paintings of gardens and a child's drawings of horses.

Sarah had never seen such a room. She had never once so much as dreamed of one. She wondered which of her sisters she had evicted. She wondered what they looked like. She had only ever known Lizzie.

She should have luxuriated in the unfamiliar comfort, the warmth, the peace. She reached over to the other side of the bed and felt her heart finally shatter. When she had fallen asleep the night before, Ian had slept alongside her, his arms around her so she could rest. The sheets were now cold. He hadn't even said good-bye.

She shouldn't have been surprised. She had felt her time

with him slipping away throughout the hours since they had climbed out of that cellar the morning before. Through interrogations, a doctor's care, and finally a visit from Lord Drake, all the while holding hands where no one could witness but the Rakes, who would never break their confidence. But Ian had to leave, and she had to let him.

She shouldn't have been surprised and she wasn't. She even understood why Ian had left without another word. It hurt too much. It hurt too much now, a universe of hurt. A hurt so crushing that the only way to breathe was to press her nose into the pillow that still held his scent. A hurt so trenchant that the only way to survive it was to remember that for at least a few days, a few searingly alive hours, she had been able to say that she had been loved by a berserker.

If she had been any weaker, she would have followed him. She would have done anything to be with him, ruin his marriage, destroy his honor, shatter his peace. But if her life had taught her nothing else, it was how to be strong. How to hold on to her self-respect, no matter what. Now that life had to teach her how to love without price. It had to teach her how to carry Ian quietly in her heart where he would always be hers.

In the meantime, surely no one would belittle her for expending a few tears. After all, no one would ever see.

She must have missed the knock on the door, because suddenly it was open, and a visitor was peeking in. "Are you awake yet, Mrs. Malaprop?"

Quickly scrubbing away her tears, Sarah slowly sat up. "Well, if it isn't Jack Absolute," she greeted her sister.

Guinea gold hair swept up in an elegant knot and clad in a periwinkle Indian muslin round gown, Lizzie looked every inch a duke's daughter. Sarah was surprised at the rush of emotion she felt at seeing her again after so long.

"Oh, Sarah," Lizzie cried, hurrying forward. "You're all over black and blue. Can you tell me what happened? There has been a lot of whispering, but the most I know is that you and Ian Ferguson came here and ran afoul of some very bad people."

Stepping up on the stool, Lizzie surprised Sarah by indecorously climbing onto the bed and sitting across from her, hands in her lap. "I understand you saved Ian's life."

Sarah did her best to smile. "And he saved mine."

But she would not be able to tell Lizzie how. It had been decided the day before that only the simplest details would emerge. Desperate criminals caught, and Ian hopefully on his way to vindication.

"You missed quite an adventure," Sarah told Lizzie. "Where were you?"

As if Sarah hadn't suffered surprises enough, Lizzie blushed and ducked her head. "Oh, nowhere interesting. But I am dying to hear about your escapades. Pip said that you scaled the balconies like a mountain goat. I wish I had seen it."

Sarah did grin this time. "Where is Pip? She had a part to play in this tale."

Lizzie didn't answer right away. Sarah was surprised at how suddenly stiff Lizzie looked. "I, uh, asked Pip to give us a bit of time. So we could...talk."

Sarah froze. There were tears in Lizzie's eyes, and she was clenching her hands together. Sarah could never remember such a thing.

"Lizzie?"

Sarah was going to ask what was wrong. But suddenly

she knew. She could almost hear the words piling up in Lizzie's head. The same words that had been collecting in hers since she had read the note and realized that Lizzie had known all along that they were sisters.

Suddenly there was so much to say; so much neither of them knew how to say. They had known each other since their twelfth birthdays, and yet they had never said the important things. They had neither admitted the truth they had obviously each known.

Lizzie looked so anxious, as if terrified of saying the wrong thing. Sarah didn't know how to help. What to do. What to say. So they sat there almost knee-to-knee, the two of them, silent and stiff and wanting so badly to speak.

And then, neither knowing how, they were hugging each other, and tears were silently streaming down their cheeks. They would never be sisters who giggled and talked and teased. They only had this small time to share before Sarah returned to her own world. But for those long minutes in the privacy of Sarah's room, the two sisters shared what they had never been allowed to before.

"I am so very glad you understood my note," Lizzie finally said, straightening to brush tears from her cheeks. "I wasn't certain you remembered."

Sarah straightened as well. She refused to let go of Lizzie's hand. Reaching up to tuck an errant wisp of hair behind her sister's ear, she smiled. "Don't be daft, Liz. How could I forget Jack Absolute?" Free hand on hip, she lifted her head. "'No, faith, to do you justice, you have been confoundedly stupid indeed.' I don't believe anyone else ever spoke the line with such panache."

"I didn't know what else to do. Chuffy and Lord Knight seemed so very anxious that no one could learn who sent the message." The smile died in her eyes. "But someone did learn, didn't they?"

Sarah frowned. "I wish I knew who. Has anyone said anything?"

Lizzie shook her head. "Everyone is very upset."

Sarah squeezed her sister's hand. "Well, it all turned out well in the end. Ian is well, I am well, and a very bad person is in the custody of the crown."

Just the thought of Minette and her knives sent a shudder through her. She hadn't even realized she set her hand against her chest until she felt the sting along the knife slash. She would go to her death, she thought, with the memory of that cellar catching her in unexpected moments.

"They all left this morning," Lizzie said softly. "Ian and Chuffy and Alex and Drake." She frowned. "They took Ronald to London with them. I have no notion why, since I cannot imagine how Ronald could be involved. But then, there is quite too much that I am not being told. Even mother has been frustrated."

Lizzie usually maintained a calm face, but now Sarah could see her impatience. "I suspect there is much we will never be told, Liz. I suspect it is safer that way."

Lizzie nodded. "I suspect. I must admit that I am frustrated that I missed all the excitement... although I would prefer you didn't say anything to mother, if you would."

"Good heavens," Sarah retorted. "Why would I speak with your mother?"

Lizzie's smile was rueful. "She knows you are here, of course. She forced Margaret to give up her room for you."

Sarah looked around. "I wondered." Margaret, if she recalled, was the youngest.

"Right now, however," Lizzie said, patting Sarah's hand. "Mother is focused on the potential disaster to her house party." For the first time since their childhood, Sarah saw an impish grin on Lizzie's face. "You must know that no party is complete without Chuffy, and the princess is due day after tomorrow."

Sarah chuckled. "I think I've never met another person quite like him."

Lizzie's expression grew serious. "Ian asked me to bid you farewell, Sarah. I don't believe he could bear to see you again."

Sarah could do no more than nod, tears welling again.

"You do love him, then?"

Sarah brushed at an escaped tear. "Oh, yes. I'm afraid I do."

"I'm so sorry, Sarah."

Sarah tried so very hard to seem content with her fate. "I remember when it was all of our goals to be a tragic romantic heroine." Shaking her head, she squeezed her sister's hand. "I fear it is not all we thought it would be."

Again Lizzie surprised her. Her own eyes suspiciously damp, Lizzie nodded. "I know all too well, my dear."

Sarah wanted so badly to ask how. She wanted to offer her sister the same sympathy. Sadly, before she could, the door pushed open again, and Lizzie's mother stepped into the room.

Sarah's reaction was instinctive. Pulling free of Lizzie, as if she could protect her sister by distance, Sarah climbed out of the bed and stood barefoot on the rug, her body harshly protesting every move.

The duchess, still tall and gentle and beautiful, with her modest brown hair and kind blue eyes, stepped up to take Sarah's hands in hers. "You should be back in bed, young lady. It seems you have seen the worst of my house."

Sarah felt herself dislocated, standing there and yet back in the sunny salon at once, a small, awkward girl who knew she was being judged and found wanting. The kindness in the duchess's eyes was the only constant. "Only your cellars, your grace. Thank you for your hospitality since."

The duchess helped her back up on the bed. "An easy matter, since you couldn't walk yesterday. I sent a message to let your family know you were here. I have just received their reply. They are glad of your safety and anxious to see you at home."

Sarah might have accepted the wishes with equanimity, if the duchess had not used that word. *Home.*

Poor Fairbourne. Could she continue to devote so much energy to it now that she knew it had never really been home? Would she fight so hard for it, or would she be happy to escape the place where she had spent the most devastating days of her life? Where she had met Ian and lost her peace.

"I will be glad to see them as well," she said, knowing it was expected. "If I might borrow a dress, I could be on my way now. I assume I am not needed anymore?"

The duchess looked vaguely surprised. "Since no one said anything to the point, I assume not. I do wish you would rest up another day before going, though, child. I could not in good conscience send you out on the road looking as you do."

Sarah smiled as best she could. "I am certain I look far worse than I feel, ma'am."

A lie, but the longer Sarah stayed here, the harder it would be to reclaim her life.

"Just until tomorrow," Lizzie pleaded. "You and Pip and I could toast cheese in front of the fireplace and tell lies, like we did before."

Even though it hurt, Sarah smiled. "'Til tomorrow."

As if she had been waiting for those very words, Pip pushed into the room. "I knew you'd say yes," she caroled, and ushered in a maid burdened with a loaded tray. Once again bestowing her gentle smile, the duchess made a strategic retreat and left the girls to their reunion. Sarah was provided with a dress of Margaret's, and a maid to do her hair, and various nostrums and creams for her hurts. But the best medicine was the laughter she shared with her friends.

Catching up took all day. Lizzie made tea, and they sat on Sarah's bed, and Sarah told as much of her story as she could. Pip spoke of her own years on the marriage market and the marriage offers she had declined in hopes that her brother's friend Beau Drummond would finally notice her. Lizzie, too, had passed three seasons without a match. She talked instead of her charities, and the help she had been able to provide her brother. There was no man in her life, she insisted, nor did she particularly care. Watching the faint shadows pass across her expression, Sarah wasn't so certain.

They toasted cheese and snuck pear tartlets from the kitchen and vowed that they would always be close. And for the first time, Sarah truly believed it. When she returned that night to her indecently comfortable bed, she lay awake holding on to her moments with Ian, with Lizzie and Pip, the people who *were* her home. And then she woke the next morning ready to return to Fairbourne.

"Are you sure you should go?" Pip asked, standing behind Sarah as Lizzie's maid arranged her hair for the last time. "How can we know you'll be safe?"

Sarah smiled at her friend. "My neighbors will help. As much as I would love to remain curled up in this room with you and Lizzie, I have work waiting for me. My animals need me. My family needs me."

"How can you call them your family?" Lizzie demanded, her serene face unusually rigid. "I have heard how they treat you."

"They are my family because I say so." And oddly, she missed them.

The duchess called her own barouche up, and met Sarah in the hall with a basket of food for the ride and a maid for countenance. Pip and Lizzie kept their silence, even though Sarah knew they wanted to protest. The only thing that made her leave-taking bearable was that Ian was already gone. If she had had to part with him in public, she wasn't at all certain she could have done it.

She was exchanging hugs with her friends in the high, echoing foyer when the great front door burst open.

"Oh, y'r grace," a footman gasped, almost knocking Sarah on her bottom, "'er 'ighness. She's 'ere!"

For a split second the duchess paled. "Oh, my goodness." Then, because she was the duchess, she smiled. "Ah, well. Have Barton gather the staff. Sarah, after the princess passes, we will be able to board you from the east door." Sharing a brief, trenchant glance with Sarah, she looked to the door of a small sitting room off the foyer. "Elizabeth, you will attend me, please."

Lizzie briefly looked as if she would rebel, but Sarah

never gave her the chance. Dropping a curtsy to the duchess, she quickly retreated through the door. It was another lesson in her proper place. As the ladies stepped through the great doors, she took her place in the little side room, cracking the door enough to see the princess pass.

She could see Lizzie give her hair a pat and follow the duchess to the top stair of the portico, Pip at their back and the majordomo behind her. From the bowels of the building, footsteps thundered up the steps, the butler directing his army like the best general. Sarah watched, enjoying the speed with which order was created from chaos. By the time the princess's ornate, crested carriage rolled to a stop before the steps, the staff, like their mistress, were in position, calm, collected, and ready to act.

Sarah found herself holding her breath. Princess Charlotte, the heir to the throne of England. Only eighteen and yet already enmeshed in international politics. The focus of a scheme to overset the government. In only a few moments, she would be close enough for Sarah to speak to. To warn.

One look at the girl settled that idea for the nonsense it was. Allowing one of the equerries to hand her out of the carriage, the princess, a prettily plump girl with speaking eyes, all but bounced up the stairs to greet the duchess.

"Cousin," she trilled, beringed hands out. "We are *delighted* to be here. Weymouth has been positively *gloomy*. It is a relief to be somewhere one can be assured of comfort and good company."

Like a strong wind, the young princess swept up the steps and into the house, talking nonstop, her hand in the duchess's as a train of staff and companions followed in her wake like the trail of a comet. Out on the front drive, what seemed a half a regiment of guards snapped to attention under the eagle eye of a tall, ramrod-straight officer.

Sarah couldn't help but shudder. Thank heavens she and Ian had not had to breach the manor after the princess had arrived. Ian never would have had a chance.

She took one last look at the princess's entourage. Could one of them be a traitor? Could someone already have the ear of the girl who would one day be queen? From what Sarah had read, Charlotte would seem an easy target for persuasion; emotional, mercurial, headstrong. The accounts had failed to mark her effervescence, however, her native intelligence. Her spirit that made one want to smile.

Comfortable that none but the servants remained in the great echoing foyer, Sarah stepped out of the small parlor and shut the door.

"Lady Clarke?" a man's voice addressed her.

She swung around to see one of the guests stepping back into the foyer. A bit under six feet, he was dark, with lustrous brown eyes, and thick, curling, almost black hair. Sarah had never met him.

"Do I know you, sir?" she asked.

He smiled, which almost made Sarah gasp. His face, which had been closed and saturnine, metamorphosed with that smile. Suddenly he was compelling, beautiful. Delicious. It was the only word one could use for him.

"I bring a message from Ian Ferguson," he said, his voice soft.

Sarah felt the air catch in her chest. "And that is?"

"He said to tell you that Raul has confessed in his part in Stricker's death, which clears Ian of any charges in the incident."

Sarah's heart stuttered. Her knees all but went weak. "The charges of treason?"

He briefly bowed his head. "That is a bit more complex. I hope that someone will let you know as soon as the matter is concluded."

Someone. Not Ian. No, that would be unwise. A sharp pain twisting in her chest, Sarah nodded. "Of course. Well, thank you very much, Mister . . ."

"Beau!!"

They both turned to see Pippin racing across the foyer. "You're here! Have you come with the princess?" Her smile grew impish. "Or did you decide you simply couldn't stay away from me any longer?"

So this was Beau Drummond, Sarah thought. No wonder Pippin had held out for him. She wondered if Drummond had an inkling of the depth of Pippin's regard.

He greeted her friend with a scowl. "Really, Brat," he said, his dissatisfaction bringing her to a screeching halt. "Haven't you learned basic etiquette yet?"

"Better than you," Pip challenged, her eyes squinted up at him. "You haven't even introduced yourself to Sarah." Quickly she turned. "Lady Sarah Clarke, may I present to you Beaufort William Villiers Francis, Viscount Drummond. Or, to those of us unimpressed with his lofty position, Beau. Beau, you have met Lady Clarke."

Sarah almost grinned. It had been a deliberate slight. It was simply not done to ask the commoner if she would be introduced to the viscount, and from the expressions on both Pippin's and Drummond's faces, they both knew it very well.

"I must go, Pip," Sarah said. "I am certain the coach is here."

"Talk her out of it, Beau."

He frowned. "Why would I ever do that, Brat? Now, if you don't mind, I am here to attend the princess."

Poor Pip. Sarah could see that she was torn between saying good-bye to Sarah and following the man she loved. Sarah made it easy for her. Giving Pip a crushing hug, she strode off toward the east portico before Pip could object. Her conveyance was finally here. It was time to go home.

*　*　*

The next three weeks were the hardest of Sarah's life. She did return to the farm and resume her duties, but everything was different. At first she was feted as something of a heroine. Word had gotten around about Ian's daring capture of a dangerous spy and Sarah's part in the adventure. The entire household clucked and fussed over the fading bruises on her face and the dowager made much of her own trials. Artemesia declared herself in love with one of the militiamen who had come to set them free.

Just as Sarah hoped, routine quickly returned. Within two days the dowager was back walking the undercliff with Rosie, and Artie was enjoying the status of Brave Victim among her friends. Willoughby greeted Sarah as if she had deserted him for a year with no food. However, he did stay closer to home.

Sarah found that she faced the usual drudgery with more tolerance and her little family with more patience. They had not become good friends overnight, but Sarah thought they understood each other better.

She failed to regain her hard-won contentment,

though. She went to bed each night aching to share all the little incidents of the day with Ian. To hear his hearty laughter at her neighbor's antics, or Willoughby's latest passion. She dreamed of his arms and woke restless and hungry for his lovemaking. But the worst was that she had been right on that night Ian had taken her from the house. When she had walked out that door, she had left the known world and entered a place she didn't recognize. She had been forced to strip away all the lies she told herself to make her loneliness bearable. What she had once tolerated now grated like sand against her skin. What she accomplished meant nothing but another day of work. What she had celebrated as victories became nothing more than another day of drudgery in a world gone gray.

At least she had been able to close one chapter in her book. Boswell finally came home from the wars.

It was George who brought the news. Grim-faced and gentle, in his best Sunday suit and shined shoes, invited into the Oriental Salon. "I wanted to bring you the news soon as I heard, your ladyship," he said, and knelt at the older woman's feet. The dowager's face went white. "I have some friends," George said. "They travel to Belgium, you see, and I asked them to look. For Boswell." He briefly bowed his head, cleared his throat. "I'm sorry, my lady. I'm so very sorry."

The dowager never wept. She simply grew still, her usual histrionics absent in the face of true tragedy. "My Boswell is coming home," she said finally, holding tightly to Miss Fitchwater's hand. "I am glad. A man should rest on his own land."

Sarah, sitting across from the dowager, saw real, raw grief briefly twist the dowager's face. Then her eyes bright with unshed tears, the older woman rose to her feet, and everyone else followed. "My thanks, Mr. Clark," she said to George. "You have been a good friend to this family."

And then, taking the grave young man's hand, she offered a smile. Just that. And Sarah could see that another lost child had been acknowledged.

It was Rosie who led the dowager from the room, quiet, solid Rosie, who had always taken better care of the dowager than the baron ever had.

They had just reached the door when Lady Clarke stopped. "Will you . . . speak to Artemesia when she returns, Sarah? She will need your strength, I think." She paused to look about the room, as if memorizing it. "And contact Mr. Clarke. He needs to know."

George cleared his throat. "Afraid that won't be possible, ma'am. Martin's gone."

Now Sarah stopped and stared. "Pardon?"

George didn't exactly smile. "Seems he was headin' up a pretty violent gang of smugglers. Been plaguing the coast for years. When the army came to arrest him, they found that he'd left the country. Jamaica, they think."

The silence in the room was profound. Had Martin been targeted because of Martin's connection with the traitors, Sarah wondered, or as revenge from Ian?

"He left Mrs. Clarke behind," George continued. "She says that she'll have enough to bring her own estate about. She'd rather not worry about this one as well."

Sarah lasted until the dowager left the room, then sat hard on a lacquered chair. She lifted a shaking hand to her mouth. It was too much, as if good fairies had suddenly decided to grant her most important wishes. The ones that could be attained, anyway.

She turned to George. "George, thank you. I don't . . ."

But all she saw there was grief for his brother. George would mourn Boswell most of all. He gave that odd quirk of the head. "He wanted it taken care of," he said. "So you'd have the chance to make the right choice."

Sarah startled. "What? Who?"

"Oh," he quietly said, an eye to the dowager as she climbed the stairs. "One more thing. There won't be no trial for Corporal Briggs. Pardon my sayin' so, it only would have hurt you. So Briggs found himself impressed in the Navy and glad for it. You'll never see him again."

Then, plopping his hat on his head, he gave her a quick nod and walked out.

From that moment, life changed. An unacknowledged weight lifted. The women put on their blacks and spent their little money on a proper funeral for Boswell, who would now rest with his father in the churchyard. They remained balanced at the edge of poverty, counting pennies and hoarding staples. But once again they worked for themselves. And it appeared Artie would indeed be able to rejoin her friends at school.

Sarah never asked George how he had managed to move Boswell, or if he knew the whole story of Boswell's last days. She didn't know how. But from that day on, he stood an even more vigilant friend to the Clarke women.

Nothing, though, lifted Sarah's loneliness. Nothing filled the aching emptiness Ian Ferguson had opened in her, or made it hurt less. Hard work at least wore her out. So she worked, coming in late to meals and getting up early to repair buildings and fences and prepare her estate for winter. And, one bright autumn day, when the sky turned the exact shade of a certain Scotsman's eyes, Sarah took up a shovel and walked out to replant Boswell's roses.

Before she sank her shovel into the loamy soil, she spent a moment considering what Boswell had so loved about this place. With gardens surrounding it and the sea stretched out endlessly before it, it stood almost out of sight of the house. The only sounds she could hear were the soughing of the wind through the firs, seagulls crying like children, the sea contentedly purling up against the shingle beach below. The sea sparkled beneath that high sun like a blanket of gems, and down below she could see some intrepid fossil hunter with his little hammer in hand.

It *was* peaceful, she thought, sinking onto the little bench. She had forgotten quite what peace felt like. So she sat in Boswell's place and said a final farewell to the man who had tried as hard as he could, and she forgave him for being so human.

She had just picked her shovel back up when she heard the slam of the kitchen door and a woman's shout. Sarah rose to see Mary Sunday running through the garden, skirts clutched above her ankles. Sarah smiled. What disaster loomed now?

Then she saw Peg follow Mary out the door. "Miz Sarah! Miz Sarah!"

Sarah began to walk their way. "Good heavens, what? Is the kitchen on fire?"

"A carriage!" Mary Sunday squealed. "A fancy one, with a seal and such!"

Before Sarah could even lay down her shovel, Artemesia popped out the door. "Sarah, hurry!" she urged. "It's coming here!"

Sarah could see nothing on the lane, but she trusted the

servant's grapevine. Reaching around to untie her work apron, Sarah quickly followed Mary Sunday back across the garden. "A seal, hey?"

"A crest!" Artemesia panted. "Old George just rode up to warn us. It should be here any minute."

Feeling an odd sense of uneasiness, Sarah led the household inside. She was expecting no one who painted a lozenge on his door. She couldn't imagine anyone like that ever approaching, unless Martin had come home. By now she knew better than to expect anyone else.

By the time she had washed up and made it to the foyer, Parker was just tugging open the front door. There was no question. Four perfectly matched grays were pulling an elegant coach to the house, its panels decorated in a very elaborate crest. Artemesia sighed in ecstasy. Sarah tucked her hair beneath her cap and twitched her skirt straight.

"Oh, who could it be?" Artemesia whispered in dread tones. "I wish *Maman* were here. She would know what to do."

Sarah smiled, deciding to forebear reminding Artemesia that Lady Clarke wasn't the only one in the house who knew how to greet someone with a title.

Then she recognized the crest. She froze in the doorway, completely speechless.

"Oh, my stars," Artie gasped behind her. "The Duke of Dorchester." She squealed. "A duke! A *single* duke! Oh, I look perfectly *frowsy* in black. What will he think? What should I say? How low do I curtsy? Oh, Sarah, I think I'm going to faint."

Sarah spun around on her. "If you do," she warned. "I shall step right over you. Now take a breath."

They stepped out onto the portico together just as a footman jumped down from the back to pull down the steps. Suddenly Sarah was afraid that she was the one who would faint. Her brother was climbing out of the carriage, and he was smiling.

It wasn't a bright smile. More a polite rictus. But he was here. And he was dressed for a formal call, impeccably turned out in a corbeau kerseymere coat and buff trousers, his hair brushed into a Brutus and at least six watch fobs dangling from his waist.

"Your grace," Sarah greeted him with a proper curtsy, which Artie duplicated.

"Sarah, my dear," Ronald said, climbing the steps toward her. "I believe I have a pleasant surprise for you."

She wasn't paying attention. There was someone else getting out of the carriage. Someone clad in a scarlet uniform jacket. Someone with shoulders the size of tree trunks and eyes the color of an autumn sky.

"*Ooooh*," Artie sighed. "Look at those *knees*."

Ian was in the uniform of the Black Watch, and his kilt swung at his knees as he walked, just as Sarah had always known it would. Stepping up beside Ronald, he gave her a crisp military bow.

Sarah was almost surprised she recognized him. He was a different person than last she'd seen him. Tailored, trimmed, barbered, and bathed to within an inch of his life, he embodied the dignity, the valor, the spirit of the Highland Brigades, and she thought she might weep.

She held out her hand. "Welcome, Colonel. You have retained your commission?"

Bending over her hand, he nodded. "I did, thank you, ma'am. Would it be possible to speak with you?"

Sarah couldn't seem to come up with an answer. She was still trying to overcome the flash of heat his touch set off, to quiet her thundering heart.

It was Artie who saved her. "Of course you can," the girl said, waving them up the stairs. "I don't know what's come over Sarah, but come, please, join us for refreshments."

Sarah kept staring. Where was her wild Scot? What had happened to the man who had laid waste to her peace of mind? Where had that mad grin gone?

Why was he here?

"Oh, um…yes." She stepped back to let them past. "Please come in, your grace. Colonel."

Ronald trotted up the steps and held out his arm for her. "You truly wish to be that formal with your brother, Sarah?"

Sarah almost collapsed on the spot. Ronald grabbed her hand, laid it on his elbow, and all but pulled her into the house. Behind them, Ian repeated the offer for Artie.

"Brother?" the girl whispered, her voice shrill. "What does he mean?"

Sarah finally came out of her stupor. Leading them all into the Rose Salon, she made formal introductions, which left Artie pink-faced and stuttering.

"We heard about Sir Boswell," Ronald was saying, sounding quite sincere. "Mother and Elizabeth send their most sincere condolences. If there is anything we can do, please let us know."

Sarah found herself staring again. What in the devil was going on?

She regained her sense to find them all clustered in a group by the settees. "Your Grace, Colonel Ferguson, may I formally present my sister, Miss Artemesia Clarke? Artemesia, His Grace the Duke of Dorchester and Colonel Ferguson."

The men bowed. Artie gaped like a yokel. "You're ... *oh!*"

Ian flashed her his best smile. "Aye, lass. I am. Oh. I'm glad ta see ya fared so well from my last visit."

Unable to take her eyes from Ian, Artie bobbed again.

"I think the duke, the colonel, and I need to speak privately now," Sarah said, gently guiding the girl to the door. "After that, Artie, I believe tea sounds wonderful."

Even when Sarah closed the door, Ian kept his distance, waiting for Sarah to sit before taking the settee opposite and balancing his busby on his knee. Ronald kept his feet. Sarah didn't know what the two of them were about, but suddenly she was having trouble breathing.

"I know you must be surprised," Ronald said, fiddling with his watch fobs. "Fact is, Sarah, the duchess and I have spoken. We think it long past time you were acknowledged by the family. Can't hurt father anymore. Can't possibly mistake you for anybody else. We would be delighted if you would come visit Ripton."

The last time Sarah had seen her brother, he had been deserting her to an assassin. The sudden *volte-face* was too much for her to take in. Gaping a bit herself, she turned to Ian for an explanation.

"Discretion and valor, lass," he said, his eyes too grave for Ian. He looked nervous, by God. "The man's trying to make amends. But only if you say so."

"And if I do not?"

Ian shrugged. "He takes a long vacation in the Antipodes for his part in the smuggling of French spies."

Ronald reddened unpleasantly. "I had no *idea...*," he protested, as if it wasn't the first time.

"I think you had an idea when you left me with that woman," she said. "I think you knew just what she was, and yet you abandoned me to her."

"She would have hurt my mother!" he protested, and Sarah was frustrated to realize that he actually sounded distressed. "Lizzie and Maggie and Caroline. How could you expect me to sacrifice them?"

She couldn't, of course. And she wasn't certain she would have been any braver.

Still, for just a second, Sarah was tempted. Didn't she deserve some revenge for all those times he had threatened her? For the insults and banishments? For selling her into marriage so he didn't have to acknowledge her?

It would mean so much to her, though, to normalize relations. She could actually visit Lizzie. She could get to know her other sisters.

Oh, she didn't understand any of this.

"All right," she heard herself say instead. "Amends are made. What now?"

Ronald actually slumped against the mantel. Pulling out a crisp monogrammed handkerchief, he mopped his brow.

"I am doing it for Lizzie," Sarah told him. "And the duchess. Not for you."

"And what about me?" Ian asked.

He actually startled Sarah. She looked up to see that he had gained his feet. "What *about* you?" she asked, her voice breathy and frightened.

She had the most unnerving urge to run out that door before he said another word. She couldn't bear many more cycles of hope and disappointment. She couldn't bear, she realized, to see him if he was only going to leave again.

"All right, duke," he said, not looking away. "Ye've done y'r job. Awa' wit' ye."

Sarah's view was taken up with Ian. Only Ian. She suddenly felt as if her heart would explode. "If you'll step outside, your grace, my sister by marriage would be delighted to serve you tea in the Oriental Salon."

He must have gone. She didn't know. "Why did you do this?" she asked, her voice trembling and uncertain.

He stepped closer. "Help the duke see the light? It was the right thing to do."

"Fustion. No one has been able to convince him to do the right thing since he was in short coats."

He shrugged, his movements stiff. "It's much easier to make the right decision if the alternative is being arrested for treason."

"Then you made him do this."

He shrugged. "I but offered encouragement."

"I assume you also had a hand in Martin Clarke's arrest and Corporal Briggs's new career."

He offered a small smile. "I am, at heart, a tidy soul."

She drew a breath. "You helped George bring Boswell home, didn't you?"

"Oh, lass," he said. "I'd do far more than that for you."

Suddenly he was on his knee.

She jumped up as if he'd hit her. "Stop that!"

She backed away. He regained his feet, blushing, of all things. "Will ye listen to me, lass? I've practiced this speech a thousand times all the way down from London."

"No," she said, truly frightened. Would he offer again? Would she have the strength to say no? "I don't think I will.

I thank you, Colonel, for everything you have done. I cannot possibly repay the boon you have granted my family."

He stepped closer. "But you can."

She stepped away again.

Suddenly Ian was laughing. "Lass, stop. Ye're beginnin' to look like y'r practicing the waltz."

She pointed at his feet. "Well, stay where you are."

He held out his hands, but he didn't move. "Could we at least sit again?"

"As long as you don't go anywhere near your knees."

His grin broadened as he followed her back to the settees. "I am exonerated," he said baldly, the minute he sat.

Sarah felt the blood drain from her head. "Oh."

How odd. She felt she was going to faint.

"Sarah?"

She looked up to see him frowning down at her. Tears burned her throat. "Oh, Ian, I am so very glad. Have you been to see Fiona and Mairead?"

He was frowning again. "Alex and Chuffy are going I...um, I cannot go just yet."

She matched his frown. "Why?"

Before she could react, Ian was sitting next to her, her hand in his. "Lass, tell me now. Do you truly love me?"

She stopped breathing. "What?"

Was he perspiring? "Do you love me? You said so, but you were under considerable stress. I need to know."

It was too much. She had dreamed this so many times, deep in the night when impossibilities seemed probable. She had spent so much of herself to sacrifice it. Before he could stop her, she lurched off the coach again and fled across the room. He stood and faced her.

"Don't do this to me," she begged, hands fisted.

She couldn't take her gaze from his face. There were new scars, at his lip and his eyebrow, still a bit raw after all this time. His nose had changed shape again, oddly enough, straightening. She hadn't thought she could love it more.

"I must," Ian said, stepping up to reclaim her hands. "If you answer me this question, lass, I'll tell you why I came. Why your brother and I dressed up all in our Sunday best to greet ye."

She laughed, the sound sore. "Of course I love you, you great lummox. Do you think I give myself to any ox I happen to run across in a hayloft?"

His smile appeared, his eyes glowing like the sky, and the dimple peeking out in his cheek. "Nay," he said. "I don't. Which is why I've screwed up my courage and come here today. To beg you to become my wife. To be my wife, my lover, my helpmeet. To soothe my temper when I have to deal with idiots and cheer me on when the cause is just. I need your sense and your humor. Oh, please, lass. Come awa' with me."

She knew she was gaping at him. "How dare you?" she demanded, the tears filling her eyes. "How *dare* you do this to me?"

He stepped back, muttering. Dragging both hands through his hair, he laughed. "Oh, lass, you make me crazed. I have this all backwards. Will you sit again if I promise to stay off my knees? They're getting' fair chapped anyway."

She couldn't think. She was so tempted to walk out the door before he tempted her beyond endurance. But she sat, just as he asked, clasping her hands in her lap where they would be safe.

Ian nodded and began to pace. "I forgot to tell you a few things. Important things. First, it seems I'm no longer engaged."

The only thing preventing her from launching back to her feet was the sudden hold Ian had on her hand. "What?"

Claiming the seat next to her, he flashed her a rueful smile. "Being dead actually worked to my benefit, if you can believe it. The marquess was so disgusted with me that he personally went to Ardeth's father and let him break the contract."

"But what about Ardeth? I thought she was going to change the world with you?"

He ducked his head. "After I explained about...well, you and me, she let me go. Ardeth may be committed to change, but not if it means she must spend her life with a man who loves someone else."

It was Sarah's turn to rub at her face as if it could rearrange the thoughts whirling madly in her brain. "But Ian," she cried. "Nothing else has changed. I am no different."

He claimed the other hand as well. She let him. "Ah," he said, "but you see, you're wrong. Everything has changed. As of today, you are the acknowledged sister of a very powerful duke. You are officially welcome at the ducal seat like the family you are. That little skint of a brother of yours will even legally give you the Ripton name if you so wish. Sarah," he said, pulling her close. "You are no longer nameless."

Tears, again. Hot, thick, clogging her throat and wetting her cheek. "You did this for me."

He laughed. "Don't be daft, girl. I did it for me. Do you know what I've been doin' the last three weeks? Minglin' with Sassenach toffs. And I tell ye, I refuse to do it again unless ye're at my side. So even if ya stay away from me thinking it will help, I still willna accomplish anything. I need my own lass with me to give me courage."

Gently he tipped her head back. "Please. Say yes. We'll bring the women with us if you want. We'll bring Willoughby the pig, and lovely Elinor and their babies, and Mary and Martha, and oh, I have a new Rachel out in the carriage. She's a grand, pretty little bird, all spruced up and waitin' to meet your rooster. We'll set our house up any way you want. Just tell me you'll have me, lass. Please."

She could barely speak through the fresh tears. "You bought me a chicken?"

He laughed. "I swear, lass, I canna think of another woman who could say those words and make it sound as if I'd dropped diamonds on your head." Suddenly his smile died, and Sarah thought he looked as if he clung to his last hope. "Sarah. Please."

After everything, it really wasn't that difficult to give him her answer. Her hands clasped in his, she looked up into those honest, loving blue eyes, and she smiled. "Only if I can be there when you break the news to your grandfather. I wouldn't miss his reaction for anything."

Ian's shout was so loud that the rest of the household poured back in the door. Before Sarah could demur, Ian called for champagne. Peg brought dandelion wine, which was all they had, and everyone celebrated, even Ronald, which didn't surprise Sarah as much as she thought it would. After all, she was saving him a very unpleasant boat ride. And then the party began all over again when Lady Clarke and Rosie returned from their jaunts and Ian formally asked permission from both the dowager and the duke for Sarah's hand in marriage.

It was only later in the early hours of the morning when Ian had snuck back into Sarah's bedchamber for a bit of private celebrating that he admitted the rest of the truth.

"Um, there is one other pesky little detail to address," he whispered, dropping kisses along her collarbone.

Sarah sighed, her toes curling with the most delightful afterglow. "It will wait 'til tomorrow."

"Nay. I'm afraid not. There will be too much happenin' tomorrow. Extra hands on the estate to meet, more victuals to sustain us all, a vicar, and a special license."

She rose on her elbow. She tried to level a glare on him, but she was too distracted by how endearing he looked with his hair tousled from lovemaking. "You *have* been busy."

He gave her a bashful look. "The fact is that no matter where we decide to live, we can't leave quite yet. I'm still in hiding." He began to play with her hair. "If you want the bald truth of it, lass, no one knows yet that I've been exonerated."

"Why?"

He slid his finger down her cheek. "Ah well, it seems there was a witness to my...tête-à-tête with Madame Ferrar. An older gentleman who looked like one of the most stiff-nosed Sassenachs I've ever met. You didn't see him, did you?"

She shook her head.

He nodded. "I thought not. The problem is, I never got a good look at him, and Drake is worried that he'll come after me before we can identify him. So I am officially still missing in action. Until I am told different, I'm to dye my hair, start growing my beard again, and remain right here on your farm."

She blinked, still trying to focus on something besides the heat of Ian's body. "Why do they think they can protect you better here?"

"Because your neighbors will spot a stranger faster than anyone will in London. Because Old George has a band of men who will be happy to help." Suddenly he couldn't look at her. "Because someone intercepted the line of carriages carrying Minette Ferrar to prison and managed to get her loose, and...well, Drake and Thirsk prefer to know where we are until they catch her."

Sarah sat up so fast she almost cracked his chin. "What?!"

His smile was weak. "They don't believe she'll try to come back here. After all, she's been seen here. She'd be recognized. They're just being cautious."

For a moment, she couldn't think of a thing to say. When he reached up to pull her back into his arms, though, she went, nestling against his shoulder, where she was safe.

"Surely someone will tell your sisters, though, and your grandfather."

He tweaked her nose. "That's what I love about you, lass. Always with an eye to somebody else. Aye, Alex Knight and Chuffy Wilde are on their way north."

She nodded, more interested in how it felt to draw her fingers down his rippling abdomen. "Well," she said. "It *would* give us more time to decide what to do here. I know Rosie and the dowager would prefer to stay. It is where their work is. But Artemesia needs a season."

"We have money for it all. You've no more worries, lass."

She nodded. She could see the sheet begin to rise, and it made her smile.

"Then you won't mind if it's a while before you move to your new home?" he asked.

That got her head back up. "New home? I don't need a new home."

He frowned. "Why?"

"Because I'm already there."

He looked confused. She gently rubbed away the worry line between his eyes.

"I dinna understand," he said, his hand on her back.

She smiled. For the first time since she could remember, she could feel joy without hesitation, without a weight to dim it. Without boundaries. "It is something I realized while we were on the road," she told him, dropping her fingers to his lips. "I have spent my entire life looking for a home. Not a roof over my head, or regular meals or people. A home of my heart."

His eyes softened, and he smiled. "You have?"

She nodded. "And to my amazement, I finally found it." Her smile grew. She knew that her heart was in her eyes, and it should have lit the room. When she laid her hand against Ian's chest, she swore she could see her heart reflected in his gaze. "*You* are my home, Ian Ferguson. And no matter where else we go, I will need no other."

Tears welled in her berserker's eyes. "Amazing," he whispered, leaning down to drop a lingering kiss on her lips. "I was just about to say that very thing."

And he spent the rest of the night proving it to her.

Epilogue

Alex Knight hoped that this was the last time he had to step inside Hawesworth Castle. Next time, they would have to get some clerk to deliver the marquess's news.

"Odd," Chuffy said next to him. "Grim kinda place, ain't it? Wouldn't think so. All marble and statues. Should look like a church."

Alex looked over his shoulder at his friend, who was concentrating on the priceless pale blue porcelain vase he held in his hands. They were back in that grim ice blue and white salon where he had delivered bad news only a few weeks ago. At least, he thought, this time he would be able to make Miss Ferguson smile again.

He realized he'd been thinking of that smile a lot. He'd been thinking how close he'd come to being the one who kept Ian from ever returning home. Chuffy had never spoken to him of that night. Alex had spoken to Drake, but he hadn't been able to tell the whole story. He would never be able to tell the whole story, and it ate at him.

"Don't much like the name either," Chuffy suddenly mused, tipping the vase upside down over his head so he could see inside. "No castle here. Not even a turret. Names should fit the place, ya know? The Ice House. Frigid Friary. Grimstone."

Alex paced. "I hope you don't plan on sharing your ideas with the marquess."

Setting down the porcelain, Chuffy shrugged. "Friend of the pater's. About as much sense of humor. Don't appreciate me."

Alex smiled. Pulling out his pocket watch, he checked the time. If the marquess didn't appear soon, they would have to leave and come back in the morning. He certainly didn't want to spend another night in this wasteland, though.

"I wonder where Miss Ferguson is," he mused. "It's been almost forty minutes."

Shoving his glasses up his nose, Chuffy shook his head. "Can't picture Ferguson here. Too rigid. Too bland. Too . . ."

"Civilized?" a cold voice answered from the door.

Alex refused to let the marquess know how startled he'd been. Turning easily, he offered a bow. "My lord," he greeted the older man.

This time the marquess had his quizzing glass, which he used to peruse his guests. "This is becoming a habit, Knight," he said. "As for you, Charles Wilde, your father would not allow any son of his to gain so much weight."

"Why I waited 'til he popped off," Chuffy said amiably. "Didn't want to cause a seizure."

"If you don't mind, sir," Alex said. "We have come to deliver some news. It's about your grandson. Will his sisters be joining us soon?"

The marquess went rigid. "They will not."

Walking by the two men, the old man sat down on one of the pale blue chairs, tugging his trousers into place as he settled. Alex sighed. With a speaking glance to Chuffy, he sat as well. Chuffy shoved his glasses up his nose and perched on the settee.

"Good to see you, Marquess," Chuffy said. "Nice to know you haven't changed. Be too much of a surprise."

Alex almost burst out laughing. The marquess went ruddy, glaring at Chuffy as if he'd soiled the floor. Chuffy was completely oblivious. He'd found another vase to play with.

Alex dragged his attention back to the marquess and his mission. "I would rather deliver this news all at once, sir. Should we come back tomorrow to see the young ladies?"

The marquess glared. "Get it done now, sir. I don't have time. Although why you have returned, I cannot say. I have a new heir. A distant cousin due to arrive within the week. As for that jackanapes with whom you associated, I have struck him from the Bible and forbidden his name in the house. Hawesworth Castle breeds no traitors."

"Nor does it now, sir," Alex said, feeling more uncomfortable by the minute. "The news we bring is good. For reasons of national security, this information may not be publicized, but the prime minister thought you would want to know. Ian is alive. I have just seen him."

Anyone else might have been thrilled. Alex imagined that Fiona would shed tears when she heard. The marquess greeted the news with a sneer.

"Alive? What am I to care? I told you. The boy is not welcome here."

Alex was beginning to lose his temper. "Considering

the fact that he was not only innocent of the charges but is helping to bring down a vicious ring of traitors, you might wish to reconsider your position." Reaching into his pocket, Alex pulled out a folded and sealed note. "The Prince of Wales has written, sharing his joy that your heir will be restored, once this business of traitors is satisfactorily settled."

He proffered the letter. The marquess stared at it as if it were a snake. Finally, he snatched it and sat back. He did not open the letter or read it.

"Good news," Chuffy said. "No scandal."

"Don't be absurd. There is scandal aplenty." The marquess paused, eying the sealed letter. "I suppose his highness wishes me to welcome the return of my grandson."

"I believe so."

Although Alex couldn't imagine Ian being delighted by the prospect.

The marquess abruptly stood. "Well then, you will have to notify my granddaughters as well."

Alex followed to his feet. "I would be happy to, sir. When may I see them?"

The marquess looked more rigid than ever. "When you find them."

"I beg your pardon?" Alex asked.

Even Chuffy stared. "Where are they?"

"How should I know?" the marquess snapped. "I threw them out right after you were here the last time. I told you. No traitors. No scandal."

And without another word, the marquess walked out the door, slamming it behind him.

Fiona Ferguson feels fortunate to have a job as a schoolteacher and a townhouse she can temporarily call home. But when she's reunited with Alex Knight, Lord Whitmore, Fiona begins to dream of her heart's true desires . . .

Twice Tempted

Please turn this page for a preview.

Chapter 1

For the fifth time that day, Fiona Ferguson thanked the education she had received at Last Chance Academy. It had been an awful school, but it had definitely beaten the maidenly arts into its students. Because of it, Fiona could draw a figure, sing a tune, play a reasonably melodic piano, sew a sampler, and set a table. All of which she was teaching the neighborhood girls, along with Latin, Mathematics, Globes, and Science.

As she accompanied the last of her students to the door, she also thanked her friend Margaret Bryan for the chance to do both, at least for now. If Margaret had not offered Fiona and Mairead this temporary haven eight weeks ago, they would have been on the streets again. Instead, at least until the lease ran out in two months, they had a roof, some furniture, and a bit of egg money.

Fiona also had a blistering headache, but that was because of the sleep she was forfeiting trying to keep their heads above water.

"We'll come tomorrow then, Miss Fee?" eight-year-old Nancy Peters asked as Fiona knelt to button her coat.

"No, my dear. Tomorrow is Saturday. Your mother will need you about the shop. But I expect you to practice your addition and your curtsies."

Giving a gap-toothed grin, the tiny girl with her white-blond braids dropped almost to the ground. Chuckling, Fiona helped right her. "You will be curtsying to the likes of Mrs. Walsh, Nancy. Not the queen."

The little girl's grin was still cheeky. "But Mrs. Walsh thinks she's queen. Will Miss Mary be here when we come back?"

"Oh, I expect so. She is just busy working today."

Nancy gave a solemn nod. "Counting the stars."

"Exactly. Now, off with you before your mother worries."

She taught children of shopkeepers and chemists, pupils Margaret had groomed and then had to leave because of frail health. Fiona hoped her friend's health would benefit from her move to Margate. She hoped they would eventually be able to sit together again, comparing notes on Fermat's Last Theorem.

In the meantime, at least for two months more, the very lucky Ferguson sisters would keep up the townhouse in Blackheath, where Margaret had run her school for children of enlightened parents. Within that time, Fiona prayed they would be able to find another place they could afford in which to move their school. If not . . . well, she had faced uncertainty before. She was certain it would happen again. And if there was one thing Fiona Ferguson excelled in, it was dealing with uncertainty.

Watching the little girl hop down the steps of the tidy

brick rowhouse, Fiona closed the door and returned to the little south parlor to clean up the slates and books Margaret Bryan had loaned her.

Anyone from Hawesworth Castle would have been appalled at her living conditions. She and Mairead had one female helper and one male, a man-of-all-work they shared with two other families, and they were more often than not paid in foodstuffs and services. With most of the furniture sent on to Margate, they taught on an old table Fiona had scrounged from the rag and bone man, and practiced their music on Margaret's old spinet. The formal salon held one three-legged faded brown settee and two spindle-back chairs, and Fiona and Mairead shared a room. They sat at the school table if they were working together, and in the kitchen with Mrs. Quick if they weren't. The only rug resided in the schoolroom, and the only artwork had been done by her students. Other than that and the roof over their heads, they had nothing.

They had everything. They were off the streets. They had food and heavy boots and heavier cloaks and a bit of coal for the fires. They had their correspondence from their friends around Europe, which was their only frivolous expense, and the Royal Observatory up the hill. And they had each other. For that Fiona was most grateful. Now that Ian was gone, Mairead was all she had left in the world.

Considering how little Fiona had seen her brother Ian while growing up, she was surprised how sharp her grief still sat on her shoulders. It was as if a foundation stone were missing from her house that threatened all stability.

No, she thought, neatly stacking the primers on a shelf.

It was as if she were left alone to provide stability, having to balance a heavy, unwieldy load on only one leg. She had done it before, of course. This time, though, there was no hope of regaining that balance. Ian was gone, and the only person left who loved her was Mairead. And Mairead couldn't help her. It was Fiona's task to help Mairead.

Over on the mantel, the little bracket clock struck four. Mairead should be home soon. Fiona's precious silence was almost over. Between the relentless enthusiasm of the children who came every day and Mairead's obsessive re-counting of her own hours, Fiona got precious little time with her own thoughts. And what time she did have she usually spent going over accounts, lesson plans, or mathematical equations.

Just now, however, there was a very pleasant gap in her schedule. A book, maybe. She had been working her way through Goldsmith's *History of Britain* in an attempt to plug the holes in her knowledge of her own country, and had just reached James I. But James was not her favorite king. Perhaps a bit of needlework, or work on the computations Mr. Pond had asked her to do.

For a long moment, she stood frozen, overcome with the possibility of being completely selfish for an entire half hour. It was inevitable, then, that she heard the front door knocker.

She should go out and answer it. She spent a moment making sure her lace collar was flat against her ubiquitous black kerseymere dress, knowing quite well that she was delaying as long as she could in the hopes she would hear Mrs. Quick's footsteps crossing the hall.

"Don't you worry yourself," she heard the strident

notes of sarcasm out in the hall. "I was just dyin' to open the door."

Fiona couldn't help it. She smiled.

And then she heard a man's voice. "Excuse me. Is Mrs. Margaret Bryan at home?"

Fiona swore she stopped breathing. It couldn't be.

Before she could think better of it, she threw the door to the library open to see Mrs. Quick poised before the open door, hand on hip, face pursed in displeasure at the sight of two rather large men on the stoop.

"Mrs. Bryan don't live here anymore," the housekeeper snapped, ready to close the door again.

"Wait!" Fiona cried, frozen on the spot. "It's all right, Mrs. Quick. Let them in."

"Don't think I should," the woman retorted with a squint at the two town bucks. "Don't need their kind nosin' around the school."

Fiona almost laughed out loud. "I sincerely doubt they're here to ravage our children," she said.

She hadn't imagined it. Alex Knight—no, Lord Whitmore, now—stood in her doorway, staring at her as if he'd seen a ghost.

She couldn't believe it. She had been thinking of him for so long. He was the only good memory she had carried away from Hawesworth. His compassion. His strength. The unshakable memory of comfort as he'd taken her hand.

She seemed to have forgotten his beauty. Wind-chapped and tousled, he exuded life, with his broad shoulders and warm hazel eyes and strong, angular features. Just the sight of them sent her heart skidding around in her chest.

She'd never thought to see him again.

"Don't look helpless to me, old lad," his companion suddenly said.

Her feet finally unfroze, and she stepped forward. "She isn't," she greeted him. "Please. Would you care to come in? I can at least give you Mrs. Bryan's current address."

Mrs. Quick only conceded ground grudgingly, finally shutting the door behind the men with an impatient briskness that conveyed judgment. The men stepped into the bare little foyer and removed their hats.

"Actually," Alex said, still staring at Fiona. "We came to see you."

THE DISH

Where Authors Give You the Inside Scoop

♥ ♥ ♥ ♥ ♥ ♥ ♥ ♥ ♥ ♥ ♥ ♥ ♥ ♥

From the desk of Roxanne St. Claire

Dear Reader,

Years ago, I picked up a romance novel about a contemporary "marriage of convenience" and I recall being quite skeptical that the idea could work in anything but a historical novel. How wrong I was! I not only enjoyed the book, but *Separate Beds* by LaVyrle Spencer became one of my top ten favorite books of all time. (Do yourself a favor and dig up this classic if you haven't read it!) Since then, I've always wanted to put my own spin on a story about two people who are in a situation where they need to marry for reasons other than love, knowing that their faux marriage is doomed.

I finally found the perfect characters and setup for a marriage of convenience story when I returned to Barefoot Bay to write BAREFOOT BY THE SEA, my most recent release in the series set on an idyllic Gulf Coast island in Florida. I knew that sparks would fly and tears might flow when I paired Tessa Galloway, earth mother longing for a baby, with Ian Browning, a grieving widower in the witness protection program. I suspected that it would be a terrific conflict to give the woman who despises secrets a man who has to keep one in order to stay alive, with the added complication of a situation that can only be resolved with a fake, arranged marriage. However, I never dreamed just how much I would love writing that marriage of convenience! I should have known, since I adored the first one I'd ever read.

Throughout most of BAREFOOT BY THE SEA, hero Ian is forced to hide who he really is and why he's in Barefoot Bay. And that gave me another story twist I love to explore: the build-up to the inevitable revelation of a character's true identity and just how devastating that is for everyone (including the reader!). I had a blast being in Ian's head when he fought off his demons and past to fall hard into Tessa's arms and life. And I ached and grew with Tessa as the truth became crystal clear and shattered her fragile heart.

The best part, for me, was folding that marriage of convenience into a story about a woman who wants a child of her own but has to give up that hope to help, and ultimately lose, a man who needs her in order to be reunited with his own children. If she marries him, he gets what he needs…but he can't give her the one thing she wants most. Will Tessa surrender her lifelong dream to help a man who lost his? She can if she loves him enough, right? Maybe.

Ironically, when the actual marriage of convenience finally took place on the page, that ceremony felt more real than any of the many weddings I've ever written. I hope readers agree. And speaking of weddings, stay tuned for more of them in Barefoot Bay when the Barefoot Brides trilogy launches next year! Nothing like an opportunity to kick off your shoes and fall in love, which is never convenient but always fun!

Happy reading!

Roxanne St. Claire

♥ ♥ ♥ ♥ ♥ ♥ ♥ ♥ ♥ ♥ ♥ ♥ ♥ ♥ ♥ ♥

From the desk of Kristen Ashley

Dear Reader,

As it happens when I start a book and the action plays out in my head, characters pop up out of nowhere.

See, I don't plot, or outline. An idea will come to me and *Wham!* My brain just flows with it. Or a character will come to me and all the pieces of his or her puzzle start tumbling quickly into place and the story moves from there. Either way, this all plays in my mind's eye like a movie and I sit at my keyboard doing my darnedest to get it all down as it goes along.

In my Dream Man series, I started it with *Mystery Man* because Hawk and Gwen came to me and I was desperate to get their story out. I'm not even sure that I expected it to be a series. I just *needed* to tell their story.

Very quickly I was introduced to Kane "Tack" Allen and Detective Mitch Lawson. When I met them through Gwen, I knew instantly—with all the hotness that was them—that they both needed their own book. So this one idea I had of Hawk and Gwen finding their happily ever after became a series.

Brock "Slim" Lucas showed up later in *Mystery Man* but when he did, he certainly intrigued me. Most specifically the lengths he'd go to do his job. I wondered why that fire was in his belly. And suddenly I couldn't wait to find out.

In the meantime, my aunt Barb, who reads every one of my books when they come out, mentioned in passing she'd like to see one of my couples *not* struggle before they capitulated to the attraction and emotion swirling around them. Instead, she wanted to see the relationship build and grow, not the hero and heroine fighting it.

This intrigued me, too, especially when it came to Brock, who had seen a lot and done a lot in his mission as a DEA agent. I didn't want him to have another fight on his hands, not like that. But also, I'd never done this, not in all the books I'd written.

I'm a girl who likes a challenge.

But could I weave a tale that was about a man and a woman in love, recognizing and embracing that love relatively early in the story, and then focus the story on how they learn to live with each other, deal with each other's histories, family, and all that life throws at them on a normal basis? Would this even be interesting?

Luckily, life *is* interesting, sometimes in good ways, sometimes not-so-good.

Throwing Elvira and Martha into the mix, along with Tess's hideous ex-husband and Brock's odious ex-wife, and adding children and family, life for Brock and Tess, as well as their story, was indeed interesting (and fun) to write—when I didn't want to wring Olivia's neck, that is.

And I found there's great beauty in telling a tale that isn't about fighting attraction because of past issues or history (or the like) and besting that to find love; instead delving into what makes a man and a woman, and allowing them to let their loved one get close, at the same time learning how to depend on each other to make it through.

I should thank my aunt Barb. Because she had a great idea that led to a beautiful love story.

♥ ♥ ♥ ♥ ♥ ♥ ♥ ♥ ♥ ♥ ♥ ♥ ♥ ♥ ♥

From the desk of Eileen Dreyer

Dear Reader,

The last thing I ever thought I would do was write a series. I thought I was brave putting together a trilogy. Well, as usual, my characters outsmarted me, and I now find myself in the middle of a nine-story series about Drake's Rakes, my handsome gentleman spies. But I don't wait well as a reader myself. How do I ask my own readers to wait nine books for any resolution?

I just couldn't do it. So I've divided up the Rakes into three trilogies based on the heroines. The first was The Three Graces. This one I'm calling Last Chance Academy, where the heroines went to school. I introduced them all in my short e-novel *It Begins With A Kiss*, and continue in ONCE A RAKE with Sarah Clarke, who has to save Scotsman Colonel Ian Ferguson from gunshot, assassin, and the charges of treason.

I love Sarah. A woman with an unfortunate begin-ning, she is just trying to save the only home she's ever really had from penury, an estate so small and isolated that her best friend is a six-hundred-pound pig. Enter Ian. Suddenly she's facing off with smugglers, spies, assassins, and possible eviction. I call my Drake's Rakes series Romantic Historical Adventure, and I think there is plenty of each in ONCE A RAKE. Let me know at www .eileendreyer.com, my Facebook page (Eileen Dreyer), or on Twitter @EileenDreyer. Now I need to get back. I have five more Rakes to threaten.

Eileen Dreyer

♥ ♥ ♥ ♥ ♥ ♥ ♥ ♥ ♥ ♥ ♥ ♥ ♥ ♥ ♥

From the desk of Anne Barton

Dear Reader,

Regrets. We all have them. Incidents from our distant (or not-so-distant) pasts that we'd like to forget. Photos we'd like to burn, boyfriends we never should have dated, a night or two of partying that got slightly out of control. Ahem.

In short, there are some stories we'd rather our siblings didn't tell in front of Grandma at Thanksgiving dinner.

Luckily for me, I grew up in the pre-Internet era. Back then, a faux pas wasn't instantly posted or tweeted for the world to see. Instead, it was recounted in a note that was ruthlessly passed through a network of tables in the cafeteria—a highly effective means of humiliation, but not nearly as permanent as the digital equivalent, thank goodness.

Even so, I distinctly remember the sinking feeling, the dread of knowing that my deep dark secret could be exposed at any moment. If you've ever had a little indiscretion that you just can't seem to outrun (and who hasn't?), you know how it weighs on you. It can be almost paralyzing.

In ONCE SHE WAS TEMPTED, Miss Daphne Honeycote has such a secret. Actually, she has two of them—a pair of scandalous portraits. She posed for them when she was poor and in dire need of money for her sick mother. But after her mother recovers and Daphne's circumstances improve considerably, the shocking portraits come back to haunt her, threatening to ruin her reputation, her friendships, and her family's good name.

Much to Daphne's horror, Benjamin Elliott, the Earl of Foxburn, possesses one of the paintings—and therefore, the power to destroy her. But he also has the means to help her discover the whereabouts of the second portrait before its unscrupulous owner can make it public. Daphne must decide whether to trust the brooding earl. But even if she does, he can't fully protect her—it's ultimately up to Daphne to come to terms with her scandalous past. Just as we all eventually must.

In the meantime, I suggest seating your siblings on the opposite end of the Thanksgiving table from Grandma.

Happy reading,

Anne Barton

♥ ♥ ♥ ♥ ♥ ♥ ♥ ♥ ♥ ♥ ♥ ♥ ♥ ♥ ♥

From the desk of Mimi Jean Pamfiloff

Dear Reader,

After living a life filled with nothing but bizarre, Emma Keane just wants normal. Husband, picket fence, vegetable garden, and a voice-free head. Normal. And Mr. Voice happens to agree. He'd like nothing more than to be free from the stubborn, spiteful, spoiled girl he's spent the last twenty-two years listening to day and night. Unfortunately for him, however, escaping his only companion in the universe won't be so easy. You see, there's a damned good reason Emma is the only one who can hear him—though he's not spilling the beans just yet—and there's a damned bad reason he can't leave Emma: He's imprisoned. And to be set free, Mr. Voice is going to have to convince Emma to travel from New York City to the darkest corner of Mexico's most dangerous jungle.

But not only will the perilous journey help Emma become the brave woman she's destined to be, it will also be the single most trying challenge Mr. Voice has ever had to face. In his seventy thousand years, he's never met a mortal he can't live without. Until now. Too bad she's going to die helping him. What's an ancient god to do?

Mimi